RUBY
REVENGE

KAY RILEY

Copyright © 2022 Kay Riley

All rights reserved. No part of this book may be reproduced in any form or by any electronic or mechanical means, including information storage and retrieval systems, without permission in writing from the publisher, except by reviewers, who may quote brief passages in a review.

Names, characters, businesses, places, events, locales, and incidents are either the products of the author's imagination or used in a fictitious manner. And any resemblance to actual persons, living or dead, businesses, companies, locales, or actual events is purely coincidental.

Designations used by companies to distinguish their products are often claimed as trademarks. All brand names and product names used in this book and on its cover are trade names, service marks, trademarks and registered trademarks of their respective owners. The publishers and the book are not associated with any product or vendor mentioned in this book. None of the companies referenced within the book have endorsed the book.

ISBN

978-1-7375674-9-3 [ebook]

979-8-9861491-0-3 [paperback]

Cover Design by: Y'All That Graphic

Edited by: Editing by Gray

Proofread by: VB Proofreads

Formatting: Wicked Gypsy Designs

For my mom
The first person who showed me the magic of living in fictional worlds of books.

NOTE TO READERS

In a unique twist, the hero of this story is a mystery in the beginning. All of his chapters are labeled 'Him', and I hope you have fun trying to guess who he is before it's revealed! Please let future readers share in the same suspense by keeping his name a secret after you find out who 'he' is

This is a dark forbidden, slower burn, stand-alone romance. If you'd like more details concerning the content, please refer to my website. Thank you!

https://www.kayrileyauthor.com/

PLAYLIST

"WHO AM I?" BESOMORPH &RIELL

"RITUALS" JIOVANNI DANIEL

"I AM YOURS" KELSEY GRAMMAR

"LOVER. FIGHTER." SVRCINA

PROLOGUE

Sage

"I'm sorry to be the one to tell you this, but her remains were found."

The air was thick with tension as a chill swept through me. Bile crept up my throat, and I fought to keep from emptying my stomach all over the nursing home floor. I was expecting those words. Yet, it still felt like I was trapped in a nightmare as the detective spoke.

This was the moment I'd feared every day for the last twenty years. The small amount of hope of ever seeing her alive again vanished. The room was unbearably hot. My red hair was slick from sweat, and the strands sticking to my neck were suddenly suffocating.

The mother I had no memory of, who was only in my life for two months, was dead.

Pulling my hair from my neck, I forced myself to look away from the conference table and glance at my sister. Lacey's usual pale complexion was even more ashen as her gaze lifted to meet mine.

"Who are you again?" My dad's voice made my stomach plummet.

His eyes, usually filled with love when he saw us, were a blank. He was not in a lucid state. Early-Onset Alzheimer's was the reason he was in this nursing home. My heart ached realizing he had no idea we were talking about the love of his life.

"It's okay, Charles," his favorite nurse murmured, helping him stand from the chair. "Let's go get some lunch."

"We'll talk to him later, okay, Sage?" Lacey mumbled, squeezing my hand. Biting my lip, I wondered if we were going to tell him when he was in a lucid state. Was it worth it? It would only crush him. Detective Thomas cleared his throat and pulled me from my thoughts.

"I know this is difficult. And I'm sorry we have to do this. But I'm sure after this long, you and your family want answers." He started the conversation. "The circumstances in which we found her remains are very unusual. She was found in Cass County, which is over a three-hour drive from here. She was buried in an oak casket. Whoever did it took the time to give her a proper burial, which leads us to think it was someone she knew."

"How did she die?" I forced the question out as my nails dug into my palm.

"The cause of death was a stab wound to her heart. There was nothing else. No defensive wounds or other injuries."

"Was it—was it painless for her?" I asked, attempting to keep my composure.

"I don't believe she suffered," the detective answered, his voice filled with compassion. "It's likely she was killed soon after she went missing. But I do have a question for you."

"Anything that could help," Lacey said before I could.

"Did your mom have short hair when she went missing?"

"No, her hair was long, at least down to the middle of her back," my sister answered, her eyebrows raising slightly.

"Your mother's remains...they were in good condition, even after twenty years," Detective Thomas said as softly as possible. "The oak coffin kept the elements out. The autopsy and the investigation of the coffin showed no evidence of her hair. That's why we want to know if she had short hair."

"You're saying whoever did this cut her hair off?" I asked in shock.

"It looks like it, yes," he said. "We dusted for prints and looked for any other evidence but didn't find anything. She was found in a field that hasn't been touched in decades. But a company bought it and started construction to build, that's when the coffin was discovered. Do you know anyone in Cass County?"

"No," we both answered at the same time.

"Are you sure? Maybe other family members do," Detective Thomas pressed as I shook my head. There was no other family that would be helpful. Our dad didn't have any living relatives. He was the youngest, and his siblings had already passed away. Our mom had one sister, but she lived in Oregon, and they were never close.

"We're positive. We don't have any other family in Michigan," Lacey answered.

"Well, if either of you can think of anything that could possibly help, please feel free to contact me. We're still investigating, but with this being a cold case for so long, and since no new evidence has come to light, we sadly don't have any leads. We will release the remains as soon as everything is completed," he said gently, pulling a small piece of paper out of his jacket pocket and handing it to Lacey. "Here's the number to arrange that."

"Thank you, I'll take care of it," Lacey promised as she grabbed the paper he held out. A small grin pulled at my lips. Lacey was my big sister and wanted to do what she could to take care of me. But we both knew I was the responsible one in the family.

The detective stood up and moved to shake our hands. "Again, I'm so sorry for your loss. If any new evidence comes to light, I'll call immediately."

I stayed in my chair as he left the room. Disappointment rippled through me as Lacey leaned over from behind me and pulled me into a hug. I wanted answers, but now I had even more questions.

CHAPTER ONE
ONE MONTH LATER

Him

Staring at the funeral from behind the tinted windows of my black sedan, I was reconsidering coming here. I should leave; being here was a risk. The others would be upset if they found out. But I couldn't help it. It was necessary to make sure the funeral happened and there would be no more autopsies or investigations of Susan Taylor. I had a personal connection to Sage and Lacey's mother.

I knew who killed her and why they'd done it.

Running a hand down my face, I convinced myself it was fine. I'd covered my bases.

The license plate didn't even belong to this car, and I would switch plates again after I left. Glancing out the window once more, I saw who I had been looking for. The Taylor sisters. Sage and Lacey stood arm in arm, facing away from me.

A minute later, the funeral ended, and people started to walk toward their cars. My foot hovered over the pedal, ready to bolt if I drew any attention. Just by being here, I'd already pushed my luck. But I needed to see Sage and Lacey's faces before I left. Finally, the girls turned to leave, and Sage glanced at my car as she talked to her boyfriend.

My heart seized as I met her eyes, even though there was no way I was visible to her. I'd checked the tinted windows before coming here. It was impossible to see inside this car. Her attention returned to her boyfriend, and I snorted.

That guy was too soft. He wasn't man enough for Sage. She had a fire that couldn't be tamed. Her fiery, ruby red hair hung in soft waves down her back. As for Lacey, she was a classic beauty. Where Sage was athletic, she was dainty. She had an aura of innocence about her. Her hair was red like her sister's. But was much lighter with an almost orange hue. Even with their differences, the fact that they were sisters was undeniable when they stood side by side.

They both had the same hazel eyes that changed color, depending on the light. Their smiles were infectious. And right now, even with their faces streaked with tears, they were both breathtakingly fucking gorgeous.

My pulse quickened when the girls began to walk toward the road. Sage stared at my car again and I decided it was time to go. I stepped on the gas and sped out of the cemetery, but my mind stayed on the sisters.

A groan escaped me as the constant ringing of my phone pulled me from my sleep. Blindly, I reached around on my nightstand until my hand closed around my phone.

"Yeah?" I answered gruffly, not bothering to open my eyes.

"What the hell were you thinking?" the man on the other end practically yelled.

I sighed and sat up while rubbing my eyes. I should have expected this, but I honestly didn't think any of the others would have noticed that I was at the funeral. Obviously, I wasn't as careful as I'd thought.

"I don't know what you're talking about." I decided to feign innocence, in case it wasn't about where I was yesterday.

"You know exactly what. Going to that funeral. Acting all shady in a car with tinted windows. That screams suspicious." He was pissed.

"Don't worry. They didn't see me, I was careful. Even if they did see me, you really think I couldn't have talked my way out of it?"

"What are you? Stupid?"

Swinging my legs over the edge of the bed, I rolled my shoulders before standing up. I took a deep breath before answering, trying to control the anger coursing through me.

"Calm down; nothing happened. I know what I'm doing. I've been taught to be discreet all my life. You really think I'd risk it if I wasn't a hundred percent sure I wouldn't be caught?" I asked, fighting to keep my voice controlled.

"Do not do anything that brings more awareness to that case. There have been no new leads in the case of that woman's death, and I want to keep it that way. Got it?"

"Yes, sir. I got it," I said through clenched teeth.

"Good," he replied, hanging up before another word was spoken.

I grumbled under my breath and stretched my arms over my head. The discovery of Susan Taylor's body made big news in the small town of Capac. She had been considered a missing person for the past twenty years, and that's how it was supposed to stay. The old guy who owned the land where she was buried kept it from the public for years. Until he died and none of the others in the group knew because he lived alone.

That wouldn't happen again. We would put measures in place

after this unfortunate incident. Couldn't have land being sold off to the public, uncovering our deep secrets. It made working toward the greater good that much harder.

The plan would happen soon. There were only a couple months to get it all together for everything to go off without a hitch. Excitement shot through me, and the thought of seeing the others instantly put me in a better mood. I only saw them when the planning started, and again on the night of the ceremony. We couldn't all be seen together; it would draw too much suspicion.

They were like family, and anything they asked, I'd do. No matter what. That included listening to the asshole who'd told me not to arouse questions about Susan Taylor's death.

I chuckled as I made my coffee. I hadn't agreed to stop going around the Taylor sisters. They were intriguing and had been on my mind more than I'd ever admit to anyone. They were so different from each other but had a bond I'd never witnessed. I wanted to be a part of their lives, at least for a while longer.

While I watched the coffee brew, the tragic fate of the Taylor family filled my head. The sisters had lost their mother when they were so young. Spent their childhood years wondering what happened to her. Then their dad got sick.

Those girls didn't know that their family was part of a bigger picture. Something for the greater good. Their mother found out what that was before her death, but she didn't accept it. Maybe the chosen sister would. Either way, Sage or Lacey was marked to share the same fate as their mother.

Maybe she'd accept it and understand why this must be done. Or not. Many of the women who were chosen didn't understand why this happened to them. Before I could convince myself not to, I pulled out my phone and searched online until I found Lacey's profile picture. I stared at the picture of the two sisters with contagious smiles on their faces. If only they knew what was going to happen once the plan was set.

One of the Taylor sisters would be dead before summer ended.

CHAPTER TWO

Sage

Every town was known for something, and my home was no exception. Capac stood for Cows and Pigs and Chickens. Laughter was the first reaction when hearing it, but people from my small Michigan town were always proud to spout off that fact to anyone who would listen. Nothing exciting ever happened here.

Except twenty years ago, when an unsolved crime created enough panic to make everyone lock their doors at night. And it stayed unsolved until a month ago when they'd finally found my mother's remains.

I was convinced happiness could only be a phase. Nothing could stay good forever. My mother's disappearance, and now her death.

My dad's illness. When life started going right, there was always something waiting to drag me back down.

"...what do you think? Sage? Sage," Lacey yelled from the back seat, finally getting my attention.

A hand closed around my thigh, giving me comfort, as if he knew what I was thinking about. My boyfriend, Alex, glanced away from the road for a moment to give me a quick smile.

"So, what do you think?" Lacey asked again, leaning forward to talk right next to my ear.

"About what?"

She sighed. "I said it three times. Jamie is going to come over to join us today. Alex said it was okay. What's wrong, Sage?"

"Nothing," I lied, not wanting to ruin the day. "It would be nice to see him."

I honestly really didn't care if Jamie came or not. He was Lacey's newest friend. She didn't do relationships and was never with the same guy for long. But I'd met him a couple times, and he seemed nice.

Alex pulled into his parents' driveway. It was so long and surrounded by trees that the house wasn't visible from the dirt road. Finally, the small ranch-style house came into view. It was Alex's childhood home, the only one he'd lived in until he moved in with Lacey and me.

"*Geia, gios mou.*" His mom greeted Alex in Greek with a big hug when we got out of the car. Both his parents had been raised in Greece but moved to the states after getting married. They were about as traditional as any marriage could be.

"Hi, Mom," he said while trying to untangle himself from her hug.

"Alexandros, how are you?" his mom asked in her thick Greek accent, and I smiled. His parents were the only ones who didn't use his nickname.

"I'm good. You remember Sage's sister, Lacey?"

"Of course, I do."

"Hi, Mrs. Rossi."

"Sage, please. Call me Caitlin, like I've told you a hundred times before," she said with a small laugh before giving me a warm hug. Her usual scent of sweet baked cookies surrounded me as sadness and longing swallowed me worse than usual. Ever since my mom's funeral, anything that had to do with mothers was hitting me harder. Pulling away from Caitlin, I pushed those thoughts away, determined to enjoy the day.

With her arm linked with Alex's, Caitlin led everyone around to the backyard. I looked excitedly at the pool that was attached to their back patio. There were a few lounge chairs in front of the pool, and closer to the house door was a patio table sitting under a huge umbrella and a small charcoal grill. Stepping onto the deck, I was ready to enjoy a day of relaxing. Too bad that meant dealing with his family.

Alex's dad, Theo, was sitting at the patio table talking on the phone to someone. My guard rose a bit as he glanced over me before looking at his son.

"Hi, Alexandros. Sage and Lacey, how are you?" Theo asked coolly after he hung up the phone. Theo was much more subdued than his wife, and I felt like I had to walk on eggshells around him. When I'd first started dating Alex, I was positive he hated me. Actually, neither of his parents seemed to like me in the beginning. But his mom finally warmed up to me. It had only taken three years.

"Nikolas is getting the meat ready for the grill," Theo said, just as Alex's older brother slammed the screen door open with a tray filled with burgers and buns balancing in his hands.

"Baby brother, you finally made it. I see you brought the lovely Taylor sisters with you." Nikolas's gaze lingered on Lacey and me. "You two look great. Been working out with Alex?"

"Hey, Niko." I fought the urge to roll my eyes but lost that battle when Niko's identical twin, Geo, walked out of the house.

"Geo, I didn't think you were coming today." Alex gave his brother a hug like they hadn't just seen each other at work yesterday.

"Geoffrey, help your brother with the food," Theo ordered, watching Niko almost drop the tray. Alex and his brothers got the food ready to cook as I sat down next to Caitlin.

The twins were two years older than Alex, and they all spent a lot of time together. If Alex wasn't with me, he was with them. They worked on the same construction crew, went to the gym when they could, and of course, spent every Sunday at their parents' house.

I tolerated Niko and Geo. For Alex. Because they were his family. We'd all grown up in this small town, but I'd successfully ignored the twins until Alex came into my life. They were arrogant and cocky. Life of the party type of guys. Alex was the complete opposite. And I loved that about him.

Lacey and I chatted with Caitlin while the guys hung out at the grill as the burgers cooked. Once the food was done, we sat around the large patio table, and silence fell as everyone started eating.

"So, Sage, how are your classes going? Almost ready to be a teacher?" Geo asked with a smirk, and I scowled on the inside. He knew full well that this was a sore spot with his parents. Niko coughed to cover up a chuckle as his gaze darted from me to his twin. Alex pushed food around his plate and his parents both looked at me.

"Almost, I still have one more year, and then a semester of in-class training," I answered as brightly as possible while shooting Geo an annoyed glance. Another awkward silence settled over the table. Theo's mouth was pressed into a thin line, and Caitlin looked over at Alex.

Taking a deep breath, I tried to ignore their obvious disapproval. They were traditional. Which meant that the women who married their sons were supposed to stay home and care for the them. Alex didn't share that belief, but he didn't like to argue with his parents about it either.

"Lacey, is Jamie still coming?" Alex quickly asked, trying to change the subject.

"He should be here soon, if he can find the house." Lacey laughed lightly in an attempt to ease the tension. I could practically hear my sister's thoughts. One of the pros of not having relationships was not dealing with potential in-laws.

"Let me help," I offered as Caitlin moved to collect everyone's dishes.

"No, no. It's okay, Sage. You came to relax and swim. I don't mind." Caitlin grabbed the plates from me and practically shooed me away.

Both Theo and Caitlin disappeared into the house while we all moved to the pool area and plopped into the lounge chairs. Immediately, Lacey took the sunscreen out of the bag and started to lather it all over her body.

I tanned as easily as Lacey burned. In the summer, Lacey went from white to red. There was no in between for her. I would never admit it out loud, but I was secretly grateful I looked more like our mother. We shared the same deep red hair and body type.

Lacey took after Dad. Freckles dotted her shoulders and back, and they looked adorable. I'd always thought Lacey was much prettier than me. Her high cheekbones could give models a run for their money. She had beautiful long legs that helped give her about four inches more to my five-foot-four-inch frame. The only feature we shared was our dad's hazel eyes.

"You want me to get your back, Lacey?" Niko asked with his usual grin. He watched Lacey pull off her floor-length purple sundress to reveal a red bikini.

"Thanks, but Jamie can help when he gets here," she replied with sarcastic sweetness as she rubbed the sunscreen on her legs. Her gaze darted between the twins before glancing at me. She still couldn't tell them apart. Almost no one outside Alex's family could. They were identical in every way. From their voices down to the way they walked. I could barely tell them apart even after being around them for the last three years since I started dating Alex.

"Why wait for him when we can help?" Geo interjected with a wink, scooting his chair closer to us.

"Is it possible for you two to not be dicks?" I grumbled, making sure to keep my voice down so their parents didn't hear.

"Is it possible for you to ever have fun?" Niko shot back, his eyes dancing with mischief as he took another swig of beer.

"Leave the girls alone," Alex yelled from the pool. "They came here to relax, not deal with you two."

I scoffed, knowing he was speaking up only so I'd come over here with him again. He spent every Sunday with his family, but this was the first time I'd been here in months. Dealing with his overbearing parents and his brothers wasn't a way I wanted to spend my weekends.

Niko laughed and took off his shirt as Geo did the same. My gaze wandered over their ripped abs before I caught myself. Alex climbed out of the pool and took a beer from Geo. I grinned, glad I got the brother who was hot and actually treated me right. The three of them were ridiculously good looking, and all had the same body type. The same solid build and forest green eyes. The twins had jet black hair like their mother's while Alex's was a dark brown.

Niko caught my gaze and gave me a lopsided grin before he jumped into the pool. Alex and Geo joined him while I helped Lacey apply the massive gobs of sunscreen. Lacey talked about her newest job at the bar as I laid back in a patio chair and closed my eyes, enjoying the sun.

Suddenly the sun was gone, and I opened my eyes to see one of the twins staring down at me. I bristled at how close he was, and I sat up and pushed him away before jumping out of my chair. Geo and Niko looked exactly alike. If I didn't know what they were wearing, I had to check for the birthmark on Niko's wrist. It was the only way to tell them apart.

"What do you want?" I noticed Alex sleeping in the chair next to me. I must have dozed off longer than I thought.

"Come on in, Sage, the water is great," the other twin answered from behind me, making me nearly jump.

"I will in a minute," I replied coolly, knowing they were up to something. I felt hands around my waist before I was lifted into the air. For a second, I thought it was Alex, until I twisted my head to see him still passed out in the lounge chair. I looked down and saw the birthmark.

"Damn it, Niko. Put me down," I yelled as he started walking forward with me still struggling against him.

"You're taking too long to get in the water. Don't worry, we'll help." Laughing, Geo walked next to us, and I glared at him while trying to pry his brother's hands off me.

"I still have my clothes on, don't you dare—" Before I could finish my sentence, Niko threw me into the pool. The water was cool and refreshing after lying in the sun. Too bad the only clothes I had were now soaked. I broke the surface of the water to see the twins rolling with laughter on the deck.

Alex had woken up and quickly put together what had happened. I treaded water as I watched him shove Niko and then Geo into the pool. Not that they cared as they still laughed over their prank. I climbed out of the water and pulled off my now wet clothes to start wringing them out.

"Seriously, Niko, how old are you? You're lucky I didn't have my phone on me," I seethed, not bothering to hide my annoyance.

"Nah, we knew you didn't have it." Geo chuckled.

Alex grabbed my clothes from my hands before pulling me in for a quick kiss.

"I'll throw them in the dryer, baby. They'll be done before we start the bonfire."

"Thanks, Alex." I gave him a smile before throwing the twins a warning look. They were not going to ruin our day.

"Need help getting back in the water?" Niko just couldn't help himself. He thought he was hilarious. I ignored him and slid into the water myself. I was already wet, might as well swim while my clothes dried.

Lacey looked over to the side of the house, and I followed her gaze. I could see Jamie's tall frame while he walked toward us as the breeze blew his shaggy black hair on his face. He had to be at least a foot taller than me. Lacey liked taller guys, and Jamie was very good looking. He had deep, serious brown eyes and a perfect smile.

Lacey left the deck and went down to meet him, then introduced Jamie to Niko and Geo once they got onto the patio. I said a quick hello as I climbed out of the pool. There was no point in investing much time in Lacey's guy friends because they never lasted long.

I was surprised they'd been together for three months. That was usually around the time Lacey started getting antsy about things being too serious.

"Time for the fire," Alex announced excitedly after he brought my now dry clothes from the house. He loved bonfires and always enjoyed the time when I came to his family's house. Geo and Niko went to the garage to get the wood while Alex went to find matches. I decided this would be a good time to find out more about Jamie.

"How are you liking Michigan? I'm sure it's a lot different from Texas." It was pretty much the only thing I knew about him.

"Yes, it's very different. I miss home, but your sister is making me love Michigan," he replied, giving Lacey an affectionate look. "I was only going to stay for a few months, but I'm thinking of staying longer."

"And he's teaching me Spanish," Lacey said with a grin.

Alex returned and pulled me against him. Niko got the fire going and his family ring hanging from his chest caught my attention when it gleamed from the flames. He wore his on a chain around his neck, just like Alex did. The gemstone was beautiful. A vibrant red-orange color, and it reminded me of a magnificent sunset. *It was a Carnelian stone*; Alex had told me. All the men in his family had one. It was a family heirloom, and he never took it off.

The ring was forgotten as Alex's hand slipped beneath my shirt, and he slowly dragged his fingers up my back. Goosebumps ran down my spine, and I turned to look at him. He raised an eyebrow and pulled away as I giggled. Such a tease. He would never try anything at his parents' house. They believed in no close contact until marriage. I was glad Alex didn't share that view with his parents. But he still would never try anything when we were here.

"You guys are so perfect together. When's the big day going to be?" Lacey joked.

"I could say the same about you and Jamie," Alex teased playfully, and I laughed. Alex was aware Lacey never wanted to get serious. Jamie pushed his thick hair out of his eyes and gave Lacey a hopeful glance. It was obvious to everyone he wanted more than just a fling.

"Does anyone want a drink?" Alex changed the subject and opened the cooler. He passed one to everyone as he sat back down next to me.

"I saw this article online about this suspension bridge that's like five hours north of here. And it connects to the Upper Peninsula. I didn't even know Michigan had an Upper Peninsula," Jamie said as he popped open his beer.

His statement was greeted with silence while everyone else just stared at him. After a couple of moments, Niko spoke up.

"You mean the Mackinac Bridge?" he asked while he suppressed a laugh. Jamie looked at him questioningly, not knowing what he was missing.

"Jamie, the Mackinac Bridge is one of the landmarks in Michigan; everyone that lives here knows about it. It's five miles long," Alex said, shooting his brother an annoyed look.

"Yeah, and only people who aren't from Michigan call it the Upper Peninsula. It's called the U-P." Geo pronounced each letter separately. "So, if you want to fit in while living here, make sure you say UP when talking about up north," he explained like he was talking to a small child.

"Ignore them. They like to make people feel stupid to make themselves feel better. You know people that aren't from here have no idea about the UP or the Mackinac Bridge," I said pointedly to the twins.

"I told you that Sage and I go up north every year," Lacey added, looking at Jamie. "That's where we go. Can't go up north without seeing the bridge."

"We should all plan a trip up there. I'd love to see it before summer is over. We could go next weekend. Lacey and I have off work," Jamie said excitedly.

Lacey nodded in agreement, and I looked at Alex excitedly. I loved to go up north and hadn't been yet this summer. We hadn't even talked about it with what happened last month. And we definitely needed a trip away.

"What do you think, Alex?" I asked.

"I was supposed to spend that weekend with my parents..." he started to say, and my shoulders sagged in disappointment. "But I think I can skip it this one time."

I gave him a huge smile and wrapped my arms around his neck. It felt good that, for once, Alex had chosen me instead of his family. A small stab of guilt went through me, but I was too excited to feel that bad about it.

"You kids have fun. Don't let the bears get you," Geo said with a grin.

"Wait—there are bears up there?" Jamie asked with a little nervousness. Everyone laughed and started talking about all the plans we had to make before we left.

CHAPTER THREE

Sage

It was hot and muggy like it always was in early August, which made the iced coffee I was drinking that much better. Rocking slowly back and forth, I withheld my laugh as Alex checked his watch for the tenth time.

"I told you she wouldn't be ready on time," I reminded him as he leaned against the porch railing.

"We were supposed to leave over an hour ago," he grumbled under his breath.

His OCD was showing. Being late or unorganized drove him up a wall, and ever since he'd moved in with Lacey and me last year, it had been a huge adjustment for him. I wasn't the tidiest person, and my sister was even worse.

"While we have a minute alone…" He shot me an apprehensive smile, making my stomach twist with nerves. "Have you given any thought to what we talked about a couple weeks ago? About getting our own place?"

I bit my lip, debating what to say. Was I ready? I wasn't sure. But I knew Lacey wasn't ready to live alone. She might be three years older than me, but at twenty-four, I didn't think she was ready to adult by herself yet. I took care of everything. Our dad's bank accounts. The bills. The house. She helped financially but hated any kind of responsibility.

"I don't know, Alex," I murmured as he shook his head. "This house is huge. I don't think she could take care of it all by herself."

He hesitated. "Maybe it's time to sell it."

"No," I snapped, not able to stop myself. "I'm not ready to do that yet."

I kept my eyes on the white, chipped wraparound porch. My parents had bought this house when they got married. It was a huge old farmhouse that they'd planned to fill with kids. Before my mom disappeared. This house was my dad's pride and joy before he got sick. I couldn't imagine selling it. Or moving. Which was why Alex had moved in with us last year.

"Lacey is old enough to take care of herself," he said gently, sitting on the swing next to me. "She's the older sister."

"I could say the same about you," I argued back. "You're more mature than both your older brothers combined."

"No. They just want different things in life. You know this. I'm ready to settle down when you are. I already know what I want in life. They're still figuring it out."

"Just like Lacey."

He wrapped an arm around me and pulled me closer. "Unlike Lacey, they don't lean on me for anything."

Opening my mouth to start arguing again, I stopped as Jamie walked out of the house. Alex gave me a kiss on the forehead before standing up. "We'll talk about it later."

"We're making good time this morning, don't you think, Sage?" Lacey asked, walking out of the house. She shot me a wink as a vein twitched above Alex's eye.

"This is going to be a long drive," I muttered, climbing into the back seat of Lacey's truck. Instead of going to college, she'd bought this beast of a vehicle with her college fund. It was so loud everyone in our small town knew who was driving down Main Street when they heard it.

"It'll be fun," Lacey corrected me as she pulled out of the driveway. "Going up north is the best part of the summer."

The five-hour drive was fun. Lacey's truck was comfortable and had more than enough room for all the camping supplies. We sang songs and talked about childhood memories. Jamie was the odd one out, not growing up in Capac. He mostly just listened and didn't add anything about his past. He was shy compared to most of Lacey's other guy friends.

Finally, we made it to Mackinaw City, and nostalgia washed over me. I had so many great memories up here with Lacey and our dad. He made sure we went every year, even if it was only for a couple of days. It was a tradition he kept even after Mom disappeared. We pulled into the hotel parking lot, and the guys started to get the bags out while Lacey and I went to check in. I rushed everyone out of the hotel room because I wanted to get the day started.

We walked down to the Mackinac Bridge first. I could tell that Jamie was excited to be here, especially with Lacey, as we all gazed at it in awe. The suspension bridge was massive. The tall cream-colored arches that held the suspension cables towered over the army green–colored bridge. It was so long that the other end of the bridge could only be seen on a clear day. The large beach was busy with all the people who had come here for vacation. Kids were running and chasing the seagulls. The water was a deep blue, and people were standing in it as the small waves hit the sand. Laughs and happy chatter could be heard over the cars driving over the bridge. A smile crept into my face as I took it all in. Up north would always be my happy place.

"We'll have to come back when it's all lit up at night," Lacey told Jamie. "It's beautiful."

The beach was rocky; the sand was full of pebbles and stones. I walked forward slowly, my bare feet stepping gingerly over the rocks until cool water ran over my skin. The sun was high in the sky, and there wasn't a cloud to be seen. Alex wrapped his arms around my waist, and I leaned back, closing my eyes as memories swallowed me.

One of my favorite photos of my mom popped into my mind. It was taken here, almost in this exact spot on the beach. I hadn't even been born yet, but the picture sat on my nightstand table. Lacey was a toddler in the picture, and she was surrounded by seagulls because she was throwing food to them. Our mom was in the background, laughing. Her smile was so genuine. So joyful. Full of life. A pang of grief speared my heart, thinking of all the things we were never able to do with her. Alex's arms tightened around me, bringing me back to the present.

With one last look at the bridge, I turned away so we could go explore Mackinaw City. There were so many little shops with one-of-a-kind items. We saw about five different T-shirt shops in the first half hour, all fighting for customers to come in and get whatever they want printed on them. We each chose a crazy colored shirt and had something funny printed on it. Lacey and I slipped our new shirts on and walked around looking like tourists instead of Michigan natives.

There was a little photo shop where we dressed up in outfits from the Old West and took pictures. We visited a fun house and got lost in the maze of mirrors. I sat on a bench to pose for a picture next to a bronze statue and nearly jumped out of my skin when the so-called statue moved. Alex, Lacey, and Jamie were in tears from laughing so hard. We finally got hungry, and I convinced everyone to eat at my favorite pizza place for dinner.

Alex held the door open for everyone, and we sat at one of the few free tables. The chairs were the cheap metal folding ones, and the tables had seen better days. But no one who came here cared about that because the food and atmosphere made up for it. There was such a friendly vibe. The walls all had colorful murals on them. One wall was full of people's signed names from all over the world who had visited.

"Jamie, how are you enjoying it so far?" Alex asked once we were all settled at our table.

"It's so much fun up here. I've never seen a town like this before. It's like this all year?"

Lacey answered, "No, only in the summer. Everything pretty much closes by the end of fall because of the weather."

"I'm surprised my aunt and uncle have never been here. They've been in Michigan for a few years now," Jamie said as he looked at the wall of names.

"What does your family do?" I asked, curious about the guy who was so smitten with my sister. I had a suspicion that Lacey really liked him. He was the first guy Lacey had ever invited up north with us.

Jamie paused for a moment. "Oh, we have a family business. They wanted to expand it out of Texas. Which is why I've been here setting it up..." His voice trailed off as he reached for his glass of water.

"His family business is a big secret. Even I don't know all the details," Lacey joked, and I shot her a questioning look. She didn't know what he did? How was Lacey okay with not knowing details about the guy she was sharing her life with? I could never do that. I was too nosey and needed to know everything about anything that interested me. My dad had always told me I was too curious for my own good. Before I could ask another question, the server came with the pizza and asked if anyone needed refills. The conversation turned to what we had planned for tomorrow, and when I glanced across the table, it seemed Jamie was relieved about that.

CHAPTER FOUR

Sage

Even though it was already nine, the sky still had a little light left. I loved how the sun set late in the summers. It gave us so much more time to enjoy the days, especially when on vacation. We were walking from the hotel to the main street to grab some drinks. Dusk started to creep up as we neared the bar. Alex held the door open for everyone and I walked in, admiring the unique interior.

It was like a log cabin, and all the walls were light sandy rounded wood logs. The tables and booths were made of the same wood, but a few shades darker than the walls. The light was dim and cast an orange glow throughout the bar. There was a small dance floor where a couple of people danced to the country music playing. The atmosphere in here was perfect for a night out.

I caught a few men glancing at Lacey as she leaned over. We were both wearing jeans with tight crop tops we had bought at one of the shops today. I thought the one I had on was low cut, but it was nothing compared to hers. Jamie noticed too but just chuckled and put his arm around Lacey, which made me smile. He seemed like a good guy.

We started with some beers but soon switched to stronger drinks. I stared at the shot glasses Jamie brought to the table and cringed, remembering the last time I'd had whiskey. It wasn't my usual choice. I gulped down the first one, shook my head, and quickly took a sip of soda to get rid of the bitter taste. Lacey nursed her mixed drink as the rest of us took a second shot. The bar had decks of cards, so we played a drinking game while more people piled into the place. I raised my eyebrows in surprise at Alex drinking so much. He usually liked to keep a level head. I'd only seen him drunk a couple of times. Jamie finished his beer, and the fact that he could still stand was shocking.

"Let's dance." Alex shot me a smile and held his hand out to me. After he led me to the dance floor, we swayed to the music with Alex's hands on my hips. The good kind of buzzed fuzziness spread through me, and Alex's touch felt even better than usual. A few minutes later, Lacey and Jamie joined us on the dance floor.

As the song changed, I turned to see Jamie inches from another man's face. Lacey was standing behind him, pulling his arm, trying to get him away from whatever was going on. Inching closer, I tried to hear their conversation.

"You touched her ass. I saw it," Jamie was saying. My stomach bubbled nervously as my eyes darted between the two men. Jamie was drunk, and from the look of the guy in the cowboy hat trying to keep steady, he was too.

"Don't know what you're talkin' about," the cowboy said with a thick southern accent. "She backed into me."

My shoulders tensed as Jamie got in the man's face. What had started out as a good night was about to spin out of control. I stepped closer just as Jamie shoved the man back. Alex grabbed my hand and pulled me back a step.

"Maybe your girl shouldn't wear things so short if she don't want the attention." The man shrugged. His eyes stayed focused on Jamie. He didn't seem like the type of man to back down from a fight, especially while intoxicated. My nervousness spiked to anger at his words. Breaking free of Alex's grip, I wedged myself between Jamie and the man.

"Don't you dare blame my sister. You're the one who touched her when you had no right," I snarled, not blinking as I stared him down. I didn't like confrontation, but when someone went after my sister, all bets were off. I was sure the whiskey surging through my veins was helping my rage show through too. His eyebrows squished together in surprise as his sour breath hit my face.

"What, not used to being told off by a woman?" I asked, refusing to be the one to back down first.

"This ain't about you. Go away and let the men talk, sweetie," the man sneered, putting his hand on my hip and shoving me away.

A cry escaped me as I stumbled to the side, but an arm swooped down and caught me before I hit the floor. I tried whirling around, livid that this asshole had put his hands on me. Alex pulled me back, and I realized it was his arm that was around me. After moving me behind him, he stormed up to the man. Alex grabbed him by the collar and shoved him hard until he slammed into the back wall of the bar. The guy's cowboy hat fell to the ground, and he looked at Alex in stunned silence. Clutching the guy's shirt, he leaned in to put his face right next to the man's ear.

"Don't you ever fucking touch her again. Don't talk to her. Don't look at her. That goes for her sister too," Alex hissed.

"Sure, man, calm down. I'm leavin' now," the cowboy said quickly. His hands were raised in surrender. Even drunk, the guy wasn't stupid. Alex was much larger and could easily take him. My mouth was hanging open as I watched. Alex had never acted like this before. He had never lost his cool on someone like that. Ever. I almost didn't recognize him. His face was pulled into a menacing scowl. His jaw was clenched, and the usual warmth in his eyes had turned ice cold. Jamie walked up behind Alex, his hands closed into fists. He looked ready to swing. It wouldn't be a fun vacation to bail him out of jail. Before I had a chance to calm the guys down, the bartender rushed over.

"You guys need to get out of my bar now," he said pointedly to Alex, who was still gripping the guy's shirt. Alex glanced over at the bartender and took a deep breath.

"Sorry," he mumbled as he slowly unclenched his fists. He looked the man square in the eyes as he backed away. The man hurriedly picked up his hat and stomped out. Lacey walked up to Jamie and tried to hold his hand, but he pulled away. Before Lacey said anything, Jamie raced out of the bar. I glanced at Alex, whose face was slowly turning back into the one I knew and loved.

His arm came around my shoulders, and he gently guided me toward our abandoned table. Lacey's face was flushed with embarrassment that all eyes were on her. Neither of us enjoyed arguments or fighting. Lacey nearly always shied away from it. Even as my hands shook, I wasn't sorry. I'd defended my sister and had nothing to feel bad about. Alex grabbed my hand as we left the bar. His breaths were still coming out fast from the encounter even though he was back to his collected self.

"Come on. Let's go get some ice cream," Alex said, keeping his tone light. "The store down the street stays open until the bars close down."

"Yeah. I can bring some back for Jamie." Lacey refused to look at me as she spoke. "I'm sure he's back at the hotel by now."

I pressed my lips together, keeping my words to myself. My opinion of Jamie had gone downhill after he just left my sister at the bar. Alex squeezed my hand and shook his head, silently telling me not to say anything. He was right. It would only start a fight, and tonight had been stressful enough.

CHAPTER FIVE

Him

Standing in the shower, I let the hot water run down my body as I thought about how the night had transpired. Soap ran down my face as I rinsed shampoo out of my hair. Luckily, I'd had a front-row seat to what happened at the bar.

Poor Lacey just looked mortified about the whole incident. She was so naïve to all the things that could happen in the world outside her small town. She needed a man in her life who would protect and speak up for her. My cock twitched when I thought about how Sage had acted. Now *she* was fearless. Got right up in that guy's face. Didn't need a man to fight her battles. Yet she was the one on the path to marry that boyfriend. Trying to ignore the blood rushing to my dick, I forced her face out of my mind. No point getting attached. The plan was in place.

My jaw ticked as another image stole my thoughts. The boyfriend, Alex, surprised me with how he came at that guy. I didn't think Alex had it in him to act like that. But I was sure I could still take him in a fight if needed. Not that it would ever happen. The girls were priority. And if everything went how it was supposed to, I wouldn't have to worry about anything.

Their lives were going to change very soon, and not for the better. Mackinaw City was the perfect vacation spot, but instead of enjoying myself, I was tasked with watching the girls. I'd known everything they'd done since they started the trip. They were happy when they got here and looked at the bridge. If only they knew what was going to happen when they crossed that bridge in the next couple of days.

Allowing myself a moment of weakness, my mind wandered back to Sage. It was fucking stupid to let myself get distracted when there were still little details in the plan to execute. Apparently, my dick didn't care, growing hard as I pictured Sage and how she'd stood up for herself at the bar. All that attitude and sass wrapped in a body that most men would commit a sin just to get a taste of. Most men. It shouldn't affect me.

Especially when I knew why she and her family were important. But I also knew more about her than just her looks. Her smart mouth could give anyone a run for their money. She was feisty. Spoke her mind. The complete opposite of the type of woman I was meant to be with. The group wanted their woman meek and obedient. Someday, I'd be expected to marry someone who shared in our belief. And I would. Because my life consisted of doing what was needed for the greater good.

So why the hell was this one girl so hard to get out of my head? Could it be that she was the forbidden fruit I wasn't allowed to taste because her life had already been chosen for a different reason? The bloodline of the women in her family was important to everything I was raised to honor.

"Fuck," I muttered, attempting to ignore my aching cock. She shouldn't be in my damn head. I had no time for distractions when the ceremony was so close. My sole focus was making sure everything went smoothly. I wouldn't let the group down. I gritted my teeth, forcing the thoughts of her away as I shut off the water.

I grabbed a towel and dried off my face. I paused for a moment, realizing why it was so different this time. I'd spent my entire life helping the group. As a kid, I did small jobs. The older I got, the more responsibility was given to me. I'd met chosen women in the past. Talked to them. Spent time with them before their time came to help the greater good. None of them stuck to me like the Taylor sisters did. Wrapping the towel around my waist, I silently admitted why I couldn't get the sisters out of my head. Why they were so different from every other chosen woman in the past.

I'd talked to Sage and Lacey. Interacted. Joked. Laughed. I *knew* them. And fuck, I enjoyed the time I'd spent with them.

The chosen women were usually strangers. We watched them and their families, but it was never personal. I saw all their faces. Heard their voices. Witnessed their tears. Listened to their last words. I remembered every name of every woman whose ceremonies I'd been a part of. They were important to the greater good. But I didn't feel for them. They were needed. I did what was asked of me, and that was it.

This time was different. The sisters' voices echoed through my head. I'd been to their home. Gotten a peek into their lives. Now an unsettling tightness swelled in my chest every time I pictured the fate one of the sisters was going to endure.

And I fucking hated it. I learned long ago feelings and emotions didn't have a place in my type of life. I was an expert at concealing my thoughts—even from myself. These new intrusive pangs of conscience would do nothing to change the plan. It didn't matter what I thought. The only thing that mattered was making sure I did what the group asked.

I left the bathroom and strode into the hotel room to grab a pair of shorts as I wondered if I was the only one with these thoughts. I wasn't the only one in the group who knew the sisters personally. Blowing out a long breath, I rubbed my temples. This whole thing with the Taylor family was abnormal. We had to be more careful than usual with the strict rules we followed to keep our tradition a secret. Once we claimed one chosen woman from a family, we left their children and grandchildren alone. Multiple people missing from one family would only raise suspicion. I didn't agree with targeting the sisters after their mother had been chosen. I'd voiced my concerns. And was ignored. It wasn't my call to make.

Grabbing a bottle of tequila off the table, I took a long swig as I made my way to the small balcony. It was time to get back to business. The big night was only a couple of days away. Separating Sage and Lacey would be difficult. But with the help of the others, it would all go accordingly.

Rolling my neck, I stared up at the cloudless night sky. It was always so peaceful up here. With no big cities, the stars could always be seen. It was such a clear night that I could see lights from the UP just across the water. Sinking into the wicker chair, I gritted my teeth when my phone interrupted my one moment of peace. Glancing at who it was made me want to swallow the whole damn bottle of tequila. But I answered it anyway. I mean, I was raised to respect my elders—especially those in the inner circle.

"Yeah?" I asked just above a whisper as I peered back into the hotel room to make sure I had dead bolted the door.

"Do you have your plan set? These next few days are crucial. Nothing can happen out of place," the man said, getting straight down to business.

"Yes."

"Why're you so quiet?"

"Because I'm at the hotel. Not much privacy here. You know where I am."

"Good. Just do exactly as we all talked about. It will work out perfectly."

"Yes."

"Do the girls have any suspicions about anything?"

"Not that I'm aware."

"Good. Most of us are already up here waiting. Everything will be in place by tomorrow."

"Okay."

"One more thing...stop talking to me like that. I've been making these plans since before you were born, kid. Show me some damn respect."

I rolled my eyes. "Yes, sir. Sorry, just don't want to talk too much about it in public."

I waited for a response but heard nothing. Looking at my phone, I grumbled under my breath; he had hung up. Tossing the phone back onto the small glass table next to me, I sucked in a deep breath to calm down. This was not the time to lose control. A clear head was essential for what was coming next. And I couldn't deny I was excited to see everyone. The group was like family. Well, most of them anyway.

They came together in many places to help with the ceremonies once a year. Always in less populated locations to not arouse suspicion and never in huge groups, only twelve or fewer at each place. We couldn't get much more desolate than the place we had in the UP, except maybe Alaska. There wasn't even cell service up there, which was a benefit. To keep things as hidden as possible.

I gazed at the bright stars as my mind wandered back to the sisters again. This was the last time I would think of them as people I knew. They were chosen, and there was no alternate option. But a feeling refused to go away when I was around one of the sisters. An unrelenting presence that made me want to shed the secret I had sworn to protect. But that would be a threat to my family, and I'd die before putting them in danger.

The plan would go perfectly. One sister would be sacrificed in two days. It was the same month every year when it had to be done. Always during the full moon. The long thought-out plan changed since they'd decided to go camping. But everything was in place.

And it would happen at the lake.

CHAPTER SIX

Sage

Rolling onto my back, I groaned and rubbed my temples. It felt like a jackhammer was attacking my brain. I didn't even remember how many drinks I'd had last night. Peeking my eyes open, I watched the brown ceiling fan spin in slow circles. I jerked in surprise when Alex's arm rested on my stomach.

"You okay?" he asked, his voice hoarse from sleep.

"Besides the hangover from hell?" I chuckled and then winced as my head throbbed.

"Last night…" He turned over in bed to face me. "I lost it when that guy put his hands on you. I'm not sorry about what I did. But I hope I didn't scare you."

Running a hand through my hair, I glanced back at the fan again. "It didn't bother me."

He caught my wrist, pulling my hand away from my hair. Sighing, I turned to look at him. He raised an eyebrow, releasing me and running his hand down my arm.

"You're a horrible liar." He shook his head and laughed as he pulled me closer.

He was right. I couldn't lie to save my life. My worst tell was touching my hair when I lied. When I was a kid, Lacey would always lie for me because I could never get a false word past my dad without him knowing. And Alex knew me just as well as my dad had before he got sick.

"Alex, you didn't scare me," I promised him. "It surprised me, that's all. You've never acted like that."

"I've never seen a man push you before."

"My knight in shining armor." I rolled my eyes but shot him a smile. "But just letting you know, I can take care of myself."

"I'll always take care of you, Sage."

"I know." I gave him a quick kiss before forcing myself to get out of bed. Damn, I was only twenty-one; hangovers shouldn't be this bad already. My head stayed in a fog as I slipped on some clothes.

"I'm going to go check on Lacey," I told Alex as I slid on my flip-flops.

"She was really embarrassed about last night," he muttered, looking a bit guilty. "She didn't do anything. It was me who made the scene."

"It wasn't that. It was how Jamie stormed off. He just left her there. I don't know. I was starting to like him until he did that."

"He was wasted. I'm sure he feels bad."

That was Alex. Always trying to see the best in people. A trait I didn't have. Second chances weren't in my vocabulary. That's probably why Lacey and Alex were the only two people I spent time with. I had no interest in making new friends who could possibly hurt me. My small circle was enough.

"Once I get back, we can get ready to leave," I said, pulling the door open and squinting into the bright sun.

"I'll pack up while you're gone," Alex replied, looking ready to fall back to sleep.

I ran to the lobby and grabbed two coffees before heading toward Lacey's room. With a cup in each of my hands, I raised my foot to knock on the door right as Jamie rushed out and nearly plowed into me.

"Sorry, sorry," he apologized as he reached for the coffees to make sure they didn't fall.

"It's fine," I replied curtly, not hiding the fact that I was upset.

"Sage, I'm sorry about last night. I've apologized to your sister so many times already. I was actually going to get coffee to surprise her with when she woke up." He glanced at the two coffees in my hands. "Guess you beat me to it."

I sighed. "Look, Jamie, I like you. But how you treated my sister last night, just leaving her at the bar, made me think differently."

I was being honest with him, just like I was with everyone else. I didn't care if Lacey loved him; he wasn't going to treat my sister badly.

"I know. When I drink, I lose my temper a bit," he said sheepishly. "I regretted it right after I left."

"Yeah, well, I just don't want to see my sister hurt."

I moved toward the door, going rigid when he grabbed my arm. I narrowed my eyes when he tried pulling me closer. After noticing my reaction, he stepped back hastily and raised his arms.

"Sorry. I really like her. And I want you to know that. I love spending time with her, and I'll do what I can to make up for this. I was an idiot."

I gave him a hard look. He seemed sincere, but I didn't know him well enough to fully believe him after this one conversation. We'd just have to see how the rest of the trip went.

I shrugged. "My sister is a big girl. She can choose who she wants to see. But I can choose to kick their asses if they don't treat my sister right."

Jamie nodded and mumbled something about getting food

before he scurried away. Honestly, I'd prefer to not deal with him anymore. But we still had a few days to spend up north, and I wasn't going to let him ruin our vacation. As long as he didn't treat Lacey like that again, I'd keep my mouth shut.

A couple of hours later, we checked out of the hotel and got back on the road. The truck was silent, with some tension from last night still in the air. Lacey had been quiet all morning, and even though she had a smile plastered on her face, it was obvious she was still upset with Jamie.

My stomach twisted with nerves as the Mackinac Bridge came into view. Fiddling with my seatbelt as Lacey drove onto the bridge, I kept my eyes on the roof of the car to avoid looking at the water below. As much as I loved coming up north, I was terrified of bridges. It didn't matter that I'd gone over this one countless times before; the fear never lessened.

My dad once told us about how a car was driving during high winds and got swept off and landed in the water below. I knew the odds of that happening were almost zero, but that didn't stop my pounding heart and sweaty palms. The smooth ride became bumpy as the concrete beneath us turned into metal grates.

Alex's hand wrapped around mine, and I shot him a tight smile. He was well aware of my fear, especially when I wasn't the one driving. After what felt like forever, the road smoothed out again, and my jumbled nerves were replaced with excitement. Trees lined the highway for miles, and I sucked in a deep breath, letting my body relax.

Reading a sign as we passed it, I grinned. *Hiawatha National Forest.* The forest was so large it took up the majority of the Upper Peninsula. If anyone wanted to escape from real life, this was the perfect place to go. Cell phones didn't work out here. There was no bustle of large cities. Just nature and silence. And it was just what I needed.

After driving for over an hour, we stopped at a small market to stock up on food and ice. The guy behind the counter rang up our items as he made small talk.

"This your first time camping up here?" he asked.

"I'm the only newbie in the group." Jamie laughed. "It's beautiful up here."

"Yes," the man agreed, putting our food in a bag. "Just be careful. Lots of wildlife in these parts."

Alex nodded. "Especially where we're staying. Up by the bay."

"Now we get to guess where the campsite is," Lacey interjected, glancing at Jamie. "I told him we wouldn't have signal up here, and we should have printed off the directions. But someone didn't listen."

"I didn't realize how cut off from civilization we'd be." Jamie shrugged. "We'll find it."

The man handed the bags to Alex. "Where are you staying?"

"Campland Bay," Alex answered. "We shouldn't be too far away—"

"That's just down the road," the guy interrupted. "Stay on this road, and you'll see a sign for it. Enjoy your vacation."

We thanked him and got back on the road. Jamie peered out the window intently as Lacey drove. After about forty-five minutes, I was beginning to doubt the guy at the store knew what he was talking about. I was hoping we'd find it soon. Spending an entire day in the car wasn't on my list of things to do on vacation.

"There." Alex pointed to a small sign. "That has to be it."

"Just down the road, my ass," Jamie grumbled as Lacey slowed down to turn into the campground.

"Be glad we found it," I said with a shake of my head. "Next time, we print off the directions."

Jamie shot me an annoyed glance, and I frowned. If things kept going how they were, I didn't think there would be a second time. I had no desire to hang out with Jamie anymore. Lacey shot me a pleading look in the rearview mirror when she saw my face. Damn, she really did like him.

"Let it go," Alex murmured under his breath, leaning close to me. "Don't let him ruin our vacation, okay?"

"He won't ruin it," I muttered, deciding to drop it. Looking out the window, my mouth dropped at the beauty of the campground. The campsites were far apart, and trees made sure each campsite had all the privacy they could want. Lacey expressed her unhappiness by letting out a long sigh. Unlike me, Lacey and nature didn't mix. It had taken me forever to convince her to go camping instead of staying in a hotel the entire trip.

As we drove through the campground, a few campers looked up curiously from their campfires. There were maybe only twenty sites in this entire park. Each secluded from its neighbors, thanks to the dense forest. Lacey pulled into our reserved spot, and everyone scrambled out. I stretched my achy muscles from sitting for so long as Alex opened the tailgate of the truck.

"There's really only two public toilets for this entire campground?" Lacey complained. "Where are we going to shower?"

"We can rinse off in the lake. I think you'll be fine for two and a half days," I said, rolling my eyes. Alex chuckled, and I looked over my shoulder at him.

"Not used to camping with such newbies?" I joked. He went camping with his family up here at least once a year and was used to campgrounds like this.

"It's okay. It'll be an adventure, baby."

Alex set up the tent by himself while Jamie looked blankly at the instructions and tried to look like he was helping. Examining our huge campsite as I lugged the cooler out of the truck, I spotted a small trail that must have lead to the lake. I set the cooler next to the picnic table as Lacey dropped the firewood next to the small metal pit.

"Need help?" I asked Alex as I glanced at Jamie. He was standing there with the instructions in his hand, even though Alex clearly knew what he was doing.

"No, I'm almost done." He stopped for a moment and gave me a quick kiss. "I know you've been waiting to go to the lake. Go. I'll meet you when I'm done."

"Want to come, Lacey?" I asked her, as she came to stand next to me.

"Actually"—Jamie tossed the instructions onto the picnic table—"I was hoping Lacey would go for a walk with me."

Lacey hesitated, and I knew she was thinking about what he'd done last night. For most of the day, she'd been acting like everything was fine. Because she liked him. Shock tore through me as she nodded to him, and they began walking down the small road, hand in hand.

"I think she likes him enough to break her three-month rule," Alex murmured, watching them disappear around a bend in the road. "Maybe your sister is finally growing up."

"I guess."

"Sage, he made a mistake. He was drunk. It happens. I think he really is sorry," he said softly. "Give him a chance. Come on, let's go down to the water. I'm done setting up the tent."

Deciding that Alex was right, I ran my hand through my hair and nodded. If Lacey was happy, then I wanted to be happy for her. Alex grabbed my hand and lead me to the small trail I'd seen earlier. I could hear the waves breaking before Alex had even pushed past the shrubs. A calm washed over me as my feet hit the sandy beach.

Lake Superior was so large I couldn't even see the other side of it. I remembered stories about the shipwrecks that had never been found because the lake was so massive. The beach went on for miles in one direction, and in the other was a small cliff a couple of miles away.

"Isn't it beautiful, baby?" Alex gazed at the water admiringly as he pulled me into his arms. "This is why I love to come up here. It's like living a different life."

"I love it here. I'm glad you came with me." I snuggled against his chest, feeling his heart racing faster than usual.

"You know that I love you more than anything? I want to spend forever with you."

"I love you too, Alex. Always." Turning in his arms, I met his gaze.

"I'm with my perfect girl—in my favorite place." He sounded nervous, and I tilted my head in confusion. "Sage, will you marry me?"

Butterflies swirled in my stomach as shock hit me. That wasn't something I'd been expecting at all. Before I could say anything, he kept talking.

"I know we've talked about it before, and you want to wait until after school. We can wait to get married for as long as you want. But I want the world to know you're mine. I've never been so sure of anything as I am knowing I want to marry you."

"Yes," I answered without hesitation. There wasn't any part of me that wanted to say no. He wouldn't push me to marry. I wanted to spend forever with him, and a long engagement would be perfect.

A smile stretched across his face as he touched the ring that hung around his neck. "This was so spur of the moment, I didn't even get a ring yet. I would let you wear mine, but it's way too big. But being here with you—I couldn't wait any longer."

"Ring or no ring, I'm still yours. And I love spur-of-the-moment things."

CHAPTER SEVEN

Sage

We walked back to the campsite and found Lacey and Jamie making out on the picnic table. They'd obviously made up from last night, and they untangled from each other when Lacey caught sight of us. Someone cleared their throat, and we all looked to see a man standing at the edge of the road near our truck.

"Hey there. I'm Bud. I keep up the campsites, so if you need anything, just ask," he said with a smile. I tried not to stare at the gaps where his teeth should be. It looked like he hadn't showered in a week, and his blue overalls were almost completely brown from dirt. Maybe Lacey had a point about there being no showers here.

"Thanks, Bud." Alex moved forward and shook Bud's hand. "I'm

Alex. We saw on the website there were kayaks we could borrow. Is that accurate?"

"Sure. They're over near the entrance." Bud pointed down the road. "Feel free. Just make sure you bring them back when you're done."

"Thank you," I told him, glancing at my phone. There was still enough time to get on the water today before it got too dark.

"You're all trolls, aye?" Bud asked.

Jamie gave him a bewildered look. "Excuse me?"

I giggled and explained, "Trolls are what they call people who live below Mackinac Bridge."

"Oh...okay." Jamie still looked like the guy had just insulted us.

"Don't worry, man. We call people from the UP 'yoopers.' Just fun nicknames." Alex chuckled and patted him on the shoulder.

Bud waved as he strolled down the road, making conversation with other campers. Alex opened the cooler and frowned before glancing at me.

"We didn't get enough ice," he said, shaking his head. "I'll go grab some more."

"I wanted to kayak before it gets dark." I bit my lip and shot my sister a hopeful glance. "Lacey, want to come?"

She groaned. "Can we just lay on the beach and enjoy the sun?"

"We won't go far," I pressed, wanting some alone time with her to tell her about Alex's proposal. "Then we can lay out."

"Fine."

"I'll get the kayaks for you," Jamie volunteered as he headed to where Bud had pointed to earlier.

Alex gave me a quick hug. "I'll see you in a bit. You need anything else from the store?"

"No, I'm good."

Lacey tossed him the keys, and he climbed into the truck. Lacey and I went into the tent and changed into our swimsuits before heading to the beach. Jamie was there with two kayaks at the water's edge.

"You two be careful," he said, looking at Lacey.

"You don't want to join us?" Lacey asked him.

"No. I'm going to try and get some sleep." He rubbed the back of his head. "I didn't get much last night."

The second he spoke, regret filled his eyes from bringing up what happened at the bar again.

"We'll see you when we get back," Lacey said brightly, ignoring his concern.

I dragged my kayak into the water, and shivers rolled through me as the ice-cold water hit my legs. Lacey came up behind me, letting out a squeal when she stepped into the water.

"It's freezing," she complained, climbing into her kayak. "I swear if I fall in—"

"You'll be fine," I cut in. "There's no waves or wind today. It's perfect."

We paddled out farther, and I pointed to the cliff in the distance. Lacey rolled her eyes but nodded as she followed me.

"Alex proposed," I blurted out, unable to wait any longer.

Lacey stopped paddling and stared at me in shock as the small waves rocked the kayaks. My heart sank when I saw no joy on her face. I wanted her to be happy for me.

"What did you say?" she asked.

I frowned. "I said yes. We've been together for over three years, Lacey. I love him."

"You're not even twenty-two yet."

"So?"

"*So*, I don't want you making a mistake and regretting it."

I rolled my eyes. "I won't regret it."

"I don't think you want to marry him for the right reasons."

I started paddling again. "The reason is that I love him. What other reasons do you get married for?"

"Sage," Lacey said gently. "I want you to be happy. But I think you're doing it because you don't want to be alone."

"I'm not alone."

"I know..." She trailed off, and we paddled toward the cliff in silence before she finally said what she wanted. "Mom left us when you were only a baby. Now Dad. I mean, he's still here, but not really. And we can't live together for the rest of our lives. I really like Jamie. I'm thinking of moving in with him."

My jaw dropped in surprise. "What?"

"He's different from anyone else I've met," she admitted. "I think I'm falling in love with him."

"That's great, Lacey." I couldn't stop the empty feeling crawling through my chest. It had always been the two of us. Living apart would change everything.

"I think you want to marry Alex so he can't leave you." Her voice was full of apprehension, but she continued anyway. "Like our parents did. Even if it wasn't their fault. You're scared of being alone."

"Alex wouldn't leave me even if we didn't get married," I shot back, getting defensive. "I'm doing it because I want to."

"I'm not trying to make you mad," she replied quickly. "If this is what you want, then I'm happy for you."

"It is."

"Okay." She smiled, even though it was a bit forced. "Then congratulations. I can't wait to be the maid of honor and throw you a bomb-ass bachelorette party."

I laughed as our conversation lost the tension. "I can't wait."

"I'm going back. My arms are killing me," Lacey said while she started turning the kayak around. "Are you coming?"

"You go. I'm going to check out the cliff first. I'll be fine. It's not far," I replied. My body was starting to hurt too, but I was enjoying being on the water and didn't want to turn around before finishing what I'd set out to do. And I wanted to think about what Lacey had said. I wasn't marrying Alex because of my fear of being alone. Yet, her words wouldn't leave my head.

I watched her head back before facing the cliff again. I was already more than halfway there. Ignoring the aches throughout my body, I slowly started paddling again. I got lost in my thoughts, and it didn't take long until I was close enough to reach out and touch the rocks of the cliff. Letting my kayak drift, I took in the view. I loved Alex. That's why I'd said yes.

Running a hand down my face, I realized the sun was setting. I sighed as I turned the kayak around and looked at how far the campsite was. I needed to get back before it got dark. Being on the water when it was pitch black was not a good idea. As I paddled faster, my arm muscles burned. I made a mental note to seriously start working out when we were done with vacation.

As I got closer to the campsite, I spotted the red kayak floating in the water about ten feet from the beach. Squinting my eyes, I searched for Lacey. The sun was reflecting off the water, making it nearly impossible to see anything. With renewed energy, I quickly paddled closer to the abandoned kayak.

"Lacey?" I yelled, panic creeping into my voice. I shouldn't have left her alone. The currents in the lake were nothing to mess with. I frantically looked up and down the beach but saw no one. With my heart rate climbing, I scanned the water around the kayak. Nothing.

My aching muscles were now locked in fear. I looked at the beach again and saw someone standing there looking at me. Paddling closer, I realized it was Jamie. Maybe he was looking for Lacey too.

I treaded water as fast as the oar allowed, splashing water all over myself. Once I was a few feet from the beach, I jumped out, ignoring the frigid water. Pulling my kayak onto the sand, I was still searching the water for any sign of my sister.

"Where's Lacey?" I yelled to Jamie, who was over by the trees.

He just stared at me before stepping closer.

"Where's Lacey?" I repeated, clutching to my last shred of calm.

"What's wrong?" asked Lacey, who walked onto the beach from the campsite trail.

My knees almost buckled from relief. Rushing across the sand, I wrapped her in a hug. My heart was still racing, and I tried to stop my hands from shaking.

"Why is your kayak in the water? I thought you got pulled away by the current." I said with my arms still tight around her.

"Oh...I guess I didn't pull it on the beach enough. It must have drifted back out." Lacey pulled out of the embrace and shrugged.

That answer would have usually annoyed me, but I was so happy that Lacey was fine I didn't even care.

"Well, someone has to get it. We have to return the kayaks to Bud." I gazed at the kayak floating farther away from the beach.

"It's not going to be me. That water is freezing," Lacey replied as she turned to Jamie.

He let out a defeated sigh. "I'll do it. A little cold water won't hurt."

He slowly walked into the water and abruptly stopped when it reached his knees. Lacey and I both started laughing, knowing firsthand how cold the water was. It barely ever hit sixty degrees, even on the hottest days of summer. Jamie glanced back at us, looking even more determined to get the kayak.

"It's okay. It's not that bad," he insisted as he grabbed the kayak and rushed back to shore. Pulling the kayak onto the beach, he was covered in goosebumps, and a shiver ripped through him as he headed back to the trail. We followed him, and I could smell the bonfire before getting to the campsite. Alex was sitting next to the fire cooking hotdogs. He caught my eye and smiled.

"Have fun?" he asked, arching an eyebrow when Jamie stood inches from the fire, rubbing his hands together.

I laughed. "Yes. And I also learned I need to start working out with you. I'm so out of shape."

"I can help with that." He winked, making it obvious he wasn't talking about going to the gym.

"Sage told me about the engagement," Lacey spoke up, keeping her voice cheerful. "Congratulations. You make her happy, Alex."

"Wow." Jamie's eyes widened in surprise. "Congratulations."

We talked about it for a while as we ate. Alex had brought beer, but after last night, no one felt like drinking. I swallowed a yawn as

Alex wrapped his arm around me. It wasn't that late, but we were all about to pass out. We let the fire die, and Alex dumped water on it before we headed toward the six-person tent.

I slid into my sleeping bag and lay down between Lacey and Alex. Slowly drifting to sleep, I listened to the soft chirp of the crickets and the waves rolling onto the beach as I thought about how amazing today had been.

"You hear that?"

I was pulled from sleep to hear Alex and Jamie talking in hushed tones.

"What's wrong?" I asked groggily while I sat up.

I froze when I heard it. Someone—or something was outside the tent. Scratching at the side. Something brushed up against the tent wall, and I whipped my head toward the noise. Another sound came from the other side of the tent at the same time.

I held my breath, trying to be as quiet as possible. There was nothing that could be seen through the darkness. Suddenly, part of the tent moved, like something was pushing on it from the outside. My mouth went dry, and the hairs on the back of my neck stood up.

This vacation wasn't going how I'd expected at all.

CHAPTER EIGHT

Sage

"Someone's out there," Jamie said calmly, and I wondered why she wasn't panicking like I was.

The tent moved again, and I reached out, trying to find Alex's arm through the darkness. Nothing bad ever happened up here. No city crime. Murders were practically nonexistent. We most likely weren't in danger. But a nagging feeling that this trip was turning bad wouldn't go away.

"It's a bear," I whispered.

Alex grasped my hand and squeezed reassuringly before he replied. "No, bears travel alone. There's more than one out there. I'm guessing a pack of wolves."

"I left my gun in the truck," Jaime said with a groan.

"You have a gun?" Lacey spoke up. The sleeping bags rustled as she sat up next to me.

"Yeah, I decided to bring one along when you guys said there were bears up here," Jamie answered defensively.

"Would have been nice to know." Annoyance overtook the sleep in her voice.

"Shh," Alex breathed out. "We don't want to attract any more attention—"

We all jumped when a loud crash came from outside the tent. Feet scampered, and then a low growl filtered through the air. It almost sounded like they were eating something. We all sat in silence until the noises were gone.

"We'll check it out in the daylight." Alex lay back down. "Don't want to go out there if they're still hanging around."

I let my head fall back on the pillow, but I was wide awake. Alex's hold on my hand loosened as he fell back to sleep. Lacey's deep breathing on my other side made it clear I was the only one unable to fall back to sleep. Closing my eyes, I tried forcing my brain to shut off. I tossed and turned for hours until the sun came up.

Everyone else was still sleeping. It was still early, but the tent was already getting hot. As quietly as I could, I slipped out. I kept it unzipped a bit to get some air flow for them as they slept. My eyes widened at the mess all over the campsite. Hearing a rustle, I glanced back and saw Alex and Jamie stepping out. They stood beside me, assessing the damage.

"Who was the last one in the cooler last night?" Alex asked.

"It was me, but I'm sure I closed the lid," Jamie said, sounding anything but confident. He rubbed the back of his head and shot us an apologetic smile.

All our food was in pieces all over the campsite. The wrappers were torn to shreds. The guys started cleaning up the trash, and I glanced in the cooler. There was only water from ice that melted.

"We should have just stayed at a hotel."

I spun around to see Lacey's face scrunched in irritation.

"Okay, besides this, the camping trip has been fun...we're going to have to go to the store and stock back up," I told her, dumping the cooler on its side to drain the water.

"Oh no, I don't think so. I am not staying here another night. One night of wolves clawing at our tent was enough," Lacey exclaimed, crossing her arms before looking at Jamie for backup.

"Uh... yeah. Maybe we should go to a motel or something tonight," Jamie said as he shifted his feet. He still looked guilty about leaving the cooler open.

"There's a place just down the road you folks can stay at," Bud said as he sauntered toward the campsite, clearly having caught the tail end of the conversation.

"Like a motel?" Lacey asked hopefully, turning to Bud.

"I guess you can call it that. It's a real nice house, a mansion really. Been here since my Gramps was a kid. But they rent out rooms, usually to hunters or people just passing through. Not sure if they'll have rooms open. You know it's the busy season, aye?" Bud said, his yooper accent coming out full force.

"Thanks, Bud, we'll check it out. And sorry about the mess. We'll clean it up before we leave. Animals got into our stuff," Alex explained, obviously not wanting Bud to think we'd trashed it.

"Happens all the time." Bud chuckled and tipped his hat before walking away. I was disappointed Lacey and Jamie wanted to leave after only one night. I wasn't ready to go back to real life.

"Maybe we could find a better campsite that's near here." Alex caught the look on my face and was trying to save the trip.

"Why don't we check out the place Bud mentioned? It's right down the road, so we won't have to drive far. It's still on the lake, so we can at least enjoy one more night up here," Jamie said, and Lacey was nodding in agreement before he even stopped talking.

"It will probably be run down if their usual customers are hunters. Might not be up to your standards, Lacey." Alex laughed.

She scoffed. "Anything is better than a tent."

We all started cleaning up, and it didn't take long to have the campsite looking as good as new. Jamie went to find Bud and get directions to the place we were going to stay at while the rest of us packed everything up. We piled into the truck and turned out of the campground.

"Turn left out of here," Jamie told Lacey as we got back onto the main road. "Bud said there's a small dirt road a couple miles down, and that's where it is."

Once we hit the dirt road, I noticed there was no sign on the main road for the hotel. No one would ever find this place if they didn't know about it. After a couple of miles and a lot of potholes, the mansion came into view at the end of the road. I looked in awe and wondered if this would be better than camping.

It was beautiful. The white two-story beauty had massive pillars supporting the long wraparound porch. There were delicate high arched windows. It looked like a southern dream house. A hidden gem in the middle of nowhere.

Lacey parked, and we made our way up the front steps and onto the large porch. The details of this old house were amazing. Each pillar had large pine trees carved into it that wrapped from the bottom of the pillar and went all the way to the top. The front door was made of solid oak and had a copper door knocker in the shape of a lion.

Before anyone could knock, it swung open. A man who looked to be in his thirties greeted us with a joyous smile. He was wearing jeans and a red flannel shirt. His dirty-blond hair was a mess, and a thick beard covered his face.

"Hello. Are you all looking for a room?"

"Yes, two rooms, please. Just for one night. This place is absolutely stunning," I said as I glanced around the front porch. There were a few wooden rocking chairs with a little white table between them. I looked at the windows, and my eyes widened.

I cleared my throat. "Excuse me, but...why are there bars on your windows?"

Before the guy could respond, Alex answered, "Maybe to keep out the bears and other wildlife."

The man smiled and nodded. "Yes, that. Also, my wife and I spend a few months away in the winter and don't want any uninvited guests making themselves feel at home."

"Oh...makes sense," I muttered uneasily. Bars on a window was not something I was used to seeing. Especially up north. I met Lacey's eyes, but she only shrugged. Apparently, she was fine with it as long as she didn't have to stay in a tent again.

"My name is Eric. My wife is down south for the week, so it's just me working up here. We have a few rooms open. Unfortunately, with my wife being gone, the kitchen is closed. So you'll have to fend for yourselves," he explained as he opened the door wider and gestured for us to come in.

Disappointment filled me as I stepped inside. It was nothing like the beautiful exterior. The dark wood floor had nicks and scratches covering it and looked like it hadn't been redone or polished in decades. The dark velvet drapes hanging from the windows were moth eaten and stained. The high ceiling had cobwebs in the corners. There was a musty smell, like the place had been empty for a long time.

A pair of large wood doors to the left lead into a great room. I could see two pale pink sofas that would have been beautiful in their time—about forty years ago. But now they looked just as dreary as the rest of the place. All the walls were a dull white and were bare of any décor or paintings. About ten feet ahead of the front door was a wooden staircase. The paint on the white handrail was coming off and left white chips all over the steps.

"All the bedrooms are on the second floor. I'll show you which two are open." Eric glanced at me, and I tried to clear the dismay off my face. "I know it's not as beautiful as it used to be. This is a big house for two people to take care of. Usually, we only get hunters as guests, and they don't mind."

"Oh, it'll be fine for one night," I said quickly, not wanting to offend him.

Eric led us up the creaky stairs and pointed to the first door. "This is the bathroom, but there is also one in each of your rooms. The fourth and fifth rooms on the left side of the hall are the ones available."

Alex and I took the first room, while Lacey and Jamie took the next one. I pushed the door handle down and opened the door with hesitation. I didn't know what to expect after seeing downstairs. A breath of relief left me before I could stop it, and I was glad Eric had gone back downstairs.

It was as dreary as the first floor, with the same white bare walls. But at least it was clean. I glanced up and didn't see any cobwebs. The bed was neatly made with a brown comforter, and there was a nightstand and lamp on each side. There was a black leather lounge chair in the corner. I peeked into the bathroom and saw a stand-up shower enclosed in glass. There was a white porcelain sink next to the toilet. Small, but at least it was clean.

"It'll do for a night." Alex set our bag down. "We can go somewhere else if you want, though."

I shook my head. "No. This is fine. It's still right near the lake."

We went to Lacey and Jamie's room, and it was almost exactly the same. Except they had a little blue loveseat sofa instead of a lounge chair.

"We need to restock up on food." Alex held his hand out to Lacey for the keys. "I'll go grab some, if you guys want to relax here."

"I'll go too," Jamie said quickly. "I'll buy it all. It's my fault we have to get more."

After the guys left, Lacey and I decided to explore the old house. We walked back down the paint chipped stairs and went into the great room. The room was huge, and the only things in there were the worn-out sofas.

"I don't think renting rooms makes enough money," Lacey muttered quietly as we entered a large dining room. The long wooden table was large enough to fit at least sixteen people. I ran my hand down it and glanced at my dust-covered hand. Wiping it off on my shorts, I kept walking until we pushed open the doors on the other side of the room.

The kitchen was as large as every other room in this place. Some of the dull white cabinets were missing the knobs. It had the same dinged-up wood floor as the rest of the house. I tilted my head to the side as Lacey and I exchanged a confused look. Something was off. There was nothing on the counters. No coffee maker or microwave. It was just bare. Footsteps approached from behind us, and we turned to see Eric.

"Like I said, no one uses the kitchen when my wife is gone. She always keeps everything put away so people don't mess with her stuff," Eric said as he leaned against the counter.

"This place is massive. How many rooms are there?" Lacey asked.

"Well, there are thirteen bedrooms upstairs. The great room, dining room, a study, and a couple smaller rooms throughout the first floor. There's also another set of stairs in the back of the house that goes to the second floor. It's a lot to keep up, but it's been in my family since it was built," he explained. "We really don't want to deal with tourism, which is why we mostly cater to hunters. They aren't here for the wine and dine experience. They just want somewhere to sleep."

I nodded as I glanced around the empty kitchen again. I could imagine how grand it was back in the day. We chatted with Eric for a few more minutes before we went out to the backyard. The house was surrounded by forest. The old trees towered over the house, casting shade throughout the yard. The clean, refreshing scent of the sprawling pine trees relaxed me, and I sank into one of the oversized wooden chairs.

There was one little opening, a trail that led straight to the lake. The only sounds that could be heard were the birds and the gentle lapping of waves. This place was so peaceful. Life was so much simpler here. Disconnected from phones, surrounded by nature. It was a place someone could find themselves again.

"What was that?" I asked, sitting up and peering through the trees.

Lacey followed my gaze. "What?"

"I thought I saw something move over there."

"Probably just an animal. Relax, Sage."

She was right. I guess I was still on edge over the incident with the wolves last night. Leaning back in the chair, I could feel my body begging for sleep since I hadn't gotten any last night. Lacey was quiet, and I closed my eyes, enjoying the silence.

The rest of the vacation would be great.

CHAPTER NINE

Him

Ripping the car door open, I slipped into the passenger seat before slamming the door shut behind me.

"The plan is fucked."

I glared at the guy who was sitting in the driver's seat. "Really? I didn't notice. Why the hell do you think I'm here instead of getting ready for the ceremony, Thomas?"

His grip on the steering wheel tightened. "This is the last night we can do it—"

"I know," I snapped. "It'll still happen. We're working on it."

"It was supposed to happen at the lake. Them leaving that campground messed everything up." Thomas stated what I already knew. It had been a hellish morning of scrambling to change everything.

"You want to go against what the elders ordered and pull the plan?" I asked, already knowing what his answer would be. "I already tried calling it off until next year. They said no. It's happening."

Thomas's face paled. "If that's what they want, we'll do it."

I thought it was a fucking mistake. We'd changed courses too many times. It was a sign that this shouldn't happen. But it wasn't up to me. If they wanted to continue with it, then I'd do whatever they asked.

"After dark," I murmured, staring straight ahead. "We'll wait until the sisters are separated, and then we'll begin."

"What if they don't leave each other—"

"They will," I cut him off. "Everyone better be where they're supposed to be when it starts. We don't have any cell service up here."

He nodded. "They know what to do."

"Good."

Closing my eyes for a moment, I took a deep breath. It had already been a long day, and it was only the beginning. I was ready for the night to be done. Usually, everything went off without a hitch. But this time was different.

In every damn way possible.

CHAPTER TEN

Sage

"The sun is going down." I pushed the plate away and relaxed in the chair. We ate dinner outside after spending the day relaxing.

"You want to go down to the beach to watch the sunset?" Alex asked.

I smiled excitedly. "You read my mind. Lacey, you guys want to come?"

"I think we're going to spend some time in our room," Jamie answered first. He gave Lacey a sideways glance and grinned. Lacey laughed and nodded as she snuggled up to him. My gut twisted, and guilt hit me. I wanted her to be happy. I was with Alex. We were both growing up and moving on. Soon, we'd end up living apart, and I wasn't sure I was ready for that.

Alex grabbed my hand, and we headed down the trail to the beach. We got there just as the sun was above the water. The sky was cast in warm orange and yellow clouds. All my troubles disappeared as I sat in the sand. It had been such a good day, and this was the perfect way to end it.

"I have a ring for you. Back home," Alex murmured, putting his arm around me. "It was my grandmother's."

"You think your parents will be happy about us being engaged?" I couldn't help but be nervous about that. His father had never seemed to like me.

"They already know, Sage. They're happy for us."

I doubted that. But I didn't want to think about that at the moment. I leaned against him, and we watched the sunset in peaceful silence. The sky lost its orange ambience after the sun dipped below the water. Darkness started setting in, and I looked up, waiting to see the stars. The moon was full and cast a dim glow on the beach. Thinking about something, I suddenly jumped up.

"What's wrong?" Alex sat up, alarmed at my sudden movement.

"Nothing. I just thought that I haven't taken any pictures since being up here. I want one of us on the beach. The vacation when we got engaged." I smiled at him over my shoulder as I walked away.

He rushed to stand up. "I'll get it."

"No, it's fine. The camera is in the truck; I'll run and grab it." I was already halfway to the tree line.

"Okay, just hurry back," Alex called after me.

The moonlight lit the path to the truck. As I reached for the door handle, I remembered that Lacey had grabbed the camera, along with her backpack. Shooting a glance at the house, I debated if I should go get it. It had been at least an hour since we'd gone down to the beach. I laughed under my breath. They should be done with whatever they were doing in the house.

I pushed open the front door and skipped up the steps. I knocked on Lacey's door and waited. After a few seconds, I knocked louder. There wasn't a sound coming from the room. No way they'd be sleeping this early. Maybe they'd gone to a different part of the beach. I knocked one more time before cracking the door open. It was pitch black.

"Lacey?" There was only silence. I ran my hand along the wall and flipped the light switch on when I finally found it. Blinking from the sudden light, I gasped when I saw the room.

It was trashed.

One of the bedside lamps was on the floor with the bulb shattered. The mattress was halfway off the bed frame with the blankets twisted on the floor. Lacey's and Jamie's bags were empty, thrown in the corner with their clothes strewn all over the room. Unease crept into panic as I took a shaky step into the room.

I jumped back when Jamie burst out of the bathroom. The wild look in his eyes caused my heart to thrash in my chest. His hair was disheveled, and his sleeve was ripped. My breath hitched in my throat when my gaze fell to what was in his hand.

A hypodermic needle.

My muscles locked up as I straightened my spine. My instincts were screaming to run, but I couldn't leave without knowing if he'd done something to Lacey. I tore my eyes from the needle and glanced into the empty bathroom.

"Jamie, what happened? Where's Lacey?" I asked, trying to stay calm. The needle was gripped tightly in his hand, and I didn't want to give him a reason to get closer to me. He just stared blankly at me, swaying back and forth, unable to stand up straight.

"Where's Lacey?" I asked again, louder this time.

"I'm gonna kill them." His tone was numb—no feeling or emotion—and I swallowed thickly.

"What the hell are you talking about?" I couldn't keep my voice steady. "Where's my sister?"

My mind was racing. Had Jamie drugged Lacey with whatever was in that needle? I thought back...it was his idea to go on this trip. To come up here and camp. It was even his idea to stay in this house for the night. I just stood there, unable to stop the fear that paralyzed my body. Jamie finally locked eyes with me and seemed to snap out of it.

"You have to come with me." He stepped closer.

"I'm not going anywhere until you tell me what's going on."

"We'll find her," he muttered, more to himself than to me.

He took another step forward and stumbled. The needle he was holding came too close when he fell toward me. Jerking away, I kept moving until I was in the doorway. All I could think about was Lacey. My stomach dropped. What if she was hurt? Or worse? I couldn't think like that. I needed to focus on making sure Jamie didn't stab me with that needle.

"I'm going to get Alex." Without taking my eyes off his hand, I backed farther into the hall before turning around.

"No. You need to stay with me." Jamie yelled from behind me as I fled from him.

His clumsy footsteps echoed through the hall as I made it to the stairs. I took the steps two at a time and started sprinting the second my feet hit the floor. Fear seized me, and my scream was trapped in my throat.

Halfway to the front door, a hand wrapped tightly around my wrist. I cried out when he yanked me backward so hard that I crashed to the floor. A sharp pain jolted up my arm as I caught myself from falling. He fell with me, and I was able to wrench my other arm free from his grasp. But now he was between me and the front door.

Not giving him the chance to grab me again, I jumped up and ran through the dining room. There was a door in the kitchen that I could use to get outside. Slamming the kitchen doors shut behind me, I ran to the outside door and pulled on the handle. It didn't open. I yanked again, harder this time, but it didn't budge. I glanced back at the closed kitchen doors, knowing Jamie wasn't far behind.

My heart was beating out of my chest, and a cold sweat covered my body. Panic was taking control of any rational thought. I needed to get out of this house and get to Alex. I scanned the empty kitchen again and made a split-second decision when I noticed a heavy-duty door on the opposite wall.

My entire body was shaking, and my hand slipped off the doorknob twice before I ripped it open. I expected it to be a wine cellar. Instead, I was met with a set of steep steps with one bare lightbulb dangling above them. Footsteps pounded through the dining room, and I hastily closed the door behind me, hoping Jamie hadn't heard the creaking. Trying to be as silent as possible, I tiptoed down the stairs, stopping when I came face to face with another door.

CHAPTER ELEVEN

Sage

The door squeaked loudly as I opened it, and my eyes slowly adjusted to the dimly lit room. The only light was coming from candles. The flames danced along the walls, and most of the room was cast in shadows. It was impossible to see how big it was.

The walls were worn-out gray cement with what looked like dozens of crosses hanging on them. The huge, elegant dark oak tables looked out of place in this run-down room. Above me were two iron archaic-looking chandeliers. The white candles on the chandeliers were unlit. Even though this room was old, it had been kept up. Not one cobweb in the corners that I could see.

I ran my hand along the table closest to me and inspected it in the candlelight. Not one speck of dust. The room was important to someone. I glanced down at the table to see scissors and a bunch of twine. To my right was another table, and on it were about five knives, all different lengths and sizes. Another table had what looked like hypodermic needles with fluid in them. My stomach dropped. The same kind of needle Jamie had.

What kind of place was this? I crept farther into the room to look for a place to hide and hoped there was no one on the other side of the room in the shadows. Spotting a door down the wall, I picked up my speed. It was the only hiding place I could see. I passed a candle perched on the wall and glanced at the cross right next to me. Freezing, I did a double take before inspecting the it.

Fear cemented me in place when I realized what I was looking at. Those weren't wooden crosses; they were made with hair. Braided hair. I examined it as nausea coiled in my stomach. Yes, definitely hair. And the color looked like red or orange. The braids were tied off with pieces of twine with another piece of twine in the center connecting the two braided pieces to make the shape of the cross.

I turned around and looked at the tables again, realizing what the scissors and twine were for. Losing confidence that hiding here was smart, I began to back up toward the door. I went perfectly still when a groan rang out through the silence. Crouched against the wall, I tried to make myself as invisible as possible when I heard the noise again.

It was coming from the back of the room, where it was too dark for me to make anything out. If Jamie had found me, he wouldn't have waited or been this quiet about it. I warily made my way closer to where the noise was coming from. As I got closer, I could make out another table. This one had something large on it and was covered in a black sheet. I gripped the top of the cloth, not sure I was ready to find out what was under it. After tugging the sheet down, I froze in disbelief.

It was Lacey.

"Oh my God. No. No. Lacey. Wake up." I was almost screaming, and even though I knew I needed to be quiet, I couldn't control my voice. I was in full panic mode as Lacey lay there, unmoving.

"Please. Wake up," I cried out, shaking her. Nothing I did fazed her. Pressing my ear to her chest, I let out a shaky breath when her heart thudded. Standing back up, I tried to pull her off the table and realized that large metal cuffs clasped around her ankles and wrists had her locked in tight.

I began to hyperventilate as I spun around, looking frantically for a key. Suddenly, a large hand covered my mouth. My scream was muffled as I tried tearing away. An arm wrapped around my body before dragging me away from the table Lacey was imprisoned on.

"Shh. It's me. We have to go," Alex whispered as he pulled me away. Relief flooded through me that it was Alex, but it was instantly replaced with fear that we were leaving Lacey. Trying to talk through his hand was impossible, so I pointed at the table, trying to show him that we needed to go back.

Ignoring me, he opened the door I had first planned to hide behind, and I got a glimpse of a mop bucket and brooms before I was thrown into darkness. The sound of a door creaking open filled the room. Lacey started to make noise then; it sounded like she was finally waking up.

Then chanting began.

There were vents in the door, and people walked past where we were hiding, heading straight for my sister. All were wearing black robes with hoods on, making it impossible to see their faces. There had to be at least ten people. The room was bright with light wherever they walked because of the lanterns they carried.

The chanting was in a different language, and although it sounded familiar, I couldn't put a finger on where I'd heard it before. Alex's arms were like chains wrapped around me, and even as I fought against him, I couldn't move. I craned my neck and peered through the vent to see the table Lacey was on.

"Wha...what's going on? Who are you people? What do you want? Let me go. Please let me go. I'll do whatever you want." Lacey was crying. She had finally woken up with the robed people circling her. Her cries were ignored while they continued chanting. I was still fighting futilely against Alex. I couldn't sit here and leave Lacey alone. Alex only tightened his grip. His breath hit my neck before his lips brushed against my ear.

"Baby, there's nothing we can do. We can't go out there. I know she's your sister, I know. And I'm so sorry, but I can save you."

He wasn't even breaking a sweat while he kept me in his arms. I watched helplessly as Lacey continued to plead and scream. She was pulling at the restraints as hard as she could. I tried blinking away the hot tears invading my vision. My sister's screams were ripping me apart, and I was fucking powerless to help.

The people continued their chanting, getting louder and louder until they drowned out Lacey's cries. One of them slowly walked over to the table with the knives and picked one up. He seemed to inspect it before he slowly walked back to join the others. The person with the knife went to the head of the table and stared down at Lacey.

He slowly raised the knife above his head, and the chants were now deafening. Lacey was struggling against her bonds, trying to free herself, while pleading as loud as she could over the voices, but it was useless. Suddenly, the knife was plunged into Lacey's heart. All that could be heard were the chants echoing off the walls.

My struggles stopped as I stared in a daze at my sister. My mind could not process what my eyes had just witnessed. Lacey lay there, motionless, with the knife still buried deep in her chest. Blood started to spill onto the table from the stab wound. Snapping out of it, I began thrashing uncontrollably. Alex grunted, actually needing to try to keep me from escaping out of his arms. The only reason my wailing couldn't be heard was because they were still chanting.

Another cloaked person walked to a table, grabbed the scissors, and cut small pieces of twine. He walked back and handed the twine to another man who was standing near Lacey's head. Gently turning her head to the side, he separated her hair into two sections and then tied them both off with twine, making two loose ponytails. Then he took the scissors and cut her hair off above the tied twine and handed the two sections of hair to another man.

He walked to another table right in front of our hiding place and set the hair down and began to braid it. He tied each end off and put one braid across the other to make it into the shape of a cross and tied twine around the center. I watched in horror and denial of what was happening. Glancing at all the crosses on the wall, I felt like I was going to throw up.

How many people had been killed in this room?

The cloaked man who had ended Lacey's life walked over to the table with a lantern and seemed to inspect the braided cross. The other who braided it held it up to show the others. A glare came from the person's hand in the lantern light. My eyes zeroed in on the hand, knowing I recognized something.

A ring. With a deep red rock on it. I stilled, swallowing the bile that was burning my throat. Of course, I'd seen that ring before. It was the same ring on the necklace Alex never took off. The same one that was digging into my back right this second. The same family heirloom that every man in his family wore. I carefully looked at each man, and at least half of them were wearing the same ring.

The echoes of the chants abruptly stopped, and the room was silent. I was barely breathing, still trying to comprehend what had just happened. The person with Lacey's hair nailed it to the wall while the others watched. Then they walked out of the room in a single file line. The door slammed shut, and the sound shocked me back into reality.

I needed to get out of Alex's grasp. His touch made my skin suddenly feel dirty. He relented and removed his hand from my mouth first and then moved his arm from my body. Flinging myself out of the storage room, I ran to my sister. Lacey looked so peaceful. Her eyes were closed, and if not for the blood, it could have looked like she was sleeping. Her beautiful red hair was gone. All that was left was a couple of inches of jagged pieces. I took Lacey's face in my hands and gave her a kiss on the forehead.

Gut wrenching sobs erupted from me with such force that it stole my breath. My sister, my best friend, was gone.

"Sage, I'm so sorry. I can't imagine how hard this is." Alex's voice was so calm. Much too calm after what we had just witnessed. There wasn't one note of alarm or fear in his voice.

He came up behind me to wrap his arms around me, but I ducked and slipped under them. Meeting his eyes, I attempted to keep the fear of him off my face.

The man I had trusted with my life. Who had been there for me over the years for anything I needed. I had planned to spend the rest of my life with him. He was the perfect person for me. Now, he was a monster.

The arms that I had found so much comfort in looked threatening now that they so easily held me captive. The last three years of my life were all a lie. But I couldn't let him know that I knew. He wouldn't let me out of this place alive with the secret I now carried.

"I can't be touched right now. I know you want to help, but right now, you can't. We should leave before they come back. We need to go to the police." My voice caught as another sob ripped through me. I fought the instinctive urge to flee as fast as possible and forced myself to meet his gaze. I was sure there was still fear in my eyes, but he didn't have to know it was fear of him. Alex stayed silent and seemed to study my face.

"I know you saw it."

My heart stopped.

"Saw what? Saw my sister get murdered? Saw those crazy fucking people cut her hair and braid it? Of course, I saw it. We need to get the hell out of here now," I tried to say without my voice cracking, as I ran a hand through my hair. I abruptly stopped when Alex's gaze fell on my hand. It was my worst tell when I lied. And he knew it.

"It's okay, Sage. I know you saw his ring." He gently pulled the necklace out of his shirt and revealed the ruby-red heirloom. "I was hoping it didn't have to happen this way. You never should have seen what happens here. This wasn't the plan," he said, more to himself than to me. He took a step toward me, and I darted around the table that Lacey was lying on. I backed up another step and hit the cold, rough cement wall.

"Alex, what are you saying? That this was going to happen anyway? How would they know we were going to stay here? This was a last-minute plan. And it wasn't even your idea to stay here." I was trying to buy time by saying anything as I scanned the room for an escape route.

He was with them. I couldn't trust anything he said. Alex sighed and walked around the table until he was face to face with me. I silently calculated the odds of being able to slip past him, but my confidence shrank each time he took a step closer. There was no malice in his eyes. He was gazing at me the same way he had a thousand times before. With love and comfort. It made me want to slap him. How could he look at me like that after what had just happened?

Anger suddenly took over my grief-filled body. He'd known what was going to happen to Lacey. He was a part of it, and he stopped me from trying to save her. With a burst of pure adrenaline, I charged at Alex and ducked under his outstretched arm. His hand grazed my hip, but I twisted away and kept moving. Without looking back, I bolted straight for the door I had come in through.

I didn't know how close behind me he was, but his footsteps seemed deafening. Turning to look wasn't an option. I needed to look straight ahead. The dim room was hard enough to move through while walking, let alone sprinting.

I made it to the door, grabbed the iron handle, and pulled it open, only for it to be slammed shut. His arm was next to my head, keeping the door closed. He was so close that his chest brushed my back. He put his other arm up on the other side of me, pinning me against the door.

"You really shouldn't have wasted your energy doing that. I grew up in this place. In this room. You thought you could really beat me to the door?" Alex asked while catching his breath. For the first time since he'd pulled me into the storage room, he wasn't calm and collected.

"Whatever you're going to do to me, just do it." I continued facing the door because it was better than looking at him.

"Sage, I'm not going to do anything to you. I told you this wasn't the plan. You shouldn't have been here."

"Wasn't the plan? Tell me, Alex. What the hell was the plan? Did it originally involve murdering my sister?" My voice broke and my eyes welled with tears as the image of Lacey's death jumped back into my mind. Alex was silent for a moment. His fingers closed around my arm, and I bristled, trying to dodge his grip. But it was too late.

"Don't touch me," I growled, attempting to break away from him. But he held on tightly to my arm to make sure I couldn't run again. I cursed myself for never making time to go to the gym and for never taking a self-defense class. I was no match for him. He pulled on my arm until I turned and was facing him.

"Look at me, baby. I want to explain it to you. I'm not going to hurt you. That was never the plan. I love you."

"Love me? You're with the people who murdered my sister and you let it happen. I don't even know who you really are. I don't give a damn what the plan was. I just want you as far away from me as possible," I screamed at him, still trying to wriggle out of his grasp.

"Let me explain. Give me a chance to help you understand what this place is. There's a reason for all of this, and I need you to see that. Come on, I need to show you something. It's on the wall over there." He motioned with his free hand to a small bookshelf. I slowly turned my head and followed his gaze toward the wall.

There was a small bookcase with one shelf filled with older books. On top of the shelf was a book on a black metal stand. I squinted to make it out in the candlelight but could only see that it looked incredibly old.

"All I'm asking is that you read a passage in that book on the top shelf. It will explain everything, and you'll understand why a place like this exists." He spoke carefully and calmly.

Instead of answering, I only glared at him. He gave me a minute to respond, and when I didn't, he started tugging me toward the bookshelf.

"Here, sit here while you read it." He pulled a stool out from under the closest table and waited for me to sit. Looking anywhere except at him, I remained standing.

"Sage, you should sit down; you need it." The caring demeanor sent rage coursing through me. I felt stupid. I had fallen for his charm. For his fake love.

"I think I'd rather just stand, or, you know, leave," I spat out.

"No, I want you to sit." Annoyance crept into his voice. "You know, I'm trying to make this as easy as possible for you. What you just went through is devastating. But if you're going to be stubborn, then I may have to do things to make sure I won't have to chase you down…" He trailed off, and I followed his gaze to the ball of twine on the table.

A shiver ran through me as I thought about my next move. He had never been anything but caring toward me. But after what had just happened, I had no idea what he was capable of. Attempting to escape would be a lot harder if he tied me up. The image of him at the bar when he charged at the guy flashed into my head. He had an angry side, and I didn't want that side of him to come out.

"Happy?" I grudgingly sat down on the stool. I hated people getting their way with me when I didn't want to do it. Being in this horrific situation made it so much worse.

"See, now don't you feel better? What you're about to read is pretty intense, so you should be comfortable." He ran his hand down my hair before resting it on my shoulder. He gripped it tightly before he reached over and took the book off the shelf.

I couldn't suppress the shudder that shot down my spine. Having his hand on my body was the last thing I wanted. I grabbed the book from him and set it in my lap. The book was black leather, and the cover was blank. It smelled musty, and the binding was worn from use, but it was still in good condition. It had been taken care of properly over the years.

"I can't see. There's not enough light in here to read it."

"Here—I have a flashlight. I'll shine it on the book while you read. You'll understand all of this, baby. Once you read this, you'll understand," he said, almost pleadingly.

Hesitating for a moment, I slowly opened the book, still painstakingly aware of Alex's hand on my shoulder. I just needed to read this and, no matter what, agree with him. He needed to believe I was on his side if I had any chance of getting out of here alive. With that thought, I started reading.

CHAPTER TWELVE

Sage

August 430 BC

A man and wife lived in Athens during the great Peloponnesian War. Athens and its allies fought against Sparta and theirs. That year a plague hit the city of Athens. It decimated almost two-thirds of the population. The man's wife was pregnant and at full term. The midwife was in the room with her getting ready for labor while the man anxiously waited outside the room. He was the last of his family. There was no one to carry on the family name or legacy if something happened to his baby during childbirth. The midwife came out to tell the man that there was something wrong. To help save the life of the mother and hopefully the baby, the midwife told him they would have to cut the baby out.

The man went into a fit of rage. The baby had to come out naturally and healthy. He was the last of his family. All others succumbed to the plague or the war. He needed this baby born healthy. The midwife told him it wasn't possible, that they had to cut the baby out. She turned to go back into the room, and the man grabbed a knife that was on a table near him and stabbed her straight through the heart. With blood on his hands, he looked at the woman with deep remorse. He hadn't wanted to do it. He'd had to. For the sake of his unborn child. With regret filling his heart, he took the knife and cut off the midwife's beautiful red hair. He braided it and tied it off with twine and made it into the sacred symbol of a cross to show his remorse. He gently laid the cross on her body. He went outside and fell onto his knees.

He looked up at the full moon and prayed to the God of Fertility and Goddess of Childbirth to have a healthy baby, even if he'd just committed a horrific deed. He heard his wife scream, and he ran to her side. She then gave birth to twins—healthy boys.

His story began circling Athens. That if a red-haired woman was sacrificed in August under a full moon, that man's family would have fertility for that generation. Soon, it spread outside Athens. To other areas that are in modern day Greece. Before most people knew how to write, it was spread by word of mouth. Now it is written and will never be forgotten. It spread outside of Greece, outside of Europe. This belief has become a society. Everyone in this society is family. If someone needs help, they will receive that help from whomever is able. Discretion is needed in this new day and age, but it must be done. For the greater good of all the families who are in need of fertility.

I stared at the last sentence in disbelief. Did Alex and all those other people really believe that killing someone would bring fertility to their family? They were crazy. Insane. What I read was only a couple of pages, yet this book was thick. Curiosity got the best of me, and I turned the page to see a list of names and dates. Realization hit, and my blood ran cold.

I was cast in darkness when Alex turned off the flashlight. As my eyes tried to adjust to the candlelight, I attempted to stand up. But he pushed me back down onto the stool.

"Hold on," he said as he gently set the book back on the stand and made sure it was just as they'd left it. This time when I tried to stand, he let me, keeping his hand firmly on my shoulder.

"Did you read it all, Sage? Don't you see? This needs to happen. If we weren't doing this, so many family lines would cease to exist. Including mine. It's for the greater good." He wanted me to agree with him more than anything.

My gaze dropped to the floor as I clenched my jaw. If I opened my mouth, I wouldn't be able to keep my thoughts to myself. He grasped my chin, forcing my head up until we locked eyes.

"We do this so families can survive. We did this for us. So when we get married, we will be blessed to have kids. I'll do anything for you. I want us to be together forever." He looked at me pleadingly, his eyes begging me to understand. It was his way of life. He'd grown up believing this. His whole family was in on this, and who knew how many others in the world.

"Did you plan to kill Lacey this whole time?" I asked quietly. This time he broke eye contact and looked away, almost ashamed. I knew I should agree with anything he said. Pretend I understood and believed him. But I needed to know exactly why my sister had been chosen.

"Your family has been chosen for a long time," he stated, still avoiding looking at me. "Honestly, years ago, I didn't care if it was going to be you or your sister. But then we started talking, and I fell in love with you. There was no way I could have let you be sacrificed."

"My family's been chosen?"

"It had to be your sister." He ignored my question.

"No, you didn't have to kill—"

"Yes, we did. You read it, Sage. It had to be done." His eyes bored into mine. "I'm just sorry it happened the way it did. Like I said earlier, how it happened was not the plan. You finding this mansion and staying here was not the plan. I don't know what happened back at the campsite. Bad luck, I guess. They were going to take Lacey when she was down at the beach by herself, and have it just been ruled an accidental drowning, and that be the end of it. I never wanted you to see this. But you were down here when the ceremony was about to start. I couldn't let you interrupt it. Tonight was the last full moon." He finally relaxed the grip on my chin, and I tore my face away from his hand and looked away.

"You planned to make it look accidental? My sister missing forever, just like my mom was." I was doing all I could to hold my composure. It was all too much. My hands curled into fists as I tried to silence the tremors rolling through my body.

"It was the best way to do it. But obviously the plan had to change when you all decided to stay here for the night. Lacey wanted to go stay somewhere farther away, where there were more people. That would have ruined the plan."

"What were you going to do with—with her body?" I choked out.

"We are very respectful with the remains of all the sacrifices. We try to inflict as little pain as possible. Usually they are still unconscious when it happens. I'm sorry she was awake," he explained. Like this was a normal conversation. Disgust shot through me when I understood it was normal for him. He continued, "After the ritual, we find a place in the middle of nowhere and bury them and give them a proper funeral. They deserve that, for their sacrifice."

"You bury them?"

"Yes, a proper burial. We get a nice coffin and have a little service—"

"Coffin. Like an oak coffin?"

"I don't know. That's not what I help with."

I stood there silently. Clips of conversation from months ago popped into my head. *Your mom was found in an oak coffin. Whoever buried her took the time. It looked like they cared.* The investigator's voice rang in my ears. *She was killed by one stab wound to the heart. There was no evidence of her hair in the coffin.*

I flailed both of my arms at Alex, hitting every part of his body I could. Shocked at the sudden outburst, he scrambled to grab me. After a couple of seconds, he managed to catch my wrists.

"What's wrong? You were so calm asking questions—"

"You son of a bitch. You and your family are murderers. You ruined my family. Ruined it. My mom was killed by your society, wasn't she? Wasn't she?" I was screaming and crying. The emotions were impossible to hold back. I couldn't pretend to agree with him. Couldn't keep calm. Not anymore.

"I really was hoping you wouldn't make that connection. Yes, your mom was sacrificed. That's why we knew at least one of her children would be too. Because of her sacrifice, my mother was able to have me." He was rationalizing, trying to make me understand. That it was all for a greater good. He brought my wrists to his chest, pulling me closer. "I know your pain is unimaginable right now, baby. But we can get through it. Now you and I can start a family when the time is right. If you hadn't seen all this happen, if your sister really had disappeared in a swimming accident, we would have driven back home and gone on with our lives. Together. We can have that again."

I barely held back the hysterical laugh that bubbled in my chest. He'd been brainwashed. He truly believed that this was the way of life. It was the way of life in his family. He really thought we could grow old together like nothing had happened. A cold sweat slid down my back at the thought of being with him.

There was no way I could lie my way out of it. He knew me better than almost everyone. With a jolt of pain, I realized he did know me better than anyone. The only other person who completely understood me was Lacey. But she was dead. Because of him and his family.

He'd pick up on my lie right away. I had to get away. Not just for myself, but for all the women who had died at the hands of his family and countless others. I needed to go to the police. To make this public.

Swiftly, and as hard as I could, I slammed my knee into his groin. He grunted and fell to his knees. He finally released my wrists, and I pushed him to the ground before racing to the door. Pulling it open, I slipped out and started running down the hallway toward the stairs.

I leaped up the steps and was about to fling the door open but stopped myself. I needed to be quiet. There were more people here, and I couldn't fight my way out. Slowly, I cracked the door open and peeked out. The lights in the kitchen were off, and there was no one in there that I could see. Knowing I didn't have long until Alex caught up, I pushed the door open just wide enough to fit through and shut it quickly.

Grabbing a chair from the small kitchen table, I shoved it under the doorknob of the basement door. It probably wouldn't hold, but it would at least slow him down. I silently made my way through the kitchen and dining room to get to the front door. I reached for the door handle and abruptly pulled my hand back. What was the plan when I left this house? There was nothing but forest around for miles. Alex had said that he'd grown up here. He knew this house and most likely the forest around it.

With a sinking feeling, I tried to clear my mind to come up with a better plan. The truck. If I could get the truck keys, I wouldn't need to run on foot. The keys were probably in Lacey and Jamie's room. My heart sank. I thought Jamie had brought us to this place. That he was the one to run from. I hoped he had escaped. Or was alive, at least. I glanced out the window and saw the truck still in the driveway. I needed to go upstairs to get the keys.

A roar of laughter sliced fear through me. A light flickered from under the door that led into the great room. From the sound of laughter and talk, it was all the men who'd been downstairs. I tiptoed past the door and made my way up the stairs. Once I was at the top, I slowly peered around the corner to see if the hallway was empty. The dim bathroom light was the only thing lighting up the long hallway, and I couldn't see the end. As I glanced back down the stairs, I weighed my options. Either sneak out the front door and through the woods or hope there was no one at the end of the hall. I wouldn't make it far in the woods by myself. I took a deep breath and started down the hall.

CHAPTER THIRTEEN

Him

I looked around the great room at all my family that had come to help. I was grateful. That had been much harder than I'd anticipated it to be. I tried to slow the shaking of my hands and glanced down to see how obvious it was. Ever since I'd held the knife in my hand, I hadn't been able to stop the shaking. The image of Lacey's fear-stricken eyes was seared into my mind.

When we were planning this, it didn't seem horrible. But actually doing it...I shook my head. This should have been like all the other ceremonies. It wasn't. I knew it was needed. It was for the greater good. My father instilled that in me when I was a child.

What made it worse was that Lacey had been awake. They were usually still unconscious from the sedative they were given. But we'd waited too long. My thoughts went back to when we went to the bedroom to get her. Jamie had put up a larger fight than we expected. We tried to knock him out too. But he only got a little of the sedative before he punched Eric. Then he pulled the needle out and locked himself in the bathroom.

I took a large swig of beer, trying to block the emotions that threatened my carefully carefree attitude. Everybody had already congratulated us. We'd done it. Our family would be able to bear children for this generation. Now the men were all celebrating with drinks and talk until they all had to go their separate ways in the morning. Two of the men were going to take Lacey's body to give her a proper burial. They planned to leave in the early morning. I wondered where Sage was right now. Eric would just tell her that there were hunters hanging out here. No reason for her to be suspicious about that.

I could only imagine what Eric's face looked like when the two red-haired sisters pulled up and asked to stay here. I couldn't believe the odds of them actually coming to stay the night. It would have happened no matter what. But this way was just more difficult. It was the last full moon in August, so it had to be done tonight. I pictured Sage again, and my heart beat faster. I didn't want to think about how she would react when she found out her sister was missing. Guilt washed over me. It was going to break her.

Standing up, I set my drink down before walking to the doorway. I needed something stronger than beer. I pushed the door open and made sure no one was in the foyer before stepping out. Jogging to the kitchen, I checked that I was alone before flicking on the light.

Confusion swept through me when I saw a chair pushed up against the basement door. Before I got close, someone started banging on it from the other side. I moved the chair out of the way, and Alex barreled out.

"What the hell happened? I thought the plan was that you were going to keep Sage out of the house," I said, bewildered.

"Yeah, well, that plan obviously didn't work. She got back into the house and found the basement. We were in the storage room for the whole thing. How did she get into the house? The front door was supposed to be locked." He kicked the basement door closed and then kicked it again.

"It was your idea to make everyone except Eric and me leave the house. You didn't want the sisters to see us. They parked near the road and waited until they thought the coast was clear. Not easy when there's no cell service up here. They must have forgotten to lock the door," I answered, annoyed that Alex was trying to blame me.

"Have you seen her?" Alex asked as he glanced around the room.

"Nope. I thought she was with you. You know, keeping her safe from knowing our little secret," I replied as I leaned against the counter. I knew Alex was upset. But I had told him again and again this would never work. Keeping someone in the dark from this is impossible. He should have fucking known better.

"She has to be in the house. We'll find her. What did you do with Jamie?" He looked at both doors on opposite ends of the kitchen, as if deciding which way to go first.

"About that. He decided to throw punches before we could give him the full sedative. He locked himself in the bathroom, and we heard him pass out. Left him there while we carried Lacey downstairs. Since it was just Eric and me dealing with both Jamie and Lacey, it was a shit show. This was not how the plan was supposed to go. The sedative wore off before we went back upstairs, but we found him here in the kitchen. Now he's locked in the wine room," I explained, replaying the night from hell.

"Has it been decided what's going to be done with him?" he asked quietly.

"No. Waiting for one of the elders to get here to decide." But we both knew what would happen. Jamie had found out our secret. He was a threat.

"Are you going to help me find Sage? I need to get her to understand before we can leave."

"You realize how small the odds are of that, right? I mean, she just saw her sister get murdered." I shook my head, blocking the images that tried to creep back into my mind of what had happened in the basement.

"I know. But there's no other option."

"There is. We can just keep her here. At least until she calms down. I can even stay here and help watch her. I can keep her company." I smirked at Alex, knowing my words were getting under his skin. I didn't even mention the other option. If she didn't come around, other members would insist she be held until next August. Until the next sacrifice. We already knew her family history. We couldn't have someone run around with our secret who didn't believe in it. I pushed away the thought of Sage being sacrificed. I didn't like it. Her spirit burned so hot. She had so much life. This wasn't how I wanted to see her life go.

"You, just like everyone else, know—She. Is. Mine," Alex growled. "I'll help her get past this."

"Who says you get to be the only one with a red-haired beauty?" I couldn't help but get under Alex's skin.

"I don't care who you fuck, as long as you stay away from her," he said as he clenched his fists.

I put my hands up. "Calm down. I'm kidding."

Alex glared at me. "We need to find her."

"Have you even told her everything? Like her mom being chosen? Or how she was in this house for months before the sacrifice?" I asked, curious about how much Sage knew. Many of the chosen women were taken early and kept until August. Couldn't have redheads go missing one month a year. That would cause suspicion. The society did everything to keep them comfortable. A nice bed, cable TV, their own bathroom, and lots of good food. The women were important; they were never to be treated badly. But, as Lacey's screams echoed in my head, I thought about how scared they must have been. I groaned to myself, running a hand down my face. Tonight had really fucked me up.

"Anyway, you might want to hurry and find her. We thought we heard the front door open a little bit ago. We didn't think much of it. Since Sage was supposed to be with you." My words were complete bullshit. "One of the guys went to check, but he never said if it was locked or not..."

Alex shoved me hard into the counter. "You waited this long to tell me? Who knows where the hell she is now."

"Relax. It's the middle of the night; no civilization for miles. You spent every summer in these woods. You'll find her."

He was already halfway out the back door before I finished my sentence. I chuckled when the door slammed shut. I knew the front door was locked. Just like every other door in this house. I had checked them myself after we found Jamie in the kitchen. I had a feeling I knew where Sage was.

I wanted to see her before Alex did. As I left the kitchen, I buried the guilty thoughts. I refused to look weak in front of anyone. Sage knew our secret, and she had to stay scared enough to do what Alex told her so she could stay alive. I straightened my shoulders and let the feeling of indifference wash through me as I walked back to the foyer to look for her.

CHAPTER FOURTEEN

Sage

I couldn't remember if Lacey's bedroom was the fourth or fifth room on the left. By the time I passed the third door, I was cast in darkness. The bathroom light wasn't helping anymore. With one hand on the wall, I stepped carefully and froze every time the old wood floor creaked under me. I finally felt the fourth door and reached for the door handle.

I pushed the door open an inch and then waited to hear if anyone was inside. There was nothing but silence. Pushing it open a little wider, I poked my head in. More darkness waited for me in the room. I slipped inside and shut the door behind me.

Blinded by the sudden change when I flicked the light on, I blinked a few times before realizing this was my room. Everything was just as I'd left it. My bag at the foot of the bed. The clothes I had changed out of were still strewn on the floor. I gazed at the disheveled blankets on the bed where Alex's clothes were lying.

Tears threatened to escape when I thought about how simple life had been just a short time ago. How could any of this have actually happened? It still felt like I was stuck in a bad dream. My phone was still charging on the nightstand, and I quickly grabbed it. The screen lit up and showed it was just after midnight. It had only been ten hours since we'd entered this hell house. I shook my head in disbelief. Life would never be the same—if I even survived tonight. The phone still showed no signal, but I slipped it into my back pocket before heading toward the door.

I stepped back into the dark hallway. With my hands guiding the way, I reached the next door and felt around until I grasped the cold metal of the door handle. Again, I slowly opened it and listened for any sound coming from inside. I went inside and felt for the light switch and turned it on. The room was just as it was earlier. Trashed. Something shiny caught my eye on the floor next to the bed. It was a needle. But this one was empty, unlike the one Jamie'd had in his hand.

My stomach knotted even more when it dawned on me that this must have been where they attacked Lacey. Still crouched over the needle, I closed my eyes and tried to clear my thoughts. I had to push the image of my sister taking her last breaths out of my head. If I didn't, I would never think straight enough to get out of here. I needed to get free. To go to the police. So all the families of the women who were killed could get closure and to keep this from happening to others. With a shaky breath, I opened my eyes and stood back up.

I glanced at the nightstand, and my eyes landed on the truck keys. I just stared at them. The room had been ransacked, and yet the keys just sat there, completely undisturbed. It couldn't be that easy. It could be a trap. Why leave a possible escape plan just out in the open? Then again, maybe they'd overlooked it. Either way, I wasn't going back downstairs without those keys.

I swept the keys up and held on to them tightly as I scanned the room. A small noise made me freeze, and my eyes shot to the door. If someone was out there, they'd definitely see the light coming from under the door. I stayed glued next to the nightstand, unable to move as fear claimed me. My ears strained for any sort of noise, but once again, it was silent.

Turning back around, I slid open the nightstand drawer, hoping to find anything I could use as a weapon. But it was empty. As I pushed the drawer back in, I heard a click. I whirled around to see a man turning from the door to face me. I sucked in a breath and backed up until my calves slammed into the nightstand.

"Hey, future sis."

One of the twins stood calmly in front of me, and my eyes shot to his arm. When they were together, it was easier to tell them apart. He folded his arms, and I caught sight of the small, oval birthmark on his wrist. That birthmark was the only way to differentiate them because Geo didn't have one.

"Niko," I muttered under my breath. Alex had said he'd grown up here, so it only made sense his brothers had too. I wondered if he knew I had been in the basement. Alex had said I was supposed to be at the beach when it happened. Maybe Niko had no idea I knew their secret. If he didn't know, maybe I could play this off. Letting confusion sweep across my face, I raised my voice. "What are you doing here?"

"I couldn't pass up the chance to hang out up north. I'm surprised Alex brought you to our favorite place to stay when we hunt," Niko replied as he glanced around the room. "So, where's my baby brother at? I can't find him, and he's usually with you."

I narrowed my eyes, not sure if he was serious or messing with me. He was lying, but I still wasn't sure if he knew that I had found out everything.

"I don't know. I was up here getting my phone and stopped to look at the pictures I took today. He's probably downstairs. Let's go find him," I answered, trying to keep my voice steady. I took a small step forward but stopped when he didn't move.

"How about we talk a little first, just you and me?" He stared at me while he leaned back against the door. "You know, my brother loves you more than anything. He made waves in the family when he decided he wanted to marry you. My family is very traditional, and you definitely weren't my parents' first choice. But he didn't budge, and now my parents are welcoming you with open arms. Well, mostly anyway. They really wanted him to find someone who shared in our...beliefs." He stole a look at my hair before meeting my eyes again.

"I'm glad they came around. Your family is great," I sputtered the words out. I was almost positive he was messing with me, but I wasn't going to give up the innocent act until I had to. My face started to get hot, and I looked down at the floor next to him. I was such a terrible liar. Luckily, he didn't know my tells as well as Alex did.

"Sage, I think there's something you should know. There are people all over this country, all over this world, who share our beliefs. There's nowhere you can go where this belief isn't practiced." His voice picked up an icy edge, and my gaze darted back to him. A small speck of remorse passed through his eyes before it was gone.

What was he doing? Warning me that there were people everywhere who would kill me because of my hair color? A chill raced down my spine. He fucking knew that I'd found out about their society. Panic engulfed me, but I attempted to keep my face blank. He continued talking. "The best place to be is with my brother and my family. They would never let anything happen to you."

"Niko, I—"

"I'm not finished," he coldly interrupted me. "People from all professions share in our beliefs. Teachers, bankers, police officers. And we're all connected by this. They are always willing to help, no matter how far away. You've been to this house, our home away from home. I heard about Alex's proposal. You said yes. You're already part of this family." He looked like he didn't agree with the last part. Apparently, he wasn't happy with Alex's choice either.

"Thanks, Niko. I'm glad you think I'm a part of your family." I forced a small smile, refusing to admit anything. I slowly started walking forward to see if he'd move. But he stayed just how he was, watching my every move until he was pushed forward when the door slammed open.

"There you are. Have you seen—"

My heart dropped when Geo popped up behind Niko. I should have known I'd see him too. The twins were never far from each other. Geo had stopped talking when his eyes landed on me.

"Sage. Alex has been looking for you," Geo murmured as the tension grew. Niko moved over when Geo elbowed his way into the room.

"I was about to go look for him," I replied, swallowing hard.

"Where's Lacey and that boy toy she came up here with?" Geo said casually, but the look in his eyes told a different story. I stilled as Niko shot his brother an annoyed glance. Geo's stare left me, and I followed his gaze to the needle that was still on the floor. I squeezed the keys tighter when they both looked at my hand.

"Going somewhere, Sage?" Geo asked, his face going cold.

"Um, no...just wanted to grab something out of the truck, and it's locked." My lies were useless. It was obvious they were playing with me, but I refused to admit anything.

"You never answered me. Where's Lacey?" Geo asked again.

"Don't know," I mumbled almost incoherently. I could not break down right now.

"You mean you didn't see what happened in the basement and then push a chair up against the door to lock my brother down there?" Geo asked in a cocky tone. I glared daggers at him as he smirked. Niko went rigid as he kept his eyes on me.

"Not sure what to say now? You know our brother is outside looking for you right now. He thought you somehow got out." There was no remorse in Geo's voice for what they'd done to Lacey. Anger began to smother my fear, and I decided right then that I wouldn't let them get away with this. I'd do whatever I could to get out of this house.

"What now? You keep me in here until Alex finds us?" I hissed, glancing around, even though the door they were blocking was the only way out.

"Of course not. You can leave the room whenever you want," Niko spoke up, his arrogance suddenly mirroring his brother's. Geo looked a bit surprised by Niko's answer but then nodded in agreement.

"Then move out of the way," I demanded, sounding much braver than I felt.

Geo stepped closer. "In a minute."

Shrinking away from him, I gripped the truck keys tighter. Niko moved into the room, standing next to his brother. The small amount of remorse I'd thought I saw earlier was gone. The twins were a unified front. About everything. In the years I'd known them, I'd never seen them bicker once. They had each other's backs for anything.

"You can at least say please." Geo raised an eyebrow.

"You said I could leave. Move," I forced out through gritted teeth. I tried to shove past both of them. Geo reached for me, but Niko caught my arm first. He twisted me around, away from his brother, and pushed me farther into the room.

"That wasn't necessary, Sage," Niko told me, his tone dangerous.

"Let me leave," I pleaded, unable to keep the fear out of my voice.

"Let's drop the act," Geo said as Niko kept his hand wrapped around my arm. "We know what you saw."

"You're part of it now." Niko shook his head. "But because you're the girl our brother loves, you have a chance to accept it. And live."

"But if you decide you don't want this life, there's always another option..." Geo trailed off as his eyes went to my hair.

"Join your family, or what? Be murdered?" I asked, my voice

shaking. They couldn't do this. They didn't just get to choose the rest of my life for me.

"That's not what we said. But I think you'll make the right decision," Niko said, releasing my arm and stepping to the side. The doorway was finally free. "By the way, if you think you can get out of this house, think again."

"I just want out of this room, away from both of you," I snapped.

"But we have what you need to leave. If you think you can get it." Geo grinned and pulled out a key ring with three keys out of his pocket. "These keys open the doors and bars on the windows. Maybe if you find Alex, you can try to convince him, since he has a set too."

"Why don't you just toss yours here?" I asked, knowing full well it was useless. It was all a game to them.

"I don't think so. That would be too easy," Geo said as his grin widened. The gleam in his eye dared me to try to get the keys from his hand.

"You get these from me and they're yours. Wrestling around could be fun; just don't tell Alex." He slid the keys back into his pocket while Niko stared at me with interest as he kept quiet.

"Fuck you," I spat out in disgust. It would be impossible to get the keys from him. I stalked past, fully expecting them to stop me. Neither moved, and I picked up my pace as I got to the doorway. I jerked away when I felt my phone being pulled out of my back pocket.

"You don't need this. Don't worry, I'll hold on to it for you," Geo said, sliding the phone into his pocket.

I glared at him but didn't say anything. Stepping into the hallway, I breathed out a short sigh of relief. I wasn't close to being safe, but at least I wasn't with them anymore.

CHAPTER FIFTEEN

Sage

I flew down the stairs and across the foyer, reaching the front door. Gripping the knob, I twisted it and then pulled. It didn't budge.

"Come on," I muttered, spotting the keyhole.

Geo was right. Only a key would open it. Maybe the kitchen door was unlocked, though I doubted it since it had been locked earlier. Eric had said there were many other rooms throughout the first floor. Maybe one of them had another door. Or a window I could slip out of.

Noise came from the great room, and I tiptoed closer to the cracked door. I needed to see the men who had murdered my sister. Because if I got out of here and went to the police, I wanted each face committed to memory. Holding my breath, I peeked through the opening.

There were five men sitting on the sofas. Two of the men looked older, maybe in their sixties. The other three were younger. A sour taste filled my mouth as my eyes fell on the guy on the edge of the couch. Not a guy—a kid. He couldn't be older than twelve. They really did raise them in this life. I recognized the guy next to him. Eric. Of course, he was involved.

After staring for a couple more seconds, I realized I knew another one of the men. My blood ran cold. It was Detective Thomas. The man who oversaw the investigation of my mom's death. Niko was right; they were everywhere. I quickly backed away from the door when Eric and one of the older men stood from the couch.

Glancing at the stairs, I was surprised the twins weren't in sight. I was sure they were going to follow me. They were so arrogant. And they'd both been convinced there was absolutely no way out of this house. The fear that they might be right wouldn't disappear as I ran into the dining room.

There were no lights on anywhere, except in the great room. I kept moving toward the kitchen, relying solely on the moonlight that was streaming in from the windows. Cracking the kitchen door open, I peeked in and checked that it was empty before stepping inside. The chair I had pushed against the basement door was lying on the floor.

My body sagged in defeat when the kitchen door was locked just like the other one. Scanning the kitchen, I looked for anything that could help me get out of here. It didn't take long since the counters had nothing on them. I opened the drawer closest to me. Empty. Going to the next drawer, I pulled the handle, but it didn't move. I brushed my fingers down the front, and I clenched my teeth. Another keyhole.

Filled with apprehension, I focused on the basement door. There were weapons down there. If anything, I could use one of those knives against anyone who tried coming after me.

The thought of going back to that room paralyzed me. Lacey's screams were still haunting me, and going back down there was the last thing I wanted. My body trembled, and I glanced around again, hoping I somehow missed something I could use instead of going back down there. But there was nothing. Swinging the door open, I looked down the steps and took a deep breath, then I began moving again.

A sob caught in my throat as I reached the bottom of the stairs. I couldn't break down yet. I had to wait until I survived this. For Lacey. Fear slid through me as I stepped into the room. It looked the same as when I had first come in here. But now I *knew*, and it would never leave my nightmares.

It was a room wrapped in evil and warped with pain.

There was a heaviness in the air that would never disappear. The back of the room was cast in darkness, and I didn't even know if Lacey's body was still down here. I forced myself to turn away, knowing I wouldn't have the strength to leave if I saw her. My tears flowed freely as I went to the table with the knives.

The one I picked up looked like a five-inch blade and had a silver hilt. Good enough. I'd never handled more than a kitchen knife before, and it felt heavy in my hand as I looked for anything else to take. There were a few packs of matches on another table. I grabbed a pack and slid it into my pocket before turning toward the wall.

Crossing the room, I stopped in front of the book that Alex had forced me to read. After hesitating for a moment, I grabbed it and flipped to the end of the book. There were four names written on it; the newest one was dated from last August. I tore out the piece of paper, folded it, and shoved it in my back pocket with the matches.

For the last time, I looked to the back of the room. I wanted more than anything to lay eyes on my sister one more time. But I couldn't. Because then I wouldn't leave. My sanity was hanging on by a thread. If I saw her again, I'd fucking lose it.

Racing up the stairs, I stepped back into the kitchen and froze when a pounding came through the silence. I spun around toward the sound with my breath caught in my throat. It was coming from a small door on the other side of the kitchen. I was about to bolt from the room when I heard his voice. Running over as quietly as I could, I pulled the dead bolt free. Jamie nearly fell on top of me after he shoved his way out. A cry left me when he raised his fist, ready to attack until he realized it was me.

He pulled me from the floor as my eyes trailed over his wounds. There was a huge gash near his temple with dried blood all over the side of his face. A rush of guilt flooded me. I had thought this was all him.

"Jamie, we have to get out of here," I whispered.

He nodded and spotted the knife in my hand.

"I was going to try and pry the door open with it."

"Nothing is going to pry that door open. It's reinforced or something. I tried," he told me, holding his hand out. "Here, let me hold on to it. I'm sure I can do more damage with that than you can."

I hesitated. "I think I'm going to hold it."

"You still don't trust me?" he hissed.

"I...would just feel better if I have it," I said apologetically. I didn't think he had anything to do with everything, but I couldn't part with my only weapon.

"Did you find Lacey?"

Pain filled my chest, and I lowered my gaze. He didn't know. I didn't know if I could even tell him what happened. Not without breaking down.

I opened my mouth to somehow tell him, but we both went rigid as a noise came from the dining room. Panic swelled, and I fought against the hysteria trying to claim me.

"Come on. There's another door," Jamie said in a hushed voice. He grabbed my hand and pulled me to the far side of the kitchen. I silently hoped the door wouldn't be locked as he twisted the knob. My heart raced as it opened, and the second I was through, I shut it behind me.

The large room was lit by a floor lamp. We kept moving, and I realized it was a library. There were five aisles of shelves, all filled with different types of books. In the corner was a reading area filled with oversized couches and chairs.

"I'm so sorry, Jamie. I feel so guilty that I thought you did all this," I whispered, unable to handle the silence anymore. And I wanted to start the conversation before he asked about Lacey again. The old wood floors creaked when we moved faster, so we went slowly. Even though every bone in my body told me to run.

"Yeah, well, it was my idea to stay here," he said bitterly.

"But I let my thoughts get the best of me. You were just acting so crazy upstairs—"

"They shot me up with something, but I didn't get the full dose. It still messed me up though."

"I'm sorry for doubting you. It was your idea for this whole trip. And the other day when you were all secretive about what your family does. It all made me think it was you when I saw you upstairs."

He laughed darkly. "My family grows pot. That's my big secret. They grow it and sell it. They moved to Michigan because it's legal here now. I didn't want Lacey or you to find out and think badly of me. Doesn't seem like such a big deal now."

I didn't answer. Nothing I said was going to change what had happened or make anything better. We saw another door as we got closer to the other side of the library. I licked my lips as Jamie pushed it open. I hated not knowing what was in the next room. This house was like a maze. But hopefully it was a way out of here.

Suddenly Jamie was gone when a hand came through the doorway and yanked him inside. I leaped back, raising the knife in my shaking hand. I didn't know what to do. Run the other way or go help Jamie. I stepped toward the door, already making my decision. I couldn't leave Jamie alone. I still hesitated to go into the room. If there was more than just one person in there, I didn't think one small knife would help. I could hear Jamie fighting with whoever had grabbed him, and it sounded like someone got slammed into a wall. Before I could make another move, a familiar voice rang out.

CHAPTER SIXTEEN

Sage

"Sage, I know you're there. I could hear you two whispering before Jamie opened the door," Alex called out to me.

I didn't answer. The rage I had for him made my entire body tremble. I shuffled farther away when he started talking again.

"Niko and Geo are in the kitchen. You can't go back that way unless you'd rather see my brothers. Just come in here so we can talk—"

"Sage, run, get out of—" Jamie yelled, until a thump and loud groan came through the open doorway. If it was just Alex in there, maybe Jamie and I could take him. I didn't think Alex would hurt me. At least, I hoped so. I crept into the room, and my hope of Alex being alone disappeared. The room was completely empty except for three people.

Eric was standing behind Jamie, and confusion hit me. He had just been in the great room. How the hell did he get in here before me? Then I remembered that Eric had mentioned a second staircase somewhere in the house. Dread coiled through my limbs as I realized how impossible it was to get out of here when being chased by men who knew this house like the back of their hands.

Jamie's arm was twisted up behind his back, with Eric gripping it tightly. Eric's other hand was around Jamie's mouth. Jamie started shaking his head, silently telling me to run. Run where? The kitchen was blocked by the twins. There was another door behind Jamie, which was impossible to get to now. Eric pulled higher on Jamie's arm to get him to stop moving, and he grunted in pain.

"Come closer, away from the door. Actually, you can shut the door," Alex told me as he eyed the knife in my hand.

I glared at him while I did what he said and moved into the center of the room. He circled around me, blocking the door I had come through.

"It's a good thing I can lie better than you can," he said quietly. His gaze was still glued to the knife. I squinted at him, not understanding for a second, until I realized what he meant. And he made sure he was in front of the door before he said that.

"They were never in the kitchen, were they?" Fury coated my voice at being tricked. I should have known to do the opposite of what he'd told me. But then I glanced over at Jamie. I wouldn't have been able to leave him there.

"I don't know where they are." Alex shrugged. "But you must have seen them if you know they're here."

"Yeah," I answered.

"Sage, give me the knife so we can talk."

"No."

"If you hurt me, then Jamie gets hurt. You don't want that, do you?"

"No."

"Then give me the knife."

"No."

His eyes flashed with anger when I refused to talk to him. I stood my ground, although my stare faltered. I knew how easily he could overpower me, and I was guessing even the knife wouldn't help much.

"You agreed to marry me. You're going to be my wife. I'm bringing you into my family, and this is a part of it. I thought reading the book would help you understand. Maybe my brother was right... maybe we should stay up here for a bit," he threatened, taking a step closer to me.

My mouth dropped open slightly as I thought about my options. No way in hell I was staying in this house with him. Niko had hinted what would happen if I didn't stay by Alex's side. If I didn't cooperate, there was nothing stopping them from killing me like they had Lacey.

"Alex, you have to understand. I just saw my sister get killed—" My voice broke, and I swallowed hard. Jamie wailed from beneath Eric's hand, and I looked at him, sending a silent apology. Tears of devastation filled his eyes, and I wished this wasn't how he'd had to find out.

"You weren't supposed to know—"

"Yes, but I do know. You can't just expect me to be okay with it immediately. I still love you, but I need time to digest," I said softly as I turned back toward him. The words were barely above a whisper. Saying them without cringing took everything I had. I matched his stare, hoping my pain was concealing my rage. He didn't say a word as he studied me, trying to see if I was lying. For once, I didn't feel my face get hot with the lie. Probably because right now, all I felt was hate.

"You still want to marry me?" he asked, some of the tension leaving him.

"Yes, I do. But we need to take everything slow."

Jamie tried to yell through Eric's hand, trying with everything he had to get away. Eric turned him around and slammed Jamie face-first into the wall with his arm still pulled tightly behind him. I grimaced when blood began pouring from his nose.

I focused back on Alex. "What's going to happen to Jamie?"

"We'll talk about everything when you hand me the knife." He came closer and stretched his arm toward me.

I nodded, not moving a muscle as he got near me. When he went to grab it the knife, I tightened my grip and swung it, slicing his hand.

"Fuck," Alex screamed as he ripped his hand away. Without thinking about it, I lunged at him, aiming for the largest part of him so I wouldn't miss. I put my weight behind it and plunged the blade into his stomach, right near his hip.

The knife sank in all the way to the hilt, and my eyes widened in shock. It was so easy. It sliced through him as if it were nothing. I'd just stabbed someone, but I didn't have an ounce of guilt. Survival was the only thing on my mind.

Alex's gaze darted from his wound to my face, his mouth opening as if wanting to say something, but no words came out. My hands shook, not from what I'd done, but from adrenaline. I pulled the knife out and pushed him to the floor before running to Jamie.

Eric's eyes flashed in anger, and he pulled Jamie back from me as if debating about letting him go so he could defend himself. Before I got close enough to do anything, Eric threw Jamie down on the ground and kicked him in the stomach. He stepped over him and advanced toward me. I raised my weapon to cut him, but he was faster. And unlike Alex, he was expecting it. He grabbed my wrist and bent it back until I shrieked in pain. The knife dropped onto the floor, and Eric kicked it under the closed door behind us.

"After what you just did to Alex, you may just stay in this house until next August. You are chosen, just like your sister," he sneered.

I tried to break his grip on my wrist, and he grabbed my other arm with his free hand. I struggled against his painful hold before I was suddenly free. Spinning around, I watched Jamie throw him to the floor. He jumped on top of Eric and started punching him in the face. Over and over.

"Jamie. Come on." I attempted to pull him off. "Before the others come. Please. We need to go."

My words caused him to stop. "You're right. They all need to pay for what happened to Lacey."

I reached for the door that led into the room where Eric had kicked my knife, but it was locked, and I hit my fists on the door in frustration. Then I remembered what Geo said. Alex had a set of keys too. I glanced across the room at Alex, who was on the floor, holding his hands to his wound.

"Alex should have keys on him. For the doors," I told Jamie.

Jamie got off Eric, and I could barely recognize the unconscious man. There was so much blood on his face, it was impossible to tell if he was still breathing. We crossed the room, and Jamie got to Alex first.

"Where are your keys?" Jamie spat.

Alex ignored him, and I crouched down next to him. Without saying a word, I ran my hands over his pockets until I felt a key and slid my hand into his pocket. As I pulled it out, Alex grabbed my arm.

"Sage, I did this for you. I love you."

Pain and hurt were all over his face, and I couldn't tell if it was from the knife wound or my betrayal. His words did nothing. All I felt for him was pure hatred. I had nothing to say to him, and I didn't have to worry about it because Jamie brought up his knee and kicked Alex in the face, knocking him unconscious.

"Let's go. We need to get to the police. Do you have the truck keys?"

I nodded as I felt for the keys in my pocket to make sure they were still there. We ran through the study and back into the kitchen. We got to the door, and I tried to fit the key into the lock. But it didn't work. Had Geo lied? I didn't think so. They had both been so confident that I couldn't get those keys from him when we were upstairs that he hadn't cared if he told me the way to get out. But his key ring had three keys. Alex only had one.

"Maybe it opens the front," I muttered halfheartedly. My hope of getting out of here was all but gone. It seemed impossible that it was still dark outside. It felt like I had been in this house, running and hiding for days. We sprinted through the dining room and burst into the foyer, only to stop in our tracks.

My eyes went to his birthmark before I made eye contact with Niko and the other two men who were blocking our way to the front door. Each one was holding a big bottle of some type of rum as Niko stared straight at me. I searched the room, wondering where Geo was.

One of the men was Detective Thomas. I glared at him before looking at the front door. We were so close—only about fifteen feet away from freedom. Niko appeared amused, but that changed when his eyes grazed my body, seeing the blood on my clothes and the key in my hand.

"Sage. Where's my baby brother? You didn't hurt him, did you?" Niko tried to keep his tone light and controlled, but his jaw ticked, and his shoulders were tensed.

"Let us get to the front door and I'll tell you," I replied, slipping the key into my pocket.

"You know that can't happen. I thought I was clear about the choices you had when we chatted upstairs. You leaving without my brother was not one of them." His tone changed to menacing as he glanced at the blood on Jamie's knuckles.

"Let us go—"

"No, you tell me where Alex is. Now," Niko demanded.

"Fine, he's in one of the rooms past the kitchen." Jamie gave me a sideways glance while I spoke, but I was confident. If Niko went to help Alex, then that only left two men in the way of the door. Better than three.

Niko rushed forward, and Jamie and I stepped out of the way so he could go through the dining room door. But as he passed me, he grabbed my arm, pulling me close.

"If anything happened to Alex—"

"You better hurry, then. He could use help sooner rather than later," I told him coldly.

"You're coming with me, to show me where he is." Niko started tugging me back into the dining room, and my fearless act disintegrated. I hadn't expected him to take me. I fought to pull my arm out of his grip, and when that didn't work, I went limp and fell to the floor. He almost went down with me as he struggled to pull my dead weight back up.

"What the hell are you doing? Get up."

"You could force me to go with you. But I'll fight you every single second. It'll take you way longer to get to Alex if you have to drag me. He might not have that much time..." I let my voice drift off and shrugged carelessly.

I knew what Niko would choose. He would choose his brother, his family. He glared at me as his eyes darted around the room. He was trying to figure out another way to make me go. To be in control of this situation. I couldn't help but shoot him a frigid smile, baring all my teeth. I'd seen his anger in the past, and right now he was furious. But there was nothing he could do if he wanted to get to his brother in a hurry.

His hand loosened and I went to step away from him. Before I was out of his grasp, he wrapped his other hand in my hair and yanked me back to him until I was right next to his face, with his lips right next to my ear.

"Even if you do get out of this house tonight, this won't be the last time I see you. Or my family's last time. We're everywhere. I told you that. No one and nowhere is safe. Your old life is gone. Remember that."

He let go of me and shoved me into Jamie as he ran into the dining room. Jamie and I looked at the two men who were still in front of us. They had already set their rum bottles on the floor.

"If you have a chance for the door—take it. Don't worry about me. At least one of us is leaving this house tonight," Jamie murmured quietly, and I shook my head. We would both leave. Together.

Jamie started after one of the men. He leaned down, charged, and then slammed into the man. He wrapped his arms around the guy's large waist and sent him to the ground. Detective Thomas started to kick Jamie, trying to get him off his friend. I ran up and jumped on Thomas's back, wrapping my arm around his throat.

He grunted, his hands going for my arms as I held on as tightly as I could. After a few seconds, he pried my arm off his neck and flipped me over him and onto the floor. I landed on my back and hit hard enough to knock the wind out of me. I lay there, trying to suck in a breath and calm myself when no air filled my lungs. Tilting my head to the side, I watched as Thomas went to help the other man, who was still in a fight with Jamie. I willed myself to stand up, but my body wasn't responding.

Something wet seeped into my hair, and I could smell it before I gazed at the empty rum bottle that had spilled all over the floor. I began to scoot to the door as my breathing slowly returned.

"Jamie," I cried out hoarsely.

He looked at me and shoved Thomas away from him as the other man lay on the floor unconscious. We were only a few feet from the door with nothing blocking our escape. Except Thomas, who was hesitating about who to come after as his eyes darted between Jamie and me. Hope filtered through me until the dining room door slammed open and two more men came barreling through.

My fingers brushed my pocket as I remembered what I'd taken from the basement. I pulled out the matches and looked at the alcohol-soaked floor. With the old wood and curtains that brushed the floor, it wouldn't take much. Without another thought, I lit the match and threw it down onto the spilled rum. The floor was instantly in flames, separating us from the two men who had come in from the dining room.

Jamie got a hold of Thomas and threw him toward the growing

fire. His screams echoed through the house as the flames touched him. I faced the front door and tried blocking everything out as I took the key out. The air was quickly filling with smoke, and it was already nearly suffocating. I started crying when the lock clicked open.

"What the—"

I whirled around to see another man racing down the stairs, heading straight to Jamie, who was a few feet behind me. I flung open the door and stepped out, sucking in breaths of fresh air.

"Come on, Jamie," I screamed, waiting for him to move. "We can make it to the truck. Forget about him. Get out of the house."

Jamie looked over his shoulder at me as he put his hand on the door. The man was off the stairs and within feet of Jamie. Panic sliced through me, and I moved to pull him with me.

"I told you one of us was getting out of here tonight. Get justice. For Lacey. For whoever else these men have hurt. Go. Now," he told me calmly. Then he slammed the door before I heard the lock click.

CHAPTER SEVENTEEN

Sage

I pounded my fists on the door, screaming Jamie's name. Smoke was billowing out from under the door, and I ran to the closest window. The bars on the window would not give at all as I pulled against them. All I could see were flames and smoke.

The front door swung open, and someone stumbled out. When he was on the porch, he put his hands on his knees and started coughing. I swallowed a strangled sob when I realized it wasn't Jamie. Taking a step back, I flinched when the porch creaked loudly under me. The man looked up, and his eyes widened.

"You," he bellowed as he rushed toward me.

Jumping over the porch railing, I started running for the truck as soon as I landed on the soft grass below. My finger stayed pressed on the unlock button until I grabbed the handle and slid in. The man got to the truck right when the locks clicked. He hit the window and kept attempting to open the door. But then he stopped. He looked to where the road was and started to go around to the back of the house. I watched him leave, my curiosity pushing through the fear as to why he'd left me alone. Once he disappeared behind the house, my gaze went back to the open front door. I silently prayed for Jamie to come outside. But only smoke kept pouring out. By now it looked like the entire foyer and great room were ablaze.

The backyard was suddenly lit up. The white lights were blinding, and I tried to squint through them to see what was happening. A blue car tore through the grass and onto the driveway. Without slowing down, it kicked up clouds of dirt as it raced down the road. Right behind that car were two more that followed suit. The taillights soon disappeared from view. I wondered where all the cars had been. I waited to see if more cars came out, but once again, it was dark. Except for the orange glow from the growing fire.

I was torn. I wanted to go back to the front door and see if there was any chance of Jamie being alive. But the terror that more men still might be out there kept me in the truck. After waiting a few more minutes, I unlocked the door and climbed out. There was no one in sight as I ran back to the house. I wasn't even able to go onto the porch because the flames were so immense.

"Jamie?" I called out, my voice filled with doubt. The house was encased in flames, and I knew there was no way he'd gotten out. With a heavy heart, I turned to get back into the truck until lights lit up the night again. Unlike last time, these lights weren't white. They were blue. My heart jumped. The police.

Someone must have called about the fire. But there was nothing around for miles. The feelings of relief and fear were both fighting within me. I could tell the police what had happened. They could pay for what they'd done. But Niko's words cut my relief short. They had people everywhere, including the police. But by then it was too late to make a decision. The police car had pulled up near the house and blocked in the truck.

The police officer jumped out of his car and ran over to me.

"Are you okay, miss? Come on, let's get away from the house." He started pulling me to his car.

"Wait. There are people inside." I dug my feet into the ground as we got closer to the police cruiser. I was not getting in that car.

"The fire truck is on its way; should be here any minute. Are you the one who called?"

"Called?"

"Yes, there was a call placed that stated their house was on fire and gave the address. Lucky you have a house phone or it would have been much longer before we arrived."

I looked back at the house, trying to remember if I'd seen a phone. It was almost impossible to even see the house now. It was concealed by the tall flames.

"How many people are still in there that you know of?" he asked as he glanced down and saw blood on my hands.

"At least one," I murmured. The fight in my head to either run or tell the officer everything was all I could think of. I didn't know if he could be trusted. He was acting normal. But so had Alex.

"My boss should be here soon. It was his night off, but I paged him. I'm sure he'll have some questions for you. Do you know how the fire started?"

"No," I lied, deciding I wasn't trusting anyone yet.

Headlights made their way down the dirt road. The fire truck had finally come. Behind it was a blue car that parked behind the police cruiser. I saw the man through the window, and a gasp escaped me as my heart thrashed. I'd seen him before. He was one of the men sitting on the sofa inside the great room. Right next to Eric.

"There's the sheriff. I'm sure he's going to want to talk to you. Let me go inform him of what's going on first." The officer started to walk back to the blue car.

"I need to get some water. From my truck. I'll be right back." I bolted to the other side of the police car and jumped into the truck. Twisting the key, I pressed my foot on the gas and drove onto the grass to get around the other cars. I made it to the dirt road before glancing in the mirror to see the two men standing and staring, making no attempt to follow me.

The sheriff was in on it. He was part of their secret. I tried to think clearly as the main road came into view. This road led straight to the highway that I could take all the way back home. Every couple of minutes, my eyes went to the mirror, and I expected to see headlights, but there was only darkness.

Before getting on the highway, I pulled onto the shoulder of the road and parked. Turning on the inside light, I twisted around to look in the back seat and felt a rush of relief when I spotted my wallet. My bad habit of leaving it in the car all the time had paid off for once.

Getting back on the road, I followed the signs for the Mackinac Bridge. The bridge came into view just as the sun started to rise. I had been up for almost twenty-four hours but didn't feel tired at all. My body was shaking, and I kept a tight grip on the steering wheel. I stared at the bridge with sadness smothering me.

Just a couple of days ago, I was right here. With Lacey. I bit my tongue. And with Alex. Now everyone I'd come up here with was dead. Well, maybe not Alex. I glanced in the rearview mirror. Even if Alex didn't survive, I was positive that others had. Which meant I wasn't safe.

Driving onto the bridge, I didn't feel the stab of fear I usually got. I barely noticed the grates as I drove over them. My eyes darted between the windshield and the mirror, knowing it was only a matter of time before they came after me. There was no possible way I could go back to my old life. Niko and Geo's conversation with me overtook my thoughts. They hadn't expected me to escape. But I did. And I wasn't going to make finding me easy for them. As I drove, I planned out everything I needed to do.

Halfway home, the truck was running on fumes. I pulled into a gas station and slipped on a hoodie that was in the back seat. It smelled like Alex, and I resisted the temptation to throw it in the trash. Blood was all over my clothes, and I needed to cover it up. I climbed out and was about to start filling up when an ATM caught my eye. Trying to act natural, I pulled out money to pay for the gas in cash. I felt ridiculous for being so paranoid. But this was my life now. If the society had the reach that Niko said they did, I didn't want them to know where I was using my debit card. I decided to only use cash from here on out.

After getting gas, I drove across the street to another store and bought a prepaid monthly phone with some minutes. My old phone was still with Geo, and I made a mental note to call the phone company and report the phone as lost. The urge to go to the police was overwhelming. But I couldn't. I didn't know who was safe. The sheriff and detective were part of them. How many more were too?

Three hours later, my hometown sign, *Welcome to Capac*, came into sight. I slumped against the seat, only to straighten again when I remembered this place wasn't safe either. There was so much to do, and it needed to be done fast. Before anyone from up north got here. I went straight to my dad's nursing home.

Rushing inside, I smiled when my dad's favorite nurse greeted me. Sarah had been working here for years before my dad came to live here. She reminded me of a perfect grandmother. Her short gray hair fell in curls around her ears. She had the nicest brown eyes I had ever seen. The care she gave my dad went above and beyond. I hesitated before going up to the counter. Trusting people was impossible right now. Sarah seemed like the nicest person in the world. But so did Alex. And Detective Thomas.

I weighed my options and decided that I had no other choice. Sarah smiled warmly at me.

"Sage, back from your trip already? Your dad is still sleeping, but I'm not sure today is a good day to see him. He didn't have a good night last night," Sarah told me sadly. Then she looked me up and down. "Are you okay? What happened? You smell like...smoke."

"I'm fine. I just didn't have time to shower after the bonfire last night. I cut myself on something." The words came out fast as I tried to explain my crazy appearance. "Something did happen, which is why I'm here now. Can I just go in and see him to say goodbye? I'm leaving for a while."

Sarah's forehead wrinkled as her eyes widened. "Leaving?"

"Yes. Here is my new phone number in case of emergency. But you can't give it to anyone. Please. I know you remember my boyfriend, Alex?"

She nodded.

"We broke up. It ended really badly, and he might come asking to see if my dad has my new number. I don't want him or anyone else to know it. That's why I came back in such a hurry," I lied as I handed the paper with the number to her.

"All right, Sage. I'll make sure this number stays between us. I'm sorry about you and Alex. He didn't hurt you, did he? I'll kick him where the sun doesn't shine," Sarah said, placing her hands on her hips.

"I'll be fine, just need to get away for a bit," I tried to say reassuringly—and failing miserably.

She didn't look fully convinced. "If you need anything, you can always ask me."

I smiled and gave her a quick hug. "Thanks. I really do appreciate it."

I followed Sarah to my dad's room and peeked in. He was sound asleep, snoring slightly. Opening the door wider, I tiptoed to his bed.

"I love you, Daddy," I whispered and gave him a kiss on his forehead. Tears were pooling in my eyes as I backed away into the hall. I thanked Sarah and reminded her again not to give out that number before heading back to the truck. Sitting behind the steering wheel, I ordered myself to not lose it. Not yet.

The next place I went to was the bank. My name was added to all my dad's accounts when I turned eighteen. Lacey used to oversee the money but hated the responsibility. My parents had us later in life, and my dad started saving when he got his first job at sixteen. Dad had made each of us a savings account for college throughout the years, and there was still enough to cover his nursing home since he'd paid off the house years ago.

There was still some in my college fund, and Lacey had barely touched hers. I took nine thousand dollars out of her savings account. I wanted to take out more but knew if I took out more than that, the process of getting it would be much longer. There wasn't time for that. I put the money in the glovebox in the truck and drove to my house.

After parking the truck in the garage, I shut the overhead door. Just in case someone drove by. The second I was inside the house, I collapsed onto the kitchen chair. My body ached. My back was still sore from being thrown to the floor. Bruises were emerging on my arms from when Eric had grabbed me. Five hours of driving had made all the pain worse. Putting my face in my hands, I sobbed. I needed five minutes. Only five minutes to release everything I'd been holding in.

I finally got it together enough to stand back up, knowing I couldn't stay here long. This was the first place they'd look. I went upstairs, stopping in front of Lacey's room. Why? Pain clawed at my chest. Why did it have to be my family? I went into her room and walked over to pick up Lacey's favorite necklace from the dresser.

In the rush to leave for vacation, she must have forgotten it. The necklace used to be our mother's. It was a simple teardrop shape with a sapphire stone in it. Our mom's birthstone. I put it around my neck before going to my room and grabbing a duffel bag. I threw in a few pairs of shorts and jeans, some shirts, and a couple other essentials. Nothing fancy. Only what was needed.

Going downstairs to the kitchen, I called the phone company from the landline. We barely ever used it, but now I was grateful to have it and not waste minutes on my new prepaid phone. I reported my cell phone as lost and asked to have it locked so it couldn't be accessed. I made a mental list to change all my passwords when I got a chance.

Before I could break down again, I locked up the house and went back to the garage. I grabbed the money out of the truck and put the truck key in the toolbox before sliding into my small car. It was more inconspicuous than a massive pickup. I backed slowly away from the house and wondered if I'd ever see it again.

CHAPTER EIGHTEEN

Sage

Sitting in my car, I stared at the apartment complex in front of me. After driving for hours, I was on the west side of the state. Still in Michigan, but far enough to feel a bit safer. Capac was the only place I had ever known. Anywhere else was scary and foreign. The decision to stay or leave Michigan tore me apart, but I decided I couldn't be too far from my dad. He was all I had left.

Somehow, I ended up in Kalamazoo. It was a large college town, and I'd visited it a couple of times. It would be easy to blend in here, to act like just another college student. The road I was parked on was busy. The streets were lined with little shops and restaurants. Even though the fall semester hadn't even started, there were lots of people my age here having fun shopping.

The outside of the complex was brown stone and was two

stories. There were landscaped flowerbeds surrounding the entire building. I entered the office to see a woman sitting behind the desk. She was nicely dressed in a black pencil skirt with a white dressy top. Her brown hair was pulled back into a strict bun. She stood up when I walked in.

"Hi, I'm Cathy. Are you looking to rent, or have you already put down a deposit?" she asked while motioning to the empty seat.

I sat down. "Looking to rent, please."

"You're lucky you came when you did. By this time next week, with everyone returning for school, this place will be full. You're starting classes next semester?"

I nodded. "Yes. I was just hoping for a one bedroom. I saw on the sign out front that you have furnished apartments and the lease is month to month? And does the rent include all the utilities?"

"Yes, I think we have one or two left. Will you be paying yourself or do you have the paperwork from the school to help with your housing?"

"I'll be paying."

"All right, well here's the paperwork for you. Start filling it out."

I chewed the inside of my cheek while she read the papers. It would be so easy for someone to trace a paper trail and find me.

"Is there any way I can just pay in cash without all the paperwork?" I asked hopefully.

Cathy raised her eyebrow and gave me a once-over.

"It's just my boyfriend and I just broke up. And it wasn't a good relationship. He abused me. I left him, and I don't want him to find me. He has friends in law enforcement. I just want to find someplace where I can pay cash and lay low while I start classes. I can't let him find me." I could feel the tears start to fall but didn't wipe them away. That lie wasn't too far from the truth. I really did need to hide.

The suspicion fell from the lady's face and was replaced with understanding.

"I have enough cash to pay for the first five months. I'll give it all to you right now," I continued quickly.

Cathy looked at me, her gaze filled with empathy. "Usually, we never let anyone rent without doing the paperwork. But I understand. I was in a relationship like that before too."

I waited for her to continue as I held my breath. I was so tired. All I wanted was a place to crash and couldn't imagine having to wait and find another place.

"All right. If you give me the money for the first five months, then we'll forget the paperwork."

"Thank you so much. You have no idea how much this means to me." I said, my voice nearly breaking.

"You're welcome. But I'll need a first name so I can put something down."

I paused. "Susan."

"Okay, Susan, here is your receipt for the first five months' rent. If you need anything, please try to get a hold of me first, since technically there's no paperwork. All right?"

I nodded and took the receipt. She handed me the keys and walked with me to show me where the apartment was. It was on the second floor, door number twenty.

"I really hope you find the peace you need while you're here. Remember, if you need anything, just call," Cathy told me softly before she walked away.

I watched as she walked away as suspicion tore through me. I felt like everyone was out to get me. But I needed a place to stay and to do that, I had to talk to people. Better to talk to only one person instead of many if I kept going somewhere new. I just hoped whoever I did talk to wasn't connected to the society. Turning the key, I opened the door and looked at my new home.

The living room was small but homey. There was a small blue cloth couch in front of a TV. All the walls were a warm beige. On the other side of the couch was a sliding door that led to a tiny balcony. The kitchen had all the essentials, with a little countertop space left over. The dark brown cabinets lined above the counters had more space than I would need. Right near the door was a small round glass table with two wooden chairs pushed in. There was a short hallway with two doors. One was a small bathroom, and the other was a bedroom. The bedroom was big enough to fit a full-size bed, one dresser, and a small nightstand. All the furniture in there was white, and the room had the same beige walls as the rest of the place.

I threw my backpack and duffel bag onto the floor and crashed onto the bed. The second my face was pressed against the pillow, my sobs were uncontrollable. Both my body and mind were exhausted. Everything I had held in for the past two days exploded as I screamed into the pillow. I hit the mattress until my fists hurt. I cried for my sister. My mom. For Jamie. For my former life. Even for my relationship with Alex. After what seemed like hours, I had no more tears to shed. I fell into a troubled sleep and dreamed of what had happened up north.

The next morning, I woke up with red, puffy eyes. My throat was scratchy, and muscles I didn't know I had hurt every time I moved. The hot water in the shower was almost scalding as I tried to wash away the last two days. After getting dressed and suppressing the anxiety about going out in public, I stepped out onto the busy sidewalk.

My hair was pulled back and put under a hat, and I slid on sunglasses. Even though I was completely covered up, my fear of being recognized was overwhelming. I walked two streets over, looking for a place to get some food. The street was bustling with families and kids, all finding places to eat lunch. I passed a pharmacy and stopped in to get a few things.

The next place I found was a small local grocery store. I bought enough food for a couple of days and headed back to the apartment. After putting the food away, I went into the bathroom. The brown paper bag from the pharmacy was in my hand, and I pulled out what I'd bought as my stomach twisted.

Semi-permanent hair dye. I sighed and got to work.

The image that stared at me from the mirror wasn't recognizable. My once fiery hair was now a dull brown. The spark in my eyes was gone. Even when I smiled, it looked forced and sad. The hair dye would wash out in six weeks, and I'd dye it again. I couldn't bring myself to make my red hair permanently disappear. It was a part of who I was. It made me feel closer to my mother, and now my sister too. I looked at my reflection and touched Lacey's necklace. Jamie had died to make sure I got away. To get justice for Lacey and everyone else. But I had no idea how to do it. Right now, I didn't even have the energy to think about it.

Situated on the small couch, I opened my laptop, and connected to the internet. Going onto the search engine, I typed in: *house fire in Hiawatha National Forest*. Only one news article popped up, and it was dated from an hour ago. My heart began to beat faster when he appeared on the screen. The sheriff. The man who was in the house, next to Eric. I turned up the volume and watched the news clip.

"Unfortunately, there was a fatal house fire. It is still under investigation. But it looks like it was an accident. Electrical wiring. This house was so old and hasn't been updated; it's a wonder it lasted this long. Sadly, there were two fatalities. Both families have been notified. Jamie Martinez and Lacey Taylor were staying a night here while on vacation. They were upstairs and unable to get out before the smoke consumed the house..."

I waited for more, but that was it. No mention of me. Or of the other men who were in the fire. I wondered if Alex and the twins were in the house when it started burning. I replayed the clip. They called it an accident. They covered it up. It was that easy. Maybe leaving the state was the best bet. But from what Niko had said, they had people everywhere. Nowhere was safe.

I logged in to my social media and saw it had already exploded with people offering condolences for my sister. Without even reading them, I made a quick post stating that I needed a break from online life and then closed the laptop. Nobody would miss me. I didn't have any close friends. Lacey and Alex were pretty much the only people I saw. And now they were both gone. I covered my face and blew out a long breath. Crying wasn't going to make anything better.

CHAPTER NINETEEN

Sage

The weeks dragged into a month, and nothing happened. I stayed in the house unless I needed to get food. If I got restless, I'd take a walk after dark. My neighborhood was always busy. College classes were in full swing, and the area I lived in was all students. A couple of people who lived in my building had tried to make small talk, but I kept to myself.

I bought pepper spray and a small pocketknife, and I carried them everywhere with me. I drove three hours away to a branch of my bank to pull out more cash. The drive was worth it, to keep where I was staying a secret. I called my dad once a week to check on him, but always made sure it was at different times. The stress of feeling like someone was watching me every second was exhausting. I was scared all the time, even when I was in my apartment.

I was enjoying the sun on one of my rare walks I took during the day, and I passed a small gym. There was a large banner promoting a women's self-defense class. Standing in front of it, I debated whether it would be worth it.

"You going to stand there all day?" asked a voice from behind me.

I whirled around, ready to bolt. The woman who spoke to me looked both a little amused and confused.

"You're blocking the door. Are you going in to join the class?"

"Sorry. I didn't realize I was in the way," I said quietly, without meeting the woman's eyes.

"If you're thinking about it, then it means you need this class. In which case, you should join. It's only a week long, but you learn a lot. It can't hurt." The woman gave me a kind smile before heading inside the gym.

I tapped my fingers on my leg, thinking of the woman's words. Two minutes later, I opened the door and went inside. I walked up to the counter and asked about the self-defense class.

"You're just in time. The new class starts tonight. In about fifteen minutes. Would you like to sign up?" the man behind the counter asked.

I glanced down at my black yoga pants and baggy T-shirt. I was already dressed for it.

"Yes, please," I answered, avoiding his eyes. I didn't recognize myself anymore. To fear everybody. I used to be strong-willed, and now I couldn't look people in the eye. My nature was fighting me every step of the way. I missed my old self. The person who'd stood up for anything I believed in. Maybe this class would help get a part of that back.

"Here you go. I just need you to fill out this liability form. And will you be paying with card or cash?"

"Cash," I responded as I scribbled my name on the line, making sure it wasn't legible.

"If you just go into that room on the left, that's where the class is. Have fun."

I moved toward the door and peered in the window. The class was all women who looked to be around my age. Probably girls from the college. The instructor walked in right after me. A man somewhere in his thirties who looked like he lived at the gym. The sleeves on his shirt were about to rip at the seams. He introduced himself to the class, and they started with warm-ups.

Sweat quickly pooled at my lower back. This was the most I had moved in a month. We went into the first self-defense technique, and I knew this was what I needed. A way to fight back. Images of being trapped in Alex's arms popped into my head. And it made me work harder. I never wanted to be in that position again. The class finished, and I was already looking forward to what we would learn tomorrow.

I finished the self-defense class and kept up with working out. It was a way for me to keep busy. I did pushups and other small workouts at home. There were evening boxing classes that I went to. The woman I had met before the first class was named Katie, and I talked to her a few times. I told her the same story about Alex that I had told the apartment manager. A couple of days after that, Katie gave me a stun gun. *You need it more than me right now*, she had told me. They were illegal without a permit, but I didn't care. I felt safer having it.

Any time I drove to take out more cash, I visited a library and logged in to my social media. I pulled random pictures from the internet and would make a post about traveling because I needed time after Lacey's death. There was no one else I was close to other than Lacey and Alex, so going absent online wasn't difficult. It might not have been the smartest, but I didn't need more people searching for me if anyone thought I was missing. One crazy cult was enough to deal with.

My old self was beginning to peek out of the cracked shell I had become. Still scared but more confident. I was ready to move on. To get justice for my sister. And I finally had an idea of where to start.

CHAPTER TWENTY

Him

Four fucking months.
 The last few months since the incident up north had been hell. I was sitting in the study, wishing I was anywhere else. My family was front and center of it all because it had happened during our ceremony. This event would be a learning tool in the future for the society, and not in a good way. The elders, who usually stayed in the shadows, were here for the meeting. Two of them had flown from Greece to be here. We were at one of the other houses owned by the society. Not as remote as the one that had burned down, but still far away from major cities.
 We'd been looking for Sage since the night it happened. Grant, the sheriff, the one who watched her drive away, blamed me. He claimed he was told not to harm the youngest sister. That she was

Alex's. He had no idea that Alex had been stabbed. By the time word got to me that she had driven away, she was long gone.

I expected to find her back in Capac. Either with her dad or at her house. But when we got there, the house was locked down. I went to the nursing home and explained that I knew Alex and asked if Sage had stopped by. The nurse had given me an icy glare and said no. Obviously, she was lying, but I couldn't do anything about it. We had her phone but got locked out, so that was a dead end.

I scrubbed my hand down my face. How could one girl cause so much trouble? There was a small part of me that respected her more now. She had seen her sister die and had still fought her way out of that house. She was clever enough to disappear without a trace.

I quickly buried that thought, focusing on the shit I had to deal with right now.

About eight men filed in and sat down around the table where I was already sitting. My father sat down next to me with a scowl on his face. He was not happy to be the center of attention, and I knew he was furious with me. We'd barely had a conversation in the past four months. He blamed me for what happened. With Sage. And with Alex.

"Is there anything new to report?" one of the elders, Samual, asked. He stroked his long white beard as he waited for someone to speak up.

My father cleared his throat before he answered. "No, sir. We have been using our local and national connections, and so far, there's been nothing."

I kept my head down as the conversation started. I was not planning on talking unless someone asked me a direct question. I was the one to blame for this. And the burden of bringing shame to my family was weighing me down.

"This is one girl we're talking about. She couldn't have gotten far. What about tracking her credit card?" Samual asked in his low, gruff voice.

"We do have someone who works at the bank she uses. But she

has been making large cash withdrawals from banks all over the state and even a few in the surrounding states. Other than the withdrawals, there's been no activity on her account," my dad answered.

"She's probably staying in the state then."

"Yes, sir. That's what we're thinking."

"Any info on her car?"

"We know what car she has, and we have our people in the police force watching out for it. But so far, there have been no sightings."

"What about her social media?"

"My son has been watching her accounts, and so far, nothing except her traveling. But we've already looked into it, and it's a false lead."

A strained hush fell over the room. The only sound was the ticking of the grandfather clock in the corner of the study.

"You already told us what happened that night. But is there anything you can think of that could possibly help? Something you've maybe forgotten?" Samual asked, his question directed at me.

I could feel the heated stares bearing down on me as I lifted my head. There was no doubt that it was my fault she had slipped through our fingers. I severely underestimated her will to escape.

"No, sir, nothing I can think of." The lie rolled so freely through my lips, a polygraph test wouldn't have picked up on it. Lying had always come naturally. Lying and acting like nothing bothered me was how I lived my life.

"You're the one who checked on her house?"

I nodded. "Yes. The house was locked up. She had been there but was long gone before I got there. I did go inside, and it looked like she had no plans to come back anytime soon."

Samual sat down and sighed. "We need to find her. We have many in our group, and they will all help in whatever way they can. We're a family. The faster we find her, the better."

All the men murmured in agreement. I wondered how long it would take us to find her. Sure, the group was big and had a wide reach. But we didn't have enough people to watch her house all the time. Or stay at her dad's nursing home around the clock. Each member of the society was a regular person with a day job. No one had time for that. They helped where they could, but it might not be enough. Either she'd have to make a mistake, or we'd catch a break.

Samual ended the meeting, and the men started to leave. My dad got up and left the room without even a glance toward me. I didn't think he would ever forgive me for this. It was our family's night. I stayed in the chair with my hands behind my head as I watched the second hand tick on the clock.

My thoughts were a jumbled mess. Part of me wanted them to find Sage. It would set things right with my family and the rest of the society. But another part didn't. She was special. So fierce and strong-willed. I knew what would happen if they found her, and I didn't want that to happen. Fuck, I shouldn't even be having these thoughts.

I was raised to dedicate everything to the society. But that night flipped something in my brain. Ever since then, I'd been questioning everything. I knew what was expected of me. What my family and the society wanted from me. Yet, I was keeping a secret from them.

I groaned and stood up, glad the meeting was over.

The thing was, I already knew where she was hiding.

I had picked up a lead over a month ago. Keeping this secret from the family had been tearing me apart. There had been three times I had opened my mouth to tell my father, but each time, I backed out. She was keeping to herself. I had checked on her a couple of times, and she hadn't made any attempts to contact the police or anyone else.

All I had to do was tell the society where she was, and that would be the end. But then her life would be over. There was no harm in just watching if she stayed quiet. But just watching was getting harder. I wanted to talk to her.

Maybe it was time to take a trip to Kalamazoo.

CHAPTER TWENTY-ONE

Sage

After going grocery shopping, I spent the rest of the day in my apartment getting my plan together. I could have done it sooner, but I'd have to leave Michigan. For the past four months, this place had kept me safe. And I was terrified to leave my bubble. The research had kept me busy, and I wanted it all strategized out before leaving.

There was a knock at the door. The sound used to paralyze me, but neighbors were always knocking to see if I wanted to join a party or barbeque. I got up and looked through the peephole, seeing the top part of a hat that had the college mascot on it. Twisting the lock, I cracked open the door.

"Hi—" I started to say until I saw his face. With a shriek, I tried to slam the door shut, but it was too late. His hand already gripped the door. I leaned my body against it, trying to make him pull his hand back. Instead, he rammed the door so hard that I flew back and landed on the floor.

"Hey, Sage." He grinned as he took off the hat and tossed it on the table.

I pulled the skirt of my sweater dress down as I got back on my feet, and I immediately tensed in a defensive pose. My heart was straining against my ribcage while that night up north rushed back to my head. I had let my guard down just opening the door like that. It had been months, and I had been so confident this place was safe.

My eyes went to his bare arm, and once I saw what I was looking for, I met his gaze again.

Niko.

He stood in front of the door with a smirk on his face. His sharp green eyes studied me as I stood rigid in front of him. He looked the same as the last time I saw him, except his black hair was a bit longer and messy from being under a hat. A flashback of being in Lacey's room at the house up north darted through my mind. Once again, I was stuck with him blocking the only exit. I glanced at my bag that was on the floor next to the couch. If I could reach the stun gun, I could have a chance. Unless he hadn't come alone.

"Nice place. Very cozy." Niko watched me closely, as if waiting for me to try to get past him to the door.

"How'd you find me?" I asked, raising my chin. I refused to cower and would fight just as hard to get out of this as I had up north.

"I have to be honest, Sage. I miss the red hair. Brown just doesn't suit you," he replied, ignoring my question.

I didn't say anything and waited for him to keep talking. Of all the times I imagined them finding me, I never pictured Niko showing up by himself. The cold demeanor he had up north was gone. Instead, he was acting like the arrogant asshole I'd known for years. Like nothing had changed.

"Sit on the couch. We need to talk," Niko demanded, losing his smile.

"If you think I'm going to leave with you—"

"Whoa," he interrupted me, throwing up his hands. "I didn't say anything about taking you anywhere. Just want to talk, okay?"

It was a standoff. I didn't trust that he just wanted to talk, and he didn't move away from the door. After a minute of silence, I broke first and backed up until I hit the couch. The only reason was because my bag was closer, and having the stun gun would dramatically change my odds for the better. I sat down stiffly, with my muscles taut and ready to move when the chance presented itself. Niko grabbed a chair from the table, set it a few feet away from the couch, and sat down. Making sure he was between me and the door.

"Smart choice," he murmured as he took a short piece of rope out of his pocket and set it on the arm of the couch.

My stomach clenched, and I inched down the couch, farther away from him. I had no idea what he had planned or why he'd come alone. But when I stared at the rope, all I saw was the reason for fighting. It was my life. Even as shitty as it was right now, I was still free. And I wouldn't give it up easily. Niko chuckled, and I looked back to him.

"Don't worry. Like I said, I just want to talk. But I wasn't sure how you'd react, so I had to come prepared. Just in case."

"You didn't think you could handle me without help?" I raised an eyebrow, wanting to get under his skin and throw him off.

His jaw clenched, and he looked at me warily. "I found you over a month ago. I know what you've been doing. Taking those classes at the gym. I don't know the new tricks you've learned. Better to be careful than a girl getting the drop on me. Wouldn't be able to live that one down."

I was stuck on the first thing he said. "A month ago?"

"Yeah. You did so good covering your tracks in the beginning. Not using your card or driving your car. I'm guessing you're using a prepaid phone?"

I pressed my lips together as my eyes darted to the door. I was sure others were waiting out there to take me away. If they had known for a month, they'd had more than enough time to plan this out.

"You even dyed your hair. Smart girl. I thought you might, but it's hard to picture you with any other color than your red."

"Then how did you find me?"

He flashed me a grin, and it sent hot fury racing through my veins. He had been watching me for at least a month. All this time, I thought it was safe. Before I could say anything else, his phone went off.

He pulled it out of his pocket and started to read the message. Looking at my bag that was less than two feet away, I knew this was it. He was distracted.

"Hey—" he protested as I lunged. My hand was inside the bag, my fingertips brushing the stun gun, when arms wrapped around my waist. He lifted me and spun me away from the bag.

"Really? I thought you wanted to do this the easy way," he said once he was between me and the stun gun. "What's in the bag, Sage?"

The second he set me down, I slammed my foot down onto his as hard as possible. His arms loosened enough that I was able to turn and face him. I grabbed him around the neck and pulled down before digging my knee into his gut. Just as I had practiced at the gym all those times. I did it perfectly, and it worked.

"Shit," Niko groaned out as he doubled over, stumbling away from me. I reached for the bag and grabbed the stun gun. He got a glimpse of it right as I touched it to his skin, and his eyes went wide.

"Don't—"

He didn't even get to finish what he was saying before I stunned him. The crackle of electricity filled the room, and I kept it pressed to him. He grunted and tried to stay standing. But after only a couple of seconds, his legs collapsed. I shoved him back and he fell onto the couch.

Spotting the rope, I quickly made a decision. The effects of the stun gun wouldn't last long. He was on his side, and I pushed him onto his stomach, with his legs dangling off the short couch. I put his hands together and wrapped the rope around them. Keeping his hands together as I tied it was difficult. I knotted it as tight as I could before stepping back.

Niko was already stirring. With a groan, he tried to move his arms. He froze and snapped his eyes open. I was near the door, ready to bolt if he got off the couch. The emergency bag that I always kept ready was in hand. My heart was pounding, and my hands trembled slightly. Not from fear. It was from the fact that I'd fought back and got the upper hand. My eyes didn't leave him as he tried again to pull his hands free. But the knot was holding.

"That fucking hurt. Really, Sage? I told you, I only wanted to talk."

"Right, and I should just believe you."

He took a couple of long breaths before speaking again.

"I still want to talk."

I hesitated, wanting to know how he'd found me so that it wouldn't happen again.

"Then talk," I said coldly.

With a grunt, he pulled himself into a sitting position on the couch. He stretched his legs out and crossed one leg over the other. As if he was just relaxing. He flashed his most charming smile at me, but it was forced. It didn't reach his eyes. The green eyes that looked much darker right now because of the fury that swam in them.

"You're stronger. I was not expecting that."

I could hear the surprise in his voice, and my lips twitched upward. I was proud I'd bested him. My fear still had me in a stronghold, but after the last few months, I learned how to fight through it.

I narrowed my eyes. "Spit it out, Niko. What do you want to say?"

He squirmed, trying to get more comfortable with his arms tied behind his back. I could tell how angry he was not to have power over the situation. He might be grinning, but the rage was simmering just below the surface. His shoulders were tensed, and he'd been gritting his teeth since I stunned him.

"I've known where you were for a while. Believe me, if I wanted to do more than just talk, I could have. Easily," he taunted.

"Yeah, but you didn't. Tell me how you found me," I demanded.

He shook his head. "That's not what I wanted to talk about."

"I don't care."

"Listen, it doesn't matter where you go. You can never let your guard down like you did here. Nowhere is safe. I wasn't lying when I told you that." His eyes bored into mine.

"So, you're here to what? Take me back to your cult?"

"No."

"No?"

"If we had wanted to take you, it wouldn't have been me coming alone."

"Then what do you want?"

"I told you. To talk."

"About what?"

He didn't answer right away, and the grin faded.

"To warn you. That we're still looking."

I tried to gauge the sincerity in his eyes. There was no part of me that trusted him. But I didn't understand why he had come alone.

"How'd you find me?"

He sighed. "You know that paper you signed when you started going to the gym? I'm guessing you didn't read the fine print. It gives them permission to use photos of you online. Imagine my surprise when I'm scrolling, and an ad pops up with you in a group class. Pure luck. I almost didn't recognize you with that hair though."

My mouth dropped open, and I shook my head, almost in denial. The one thing I needed. The thing that had already helped me was what had gotten me caught. He was right. I didn't even glance at the paper when I signed it.

"That gym only has three locations. Scouted one out for a few days and then came here. On the second day, I saw you. Followed you here, and that's pretty much it."

"You've been here watching me for a month?"

His usual attitude returned, and he grinned.

"Don't give me that look. I only checked up on you a few times to make sure you weren't doing anything stupid."

Confusion rocked me. If they had known for a month, then why had they been letting me stay here. Why not just take me? Niko's words broke through my questioning thoughts.

"They don't know you're here," he said quietly.

"What?"

"No one knows but me."

I gaped at him in shock. I didn't know how to respond or if I could believe him. I slowly sat down in the chair Niko had moved with the stun gun still firmly in my hand.

"You haven't told anyone?" My voice was full of doubt.

"You really think you'd still be here if they knew? No. You'd be at one of our houses."

A shiver of fear ran through me, but I tried not to show it. He raised his eyebrow.

"Don't act like you're not scared. You made yourself completely disappear."

"Yes, I did. Thanks to what you told me up north. If you're the only one who knows, then I'm fine. You're not going anywhere anytime soon. I could be out of here and long gone before you're even off that couch," I said with bolstered confidence and a dismissing wave of my hand.

"You're lucky it was me who found you," he sneered. The lack of control was getting to him.

"Thanks for the head start. I'm sure you'll get out of that rope eventually." I stood back up.

"You're just going to leave me here? I didn't even get to say what I wanted." He uncrossed his legs and sat up straight.

"I disappeared once. I'll do it again. More carefully this time."

I turned to the door, and out of the corner of my eye, I saw him jump up. His hands were no longer tied. He got to me so fast I didn't have a chance to turn back around. I blindly swung my arm around to try to touch any part of his body with the stun gun. My wrist was the first thing he went for.

CHAPTER TWENTY-TWO

Sage

"I don't think so. You surprised me once. That's not happening again," he growled as he grabbed my other wrist, twisting me around until my back slammed into the door. He raised my arms above my head and used one hand to hold them while he pried the stun gun out of my hand. Terror seized me as he gripped it. He glanced down and read my expression.

"Don't worry, Sage. I can handle you without the help of this." He mocked my words from earlier.

He threw my weapon down the hall, and it landed in the bedroom. I struggled to get free of his grasp, and he pressed his body onto mine. It was almost impossible to move, let alone attempt to kick him.

"I could hold you here all day. Just quit moving so we can talk. You know, the whole reason I came here."

"Let me go, you son of a bitch." My voice was rising from the panic of being trapped again. His free hand covered my mouth.

He leaned closer. "You might want to stop yelling. I only came here to talk. If someone else sees me here, then I'll have no choice but to take you back with me. And you know we don't like our secrets to come out. If someone saw this, they would have to be dealt with."

His words were just above a whisper, but the threat was loud and clear. I weighed my options. If he had really come here alone, getting attention could help me escape. But what if he really wasn't here alone? I didn't want anyone else to die. I stopped talking, and soon after, stopped trying to escape. I was getting nowhere, except exhausting myself.

"How is it that you grew up surrounded by the Great Lakes and never spent time on a boat?" he asked once I stopped squirming. He removed his hand from my mouth so I could answer.

"What are you talking about?"

"That knot you tied. It took less than five minutes to undo. Even with my hands behind my back. If you'd ever spent time on a boat, you'd know how to tie a knot." He chuckled.

I didn't give him the satisfaction of a response.

"You surprised me, Sage. I never would have guessed you'd be able to take me on. I mean, you kind of had an unfair advantage with that taser. Never been hit with one of those before. Hurt like a bitch." He backed half a step from me, still keeping my arms locked in his grasp.

"Sorry," I replied smugly.

"We're going to try this again. You're going to sit on the couch so we can finish this conversation. If not, I'll show you how a real knot is tied," he warned as his eyes flashed to mine, as if daring me to call his words a bluff.

He brought my wrists down but didn't loosen his grip. I instinctively tried to pull away, but he turned me around and held my arms behind my back. He pushed me down onto the couch, grabbed the bag on the floor, and threw it to the other side of the room.

"Get comfy, lean back, and relax. You're not getting off that couch until I say so," he told me as he sank back into the chair. I noticed he was much more alert than before.

"I don't get you," I said as I rubbed my wrists.

He raised his eyebrows. "What?"

"These last four months have been crazy. My life is gone. Your society killed my sister. I saw her die. And you come in here and act like this is all normal with your jokes and sarcasm. What do you want from me? Why did you come here?" I was going to ask him whatever came to mind. If I could find out anything about his family and group, then it would help in the future.

If I got away from him.

Niko stared at me, but he seemed lost in thought. His arrogant bravado seemed to vanish.

"I feel bad. About what happened to Lacey. And I don't want that to happen to you. We've taken enough from your family. I really came here to warn you. To show you how easy it is to be found."

I was speechless. I had never heard him talk so seriously before. And the sincerity seemed real. He was always all jokes. I still didn't trust him but couldn't think of one other reason why he would be here by himself.

"As for my amazing personality, it's who I am. I like making everything fun. Even situations like this. Though I have to say, this is my first time doing this." His usual grin was back as he finished talking.

I rolled my eyes. "Warning received. I'll be more careful next time. Can you leave now?"

"I'm surprised you haven't asked about Alex."

"I don't care."

"Really? Because he didn't make it. He's dead, thanks to you," he said coldly.

My stomach dropped. My mind went back to when I had stabbed

him. I did it so fast, I hadn't even thought about it before I'd sunk the knife into his stomach. I'd wondered whether he had survived. An unexpected rush of grief hit me. Grief for what, I wasn't sure. Killing him or because he was dead. I didn't know anymore. I let the feeling of anger overtake the grief as I looked back at Niko.

"What do you want me to say? I'm sorry? Because after what happened that night, I don't think I am," I snapped.

"Kind of poetic justice. We take your sister, and you take my brother," he murmured.

"No, it's not. You people are insane and murdered my sister. I killed him defending myself."

"Geo made it out, in case you were wondering. Just barely, but he did."

"I wasn't wondering," I was surprised Niko was here without his twin. They were never far from each other. But I wasn't sharing my surprise with him.

"You've learned to control your emotions. Usually you're an open book, but not anymore." He looked at me curiously.

"That night changed everything," I shot back, my voice filled with venom.

"Okay, well, this conversation is too heavy for me—" He was about to leave when I interrupted him.

"Wait. I need to know. Your group. They kill people every year. Only redheads," I forced myself to keep going, "how is it that no one has caught on? Was that house up north the only place it's happened?"

My question hung in the air as silence filled the room. I fully expected him to ignore it and just leave. But then he answered.

"It's not every year. There is only a sacrifice for each family. And that's once a man in the family gets old enough to start bearing children. It wasn't a lot in the beginning. But once it spread through Greece, through Europe, and now even here in North America, there are a lot more. Sometimes we go two or three years between them. And no, that wasn't the only house. There are more where the ceremonies are held. It's a belief. You read the book, Sage. It's been happening for centuries."

He stopped, and I stayed quiet, curious to see what else he'd say.

"We are all families with normal lives. Normal jobs. I keep telling you we have eyes everywhere. It's people doing their jobs. A police officer. A bank manager. It's an endless list. We get together to help with the ritual once a year if it's needed. And to help out with situations. They're all looking for you. You need to stay under the radar like you've been."

My heart was beating erratically, and every time I tried taking a deep breath, my chest got tight. Hearing him explain everything was sending me into a spiraling panic that I couldn't escape from. My vision went blurry, and I was suddenly back in that basement, watching the knife go into my sister's heart. My hands clenched into fists as I rocked back and forth on the couch.

"Sage. What's wrong?" Niko's voice sounded far away, and I turned, trying to focus on him, but couldn't. My hands flew to my chest as a searing pain shot through it. A crippling weight hit, and I gasped for air, unable to take a breath. During this entire time, flashes of what happened up north filled my mind. And thoughts about how I was going to end up the same way. A piercing noise echoed in my ears, and it took me a moment to figure out it was me who was screaming. Or trying to.

A light touch landed on my arm, and I jolted away. I locked eyes with Niko, who was sitting on the couch next to me. Panic filled his gaze as he looked from me to the door. I threw myself to the other side of the couch.

"Don't fucking touch me," I forced out in nearly a whisper. "You did this. Your cult. My life—and everyone I loved—is gone because of you."

"You're having a panic attack." He reached over and grabbed me around the waist. "You need to calm down."

Is that what this was? I frantically tried to suck air into my lungs as I attempted to push him away when he pulled me closer.

"Your hands on me will not calm me down," I hissed, trying to force myself to make it all go away. But my body wasn't responding.

"Talk to me. What do you hear?" he asked, his voice soft.

"Let me go," I cried out, the pain in my chest tightening as I flailed my body, trying to get away from him.

His grip tightened, and he lifted me up and set me on his lap with my legs straddling one of his thighs. He trapped my wrists in one hand, and then reached up and grabbed my chin with the other. He tilted my face until I was staring straight at him.

"I'm helping you," he murmured gruffly, his jaw clenched with tension. "Forget that I'm here. Focus on one thing. What do you hear?"

My body rocked as he spoke. I couldn't sit still no matter how hard I tried. Bits and pieces of memories were still fogging up my brain, and tears rolled down my cheeks. His fingers tightened on my chin.

"Get out of your head," he ordered, his voice softening. "You hear my voice. You're not wherever your thoughts are. You're here. In your apartment. What else do you hear?"

His words cut through my racing thoughts, and I squeezed my eyes shut. He kept talking quietly, and another noise joined his voice. The TV was on, and I could hear a child laughing. Cars bustled down the street, and the quiet hum of engines came in through the open window. The pictures in my head grew dimmer as real-life noises surrounded me.

"Now tell me what you see." His fingers disappeared from my face. "Open your eyes, Sage."

My body was still rocking back and forth, and when I opened my eyes, I found myself staring at him. He was frowning, but concern was etched on his features as his eyes bored into mine. My chest heaved as my anger climbed, remembering I was still sitting on his lap.

He took a deep breath, realizing what had happened. "Don't focus on me."

"Please," I breathed out, my heart pounding out of control again. "Just leave."

"What do you feel?" he asked, obviously not having any intention of doing what I asked.

"Hate. I feel hate. For you."

"Jesus," he muttered, looking unsure. "Physically. What is touching your skin right now?"

I wriggled my wrists against his grip, feeling the warmth from his hold. My panic increased and so did my struggles.

"Do you feel the wind from the window?" he asked. "The cool air hitting your skin?"

Closing my eyes again, I tried breathing through my nose, finally understanding what he was doing. Helping me use my senses to pull me from my head. And I had a feeling he wasn't going to let me go until I calmed down. The breeze blew over my skin, and I focused on the sounds from around me. The pain in my chest eased a fraction, and the fear I was trapped in slowly began fading away as I concentrated on what I was listening to. And what I could feel.

"What else can you feel, Sage?" His voice was tense, as if he was trying to stay in control. But I refused to open my eyes, knowing I would spiral again.

A hot rush shot through my lower stomach, and I went rigid, realizing what I was responding to. I was still straddling his leg. In a dress. Where I'd been rocking back and forth for who knew how long. A feeling I hadn't felt in months was burning through me, and as much as I wanted to stop, I couldn't. The hot feeling was the only thing keeping me grounded.

My thin pair of panties did little to stop the friction between his jeans and my clit. I didn't dare open my eyes, because then this would be real. I couldn't look at him. I shouldn't be doing this. It was wrong. Fucked up. I hated him with everything I had. But I was more terrified to sink back into the nightmares that had been consuming me.

My breathing became heavier, and I relished having air in my lungs again. My moves became faster, and instead of rocking against him, I was grinding, feeling something other than misery for the first time in what felt like forever. Waves of pleasure rolled through me as I sped up. His hand released my wrists, and my palms fell onto his chest.

My muscles tightened, and my knees dug into the couch as my ecstasy got closer to the edge. I faltered when my palms drifted over his shirt, and I felt something hard. I pinched it with my fingers, realizing what it was. His chain necklace. Where he wore his ring. What was I doing? He was with *them*. He was a part of it all.

I forced my eyes open as I went still. He was staring at me, his shoulders tense as both of his arms were spread across the top of the couch. The second I stopped moving, panic was waiting to take its place.

"Keep going," he grated out. "It's helping you."

"No. What the fuck am I doing?" I muttered under my breath as my chest constricted again.

"You're going to finish," Niko demanded, making my face flush. "Because it's the only thing calming you down."

"I'm fine—"

"Right now," he cut me off, "I'm learning about self-control I didn't know I had. But if you don't finish, then my hands are leaving this couch to help you. Do you understand?"

My gaze darted to his hands that were gripping the couch so hard his knuckles were white. He sat perfectly still, his eyes never leaving me. My clit was throbbing, and the tiniest movement of my hips had my body ricocheting with pleasure again.

After giving him one last glare, I slammed my eyes shut again. He was right. It was helping me. But I refused to look at him when I did it. I blocked him out as I ground against his leg again, letting my mind go blank as I focused on the enjoyment my body was receiving.

I climbed to the edge again and cried out as my orgasm consumed me. My body locked up as it slowly ebbed away. Reality crashed into me, and I froze in place. I couldn't believe that had just happened. My mind was finally clear from the past, and I tore myself off him. His last words of the conversation we were having before my panic came rushed back to my head.

Things clicked into place from what he said and what Alex had told me about the society when we were up north. My gaze shot to him as I realized something I had been missing. Disbelief and terror kept me rooted to the spot as I stood in front of the couch. The pleasure that had just consumed me was long gone. Niko tilted his head to the side, confused at my sudden change.

"A man gets old enough to bear children." I repeated his words from earlier.

"Sage—"

"Who's older? You or Geo?"

Niko didn't answer. For once, he wouldn't look at me.

"How did I not see it before? Alex had said it was for his family. For him. For you." My voice was getting higher with each word. "For Geo. Who did it, Niko? Who killed my sister? You or Geo? It had to have been one of you. Alex is the youngest."

He stood up, not saying a word. His eyes were clouded over with anger and what looked like a small amount of guilt.

"Who was it?" I yelled, shoving him in the chest. "Did you do it? And then come here to taunt me with it?"

"I told you, I came to help—"

"Tell me," I snarled. "Was it you or Geo?"

He bowed his head, backing away from me. "Knowing who did it isn't going to change anything."

"Get out. Get out," I screamed, knowing he wasn't going to answer me. For the first time in months, I completely lost it. Tears were pouring down my face, and disgust nearly had me heaving from what I had just done with him. His family was the reason Lacey and my mom were dead. There was a fifty-fifty chance he was the one who'd killed my sister. And I'd gotten pleasure from him.

My rage exploded, and I raised my arm to slap him, but he caught my hand inches from his face.

"I'm going to leave. But you need to hear this first." My hand stayed locked in his grip as he spoke. "I came here to warn you. So you can *literally* keep living. Don't be stupid. Keep your head low. You can't beat the society, no matter how badly you want to."

He talked fast as I pulled away from him.

"Sage, if someone else other than me finds you, then you will end up like your sister. There can't be loose ends. People knowing that aren't part of our group. I can't help if they find you. It's all on you."

I froze and met his eyes. "Can't help me, or won't?"

He seemed to deliberate on what to say. "There will be nothing I can do for you if they find you. I came here and warned you. Something I could do. Now you're on your own."

He let go of my hand and backed up toward the door, keeping his gaze on me until he twisted the handle and opened it.

"I'm sorry about Lacey. I wish it hadn't been her who was chosen. Be careful, Sage. Stay hidden." With his last words, he stepped out of the apartment and shut the door behind him.

CHAPTER TWENTY-THREE

Him

Sitting on the black leather couch in my living room, I was scrolling through my phone, like I'd been doing every morning for months. And like every other day, there was nothing new on Sage's social media. I typed a quick email explaining there was nothing new and sent it to Samual. The guy wanted daily reports.

I set my phone down and stared absentmindedly out the window. It was six in the morning, and I had no plans for the day. Usually, I would go visit my parents, but a lot had changed this year. My relationship with them was now strained. My dad still hadn't forgiven me for what happened. The elders were still making sure the search for Sage was ongoing. Although, many of the members had gone back to their lives. Sure, they would say something if they saw her. But they weren't going out of their way anymore.

If Sage were to move across the country right now, she could probably lead a decently normal life. There weren't many people in the group that lived out west. Most were on the East Coast and in the Midwest. I'd been fighting with myself for the past week about whether I should tell her that. To move on and leave Michigan. Start a new life. She could do it. She had the motivation and the drive to make it happen.

No. What I should have fucking done was go tell my dad exactly where she was so I could get back to my life. What was I thinking, letting one girl make me question my way of life? She was the reason I'd pulled away from my family. From the society. I'd been doing everything they'd asked. Except admitting that I knew exactly where she was.

The grief I'd witnessed in her eyes was haunting me. The conversation we had in Kalamazoo had gone completely different from how I'd expected. I shared secrets that I had been sworn to protect. Why? I had no damn idea. The less she knew about the society, the better. But when she'd asked, she'd looked so broken, and something inside me wanted to help her understand. I should have known that anyone who hadn't grown up in this life wouldn't get it. And by telling her, I'd fucked up the entire situation even more.

If the society found her, I was screwed. There would be nothing stopping her from telling them that I'd known where she was. Especially since she now had information that only people in our group knew. If the elders found out what I'd done, there was no coming back from that. They'd see it as a betrayal. I'd be a liability.

The front door swung open, and I glanced over my shoulder as Geo walked in. Even my relationship with my twin had changed since everything happened up north. He knew me better than anyone and could tell I was keeping things from him. We used to share everything.

"Hey," he muttered, going straight to the kitchen.

"No food at Mom and Dad's house?" I asked, raising an eyebrow. We used to live together, but he decided to move back in with our parents until everything calmed down. He was trying to prove he was dedicated to fixing the tension after what happened. Our dad wasn't happy with either of us, but it bothered Geo more than it did me.

"Mom is on another health kick. There's nothing but vegetables and fish in the fridge." He grabbed a bag of chips before falling onto the couch next to me. "You didn't come over for dinner last weekend."

"I was busy."

He narrowed his eyes. "I stopped by, and you weren't home."

"I needed to clear my head for a couple days."

"What's going on with you?" His food was forgotten as he faced me. "You keep disappearing for days at a time. Ever since that night up north, you've been different."

My stomach clenched, but I forced myself to stay relaxed. I had perfected the exterior of acting like nothing bothered me. I could fool anyone. Except my brother.

"Are you looking for her?" Geo asked, cocking his head to the side.

My jaw ticked. "It was our ceremony. If I find her, I can fix it."

He swallowed my lie, and my tension eased a bit when he went back to eating the chips. I didn't need to find her again. She might have left Kalamazoo, but I knew exactly where she was holed up. It had been three weeks since I watched her pack up her two bags and drive from the apartment she had been hiding out in. Following her wasn't hard. She drove a few hours to another city and checked into a ratty motel. I'd driven out there four times already, and her car hadn't moved from the spot she had parked in the first day.

"We'll find her." He shrugged. "Everyone is looking. And even if she did try to tell someone, she doesn't have any proof. She fucking burned all the evidence when she lit up the house."

I nodded in agreement. Everything had burned. Well, almost

everything. Geo had managed to save the book in the basement before the flames hit the kitchen. Obviously, the group had other houses, but none that she knew about.

"How's Dad?" I asked, steering the conversation off Sage.

He sighed. "Still pissed."

"Shouldn't have chosen a woman from the same family," I muttered under my breath. "It should have been a stranger. The Taylor family is too closely connected to us."

"No suspicion fell on us. They covered up everything up north," he argued, getting defensive. "What's with the doubts? The elders know what they're doing."

"I know they do." I stood from the couch and rolled my shoulders. "I'm just sick of everything. These last five months have been hell."

"It's not going to last forever. One of us will find her. Or she'll run out of money. It's only a matter of time. Until then, maybe you should try to get back in Dad's good graces like I am."

"I've done everything he and the group have asked," I snapped, feeling my anger rise.

"I might be the only one who can tell, but if you're doubting the group, they're going—"

"I'm not," I cut him off, deciding right then what I needed to do. "The group comes before anything. Like it has my entire life. Don't fucking question me, Geo."

"Where are you going?" he asked as I grabbed my keys.

"Out."

I'd been driving for a few hours and was almost there. She wasn't going to be happy to see me again. Especially after what happened last time. I didn't care. We were going to talk, whether she liked it or not. I was going to fix what I'd messed up.

I couldn't let the group find her. Not after what I'd told her. And knowing where she'd been all this time. I couldn't chance her outing me to the group. I was going to help her disappear. Get her out of Michigan. Give her money. Or whatever else she needed so she could get out of my life. And out of my fucking head. I gritted my teeth as another feeling came over me. She was messing with more than just my head.

Ever since she'd come all over my leg, my dick couldn't forget about her either.

That wasn't supposed to happen. She'd been freaking out, and I was trying to calm her down before she got loud enough to attract attention. Her grinding on me was not what I'd expected. Taking my hand off the steering wheel, I changed the radio station to distract myself from those thoughts.

I needed to be more careful this time. She'd surprised the hell out of me with that stun gun. For the months I'd been watching her, the spark of life had been absent from her eyes. But she was still feisty—even more than before. She was fighting for her life, and I had a feeling she'd never stop.

Geo was right. She had no evidence. If she went to the cops, someone in the group would hear about it. Her only choice was to hide. I was going to help so I could mend things with my family. I couldn't take the guilt anymore. The group came first. They always would. I never should have gone to see her in Kalamazoo. I should have told them right away. Too late for that. But I'd fix it.

My phone rang, and I sighed when I looked at the screen. He'd keep calling if I didn't answer.

"Yeah?" I answered while putting it on speakerphone.

"Where are you? Got to the house, but you're gone,"

I paused. "I needed to get away for the day. I'll be back tomorrow. I needed some space."

"Space from what? Us? We're just trying to help you fix what you screwed up—"

"What I screwed up? I wasn't the only one in that house when everything went to shit," I snapped, my temper reaching a boiling point. This was why she needed to disappear. I wouldn't feel torn when she was gone.

"Calm down. I called with good news. One of our guys, who is a state trooper, thinks he saw her car. Heading south out of Michigan. First lead we've had in months."

My heart sank. It wasn't possible. It had only been a couple of days since the last time I'd checked on her. The car hadn't moved in weeks. She felt safe; there was no reason for her to leave. I calmed myself down before responding.

"This isn't the first time someone has thought they saw her car. It always turns out to be a dead end." I controlled my voice to sound nonchalant, but my grip on the steering wheel tightened.

"I know, but he seemed pretty positive it was her car. Me and a few other guys are going to check it out. You going to come?"

I hesitated. "Tell me where you're headed, and I'll meet you."

"What the hell is so important compared to finding her?" The guy was getting mad. "This needs to be handled, and you're supposed to help do that."

"I know. I said I would meet you. What, you don't think you could take care of it without me if you do find her?"

"Just hurry up and come meet us."

I tried to push the dread away as I veered onto the exit ramp to get off the highway. She had to be there. If she was gone and they had gotten a lead on her car, then it was only a matter of time before they caught up. There was nothing I could do if they found her. Except pray that she kept her mouth shut about me knowing where she was this whole time. Something I seriously doubted she'd do.

My anger built as the motel sign came into view. She had tased me, and I'd still warned her. I hadn't told anyone where she was. Why would she jeopardize that to drive around? What had changed? I pulled into the parking lot and looked at the spot where her car had been.

It was empty.

CHAPTER TWENTY-FOUR

Sage

My nerves were fried. Leaving Michigan two weeks ago had reignited all my fears. Actually, Niko finding me did that. And I decided I couldn't try to survive by hiding anymore. It was time to do what I should have done months ago.

I was going to do what I promised and get justice for Lacey. For my mom. For all the other women.

After doing research, Chicago was where I ended up. My hands shook as I pulled out the paper I had ripped from the book that Alex had forced me to read. It only had four names on it, but it gave me more information to go on. My eyes went back to names scrawled on the page as their stories and my notes ran through my head.

Charlotte Miller: August will be two years missing. Was forty years old when she went missing. Went on a hike during vacation and disappeared. No foul play suspected. No living close family. No leads.

Anna Dailey: Disappeared in June. Missing for three years. Mother. Age thirty when she went missing. Never picked her son up from school. Last place seen was leaving the grocery store in her car. Foul play possible. No leads. Husband seems to have given up looking for her.

Valerie Taft: Disappeared in February. Missing for five years. Thirty-three years old. Was traveling home from a work conference in another state and never returned home. Car was never found. Foul play possible. Had longtime girlfriend who is still searching. Missing pictures are still circulating online.

Michelle Pemble: Disappeared in July. Missing for seven years. Twenty-three years old. Was an addict and prostitute. Homeless. Estranged from family for years. Missing date is best guess. No clues for disappearance. Don't know where she was last seen. Presumed dead.

After searching them all online, I realized these were all the women who were killed before Lacey was. Sadness clung to me as I reread the notes because I knew exactly what had happened to them. Researching their stories proved how far a reach the society had. All from different states, all through the Midwest. Missing at different times of the year. The only thing they all had in common was red hair.

I used to think how it was impossible that this went unnoticed. But now it made sense. Four women in seven years. People went missing every day and were never found. I didn't know whether the book was for the women who were killed in that house up north, or if it was every woman who was sacrificed for the society. I wasn't sure if I wanted to find out how many other houses they had. It was terrifying.

What I'd been obsessing over was how the women disappeared at different times of the year. My mom went missing in July. The barred windows ran through my mind. It was to keep the women inside until the full moon in August. It was hard not to think of the pure fear that my mom and the other women must have felt while being trapped there.

I had stalked their lives as much as I could through social media. The plan was to go talk to the girlfriend of Valerie Taft and the husband of Anna Dailey. Anna Dailey's husband was a bit of a mystery. Robert Dailey appeared to not use social media. I only knew what he looked like from the news articles I had found about his wife. And I knew that he was from Wisconsin. It was possible he had moved, but there was no way to know. There was no one I could talk to about the other two women. All I found were deceased family members.

Which left Kiara Jones. She was the girlfriend of Valerie Taft when Valerie went missing.

Kiara kept her social media locked down. All I was able to find out was that she lived in Chicago, was African American, and she had a kind smile. Her picture was the only thing that wasn't private. I knew she went to a book club every week because another lady would tag her in a public post.

That's why I was sitting in a coffee shop in Chicago. It was where Kiara went for book club. She was here last week, and she was here right now. I glanced across the café at her as I sipped my iced coffee. The bustling café was bright and airy. The tables and chairs were a rich white, and the floor was a beautiful copper color. I loved it and had spent a lot of time here since coming here.

My stomach was in knots, trying to find the courage to talk to Kiara. I had thought of how to introduce myself a hundred times, but the thought of talking to somebody and trusting them petrified me. Would it even help? I didn't know what I would say. Or how it could help expose the society. But at the same time, I felt a connection to her, even though she had no idea who I was. We'd both lost loved ones because of the same people. I didn't want to be alone with my sadness anymore.

Last week, I followed Kiara back to her house. She lived in a nice neighborhood, seemingly by herself. Her schedule was usually the same. Go to work, come home around dinnertime, and sometimes go for a jog if the weather cooperated. And of course, book club every week.

I absentmindedly flipped through a magazine, deciding I'd wait to talk to her. I wasn't ready yet. A shadow fell across my table before someone sat down next to me. My head shot up in alarm; I was ready to run. It was Kiara Jones. Her black shoulder-length hair was pulled back into a loose bun, and her brown eyes seemed to be sizing me up. The kind smile that I remembered from her picture online was replaced with a suspicious frown.

"Who are you?" she asked in a firm, direct voice.

"Uh...what?" I tried to play dumb. After coming all the way here, I didn't know if I was ready to trust anyone.

"You were here last week. And I saw you in your car a block from my house when I was running. Now, here you are again. So, tell me. Who are you and what do you want?" Her eyes narrowed as she waited for an answer.

"I'm sorry. Nothing. I don't want anything." I tried to think fast, but the shock from talking to her was causing my mind to go blank. I stood up, about to leave, but Kiara shook her head.

"You aren't leaving until you tell me why you're following me. See this? We can either have this conversation here or at my work." She flashed a badge.

Blood drained from my face. "You're a cop?"

"A detective," she replied curtly.

"I wasn't following you—"

"Yes, you were. And I ran your plates. You came all the way from Michigan. Why are you here?"

"Listen, I'm sorry," I said, close to tears. She'd run my plates. A stab of fear sliced through me. I had tried so hard to stay away from this. To keep hidden.

"Just tell me what you want." Kiara was not a woman who liked being messed with.

I paused for a long minute while Kiara looked on with impatience. I had to say something. She wasn't about to let me walk away, and I couldn't chance going to a police station.

"My mom disappeared over twenty years ago, and her body was found last year. No new evidence, no suspects, no leads. And I believe it's connected to the case of your missing girlfriend. Valerie Taft."

Her hard look transformed to absolute shock as I waited for her to respond. I didn't tell her the whole truth and wasn't sure if I was going to. Kiara being a detective changed things. What if she told someone on the force who was part of the society? It was a chance I wasn't willing to take.

"You're here because you think you have new evidence about Valerie?" she asked, nonplussed.

"Not new evidence. I think they're connected. I shouldn't have come here," I mumbled, changing my mind about telling the truth. I couldn't do it. Couldn't rely on anyone but myself.

Kiara raised an eyebrow. "You came all the way here just for that? After I ran your plates, I looked into you. You seemed to have disappeared for the past five months. Your life was going great, until your sister died, and then you just up and left. Why? What are you running from?"

I snapped my mouth shut. This woman was asking questions I did not want to answer. How many other people knew about the search she had run? My heart raced as panic swamped me. I needed to leave Chicago. As soon as possible.

"This was a mistake. I have to go," I rushed out as I stood up.

"Wait, please. I'm desperate for anything that could help with the search for Valerie. I'm sorry I came on so strong. But even the smallest thing could help." Kiara stood, and her pleading look tore at the seams in my heart.

"I can't stay. I need to leave—"

"Come to my house; we can talk. You already know where I live. Please, if you think you can help in any way. I can try to look into your mother's case if you want."

I thought about it. I had a feeling she wouldn't leave me alone after this, and I didn't need anyone else trying to track me down. Especially someone who had police backing them. I could go and talk to her without telling the truth.

"Okay, but only for a bit." Fear coated my voice, but Kiara didn't seem to notice.

She nodded. "Great, you can follow me back in your car if you want."

I agreed, and we left the café. I had to think of what I could tell her to get her to stop asking questions. The whole truth wasn't an option. It was too big a risk to get the police involved. I followed Kiara for twenty minutes until we arrived in front of the brick townhouse. I took my stun gun out of my bag and slid it into my hoodie pocket. Couldn't be too careful. Meeting Kiara on the sidewalk, I followed her to the white front door.

I walked in after her and glanced around. Kiara obviously liked things organized. There was not a thing out of place in her living room. The carpet was a crisp white, the same shade as the walls. There was a large brown leather sectional couch that wrapped around a glass coffee table. A large flatscreen was mounted on the wall above the fireplace. The walls all had collages of picture frames showing happy faces. The only pop of color in the entire room came from the purple flowers sitting in a vase on the coffee table.

Kiara motioned to the couch, and I sat down, keeping a hand in my hoodie pocket with a tight grip on the stun gun. The feeling of unease that was creeping inside me was heightened. It felt surreal to be sitting on someone's couch and about to have a conversation. In a nice house instead of a cheap motel. It had been so long since there had been any sort of normal in my life. Not that this was normal, but it was closer than anything in the past few months.

"Do you want anything to drink?" she asked before sitting down.

I shook my head. "No, thank you."

"Okay, tell me why you think the two cases are connected."

I opened my mouth and planned to say some random thing. Something that could be a lead, but knew it wouldn't be helpful.

"Valerie is dead."

It was hard to tell who was more shocked. I couldn't believe what I'd blurted out. The plan was to lie and leave. But the fact that she was still searching for her girlfriend was gut-wrenching. I wanted to give her closure. The unknown of my mother's fate for over twenty years had broken my dad. I didn't want it to happen to Kiara too.

"Excuse me?" she asked, her voice shaking.

I started talking. Fast. Once I started, there was no stopping the words tumbling from my mouth. It had been held in for so long. Keeping this to myself had been so hard, and I'd had no idea how much I wanted to shed my secret until now.

I told her everything. About my mom. My sister. Jamie. What happened up north, and what I'd been doing since I got away. Kiara didn't interrupt; she just sat there with wide eyes and an astonished stare. Tears started falling onto my cheeks as I spoke. About Alex and his family and the whole society. The Greek story and how it all originated. I pulled out the paper from the book and the research I had done. It had been at least an hour by the time I stopped talking, and by then, we were both crying.

Once I finished, we sat in silence. Kiara looked like she was trying to absorb everything. I didn't know whether to feel relieved or petrified about what I'd shared. What if this was it? My undoing? I didn't even know this woman, and regret seeped in. It was time to leave.

"I need to know. Did you tell anyone else about me when you looked into my life?"

Kiara shook her head. "No. I didn't tell anyone. I did it on my own time. I wasn't about to share that some young girl was following me around."

I nodded. "Good. I need to leave—"

"Leave? No, you're staying here."

My eyes narrowed and I gripped the stun gun. I was tired of

people controlling me. First Alex, then Niko, and now her. I was done.

"You can't keep me here," I snarled, leaping off the couch.

She opened her mouth in shock at how I was acting until understanding dawned on her face.

"Sage, wait. No, I wasn't threatening you. I want you to stay so I can help you. Help keep you safe. Help bring those people to justice."

I stared at her doubtfully. I had relied on myself for so long. Trusting another person seemed impossible.

"You believe me?"

She paused before answering. "The story sounds crazy. But there are so many details. With all the other missing women. The red hair. The paper you showed me. It's worth checking out."

"You can't tell anyone else. You don't know if there's anyone in your department who is part of it," I explained earnestly.

"I could tell my—"

"No. You can't tell anyone. At least not until there is something concrete. I know there's not enough evidence right now. But we can find it and then take it to more people." I was adamant. I did not hide for all this time only to go public with no evidence or to get caught by them.

"Okay. We'll wait," she agreed. "We'll do it your way if it makes you feel better. You're the one who has the most to lose."

My muscles relaxed, and I sagged onto the couch. Maybe this was it. The answer I needed to get my life back. The weight was already starting to fall off. But the fear was still just a thought away.

"I'm going back to my motel for now," I said, suddenly exhausted. The conversation had wiped me out. This was the most human interaction I'd had in months.

"You could stay here, if you'd like," she offered kindly.

I hesitated. "No offense. But I've been on my own for so long. I can't trust somebody so soon."

"I understand. Here's my number in case you want to get a hold of me," she said as she scribbled it on a piece of paper.

"Thank you."

"Of course. I'm going to try to find the address of the husband, Robert Dailey."

I nodded as I started toward the door. We said goodbye before I climbed into my car and rested my head on the top of the steering wheel. The reality of what had just happened came crashing down. I'd done exactly what I didn't want to do. Trusted a stranger. Kiara seemed sincere. But so had Alex. So had Detective Thomas. The more the thoughts came, the more I regretted it. Getting out of Chicago seemed like my best bet. But Kiara didn't know where I was staying; my name wasn't on the motel room. A few more days would be okay.

For the next few weeks, I would meet with Kiara at the coffee shop. At first, I was apprehensive about letting someone in. But that soon changed. We didn't talk about the society in public. Instead, for the first time in what felt like forever, I had regular conversations. I told Kiara about my life. My dad and my adventures with Lacey. Kiara talked about her girlfriend, Valerie. She told me about her career and her life growing up.

We went back to Kiara's house a few times and talked about the more serious matters. We couldn't track down Robert Dailey, not without a more extensive search that could cause questions. But I didn't care. I had no motivation to find anyone else. Not at that moment, anyway.

I felt safe in Chicago. It was such a busy city and seemed far away from the horror of back home. I was still staying at the motel but saw Kiara nearly every day. For some reason, Chicago felt freer. Like I could do more without having to worry as much. I was still paranoid about most things but didn't stay cooped up in the motel nearly as much.

There was public transit, so I didn't have to use my car often. The thought of staying here long term entered my mind more than once.

Kiara was a big factor in that decision. It felt safe to have someone around who knew what was happening. She already felt like family. We shared everything about our lives with each other. Connected by the grief of our missing loved ones.

CHAPTER TWENTY-FIVE

Sage

I pulled a flyer off my motel room door with my free hand as I talked to Kiara on the phone. This wasn't the first one I'd gotten. A major college was only a couple of blocks away, and apparently, they were inviting anybody who wanted to come. I'd seen some college kids at the motel here and there. They would rent rooms to party because this motel didn't really care who stayed. That was the whole point of why I'd chosen it. When they saw me, they always invited me to the party, figuring I was just another college student. My answer was always no.

"You should come," a voice said from behind me.

Kiara stayed quiet on the phone as I turned around and saw a couple of girls from the college staring at me. They both looked to be about my age. I was about to tell them no but hesitated. It would be so nice to talk to people my own age again. Enjoy some drinks. Have fun.

"Where is it?" I asked timidly.

One of the girls smiled. "About fifteen miles away. Where there's more space. We're having a huge bonfire and everything. It's supposed to be fun. Pretty much the whole college is going."

The other girl chimed in. "We're leaving in a half hour if you want to come with us. Or you can follow us in your car. I'm Hannah and that's Jordan."

"Thank you for the invite. I'll think about it."

"Great, if you're out here when we leave, then you can follow us," Hannah said as the girls turned and went back into their room.

"You should go," Kiara told me through the phone, having heard the conversation.

"I don't know."

"Go. You need some fun in your life. It's one night. I'm only a phone call away. Drink and party, and I can come get you if you need," Kiara tried convincing me.

I sucked in a deep breath as I stepped into my motel room. She was right. It had been forever since I'd laughed. Or had fun.

I gave in. "Fine, I'll go. But keep your phone on loud, please."

"Of course, Sage. Call me if you need anything."

I hung up the phone and tossed it on the bed. For the first time since I had disappeared, I decided to do something reckless. It had been six months. Chicago was hours away from home. I could forget my troubles for one night.

I pulled out a pair of jeans that I hadn't worn in forever. They were the nicest ones I had. I threw on a white cropped shirt and a blue jean jacket. It was February, and even though it had been a mild winter, it was still cold. I glanced in the mirror and made a mental note to stop at a drugstore. I hadn't dyed my hair since coming to Chicago, and the red was beginning to show through.

Once I was ready, I stepped outside to see Hannah and Jordan. They were both nice and made small talk for a couple of minutes before we got ready to leave. I got in my car and followed Hannah out of the city limits to a house with a huge yard. There were already at least forty cars parked there.

Laughter filled the air as soon as I got out of the car. It made me yearn for my old life. Hannah got out of her car, and I stared at her hair. It was so blond it was almost white. Hannah was about the same height as me, while Jordan was shorter. Jordan had jet-black hair, and it was cut in a short pixie cut. Both girls were wearing blue jeans with different color cropped shirts under their jackets. It was more than a little cold out, but it was nothing alcohol and a bonfire couldn't fix.

"You can stick with Jordan and me if you don't know anyone else. As long as you're up for fun and some drinking," Hannah said before she and Jordan laughed and led the way around the back of the house.

My eyes grew wide as I realized how many people were here. At least a hundred, if not more. The girls hadn't lied when they said the whole school was coming. I wondered whose house this was. There were three different bonfires blazing. All had random chairs surrounding them. Metal folding chairs, camping chairs, and even a bean bag. There was a barn behind the house with the doors wide open. Music was playing, and the kids had made a dancefloor inside the barn. The house looked like a perfect farmhouse from the movies. It was two stories, with white siding, black shutters, and a huge porch. They walked over to a group of tables that had more alcohol than I'd ever seen in one place, along with stacks of plastic cups.

"Here's to new friends." Jordan smiled before we all downed the first drink.

It wouldn't take much to get me drunk since I had barely touched alcohol in the last year. But a couple of drinks wouldn't hurt. If I was going to spend a night being reckless, I might as well live it up. After another drink, we walked over to one of the bonfires and met up with a few guys Jordan and Hannah knew. I was shy at first. It was overwhelming to be around so many people after spending so much time alone.

We all moved to the barn and started dancing. I danced and laughed with the group of people I was with. One guy's hands landed on my hips as I danced. My first instinct was to pull away, but I fought it. I hadn't been touched like that in a long time. Niko's face popped into my mind, and my stomach heaved as I shook my head. What I'd done with him was something I wanted to forget.

We danced through four songs before deciding we needed another drink, and we walked back near the fires.

"Come on, let's go to the bathroom," Hannah said as she set down her cup.

"See you boys later," Jordan called out with a flirty grin to the guys as we walked away.

I was feeling great. Only three drinks in, and I was in my happy place. Still functional but fuzzy enough to enjoy the night.

The farmhouse didn't have a single light on, and Hannah pulled out her phone and turned on the flashlight when we walked inside.

"There's a bedroom back here that has a bathroom in it," she said, leading the way. "The guy whose parents live here made sure to tell everyone the house was off limits. But he's a good friend, so we're good to use the bathroom."

"Yeah, just a friend," Jordan joked.

A stab of sadness hit me as they laughed together. Best friends who were living life and having fun. That used to be Lacey and me. I pushed the feeling away. Tonight was about fun. Tomorrow could be real life again.

"You can put your bag in here if you want. No one will be in here," Hannah offered.

I hesitated. I never went anywhere without that bag. It was my lifeline. But it was a hassle carrying it around all night and needing to find a place to put it when we danced again. I put the bag down and slid it under the bed. It would be fine for a couple of hours. I went to use the bathroom after Hannah and saw it connected to another bedroom.

The second we were back outside, more drinks were passed around, but this time I declined. I didn't want to get drunk. As much fun as I was having, I really didn't know these people. I needed to keep a decently clear head.

We danced some more and watched a dance contest break out. I joined everyone else and cheered on my favorite dancer. For a second, I felt like just another college kid. It was an amazing feeling. If only it were true.

We went to sit around the fire, and I listened to everyone talk about college life and the parties. It made me realize how much my life had changed. I used to belong at places like this. But not anymore.

"You smoke?" A guy was holding something out to me, and I was about to say no until I realized it wasn't a cigarette. It was a small joint. I nodded and took it. I rarely smoked weed but could keep a better head on it than with alcohol. And it would help keep the fear away for a little while. If I was going to smoke, tonight would be the night to do it.

"Smoke the rest of it. I'm more than good." The guy laughed and walked away before I could thank him.

"We're going to check out what's going on at the other bonfire. Want to come?" Jordan asked me.

I shook my head. "In a few minutes. I think I'm going to sit here and smoke this first. Do you have a lighter?"

One of the guys we'd been hanging out with gave me his lighter, and the group walked away. I stared into the flames and smiled. This night had been amazing. The effects of the drinks were pretty much gone, but I still felt like I was on cloud nine. I needed a night like this. A night of fun and interaction with other people.

Hannah and Jordan were so nice. People I could see being friends with in a different life. There were roars of laughter coming from the other fire. I glanced around to see that there was no one near me;

they were all crowded at the other bonfire. I flicked the lighter, but it didn't light. I tried again, but it only sparked. I was about to get up and join the other fire until someone sat next to me.

"Here." An arm reached over, a lighter in hand.

"Thanks—" I froze when I recognized the voice.

I lifted my head up, and the joint fell from my hand. My heart lurched as my body went cold from dread.

"Hey, baby."

CHAPTER TWENTY-SIX

Sage

All the color drained from my face as I stared into his chilling green eyes.

Alex.

This wasn't possible. Niko had told me he'd died. That I'd killed him. The shock had me paralyzed. I looked past Alex across the fire and saw Niko. He wasn't looking at me; his gaze stayed fixed on the ground. Next to him was Geo, who was grinning like he'd just won the lottery.

There were at least five other guys surrounding me. They must have all been part of the society. They had found me. My stomach twisted painfully as my mouth went dry. Finally snapping out of it, I moved to stand. To run. To do anything.

"Aw, come on, Sage. Let's talk for a minute," Alex said as he grabbed my arm and pulled, forcing me to sit back down.

"You're going to do this at a party? In front of all these people?" My voice was shrill.

"We finally found you. It's been six months. It doesn't matter how many people are around. Why do you think I brought so many friends?" Alex was speaking quietly. I figured they wanted to do this as discreetly as possible. No way I was going to make it easy for them.

"I'm not going to go quietly—"

Alex interrupted me. "You *are* going to come with us. With me. This is a party, baby. Everyone here is drunk or high. And you don't know anyone. It's not going to be hard. Once we're out of here, we need to talk."

Surprise hit me. Alex was so cold. So angry. I guess it made sense with how our last encounter had ended. Not something someone could easily forgive. I thought quickly, trying to come up with anything to get away.

"I'll go with you. Without fighting. I will. If I can grab my bag. Please. It has pictures of my dad. Of Lacey—" My voice broke as I tried to sound as pitiful as possible.

Alex gave me a hard stare, but his gaze softened a little. Maybe he still had feelings for me. That could be helpful.

"Fine. But you're not leaving my sight. Where's your bag?"

"In the house. I can't really remember. I have to look, but I won't take long," I lied. The bag was in the bedroom, exactly where I had left it.

Alex nodded to the guys around the fire, and they started walking toward the house. I got up and tried to pull my arm out of Alex's grip, but he stood up, yanking me closer to him.

"I know you don't want me touching you, but I'm not letting you go until we're in the car. Deal with it," Alex told me with no emotion.

He was completely different from the Alex I had known. He had been caring and kind. Now he was chillingly indifferent. I couldn't remember a time he had ever talked to me like that. Even that night. Or when I attacked him. I needed him to have those old feelings if I wanted to get away. I looked back and saw Niko walking behind us. He still wouldn't look at me. It wasn't like him to stay silent. He always had something to say. Maybe he was scared I would tell them that he had found me months ago.

Geo and the other guys stayed outside while we walked inside the house. Niko waited in the living room while Alex and I went to one of the bedrooms. My bag was under the bed but was easily seen from the door. My weapon, the one I had used on Niko, was in there. If I could get to it and make a dash for my car, then maybe I could get away. Alex grabbed the bag before I could.

"Okay. Let's go."

"My bag—"

"I'll hold it for now."

"Alex, I have to pee."

His eyes narrowed.

I continued quickly, "I really do. If you've been watching me, then you know I drank tonight. I can go now, or you can to stop on the way to wherever you're taking me."

He sighed. "Fine."

He started pulling me to the bathroom door on the other side of the bedroom.

"You're not coming in with me." I again tried to pull away. "Where am I going to go in a bathroom? Just give me five minutes. Please."

He paused and then slowly let go of me. "Five minutes. If you're not out, then I'm coming in."

I glanced at my bag in his hand. There was no way I was getting it now. I would have to do it without the stun gun.

"Thank you," I said, forcing sincerity across my face.

I shut the bathroom door behind me and turned on the water before going to the other side where another door was waiting. I remembered from earlier that this bathroom connected two bedrooms. If I could slip out from the other bedroom, I could have a chance. Not that I knew what I was going to do. The car keys were in my bag. But it didn't matter. I would do anything I needed to get away. I slowly opened the second door, trying not to make a sound. But when the door opened, someone pulled me into the bedroom.

Hands gripped my arms, and I was forced face first against the wall. I craned my neck to make out who it was, but the bathroom door had shut behind me and the room was pitch black. He forced one arm behind my back, pulling it high enough that I couldn't move. Another hand fisted my hair and pulled my head to the side until my cheek was pressed against the wall.

"I warned you, Sage. I told you if they found you, there was nothing I could do. Why the hell didn't you just stay hidden?" he hissed in my ear.

"Niko—"

"You should have listened. They found you. There's no getting out of it."

"You can let me go. I'll go out through the window. They would never have to know you helped me," I pleaded.

He didn't say anything, and I could hear his rapid breathing.

"Please. You came and warned me. You don't want me to go back with them. You can make this right. You told me you feel guilty about my sister. If that's true, then show it." I was trying anything to get him to let go of me.

"I did help. I warned you. This is my family. I can't just let you go. Five other guys are outside the house. There's no way out of this."

"Please let me try," I cried.

"You have that taser of yours on you?" he asked with apprehension.

"No, it's in my bag, and Alex has it." His grip loosened slightly at my words.

"If you go through that window and get caught, you better not say a word that I let you go," he growled in my ear.

"I won't." I was telling the truth. As much as I despised him, he was the only one who had helped me—in his own twisted way. And he was willing to do it again. I wouldn't turn on him; this might not be the last time I needed him. Suddenly, the bathroom door opened, and Alex walked in. Niko quickly let go of my hair but kept me pressed up against the wall.

"Your girlfriend thought it would be a good idea to make a run for it," Niko sneered. His demeanor completely changed the second his brother entered the room. I gazed at Alex and met his unrecognizable cold stare. In his hand was the stun gun.

"You've changed. I used to be able to tell when you lied," he said as he slid the stun gun into his pocket.

I didn't respond and leaned my head against the wall. I couldn't see a way out. All these months had been for nothing. When I'd found Kiara, there was a chance. To expose them. But not anymore. Now I would become another missing person.

An idea flashed into my mind. It probably wouldn't work. But I had to try. I just needed to get Alex alone. Niko stepped back from me but kept me in his grasp.

He looked at Alex. "This is your thing. Where do you want her?" He talked as if I wasn't standing right there.

"She can go with us in her car. Geo will take your truck back home."

Niko nodded and led me back outside with Alex on my other side. They knew exactly where my car was parked, and it made me wonder how long they'd been watching. Alex dug for the keys in the bag. He was about to get into the driver's seat as Niko opened the back door for me.

"Wait. I don't want to sit near Niko."

Niko glared at me. "You're not sitting back here by yourself—"

"I figured that," I interrupted sharply. "I'd rather sit near Alex. At least I know for sure he didn't murder my sister."

The brothers looked at each other, and Niko shrugged as Alex handed him the keys. I slid into the back seat, and Alex followed close behind. It was surreal—to be in the back seat of my own car.

Next to my old boyfriend, who I had thought was dead. Niko pulled onto the main road and started driving.

The motel sign flashed as we entered the parking lot, and a shiver ran through me. They knew where I was staying. Niko dug through my bag until he found the motel key and then got out of the car. I looked at Alex, but he was staring straight ahead. His body was tense, probably to be ready if I tried anything. Niko was back in a few minutes and threw my two bags into the passenger seat before he headed toward the highway.

No one spoke. The tension was almost tangible. I didn't even know where we were going. Or how long I was going to be stuck in the car with them.

"I thought you wanted to talk," I said quietly, wondering what they planned to do with me. I needed time to work out my new plan.

"We'll wait until we're alone and out of the car," Alex murmured as he kept looking out the window.

"We're just going to sit in silence for the whole drive? Where are we going?"

"Back to my place, for now. It's just outside Capac."

"Alex, I'm sorry."

"You're sorry?"

"For hurting you—"

"Sage, you stabbed me."

"I know. But that night was...I barely remember half of it. I saw my sister get murdered. How did you think I would react?"

Alex finally pulled his eyes away from the window and looked at me, his cold stare still in place, but there was a shadow of his old look.

"I thought you were dead."

"You thought one stab wound killed me?"

Niko glanced at me in the rearview mirror.

I swallowed. "I didn't know. But the whole place caught fire so fast. I didn't know if you got out in time."

"The fire you started. No, Niko got me out. He even called from the landline to try to get the fire department there faster. We almost didn't make it out."

I stayed quiet, not sure what to say.

"I almost did die. Do you know how far a hospital is up there? By the time I got there, I had lost almost too much blood. I had a lot of internal injuries. I was in a medically induced coma for a few days. Spent a lot of time in the hospital and even more on bed rest before I got back on my feet."

"I'm sorry."

"Are you? Because you didn't seem to be when you attacked me." His eyes flashed to mine.

"I thought I was going to die in that house. I would have done anything to get out." I didn't need to lie about that.

"Yeah, I know."

The tense silence came back, and I wasn't sure how much time had passed. Niko hadn't said a word since we got in the car. Alex went back to looking out the window. I couldn't do this. I had spent the last six months being quiet.

"What are you going to do with me?" I asked, ignoring the unrelenting terror that was spreading through my limbs.

"Why don't we wait—"

"Wait for what? What's the difference between telling me now or in a few hours?" I snapped, unable to handle the suspense anymore.

Neither of the brothers said anything. I stared at Alex, waiting for him to answer. After a minute, I turned my glare to the front.

"Niko, you usually can't shut up. Why don't you tell me?"

He shot me an annoyed look in the mirror but didn't say a word.

"Are you going to make me disappear? Like my mom? Like you were going to do with Lacey? Like all those other women?" Questions poured from my mouth, and it was impossible to stop now.

"Sage—"

"Just tell me."

"I wanted to avoid this. I planned to marry you. Even after you found out our secret. I thought you would understand. But then you set our house on fire. Two of our guys died. And then you disappeared." Alex was looking at me like I was to blame.

"What did you expect me to do?"

"I don't know. But I still don't get how you knew to go into hiding. You planned everything not to be found."

"Well, no one can say she isn't smart." Niko finally joined the conversation. I knew he was trying to avoid that subject, since he was the reason I'd fled.

"I saw the sheriff outside the house that night. The same man who was in the great room with everyone else. I figured your cult had reach." I thought my explanation was good enough for Alex to believe.

"It's not a cult," he growled. "It's a belief and our way of life."

"I didn't grow up in it, Alex. It's different for me," I said softly, not wanting him to get angry. I needed him to understand why I did everything. "Don't you think it's going to cause suspicion if I disappear after what happened to my mom? And my sister? Almost a whole family just gone. It's bound to raise questions."

"You've disappeared for the past six months and there's been no suspicion."

"Not fully. I was still calling my dad every week. I still pay bills for my house and make withdrawals from my bank account. If I stop calling my dad, then his nurse will know something is wrong."

He didn't answer, appearing deep in thought. Deciding what to do with me. I knew him well enough that I could play on his emotions. If I could twist this conversation just right, there was a chance of me surviving.

"What if I didn't have to disappear?"

Niko glanced back at me with questions in his eyes while Alex slightly shook his head.

"We can't let you go," he said, almost sadly, and my heart jumped. It was the reaction I wanted. He still cared.

"I know. But what if I chose to be with you? Be together. Like it used to be."

"Be together?"

"Yes. What if I chose to marry you? Like it was supposed to be. Before going up north. I could learn to accept your beliefs," I said in the same soft voice. My head was screaming at me. This wasn't right. But this was it. If I got away, they'd only find me again. It was time to change up the plan. His stare felt like he was trying to read my mind. I was relieved it was dark, even though I lied better than I used to. Reaching out, I grabbed his hand.

"You were my soul mate. My one and only. This past year has changed me, but we could get back to it again. It might take me a while to feel the same. But I could love you again."

I held my breath as I waited for him to say something. My life depended on it. Even if I did get away, I couldn't live how I had been. It was too lonely an existence. There had to be another way. And this was it.

"You would be mine again?" Alex finally asked after minutes of silence.

I ignored the pit in my stomach. Ignored the loathing I had when I looked at him.

"Yes. I'm not saying it would be like before right away. But I would make you happy. We'd be happy."

I caught Niko's expression in the mirror; his jaw had dropped.

"And what if you're just saying this until you have a chance to run again?" Alex asked with a frown.

"I'm not. I'll stay with you. Living in hiding was horrible. I can't go back to that. I wasn't even able to hide for a year. You would just find me again anyway. Disappearing isn't an option anymore," I said as tears sprang to my eyes. It wasn't hard to force emotion when I had so much built up inside.

"I don't know if I can trust you."

"We're both going to have to build up trust again. We can do it together."

Alex looked back out the window, signaling that the conversation was over. I let him think about it in silence. He had to come to the decision on his own. But I kept holding his hand. To show that I still cared. That I could touch him without cringing. We sat like that for two hours until stopping at a rest area. It was only us and one other car. I moved to climb out but was pulled back.

"Don't try anything."

"I told you, I'm not running anymore. Even if I did, we're at a rest stop. There's nothing around for miles."

Alex still walked with me to the unisex single bathroom and waited outside the door for me. He took me back to the car and waited for me to get back in.

"I'm going to run to the bathroom." Alex gave Niko a knowing look. Niko nodded and slid into the back seat next to me.

I rolled my eyes. "I already said I wasn't going to try to leave."

"Yeah, we'll see if that holds true," Niko muttered as he sat down.

I watched as Alex shut the car door and, for a split second, debated convincing Niko to give me the keys. It was a fleeting thought. There was no way he'd go for it.

"What the hell are you doing, Sage?" Niko asked the second Alex left.

"What?"

"Oh, I don't know. How about that entire convo you just had with Alex? You're going to marry him?"

"If he wants to, then yes," I answered as I stared out the window.

"I don't believe you. You're playing at something; what is it?"

"I'm not playing at anything." I turned my head and met his eyes. "If I have the choice of living or dying, I'll choose to live. I can be happy with him."

He laughed cynically. "No, you can't. You'll fight until your last breath. So, I'll ask again. What are you planning?"

"You don't know me. You have no idea what I'm thinking. I'm making a choice to have a life." Impatience was clear in my voice. I didn't want anyone getting in the way of Alex saying yes to me.

"I know you better than my baby brother does if he actually

believes you'll ever love him again," Niko said with suspicion written all over his face.

I didn't answer and watched as Alex walked back and got behind the wheel. Niko was right. Not that I would ever admit it out loud. I could never love him again. Could never feel comfortable with his touch. I did have a plan. I couldn't uncover their secrets when I was in hiding. But now I possibly had a chance to get a personal look at the society.

And try to expose them from the inside.

CHAPTER TWENTY-SEVEN

Sage

Two hours later, we arrived at Alex's house. It was on a dirt road a few miles out of Capac. It was a small one-story home. The siding was white, and it had a small porch with one chair on it. It was surrounded by trees on one side and had a cornfield on the other.

"You bought a house?" I asked as we pulled into the driveway.

"No, I rented it."

Once Alex parked, we all got out. Niko grabbed all my bags, and Alex took my hand before heading to the front door. I fought the instinct to pull my hand away. I had to show him that I was okay with being touched. He opened the door, and I stepped in and looked around. The living room was bigger than it looked on the outside.

There was one black leather couch in front of a big-screen TV. The carpet was gray and looked worn. The kitchen was right across from the living room, and it was small. Only one counter with a small sink and a couple of black cabinets. There was a card table and folding chairs in place of a kitchen table. I glanced down the short hallway and saw three doors.

"How many bedrooms?" I asked, scared for the answer. I wasn't sure I could stomach sharing a room with him.

"Two. You can take my room. Niko and I will take turns sleeping on the couch."

"Niko lives here?"

Niko chimed in. "You didn't think we'd leave you with only one person watching over you, did you?"

I glared at him, wanting to get Alex alone. To help him choose to be with me. Niko could make that difficult.

"I told you, I'm not running."

"I know, but we can't really trust you right now," Alex said as he motioned for me to go down the hall. "And Niko got me back on my feet after what happened up north."

At least only one of the twins lived here. It was better than both of them. I followed him and went into the bedroom after he opened the door. There was a queen-size bed with a dark blue comforter on it. A tall light wood dresser with a small flat screen on top was in front of the bed on the opposite wall. Other than those things, the room was empty.

"This is where you're staying. The remote for the TV is on the dresser. Here are your bags." He handed me the bags and turned to leave.

"Alex, I was serious in the car. I want to be with you." I tried to sound as natural as possible.

"It's not up to just me. I have to talk to some people first. Until then, you're staying here." His eyes softened, almost back to his old self, and I smiled. There it was. The look I'd been waiting for. He was going to say yes. My excitement faded when I realized what he'd said. Who was it up to? People in his society? The choice to leave again flittered through my mind. If the others weren't going to say yes, then I'd have to find a way to flee before it was too late.

Alex had shut the door as he left, and I looked again at the room. My own personal prison. The door didn't have a lock. There was one window, and I rushed over to it, pulling on it, but it didn't budge. It wouldn't be possible to get out that way if I needed to. Going back to the bed, I dug through my bags.

"You're not going to find what you're looking for."

I spun around to see Niko leaning against the doorframe with his hands in his pockets. I hadn't even heard the door open.

"I figured, after that stun gun, that you'd have more stuff with you. I took the pepper spray and knife out of the bag back at the motel," he said, watching me closely.

"Privacy would be nice. The door was shut," I snapped, crossing my arms.

He scoffed. "Sage, there's no such thing as privacy for you anymore."

Alex appeared next to his brother at the door.

"Quit it, man. This isn't easy for her, or for any of us. Give her a break," Alex told him, and I flashed him a grateful smile. There was the guy I remembered.

"Alex, can I please go see my dad? I haven't seen him since I left," I pleaded. It was the one thing good that came out of this. I could finally visit him.

He hesitated and looked at Niko, who shrugged.

"We're supposed to keep you here."

"Please, just a short visit. I need to see him," I begged.

Alex sighed and ran a hand through his hair. "Okay. But we can't be gone long."

I beamed and didn't even care that Alex was going with me. I just wanted to see my dad. We got back in the car, and Alex drove to the nursing home. It was early in the morning, but I knew my favorite nurse would let me in. We got out of the car, and I nearly sprinted to the door. I saw Sarah first. We hugged, and for a moment, I felt like I was back in my old life. How amazing it felt to be home. To have a bit of normal again. Sarah looked happy to see me, but that looked changed when she saw Alex.

"I thought you two were done," she whispered, her arms still around me.

"We're attempting to work it out. It's okay," I assured her, giving her a half smile.

Alex and I followed Sarah to my dad's room. He was already up for the day. Sarah opened the door and started to walk back down the hall while giving Alex a death glare. He stayed outside the door as I went to greet my dad. Tears were pouring down my cheeks before I said a word. He looked like he had aged years in just the six months I'd been gone.

"Sage, how are you?" He wrapped me in a hug.

I openly sobbed as I squeezed him back. He remembered me. I was so thankful he was having a good day. Sarah had told me they were coming less and less.

"Hi, Daddy. I've missed you so much," I managed to say between tears.

We sat down and talked for the next half hour. My dad talked about Sarah and the seniors who lived here. His mind wasn't the same as it had once been, but I didn't care. He remembered me. I could have sat there all day, but Alex cleared his throat. I looked up and saw him staring impatiently at me.

"Dad, I have to go. But I'll be back soon. I love you." I gave him a long hug and peck on the cheek before leaving. Swallowing the anger I had toward Alex, I walked out of the room. Gone for six months and I only got to see him for a half hour. Sarah said goodbye to me and completely ignored Alex before we left the building.

"Thank you, Alex. That meant so much to me," I said gratefully, being completely honest for once.

"What was that back there?" he asked as we got into the parking lot.

"What was what?"

A hand suddenly closed around my arm. "Sarah. She used to love me. What did you tell her?"

I turned and looked at him. His cold stare was back.

"After I drove back from up north, I came here. I gave her my new phone number, and I didn't want her to give it to you. So, I told her we had a bad breakup."

"Abusive bad?"

I shrugged. "No, I didn't say that. But I'm sure I didn't look very good after that night."

Alex's eyes bored into mine as I yanked my arm away, but he didn't let go.

"She thinks I'm abusing you—"

"I told you, I didn't say that."

"Yeah, well, it seems like you might have implied it. She looked like she hated me." His eyes darkened in growing anger. "What was this? A plan for me to be a suspect if you ever did go missing?"

"No. I never thought I'd be back here with you. It was a story so that she wouldn't give you my phone number."

"Right. Let's go." Alex was still closed off as we got into the car.

After we got back to the house, I went straight to the bedroom and shut the door. It was only eight in the morning, and I'd been up over twenty-four hours. I dumped my bag onto the bed and was surprised that my cell phone was there. I thought Niko would have taken it. Looking through it, I was glad I hadn't kept any research about the society on it.

I sent a quick text to Kiara, telling her what happened, but that I had a plan and was right where I wanted to be and to not contact me. There wasn't much she could do anyway. Kiara had absolutely no proof of anything. I didn't want her getting involved while I was here. It was too dangerous. After the text sent, I deleted her number and turned off the phone.

There wasn't anywhere in this room that would make a good hiding spot. I put it in a hoodie pocket and shoved it in a dresser drawer under other clothes. The paper that I had ripped out of the book all those months ago was still folded up and in the pocket of a pair of jeans. I put those in a different drawer, not wanting the phone and paper to be too close in case one was found.

The bed was calling me. Even as fear invaded my bones, I still couldn't stop my eyelids from falling. The comforter was soft and fluffy, and I got comfy under it. With Alex showing up and me being found, it had been a long damn night. I slowly fell into a light sleep, thinking about what the society would decide to do with me.

I rolled onto my side, and my eyes flew open when I hit something solid.

"Mornin', sunshine." Niko was sitting on the bed, right next to me.

I scrambled out of bed, putting space between us. "What the hell, Niko?"

"Hey, I waited for you to wake up. You slept for almost four hours. We need to talk before my baby brother comes back." He flashed me a grin as he patted the bed. "You can sit down. It's not like you have anywhere else to be."

I bit my tongue, not moving a muscle. The last time we were alone in a room, I had been on his lap. That was never happening again. I didn't want to be anywhere near him.

"Where did he go?" I asked, stepping farther away.

He paused. "He has some people he has to talk to."

"People. Like the people who are going to choose what happens to me?"

"Yeah. Those people. You really got to Alex, because he's going to beg them to let him be responsible for you."

My face scrunched in disgust. "Responsible for me?"

"What did you think was going to happen? You give Alex your

best loving smile and everything goes back to normal? No. You'll be watched for the rest of your life. By Alex, by a lot of other people."

"It still beats dying or running my whole life."

He frowned. "You're lying."

"No, I'm not," I snapped.

"Alex told me what happened at the nursing home. Trying to make him look bad in case anything happened to you."

"That's not what happened. You think I would have expected to be back there with Alex hanging on to me? I never thought I'd see him again. I wanted to cover my tracks."

"Either way, that's another reason for him to keep you alive. No one will want him or the family being suspects. I'm sure the elders will take that into account." He stood from the bed.

"Elders?"

He ran a hand down his face. "Forget you heard that. You don't need to know anything more about it."

"I'm going to live in the dark? I told Alex that I'll learn to accept your beliefs."

He snorted. "After everything you've done, you think we'll just roll out all our secrets? Is that your big plan?"

My confidence shattered as my glare faltered. That was exactly my plan, not that I would say it out loud. Niko might not fall for it. But Alex was much easier to talk to.

"No, I just want to know how it works. To help me better understand," I told him as I tried to keep my face blank.

"Sure, Sage," he replied sarcastically.

"What do you want to happen to me? It almost sounds like it would be easier for you if I did just disappear."

"Really? After all I've done for you?" he hissed, anger filling his gaze. "I came and warned you. I went behind my family's back to help you. I even made sure you were nice and safe in that crappy motel. Any word of them finding you, and I was going to warn you again."

My eyes widened. He had known where I was all this time. I

opened my mouth to speak, but he kept talking as he advanced closer.

"That was stupid. Leaving Michigan to go do what? What were you doing in Chicago? You don't know anyone there. It doesn't make sense."

He was only a foot away, standing in front of me. His eyes stayed locked onto mine, as if looking for the answers. I backed up until I hit the wall. I knew how bad his temper could get and didn't want to make it worse.

"I was just trying to find a better place," I muttered as I broke eye contact and looked at the floor.

"Right. I can't do anything else to help you. I have to help my family now. You're lucky Alex still cares about you."

"I thought you felt bad. Not bad enough to still make sure I stay alive, though, huh?" I couldn't help but provoke him. Who was he to try to make me feel grateful for what he'd done? He had no right. He gaped at me, and his hands balled into fists.

"I've done everything I could. This is my family we're talking about." He took a deep breath as he backed away, as if trying to calm down. He glanced around the room and saw my empty bags.

"Who did it, Niko?" I asked him quietly, needing to know if I was looking at a murderer or just a monster. "Did you kill Lacey, or did Geo?"

His jaw clenched. "Would it make a difference if you knew?"

"Probably not. I still want to stab you in your sleep."

"Good thing the knives are locked up tight." Surprise filled his voice. "Might want to watch your attitude around Alex. He won't fall for your fake love if you talk to him like that."

"I guess I'll save it for you then." I raised my chin, refusing to back down. I wasn't sure if he realized it yet, but I had something on him. I doubted he wanted the society to know he'd found me months ago. A reminder of that threat could help me—I stared at the rage building on his face—or it could drag me deeper into this hell.

"Where'd you put that phone?"

The sudden change in subject jolted me. I didn't say anything as I stepped around him and sat on the side of the bed, closer to the door.

"I know you have one. I saw it in there when I took out the pocketknife."

"Why does it matter?"

"I didn't tell Alex. But if he finds it, he's going to look through it. Same with your laptop. Actually, he's probably going to take your laptop. If you have anything on there you don't want him to see, you better get rid of it before he gets back. Or it won't be good for you," he threatened.

My stomach dropped to my feet. The laptop had all the research on it.

He continued, "I said earlier you don't have privacy anymore. I wasn't kidding."

"Why'd you tell me he was dead? Alex."

It was his turn to be surprised. For once, he looked flustered and lost his usual confidence.

"I don't know. Maybe I just wanted to see your reaction," he said slowly. It sounded like a bad lie, but I didn't say a word. If he didn't want to tell me, I wasn't going to be able to get it out of him. He started to walk out of the room but turned back around. "This probably doesn't have to be said, but you better keep these conversations to yourself. Or I'm done with the helpful tips."

I nodded and waited for him to leave so I could pull my laptop out. I wouldn't tell anyone about what he'd done. Not yet, at least. Unless I could spin it in my favor.

"Dinner menu tonight is leftover pizza. It's in the fridge if you're hungry," Niko called from the hall.

Ignoring him, I opened the laptop to delete everything. My fingers hovered over the keyboard as I thought of sending everything to Kiara but chose not to. The less she was involved, the better. I didn't want her to become a target for knowing too much. I cleared my search history and got rid of anything that came to mind.

I double checked everything, making sure nothing was missed

before shutting it off. Alex wasn't a tech-savvy guy. He wouldn't dig deep, and I was confident nothing would be found if he did take the laptop. As confident as I could feel anyway. Nothing more could be done about the phone; there was no better hiding place. I just had to hope he wouldn't find it.

CHAPTER TWENTY-EIGHT

Him

I sat on the metal chair on the front porch, wondering what Sage was deleting from her computer. I heard her tapping on the keyboard before I left the hallway. Rubbing my temples, I let out a long sigh. What a long fucking night. I hadn't slept since the night before, but I was on babysitter duty until Alex got back. This was exactly what I didn't want to happen. They finally found her. Now, on top of everything else, I had to make sure she didn't spill that I'd been helping her for months. My family would never forgive me.

But I had a feeling she wouldn't be going anywhere.

Alex still loved her. I knew it, and now Sage did too. And she was going to use it to stay alive. Smart on her part. Alex was talking to the elders about it. Our dad had pull in the group, and Alex was the baby of the family. There was no doubt they were going to let him keep Sage alive. I had no idea where that left me. I really didn't want to spend the next year watching my brother and Sage play house. But there was no way the elders would allow it to just be them with no other supervision. Not after all the trouble she had caused.

A thud came from inside the house, and I looked through the window. Sage was getting the pizza out of the fridge. She saw me, and her glare turned frigid. With a chuckle, I turned back toward the front yard. She had so much fight in her. I couldn't imagine her living with Alex, pretending to love him for the rest of her life. She had a plan. I just didn't know what it was yet.

Alex's Jeep came down the driveway. His smile was obvious even from where I was sitting on the porch. The meeting must have gone well. Alex came onto the small porch and leaned against the iron railing.

"How'd it go?" I asked, already knowing the answer.

"Good, they agreed."

"Figured they would."

"They want me to have help for a while. Just to make sure things go well."

I groaned, realizing where this was going.

"Can you stay here longer? So I can tell them that we don't need anyone else watching her?" he asked. "You won't even have to work. We'll cover everything."

I didn't answer right away. My heart beat a bit faster thinking about spending time with Sage. But not when she was going to be cozying up to my baby brother.

"Please, man? I trust you with her more than anyone else. And she already knows you. It'll make it easier on both of us."

"I think I'm the last person she wants hanging around. She knows it was me or Geo who killed Lacey."

"She really doesn't have a choice about anything right now. She'll deal. It was for the greater good. She wants to learn our beliefs. It had to be done."

I barely stopped myself from rolling my eyes. He really thought Sage was going to be fine with her sister's death because he'll teach her about the greater good. I loved my brother, but he was naïve sometimes.

"Yeah. I guess I'll stay for a while," I muttered with apprehension. It was going to be an interesting next few months.

Alex shot me a grateful look. "Thanks."

I nodded and watched as the sun started to set over the trees. The smell of early spring was in the air and being out here in the country was peaceful. Even though this house was going to be anything but peaceful now. I didn't know what was going to happen, but I knew Sage was planning something. It was only a matter of time before she did something to make trouble.

"Where is she?" Alex asked, pulling me out of my thoughts.

"She was just in the kitchen grabbing pizza."

"You've been checking on her, right?"

"Relax. The windows don't open. The back door needs a key to be unlocked. All the sharp objects are locked in the drawer. And I'm sitting right next to the only way out. She's fine. Probably in her room with the door shut," I answered, trying to keep the annoyance out of my voice. He was going to want one of us watching her all the time. Alex might love her, but the trust obviously wasn't fully there. Well, there was good reason for that. She did stab him. Alex followed my gaze and watched the sunset.

"How'd she know?" he asked.

"Know what?"

"That it was one of you who killed Lacey?"

My stomach twisted. "I don't know. I thought you told her."

He shook his head.

"She probably just figured it out. You did tell her it was for your family, right?" I lied smoothly. It was second nature for me.

"Yeah, I did. I didn't think she'd remember what I told her that night. She wasn't thinking straight."

The door swung open, and Sage walked out nervously. Her eyes flashed to Alex, full of questions. She wanted to know what the elders said. I waited for Alex to tell her the big news. He didn't say anything, and I swallowed my surprise. He was going to make her wait. My brother had changed too. He used to do anything to make sure she was happy.

"Need something, Sage?" I asked with my usual grin.

"Not from you," she spat out.

"Fine, I was just asking."

She ignored me and looked at Alex.

"Alex, can we go visit my dad again tomorrow? Please?" Her voice was soft and sweet, and I couldn't detect a hint of deceit. She had definitely gotten better at covering her true emotions.

"I can't. I have to work," Alex replied.

"I could just go, I'd come right—"

"No," he interrupted sharply. "You can't go anywhere alone. I'm sorry."

The crushed look that covered her face must have hit Alex hard because his gaze softened before he glanced at me.

"But maybe Niko could. He's going to be staying here with us and doesn't work nearly as much as me."

"Hey, I work, thank you," I interjected.

Alex shrugged. "Yeah, but I do more for…you know."

I did know. Alex was an up and comer in the group. He worked with the elders. If he wasn't working construction, he was doing anything the group needed. Alex felt like he needed to do more to make up for what had happened. Even though he wasn't who my dad blamed. It was Geo and I who took the brunt of it. We were the oldest. It was our ceremony. Our planning. Our fault it all went to shit. Since Alex had recovered, I'd taken more of a back seat with the group, tired of the judgments from others. I had gone to the meetings and did all I could when Alex spent those months recovering. I did my part.

Sage looked at each of us with some confusion but thought better than to ask. "Niko, will you take me?"

Her sweet look turned into a glare when she faced me. She needed to be nice to Alex. To pretend she still cared. She didn't have to pretend anything with me. I'd be getting all the hate in the months to come. Fucking great.

"You didn't say please." I smirked at her.

She scowled. "Please."

"Sure, Sage."

She rolled her eyes and stomped back into the house. Dropping my attitude would probably make both our lives easier. But I couldn't deny the heat that rushed through my veins when her sass came out and she matched her attitude to mine. And there was no way I was going to stop acting like myself around my brother just because she was living here. I didn't want Alex to ever think that I had thoughts about her. Once again, she was Alex's girl.

Alex glanced at his phone before meeting my eyes. "Dad wants to see me. You good to stay here?"

"It's going to get old fast if you ask that every time you have to leave." I put my hands behind my head and leaned back in the chair. "If you're not here, then I will be."

He nodded before heading back to his Jeep. The second he disappeared down the road, Sage peeked out the window before coming back outside. She was biting her lip as she stood on the opposite end of the porch.

I arched an eyebrow. "Need something?"

"What did they say? The people Alex talked to."

"You're still here, aren't you?"

She frowned. "Are you incapable of giving me a straight answer?"

"Anything about the group is off limits. You want to ask me about something else, then go for it." I never should have shared anything with her when I caught up to her in Kalamazoo. She had it in her head that I was a way to get information, and I needed to shut that down.

"Where'd Alex go?" she asked through clenched teeth.

"To see our dad."

"For what?"

I shrugged. "No idea."

The hum of an engine brought my focus to the road, and I stiffened when my truck pulled up. I'd been wondering when Geo was going to bring it back. Sage sucked in a breath when she caught sight of my twin as he got out. Her spine straightened, and she looked ready to bolt into the house until her eyes shifted to me and then back to him. My jaw ticked as she leaned against the railing and crossed her arms. I wasn't giving her the answer she wanted, so she was going to try to get it out of Geo.

"I just got off the phone with Alex. He'll give me a ride when he gets back." Geo tossed me my keys before turning his attention to Sage. "For being on the run, you look great. Besides the brown hair."

She scowled, her hazel eyes going dark. She was nearly vibrating with rage. I didn't blame her. She knew we were responsible for Lacey's death. And she looked determined to find out exactly who it was. Hopping up the steps, Geo advanced closer to her, causing a flicker of fear to pass through her gaze.

He reached out and spun a piece of her hair through his fingers. "You really did everything to hide, didn't you?"

"Don't touch me," she hissed, pressing her body into the porch railing, having nowhere else to go as he cornered her. I went rigid, shooting to the edge of my chair. Seeing his hand on her made my pulse spike, and my hands balled into fists. My sudden anger completely blindsided me. That shouldn't bother me. She was a problem. A problem I was stuck with.

Yet, as Geo ran his hand down her face, I'd never been more fucking pissed at my twin than I was in this moment.

"Did you really think you could disappear?" Geo murmured, grabbing her chin when she tried pulling away. "I'll give you credit though. Six months was a good run."

I gritted my teeth, forcing myself to stay sitting. I knew what he was doing. It had come down from the group. They didn't trust her. They were letting her stay with Alex as long as she behaved. But they also wanted her too terrified to try to leave again. I told them I'd do it. And I was going to. She hadn't even been here a day. Apparently, they wanted the threat to come from more than just me.

"I was just trying to survive." Her hands were grasping the railing as she leaned back as far from Geo as she could get.

"We're everywhere, Sage." He finally let her go, and she flew past him.

The chair scraped against the porch when I shot up and stepped to the side, blocking the door before she reached it. Unable to stop in time, she slammed into my chest. Whirling back around, she attempted to bound down the steps, but I caught her arm and pulled her back. Keeping my expression blank, I pushed her forward until her back hit the side of the house.

"What are you doing?" she cried out, her eyes darting between the two of us.

She was in the corner where the railing connected to the house, and I stood in front of her, not leaving enough room for Geo to stand beside me. He brushed against my shoulder, trying to shove me to the side, but I planted my feet, staying where I was.

This conversation was going to happen. The elders wanted it done. Geo wouldn't leave until he said whatever was on his mind. And his favorite way to intimidate people was by getting in their personal space. Me staying between them while it happened would make this talk more bearable for everyone.

Because fuck me, I didn't want to see him touch her again.

"Did Alex and Niko tell you how we found you?" Geo asked, still standing behind my shoulder.

Her gaze darted to me, and my heart thrashed. If she blurted out anything about me knowing where she was, I wasn't sure Geo would keep that secret for me. Twin or not, the group came first. I caught the smallest flash of betrayal before she raised her chin. My nostrils flared. Did she really think I'd given her up? After everything I'd told her?

"No. They didn't," she muttered after a few moments of silence.

"Someone recognized your car when you left Michigan," Geo told her as my breathing returned to normal. "We lost you again. For weeks. I'm guessing you were in Chicago that whole time?"

She swallowed hard and didn't answer. She hadn't moved a muscle since I had pushed her into the corner. I could tell the fear was there, but she was doing a better job hiding it than I thought she could. She was learning to lock up her emotions while mine seemed to be all over the damn place.

"When you stayed at that motel, you went to a small market to shop," Geo said as her eyes widened. "It took him a couple weeks to place you, but he finally realized who you were."

"Who?" she snapped.

"The manager of the market." His voice turned deadly. "He's in the group. Still searching for you, like everyone else was."

"Imagine that luck," I spoke up, knowing Geo was going to wonder why I was being so silent. Sarcasm was what everyone expected from me. One girl wasn't about to make me start acting any differently.

"You didn't find me because of the party I went to?" she asked, confusion crossing her face.

"We knew where you were the second you stepped into the market that morning." I shifted when Geo tried stepping closer. "We followed you back to your hotel. You must have felt really comfortable there, because you didn't look like a girl who was hiding."

"No, she didn't," Geo agreed. "Is that where you stayed the entire time? Thinking you were safe?"

"I can't exactly survive without food. I needed to buy it somewhere," she said snidely. "Believe me, I knew I was still hiding."

"Then you drove to some café." The fear returned to her eyes in an instant, and Geo might be clueless, but I knew exactly why. We had almost lost her. She drove into the city and parked on the street, then disappeared into the crowd when she walked away. Alex was pissed. All three of us went searching for her. I was hoping to get to her first and somehow get her the hell out. I saw her through the café window hugging another woman. Alex had caught up to me as Sage left the café.

"Why'd you wait until the middle of the night if you knew where I was?" she asked, obviously trying to get off the subject of her talking to the woman. My curiosity was burning. When I took her bags from the hotel, I searched her phone and saw a number other than her dad's. I bet it was the lady's number.

"Don't you get it, Sage?" Geo managed to squeeze in next to me, and our shoulders touched as he kept speaking. "Nowhere is safe. A market. A motel room. A party. We can get you anywhere."

Understanding dawned over her features. "You waited until I was in public to prove a point?"

"Did it work?" I asked her, my voice going cold. "Do you realize that if you leave again, we'll find you?"

"I'm not going anywhere." She crossed her arms. "I'm staying with Alex."

"Your hate for us is almost tangible." Geo cocked his head to the side. "How can you despise us and love our brother?"

Like me, he was suspicious of her. He didn't believe she still loved Alex. He wanted to make sure she had enough fear to stay with Alex anyway. And a part of me agreed. Because if she didn't...she'd end up like Lacey.

"Unlike you two, I know Alex had nothing to do with Lacey." Tears filled her eyes. "He was protecting me."

"That almost sounds believable." Geo shook his head. "If you hadn't stabbed him."

"Fuck you. You have no idea what I'm thinking," she snarled, not realizing she was playing right into his hands. Geo wanted her mad. He wanted to play with her emotions, to get her to slip out truths. Ready for this conversation to be done, I opened my mouth to say the words I knew were going to push her past the brink. But it was better than Geo dragging this out even longer.

"You're here because Alex loves you. Not because of anything you've said. It's because he still wants you. All he needs to do is say the word, and your life is gone. You *will* become another missing person. Like your mom." My gut twisted at the pain building in her eyes, but I kept going. Because my words would be better than anything Geo said. "You're going to be the girlfriend he misses. The love of his life. You're going to obey, Sage. You belong to the group now."

The only reason I caught her wrist before it collided with my cheek was because I was expecting it. Damn, she was quicker than I remembered.

"You really need to stop trying to hit me," I ground out, yanking her closer when she tried pulling away.

Geo laughed. "She hasn't even been back a day and she's already tried hitting you before this? I don't remember her ever being so violent."

As fast as I grabbed her, I let her go and backed up, giving myself some space. What the hell was she doing to me? I never let anything slip out that I didn't want. The last time she tried slapping me was in Kalamazoo. Something I would never mention in front of anyone. She was messing with my head. Geo claimed the space I had moved from, and Sage glared at him.

"You're not going to break our brother's heart, are you?" Geo asked, his voice going quiet.

"I love him. I'll admit, I'm not over everything that's happened. But I'll get there." Her words were slathered with truth. If anything, she'd learned to lie while she was gone.

"Good." Geo's hand went back to her hair, and my heart seized, knowing exactly what he was about to say. "Because I would hate to see someone put a knife through your heart like I did to Lacey."

No one spoke. All that could be heard was the crickets as emotions raced across her face. Heartbreak. Pain. Then rage.

"You did it," she breathed out, hatred gleaming in her eyes.

"I did. It fell on me since I'm two minutes older. Of course, Niko helped. He was part of the ceremony. He handed me the knife. Alex would have been part of it too if he hadn't needed to keep you distracted." Geo was calm as he told her the answer she'd been desperate to know. "You going to try to hit me, Sage?"

"Move," she demanded, shoving him in the chest. "I can't fucking look at you—"

"Does this change things?" Geo asked. "Do you think you can still be with Alex, knowing his brother killed your sister?"

He was pushing her, trying to see what she'd admit. It was what the group wanted. To see if she'd snap and admit she'd rather run than stay with Alex. She froze and locked eyes with me before looking back at Geo.

"Alex didn't kill her. You did." She took a deep breath. "I can hate you. And still be with him. But you better stay the hell away from me, Geo. Because you're right, I'm a lot more violent than I used to be. And you might be Alex's brother, but you're nothing to me."

"That's all I wanted to know." In a dramatic move, he slid to the side and let her pass. Without another word, she fled into the house, and the bedroom door slammed shut. I sank back into the chair, running my hand down my face.

"I thought you would have already told her it was me who did it," Geo said, shooting me a questioning glance. "It would make living with her easier for you."

"It's been a long fucking day," I muttered. "I was waiting until everything calmed down."

Truthfully, I hadn't wanted to tell her. The more I was around her, the more I began questioning things I should never be thinking about. I didn't know if it was the guilt. Or her tears. Or how my heart raced when she was close to me. But I couldn't fucking deal with it. I hadn't been raised to question anything. And her having that power over me was driving me insane. If she thought I'd killed Lacey, she'd stay far away from me. Me being part of the ceremony was probably just as bad to her. But I had a feeling she would try to get me to open up about the group now that she knew I hadn't done it.

"Alex is on his way back." Geo was looking at his phone. "What do you think Sage would think if she knew he knew about this? It was the reason he left. So we could talk to her."

"I know. That was the plan. I didn't expect you to show up."

"They thought it would be better with more than one person. You think she'll run again?"

"No. I think she understands that anywhere she goes, there's a chance someone from the group will see her." I stood up and headed toward the door. "She'll stay with Alex. She wants to live."

"Have fun with your new babysitting job." Geo laughed as he jumped off the porch when headlights lit up the driveway.

It was going to be anything but fun.

CHAPTER TWENTY-NINE

Sage

Hiding out for six months was bad. The two weeks since being back were even worse.

I was still getting used to my new nightmare of a life. I barely left my room when Alex was gone, which was often. He worked almost every day and spent a lot of time with his parents or the society. It had been much harder than I expected to get him to open up about their secrets. He was so tight-lipped about everything. The trust wasn't there yet, and I was worried it never would be.

My plan seemed farfetched now. Every night when he came home, we spent time together. I forced myself to act how I used to before everything happened. It was more difficult than I could have imagined. He seemed to want things to be how they used to be. He was sweet and loving toward me but guarded at the same time. A new habit of downing a couple of glasses of wine before he came home helped. It took the edge off and made me more agreeable.

Niko was here all the time, and I was never alone in the house. Other than asking to go to the store and to see my dad, I hadn't spoken more than two things to him since the night Geo was here. The words they had said to me played in a loop in my head. I knew they were trying to scare me into staying. And that night, it worked. But now I was more petrified about this being my forever life. I couldn't do it.

I groaned as I lay on the bed and stared at the ceiling. As much as I hated being around Niko, I couldn't stay in this room anymore. I was going crazy. There was only so much TV someone could watch without going insane. Even working out didn't help. He was the only person to talk to. And maybe I could get him to open up more than Alex about the society. It was worth a try.

Walking into the living room, I sat on the opposite end of the couch from Niko. I rolled my eyes when he did a double take. Avoiding him like the plague had been my plan for the past two weeks. He quickly covered his surprise and flashed a grin.

"Finally got bored with the room?"

"If you're going to be here, then I might as well get used to it."

"Wow, what a way to make a guy feel special."

"Are we going to talk about our last conversation with Geo? You know, when you told me your cult owns me? Or are you planning to ignore it and be your usual sarcastic, dickish self?" He turned his attention fully on me. I hadn't been planning on talking about it, but after stewing about it for two weeks, I couldn't hold it back anymore.

His eyes went cold. "How do you want me to act, Sage? Do you want me to treat you like the prisoner you are? Or do you want the pretense of having a semi-normal life of living with your boyfriend and his dickish brother?"

Shock coursed through me. I didn't know what kind of answer I was expecting, but it wasn't that.

"Which is the real you?" I whispered, regretting it the second the words were out. I was used to the arrogant jerk I'd known nearly my whole life from living in the same small town. I feared the cold monster I'd seen him turn into. What terrified me more was the face I'd seen in Kalamazoo. The one that pulled me from my panic and grounded me. Because it was a side of him I didn't completely loathe.

His eyebrows raised in surprise, but he stayed silent. We stared at each other for a tense minute before I faced the TV again. Apparently, he wasn't done with the conversation because he asked another question.

"So, how's your plan going?"

"Plan? I told you, this was my plan. To stay with Alex."

"That's why you need to drink every night before he comes home?"

I shot him an irritated glance. He watched everything I did. Nothing went unnoticed in this house.

"It's been a long year," I mumbled, folding my arms around my legs.

He nodded and seemed to wait to see if I wanted to keep talking. The whole plan was to get him to talk, but my mind was blank. He was on edge. I doubted he'd share anything useful with me. We sat in silence for a few minutes until I broke it.

"How come you don't ever go to those meetings with Alex?"

"Someone has to be here."

"I know that," I snapped. Of course I knew I had to be watched. "Why does he always go instead of you?"

He narrowed his eyes. "Why so curious all of a sudden?"

"I told you, might as well get used to you being here. I'm tired of not talking to anyone all day," I said. And unlike with Alex, I didn't have to act around Niko. I could say and do whatever I wanted.

"What did I say the night you got here? Talk about the group is off limits. I'm doing my part by being here and babysitting you."

My fists clenched as I jumped off the couch. "I'm not a kid. It's been weeks, and I haven't tried once to run."

"I haven't given you a chance to try to run, Sage."

"I could have if I wanted to." I held my ground, refusing to feel intimidated by him as he stood up and towered over me.

He chuckled. "Really? How? Because the only time I leave this house is when Alex is here. You don't have car keys. You have nowhere to go."

I was regretting coming to talk to him. He always found a way to get under my skin. To control the conversation. I could play that game too.

"You came and warned me all those months ago. You knew I was in that motel but didn't say a word. Warned me to clear my laptop. If I wanted to leave, why wouldn't you help me now?"

His body tensed, and his face turned stone cold.

"If you want to go, then go."

I gaped at him, knowing there was more to it.

"But you won't get far if I'm the one watching you. I told you. If they found you, there was nothing I could do. I'm in hot water from what happened up north. I'm still making it up to my family. To the group. Not you. I won't let you or anyone else ruin everything I've ever known."

He was dead serious. My heart sank when I realized that my small hope of getting help if I needed it was gone. He wouldn't help me. His loyalty was to the society above everything.

"I thought this was what you wanted. To be with Alex and not have to live life on the run," he said mockingly.

"It is," I quickly replied. "I was just curious about what you'd say."

"Right."

After taking a couple of steps back, I sat back on the couch and waited for him to do the same. After a few moments, he relaxed and sat down. Only a foot away from me. It was too close for comfort. Deciding to ignore him, I just stared at the TV. This was going nowhere. He wasn't opening up. I could be doing the same thing in my room without having to deal with him. The longer I sat, the more my panic washed through me. I didn't have a backup plan to leave. That needed to change.

"Listen, we're both stuck here. Are you really going to act pissed off all the time when Alex isn't here?" He tossed me the remote. "Here, turn on whatever you want."

"I'll just watch whatever you were watching," I muttered, pushing the remote back toward him. He was trying to raise the white flag, but my stubborn nature wasn't backing down. I didn't want to get along with him. He might not have killed Lacey, but he was still a part of it.

"Fine. I hope you like documentaries." He picked up the remote and turned up the volume.

With each minute that passed, the anger I'd been storing seemed to seep through my skin and create a tension that filled the room. Maybe it was all in my head, but the stiff way Niko was sitting and the side glances he was giving made me believe he felt it too. I wanted to tackle him and punch his face over and over. I wanted to scream everything I was thinking until my voice was gone. But I didn't.

I might need him again. I wasn't ready to burn that bridge until I had to, or if he stopped helping. I slowly relaxed my fists and rolled my neck, attempting to get comfortable. Gazing at the screen, I got lost in thoughts about how the hell I could get out of here. Finally, a thought came. I glanced at Niko, trying to gauge if I should bring it up now or wait.

No time like the present.

"Will you take me to my house?" I asked, trying to be as nice as possible.

"For what?" He didn't even attempt to hide his suspicion.

"I haven't been there since before. I want to grab a few of my things. And of Lacey's."

A tiny flicker of guilt crossed his face before he answered. "Fine. But if you're going to try something—"

"I'm not. I just want to get my stuff," I promised.

The glare he gave me showed he didn't believe me, but he got up and grabbed his keys anyway. Nerves bubbled in my stomach. It wasn't huge, but if I could get what I needed, then I at least had a way to leave if I needed to.

My childhood home came into view as Niko pulled into the driveway, and I immediately noticed something was different. The old, chipped white paint that used to cover the porch was gone. It looked freshly painted. I hadn't been gone that long to forget what my house looked like.

He glanced over and saw my expression. "Alex has been coming over here and keeping the place up. Just in case you two ever move back in."

The thought of sharing this house with him again was repulsing, but I kept that to myself as we got out of the car. Niko fumbled with my key ring that had my car and the house key on it. Following him to the door, I gritted my teeth as he unlocked it. I couldn't even go into my own house by myself. Hiding out was better than this.

The second he opened the door, I pushed past him and ran up the stairs. The first room I stopped at was my own. It looked the same. Everything was in place. Alex must have been keeping up with the inside too. It was spotless. There was no dust, and the carpet had been vacuumed recently. I heard Niko walk in but ignored him as I sat on my bed and looked at the picture of my mom on the nightstand.

After a minute, I glanced at him. "Can you go down to the coat closet at the bottom of the stairs and grab the backpack?"

He raised an eyebrow, making no move toward the door.

"Where do you think I'm going to go, Niko? I'm upstairs. Can I have two minutes to take this all in?" I snapped.

"Fine," he muttered as he turned for the stairs.

The second his footsteps hit the steps, I rushed to my desk. The top drawer was my junk drawer, and it kept a key ring with spare keys for both Lacey's truck and my car. I could hear him opening the closet downstairs and knew I only had another minute, if that. I quickly slid my car key off the ring and shoved it far down into my shoe. Then I put the key ring with the truck key in my jeans pocket. I was back on the bed before Niko reached the door.

"Here," he said as he tossed the bag to me.

I put the picture in the bag, along with some of my books. Hoisting the bag over my shoulder, I walked to Lacey's room with Niko trailing behind me. I swallowed the sob that threatened to come out. Crying in front of him was not going to happen. I gazed around the room and grabbed a picture and Lacey's favorite shirt. Lying on the bed, I gazed at the collage of pictures on the wall. There were so many pictures of us smiling and laughing. He just stood in the hall without saying anything. I didn't know how much time passed, but I didn't get up until the room started to get dark. After taking a long breath, I stepped back into the hall. Niko was sitting against the wall and scrambled up once I came out.

"Ready?" he asked—without his usual attitude.

I nodded and made my way down the stairs. I passed the bathroom and stopped short, causing him to run into me.

"What?" he asked, glancing into the bathroom.

"Nothing," I muttered as I kept walking. "I need you to take me to the store later."

He gripped my elbow, spinning me around. "What are you up to? You talk to me for the first time in weeks. The same day you want to come here. And now you want to go to the store. What the hell are you trying to do?"

"Tampons. I need tampons." I tore my arm away as his suspicion dropped and his eyes grew big.

"Oh. Right."

Enjoying the blush that was creeping up his face, I leaned against the wall and crossed my arms. "Unless you and Alex have female products at the house?"

"No, we don't," he mumbled. "You need to go now?"

Wanting to hide the keys I had on me before doing anything else, I shook my head. "No. But I'll need to in the next few days."

He nodded, and we headed out the front door. He locked up the house, and we got back in the truck. The ride was silent as sadness and nerves swarmed me. Going back to my house had brought up more emotions than I thought it would. But I got what I wanted.

"Thanks. For taking me," I said, as we pulled up to the house.

"Sure," he replied in a monotone voice. I wondered if his guilt was worse now that he'd been to our house and saw Lacey's room. Maybe he'd have a change of heart about helping me if I needed it. Going into the house and going straight to my room, I pushed the door shut, only for it to swing back open.

"What—"

"Really, Sage? You think I'm that stupid?" Niko said quietly as he stood in the doorway.

"What are you talking about?"

"I felt bad. I gave you space. I heard you shuffling in your room when I got the backpack. I gave you the benefit of the doubt. Until we got back here, and you ran in here, trying to hide whatever you took." He stepped into the room, and I stiffened.

"All I took was personal stuff. I came straight to the room so I didn't have to be around *you*."

"Give it to me."

"I don't have anything."

He sighed. "Are you really going to make me frisk you?"

"You wouldn't touch me now that I'm back with Alex."

His jaw clenched. "Would you rather we waited for him to come home so you can explain that you took something?"

He waited for me to answer, his threat hanging in the air. My eyes widened, and fear heated my veins. Alex couldn't know about this. He had to believe I was happy to stay here and be with him. Keeping my eyes on his, I dug Lacey's truck key out of my pocket and threw it at him. After catching it, he held the key up.

"What car do these go to?"

"Lacey's truck."

He nodded and put them in his pocket.

"That wasn't so hard, was it?"

I bit my tongue, not saying a word. The key in my shoe was pressed against my foot. At least I still had one of them. I stalked past him to leave the room when he grabbed my arm and pushed me into the wall.

"That was all I took," I screamed as he got a hold of my wrists.

"You gave that up way too easy."

"I didn't want Alex to find out." I struggled to twist my arm out of his grasp.

"Then you won't mind if I just check the rest of your pockets?" he asked, holding my wrists with one hand.

"Not getting enough attention from other girls since you've been stuck here with me? Need to get off somehow, huh?" I snarled.

His grip tightened. I debated about using some defense tactics I had learned but thought better of it. No matter what I did to him, I was still stuck in this house. It would only get worse if he told Alex any of this. I could see him trying to calm himself down. A minute went by without a word being said.

Finally, he forced a grin. "It's all right, Sage. Say whatever you want. I know you need to get it out. And you sure as hell can't say what's on your mind to my brother. You need him to be happy with you. It doesn't matter what you say to me. I'm going to do what needs to be done anyway."

He quickly patted down my pockets with his free hand as I writhed away from him. Satisfied I didn't have anything, he released me.

"I only took the key."

"Or you hid it somewhere else. But if you do have something, better not let my brother find it."

"I didn't take anything else."

"I told you that you weren't going to run on my watch. Don't try that shit again." A cry of surprise left me when his hand slid up the back of my neck before fisting my hair. He tilted my face up, putting his own inches away. His other arm wrapped around my waist and pulled me closer. "And for future knowledge, I have no issue with touching you."

My face flushed as I scowled. "For someone who puts family first, you're awfully close to crossing a line with the girl your brother loves."

"I think we already crossed that line when you soaked through my jeans." My cheeks grew hot as his eyes stayed locked on mine. "We both know you aren't Alex's girl. Not anymore. I'm curious. Whose hands would you rather have on you? His or mine?"

"His," I forced out through clenched teeth. He might have his suspicions, but I'd never admit that Alex's touch shot disgust through me. What was worse was the way Niko's closeness wasn't revolting me like it should be.

"Interesting," he murmured as his arm stayed locked around my waist. "Because when he's home, you don't go within arm's reach of him unless he initiates it. Yet, you haven't made a move to get my hands off you."

My body went rigid. "The grip you have on my hair makes that difficult."

He chuckled. "Both your hands are free, Sage. After all those classes you took at that gym, I have a feeling you'd be able to free yourself. Or at least try. But you haven't."

He was trying to get under my skin. My words had pissed him off, and he was attempting to regain control. But as he shifted his hips away from my body, I realized he wasn't as unaffected as I first thought. If I was going to be spending every damn day with him for the near future, he needed to know I wasn't going to act however he wanted without me pushing back.

His eyes widened in shock when I pressed against him, right into the rock-hard evidence that he was feeling something other than anger. I grinned through my nerves as his grip on my hair tightened.

"Hmm," I purred out as tension saturated the room. "It doesn't *feel* like you want me touching Alex. Do you want me touching you instead?"

His eyes narrowed, trying to figure out what I was playing at. "And if I said yes?"

My heart hammered against my ribs as we fell deeper into whatever kind of standoff this was. I should have known he wouldn't have backed down. Was he saying it to prove his theory that I didn't really want to be with Alex? Or did he really feel something toward me? Both of those options had my stomach lurching. For two different reasons. Fuck. Being alone for all those months was messing with me. Being touched, even by someone I couldn't stand, had my body going haywire.

"I say since you'll be stuck with me for the foreseeable future, you better get used to your hand." My smile grew as his eyes darkened.

"Excuse me?"

"It's the only way you'll be able to fix the hard problem you have." My gaze drifted to his jeans. "Because touching you is something I'll never do."

He arched an eyebrow, trying to hide his surprise. We were dancing on a dangerous line. The tension in the room wasn't from anger anymore.

"I could say the same about you." His voice was low and gruff. "It's obvious you don't want Alex's hands on you. That means you'll have to take care of yourself."

"I've been alone for months. I can take care of myself better than any guy can."

"You want to test that theory?" he murmured, keeping his body flush with mine.

I swallowed, knowing he was trying to push to see how far I'd go. He wasn't going to back down until I did first. Diving out of my comfort zone, I took a deep breath.

"Sure. You can sit and watch while I take care of myself." Shock lined his features as I spoke. "And you'll still be stuck using your hand."

Our stare down continued as I waited for him to say another smart remark. A car door slammed outside, shattering the silence. Niko's eyes darted to the door, his face going blank in an instant.

He scoffed, releasing my hair. "You're hilarious."

"You think Alex would find your words funny?" For the first time, I voiced the one thing I could hold over his head.

"He'll never have a chance to find out." He placed his palms on the wall on either side of my head and leaned closer. "You're not going to tell him anything."

"You can't threaten me." I raised my chin to meet his stare, keeping my words quiet in case Alex walked in. "I know you didn't tell your society about finding me. You have your own secret to protect. So be nice to me, Niko. Or that secret might slip past my lips."

"Sage. You really think you have any kind of pull with me?" he asked softly, his voice filled with danger. "You spill what I did, and I won't be your problem anymore. Instead, Geo will take my place."

My stomach plummeted as anger raged through me. As bad as Niko was, he was tolerable. And he'd helped me in the past. The fact that he was part of my sister's death never left me. But being stuck with the person who'd actually killed her was something I couldn't handle. I'd end up trying to kill him. Then I'd die. And I'd never be able to do what I'd planned all along. The society needed to pay for everyone they'd hurt.

"That's what I thought." Niko took my silence as an answer. Taking his hands off the wall, he gave me one last look of warning before walking out of the bedroom.

CHAPTER THIRTY

Sage

My stomach rumbled loud enough for me to hear it, and I groaned as I rolled onto my side. I told Alex I had a headache and went to the bedroom to go to sleep hours ago. It seemed like a good idea at the time. I really should have eaten dinner first. I'd been stuck with Alex all weekend because he decided he was working too much and wanted to spend time with me.

I'd gone through two bottles of wine in the last two days, and it still wasn't enough to keep my skin from crawling every time he got too close. He was trying to make things normal. He took me out to dinner and then to the movies. The conversation was stagnant.

What were we supposed to talk about? The time I stabbed him? Or about watching my sister die? Maybe we could talk about how I was tethered to him for the rest of my life unless I somehow found out enough about the society. Or I could bring up the thought that's been consuming my mind the most.

That I'd rather spend all day fighting with Niko than pretend for one more second that I was enjoying Alex's company.

Shaking my head, I rolled onto my stomach and buried my face in the pillow. How could I detest Alex with my whole heart but not feel the same about Niko? They both shared the same secret. Both part of the same fucked-up society. They were family. Brothers. I mean, I didn't particularly like Niko. He made my blood boil every time we were in the same room.

Speaking of the asshole. My eyes went to my closed door when I heard voices in the living room. Niko had made himself scarce the entire weekend. We'd barely talked since that whole conversation a few days ago. I brought my hand to my chest and felt for the key I had stashed in my sports bra. Keeping it on me at all times was the best way to hide it. I had no intention of taking my clothes off in front of anybody who lived in this house.

Cupboards slammed in the kitchen, and I wondered where Niko had been. He'd left early this morning and was gone all day. Footsteps clamored down the hall, making me tense. I blew out a long breath when the bathroom door shut. Every time someone came down the hall, I was worried it was Alex coming to talk to me. My stomach growled again, and I downed my water bottle, hoping it would satisfy me.

"Yeah, I'm going to bed," Alex said as the bathroom door opened. "See you tomorrow."

"Night, man," Niko called out from somewhere else in the house.

The other bedroom door closed, and a calm washed over me, knowing I was free from him for the rest of the night. Flicking on the TV, I watched a few episodes of an old sitcom with the volume muted, ignoring my hunger pangs.

"Shit," I muttered as a new pain shot through my lower stomach.

Cramps. I cursed under my breath as I got off the bed. I'd completely forgotten that I still needed tampons. After what happened with Niko, it had totally slipped my mind. Quietly cracking my door, I slipped through and went straight into the bathroom. Hopefully, there was something I could use until I was able to go to the store. Niko was going to be pissed when I woke him up. But I wasn't going to ask Alex, and if I did start my period, I couldn't wait until morning to get what I needed.

Crouching down, I pulled open the cabinet doors under the sink, and my jaw dropped. It was packed full. Tampons, pads, panty liners. It was everything I needed and then some. There were about five different brands of tampons and all different sizes of pads. Rifling through them, I pulled out the ones I usually used.

Was this Alex or Niko? In the past, I would have guessed Alex. This was something he would have done before everything happened. Well, maybe not to this extent. But he would have bought me what I needed. Seeing as I didn't tell him I needed tampons, I had a feeling Niko did it. After our last conversation, I was shocked he'd do something nice for me.

After going to the bathroom and washing my hands, I peeked down the hall, not hearing a sound. I didn't have any medicine to help with the cramps. But wine could dull that. And the thoughts swirling in my head right now. Plus, I was still starving. With one last glance at Alex's closed door, I tiptoed to the kitchen. The couch was empty, which meant Niko wasn't here. My heart thumped erratically as I glanced out the front window. I couldn't see my car in the pitch black, but I knew it was parked there. With the key I had shoved down my bra, I could walk out the front door and disappear.

But I didn't have a plan. I could go back to Chicago with Kiara. And live in fear that they'd find me again. A glow from the kitchen counter interrupted my thoughts, and I moved closer to see that it was a phone. An unlocked phone. Spinning in a circle, I scanned the house again, making sure I was alone.

It had to be Niko's. Alex's was smaller than this one was. Reaching out my hand, I pressed *Notes*. Everybody had important stuff stored in their notes. I skimmed over the titles until one caught my eye. My hand trembled as I hit the folder titled *Addresses*. There were four. And two were in the UP of Michigan. Were these where the society's other houses were located? I wished I had a damn pen and paper. I was horrible at remembering numbers.

The screen door creaked, and I nearly leaped out of my skin. Swiping up, I cleared out the notes and made sure the phone was back on the home screen. I backed up and took two steps to the side before reaching for the cabinet that had my wine. Pretending I didn't hear the door, I moved to grab the bottle until I realized my wine cabinet had new additions too.

There were all sorts of chocolates. From *Twix* to the expensive kind. Next to the candy were two different kinds of over-the-counter pain medication. I ran my fingers over a blue cloth, and I narrowed my eyes. Was that a heating pad? Seeing the cord connected to it, I realized it was. There was no way he had bought this all for me.

Someone cleared their throat, and I whirled my head away from the cabinet, locking gazes with a very pissed-off Niko. His eyes swam in fury as they drifted to the phone. I opened my mouth but snapped it closed when the door behind him opened again. My blood ran cold as Geo walked in.

I studied them both, making sure it really was Niko who'd walked in first. They were both wearing jackets, making it impossible to see the birthmark. But my first thought was right. I was getting better at telling them apart by just looking at their faces.

"What are you doing up?" Niko asked, not hiding his irritation. "Alex told me you had a headache."

"I did," I muttered, glancing back at the chocolate. "I was hungry."

"Hey, Sage," Geo greeted me as if we were the best of friends.

Grabbing the bag of *Twix*, I strode out of the kitchen with absolutely no intention of talking to him. He was Alex's brother, and I needed to prove I could get over what happened to Lacey. My plan was to act like he didn't exist. He had other ideas as he jumped in front of me, cutting off my exit route. I ground my teeth as anger and fear intertwined, making my heart race.

He leaned against the side of the fridge and grinned when I met his gaze. "Let's chat for a minute."

CHAPTER THIRTY-ONE

Him

She was fucking lucky I had been sitting in front of the window when she decided to peek at Geo's phone. If my brother had caught her, his suspicion would have heightened. With good reason. When I watched her scroll through whatever she was looking at on the phone, determination had lit up her face. She had been searching for something.

I hadn't planned on coming in until I realized the phone was unlocked. Geo had stuff in there about the group that Sage shouldn't be seeing. I didn't know what she'd find, but digging deeper into the group wouldn't be good for anyone. Especially her. Even if she did find something, she'd only obsess over it. Did she really think she could dig up dirt and use it against the group? It wasn't possible. I wasn't lying when I told her we were everywhere. There was no getting away from it.

"I don't feel like talking," she snapped at Geo, pulling me from my thoughts.

Geo stood in front of her, leaning against the fridge with a wide grin on his face. I inched forward, ready to get between them if I needed to. My twin wasn't exactly sober right now, and when he drank, he liked to stir shit up. Obviously, that included getting under Sage's skin. The whole reason I got Geo out of the house was so she wouldn't see him. That fucking backfired. I thought she was sleeping for the night.

"Aren't you bored with not talking? You've been here almost a month, and you've become a hermit," Geo said with a small laugh. "Do you see anyone other than my brothers?"

"Seeing as you killed the only other person I talked to—no," she snarled, anger etched on her face. There wasn't a hint of pain or sadness. She was getting better at burying her thoughts. Or this life was already numbing her.

Geo's grin faded. "It's not like I murdered her in cold blood. It was for the greater good. I thought Alex explained this to you."

"He did." A bit of anger left her and was replaced with curiosity. I refused to talk about the group with her, and I was pretty sure Alex hadn't brought it up either. "Alex made me read the beginning of a book...that night."

"How much did you read, Sage?" Geo's voice picked up a hard edge, and I raised an eyebrow as I stopped a couple of feet away from them. Usually, I knew what my twin was going to say the second he spoke the first word. This time, I had no idea where he was going with it.

Her gaze went to me for a moment before looking back at him. "The story of how it started."

"You didn't read any other pages?" he pressed as he leaned closer.

Backing up until she was back in the kitchen and leaning against the counter, she set the bag of chocolates down. Her reaction had me studying every inch of her face. She was hiding something.

"No, I didn't," she answered curtly. "Ask Alex. He took the book from me before I could."

"We know you went back down to the basement after you ran from Alex that night," he replied, stumbling a bit as he crossed the small space that separated them. "The knife you stabbed him with. And the matches you used to burn our house down. Those came from the basement. You didn't have those when Niko and I talked to you upstairs."

"So?" she asked, keeping her voice steady. But it was the panic building in her eyes that had my stomach clenching.

"I was able to grab it before the house burned down," he said casually. "That book is a huge part of our beliefs."

"Good for you," she spat out, but it lacked the vigor she had only a minute ago. "Move. I'm going back to bed."

Thanks to the beers he'd downed all night, Geo was slower than usual. She darted away from his outstretched hand, only to slam into my chest. Grabbing her upper arms, I held her in place as she raised her head to look at me.

"Please," she breathed out, her pupils dilating from panic. "Just let me go back to my room."

Glancing up at my brother, I clenched my jaw and walked forward, bringing her back into the kitchen. Whatever she was keeping to herself, I couldn't help her this time. Because as my twin's glare zeroed in on her, whatever secret she was hiding—Geo had already found it out. Tearing away from me, she spun around and glared at us as we stayed in front of her.

"What did you do, Sage?" I asked her, hoping we'd be able to end this quickly.

"I have no idea."

"All those other pages in the book. It's a list of names," Geo murmured as my gaze cut to him. *What the hell was he doing?* "Of all the women who were part of a ceremony."

She stayed silent, letting surprise cover her face. But I'd gotten better at reading her tells. And Geo's words weren't news to her.

"It was my job to write Lacey's name in the book since I was the one to complete the ceremony," Geo continued as her face began to pale. "But do you know what I found when I opened the book?"

Shock coursed through me even as I kept my face expressionless. Geo and I never used to have secrets from each other. Now it seemed we were both keeping them.

"A page had been ripped out. The newest page where I needed to write Lacey's name." Even drunk, Geo's voice radiated with threat and anger. "Tell me, Sage. Who do you think did that?"

My eyes widened as my head swung back to her. Shit. If that were true, she had evidence. It wasn't much. Not enough to start an investigation. Or implicate any of us. But it could raise questions. The elders would be furious if they knew. Seeing as I just found out, I doubted they were aware. For now, at least.

"I don't know."

The words weren't even out of her mouth when Geo shot forward and wrapped his hand around her neck before slamming her back against the wall. Her hands flew to his wrist, and her mouth opened in a silent scream as he cut off her air.

My body moved before my brain caught up. I grabbed his arm that was choking her and wrenched it away. He turned, and the side of my face exploded in pain when his punch landed on my cheek. I swung back and clipped his chin before he rammed into me. We landed on the floor near the table as we wrestled for the upper hand.

"What the fuck are you doing?" he hissed as I blocked his next hit. "She took it. She has something on us."

"Strangling her isn't going to get it back," I argued back. "Calm the fuck down. She's still Alex's girl. He would have done worse if he was awake."

I wasn't sure if that was true. If Alex found this out, he'd want answers as badly as Geo. The group came first, especially for my baby brother. But that was the only logical thing I could say to explain what I'd just done. I couldn't exactly tell him that I'd seen red when he touched her.

"It burned," Sage spoke up, making us both freeze. "I lost it when I was fighting to get out the front door. It was in my pocket. When I got out of the house, it wasn't there anymore. I don't have it."

Shoving Geo away, I got off the floor. She was rubbing her throat as she stayed pressed against the kitchen wall. Fear swam in her eyes as Geo advanced toward her again. My hand landed on his shoulder, halting him.

"Back off. I'm only going to talk to her," Geo growled, his anger for me radiating off him. We'd gotten into fights before, but not for something like this. No matter what happened, we always had each other's backs. This time was different. He wasn't fucking hurting her again.

"I don't have it," she repeated, her voice shaking. Geo stayed a couple of feet away from her with me right behind him.

"You promised you were here because you love Alex," Geo said, still catching his breath. "If you're lying—"

"I'm not," she cut in, her voice rising. "It's gone."

"Then you won't mind if we go look in your room?" he asked, tilting his head.

I stepped up next to him. "I'll look for it. You're drunk as fuck. It's affecting your decisions."

I didn't know if she had the paper. But I knew for sure she still had that damn phone. I should have taken it the day she got here.

"It's not my decisions I'm worried about." He turned to shoot a glare at me. "Spending all your time with her is getting to you."

"I'm doing what needs to be done," I snapped. "Including making sure you really don't murder a woman in cold blood."

He laughed. "I wouldn't kill her. Unless the group deems it necessary."

His attention went back to her as I went rigid. Sage shrank away, not wanting to be anywhere near him.

"If you're keeping secrets. Or planning anything that isn't staying with Alex, then you're going to end up locked in a house until next August," he threatened in a low voice. "And guess what? I'll stay with you the entire time. I'm sure we could have some fun. What do you think, Sage?"

He only took half a step closer before she whipped her hand up, and her flat palm smashed against his nose.

"Shit," he nearly yelled as he lurched backward with blood flowing down his face.

"Don't touch me again," she hissed, her eyes darting around for a way out of the kitchen.

"You bitch," Geo ground out as he raised his hand. I snatched his wrist and twisted him around until I was in front of her.

"What the hell is going on?"

Alex stood behind Geo, his eyes widening as he caught sight of the blood dripping onto the floor.

"Ask your girlfriend," Geo spat out, grabbing the roll of paper towels after I released his arm. "I'll tell you one thing. She's not as innocent as she acts."

I explained everything that happened, knowing he was going to find out anyway. Alex's face went cold as he stared at Sage.

"I don't have it, Alex," she promised as tears pooled in her eyes. "I didn't say anything because it burned with the house. I told you; that night was insane."

"I'll look while Niko drives you home," Alex said, running a hand through his hair.

"I don't have—"

"Then you won't mind if I look," he interrupted her, leaving no place for arguments.

"I'll stay and look," I spoke up. "Geo and me in the same car right now isn't a good idea."

Geo's chuckle lacked any humor. "I never thought I'd see the day when my twin protects someone over me."

"You're drunk." I softened my voice. "Sleep it off, man. We'll talk about it in the morning."

Alex looked between us and grumbled as he grabbed his keys. He was used to being in the middle the few times we fought. With one last glance at Sage, he headed to the door.

"Don't let her in the room until you search it," Alex ordered before disappearing outside. Without another word, Geo followed him, keeping the paper towel against his nose.

Tension smothered the silence as I rinsed off the blood that had smeared on my hand. Sage didn't move a muscle, staying in the kitchen as I yanked the towel off the oven handle. My pulse was still racing from everything that had just gone down, and I was trying to calm down before I faced her.

"Thank you." She broke the silence. "For stopping him."

"Don't thank me for doing what any other half decent person would have done." Spinning around, I met her gaze. "Do you have the paper?"

My words were sharp, and the gratefulness in her eyes disappeared. Geo had been right. I was protecting her. Over him. Over the group. She couldn't live here thinking I'd save her every time she needed it. Then her courage of trying to find a way out of this would grow. And she'd end up right where Geo had told her. At one of our houses. Whatever the fuck I was feeling, I needed to lock it down.

"No," she told me, crossing her arms.

"I'm going to have to look. Because if you're lying and the paper is found later, then it's my ass on the line."

She bit her lip, and I blew out a harsh laugh. "You do have it. Jesus. Are you trying to get yourself killed?"

"Yes, that's what I'm doing. I ran for six months because I have a death wish."

I ignored her sarcasm. "Give it to me, Sage."

"Are you going to tell Alex?"

"Go get it."

She hesitated, as if still trying to figure a way out of this. Leaving the kitchen, I strode to her room, and she caught up to me as I passed through her door.

"Get it. Or I'll search for it. And I'll find the phone you still have too."

Her eyes narrowed. "The phone's dead. I can't use it anymore."

"Right now, all I want is the paper."

She gritted her teeth as she moved to the dresser and pulled out a pair of jeans. After taking out a small folded up piece of paper from the pocket, she crossed the room and shoved it into my chest.

"Here." She pulled her arm back, but I snatched her wrist, keeping her in front of me. The paper fell to the floor as we glared at each other.

"Your mouth and attitude are going to get you in trouble." The blush on her cheeks made it clear she was thinking of our conversation from a few days ago as I spoke. "But it's all talk. We both know you won't do anything. There's no way out, Sage. Stop trying to get yourself killed."

Letting her go, I didn't wait for a response as I grabbed the paper and left her room. Flicking off the light, I fell onto the couch and unfolded the paper, shining my phone light onto it. My gut knotted as I read the four names. She'd had this for months. My panic increased when the image of her hugging the woman in Chicago flashed through my mind. What if she was connected to this? Footsteps in the hall broke through my thoughts.

"Are you going to tell them?" she asked softly through the darkness. "I need to know. I don't want to be blindsided."

After a minute, I sighed. "No."

More silence. I lowered my head back onto the pillow, figuring she'd gone back to her room until she spoke up again.

"Thank you. For the chocolates. And everything else."

"You're welcome."

CHAPTER THIRTY-TWO

Sage

I'd been walking on eggshells ever since Niko took the paper. Every day, I waited for the bomb to drop that he had told Alex that I had it this entire time. But it never happened. Alex went back to acting like everything was normal, never bringing it up again. Geo hadn't come back, and for that, I was grateful. He had scared the hell out of me when his hand went around my neck.

And Niko...ever since that night, he'd been distant. He was with me all damn day, but he really wasn't here. He didn't interact with me unless I spoke first. And as much as I hated myself for even thinking about it, I missed our heated arguments. It was better than living in silence. The first week, I hadn't really cared since I spent most of my time dying from cramps. But now that I was feeling better, I was going crazy. I couldn't live like this anymore. Wine and lies had become my life, and I was beginning to fear my mask was going to turn permanent if nothing changed.

I sat on the couch, and Niko stiffened as he stayed focused on the TV. I knew what he was doing. I was the reason he'd gotten into a fight with his brother. He was hiding things from his family. And by keeping me at arm's length, he was choosing them. That hurt more than I wanted to admit.

"Can we go see my dad later?" I asked, pulling my hair into a ponytail. A red strand fell on my face, and I brushed it back. The brown was almost gone since it had been months since I'd last dyed it.

"Sure."

The narrator's voice from the show he was watching droned on as I glanced at him. I shifted, feeling the key move in my bra. Trying to leave was becoming a larger possibility if I couldn't get the information I needed soon.

"How old were you when your parents told you about the society?"

My question caused the largest reaction I'd seen from him in over a week. His eyes shot to me, suspicion filling them.

"I'm not talking to you about the group—"

"I'm asking about your past," I cut in. "How would that give any secrets away? I'm just curious."

After studying me for a moment, he only shook his head and turned back to the TV. I rolled my eyes, leaning back to get comfy for another fucking day of muted tension.

"I don't know when they told me," he muttered without looking away from the TV. "I've known about it for as long as I can remember."

I stared at the side of his face. "As a kid? Weren't they worried you'd tell people?"

"It was our normal. We were taught the importance of secrets. Telling a five-year-old that his parents would be taken away if people found out worked like a charm."

I hadn't expected the harsh truth from him. "That sounds horrible—"

"Don't feel bad for me, Sage," he ground out, finally meeting my gaze. "I didn't have a terrible childhood. We went to school. Played sports. Had loving parents. Each year, we gradually learned more until we were fully immersed in it. By then, it was already ordinary for us."

"When was the first time you," I paused, not sure if I should keep pushing, "were part of a ceremony?"

I tried wording it as nicely as possible instead of asking about the first time he was a witness to a murder. I had a feeling he wouldn't keep talking if I went that route.

"I was eleven."

He mumbled it so quietly it took me a second to digest what he said. It was hard to imagine learning something like that so early in life. They were raised to accept that it was the right thing. It was like their religion. It was more of a fucked-up cult. But still normal to them.

"Your dad did the ceremony before you and Geo were born?" I asked, curious to see how much he was willing to share.

He hesitated before his face went blank as if he were going to close up again. Now I wanted to know even more. Taking a deep breath, I scooted closer to him.

"I'm not judging. I want to understand." My words weren't a complete lie. I wanted to understand how a belief could be instilled so deeply that killing someone was considered normal. It made sense when it started centuries ago. In those times, sacrifices were prominent in many societies. The fact that this belief survived this long was the unbelievable part.

"No." He blew out a breath as he ran both hands through his black hair. "He didn't."

"But Alex told me—"

"My parents got married young." His voice was tight as he explained. "My mom got pregnant with Geo and me before my dad did the ceremony. Then she couldn't get pregnant again. After two years of trying, they decided a ceremony was needed. She got pregnant with Alex that month."

"She got pregnant with you before," I repeated, unable to hide my surprise. "But that completely contradicts your entire belief. She got pregnant without having a ceremony. You don't need to kill to—"

"Drop it, Sage," he snapped, his green eyes darkening. "It only further increased my parents' faith when Alex was conceived. It showed them that it is necessary."

"And you?" I whispered, not sure if I wanted to hear his answer. "Do you think it's still necessary?"

"There are a lot of things I think about that I never used to." His eyes pierced mine, sending an unwanted flutter through my stomach.

"Why are you protecting me?" The words were out of my mouth before I could stop them.

"Does it bother you?"

I frowned in confusion. "Does what bother me?"

"That every time you look at me, you're seeing the face that killed your sister."

Shock rocked me as I stared at him, speechless. Did it bother me? Before all this happened, I used to lump Geo and Niko together as one. They were Alex's annoying twin brothers, who I ignored whenever possible. That all changed the day Niko found me in Kalamazoo.

When Geo stared at me, I only saw coldness. Cruelness. Ridicule. He looked at me like I was nothing more than something he could toy with until he got bored. Niko kept his emotions to himself most of the time. But I'd seen them break through since I'd been here. Concern. Guilt. *Desire*. Niko and Geo might be identical, but I didn't see them in the same way. They weren't the same. And I didn't know how the hell I felt about that.

"No," I breathed out before speaking more firmly. "No. I don't see you the same."

A bit of surprise lit up his eyes, but he didn't say anything. I turned away from him, back toward the TV, even though my mind was a million miles away. A lump grew in my throat as I thought of Lacey. Niko hadn't killed her. But his family had. I should hate him. Like I did Alex. And Geo. It felt like I was betraying her. A hand gripped my thigh, and I jerked my head up.

The second we locked eyes, he ripped his hand away. "I thought you were having another panic attack."

"I'm fine. Do you get panic attacks?"

He raised an eyebrow. "No."

"Then how did you know what would help me?"

I expected him to say something dirty after he had mentioned me soaking his jeans last time. Instead, he pressed his lips into a thin line as he grew somber.

"The women." He said it carefully, as if he didn't know what my reaction would be. "Up north. If they were there a while, some would get panic attacks. I researched what to do to help them."

Tears welled in my eyes, and I quickly wiped them away. It was hard not to imagine my mom going through that. Taking a shaky breath, I managed a small smile, deciding I was done with the depressing talk today.

"You know, you're not the asshole you let everyone think you are," I stated.

He let out a snort of stunned laughter. "And you're a lot stronger than everyone thinks."

"I'm not all talk." I repeated his words from when I'd given him the paper.

"Don't go digging around, Sage." His humor faded. "You won't find anything. And I can't keep protecting you without someone catching on."

Rolling my eyes, I stood from the couch before crossing the living room. I glanced over my shoulder to see his gaze right on my ass. After all the anger, I'd gladly take sexual tension over the silence. At least it made me feel something.

"I didn't say anything about digging around," I said as I walked down the hall. "I only said I'm not all talk. And I can take care of myself."

I couldn't help but peek back at him, and my stomach flipped at his heated gaze. He was thinking of our past conversation, like I was.

"Test your theory, Sage," he murmured gruffly.

Without another word, I slipped into my room and leaned against the door. At some point, one of us was going to cross the line, and all these words were going to turn into actions. Making my already complicated life even more twisted.

I didn't care nearly as much as I should.

CHAPTER THIRTY-THREE

Him

The wine bottle clinked onto the glass as Sage poured her third drink. Gritting my teeth, I kept my thoughts to myself. It wasn't my place to tell her what to do. If she wanted to drink herself into a fog before Alex came home, it was her decision. I still didn't fucking like it.

The weeks had been creeping by, and I'd kept my distance. Physically, at least. If Alex wasn't home, we were always together. Talking. Playing cards. Binging random shows. Working out. She'd been keeping up with everything she learned when she went to that gym. Now that the weather was getting nice, we spent time outside. For the first time in my life, I let my guard down, and I let her see parts of myself I didn't show to anyone else. About most things. I didn't talk about the group. Or Geo.

Because even if it seemed like everything was going peacefully, it was only a curtain blocking out real life. And it wouldn't last forever.

That's why I'd made sure to keep my hands off her. She had enough going on in her life; she didn't need me to fuck it up even more. I couldn't give her what she wanted. I could protect her in the small ways I had been, and that was it. The only way she was going to survive this was by staying with Alex. I couldn't turn my back on the group or my family, no matter how much this one girl was slowly consuming my every waking thought.

"What are you thinking so hard about?" she asked, sitting on the couch next to me. Inches from me. She'd been pushing me, seeing what I'd do. The wine gave her extra courage. The scent of her lilac lotion drifted over, and like it had been each day, my self-control took another dip.

I was trying to not be an asshole. She was making it hard. She was already stuck with me. I didn't need to make it any more difficult by adding sex to the equation. I turned to look out the window as tires crunched over the gravel in the driveway.

"He's home early," I muttered, glancing at her. "Better put that away before he sees. Unless you want to explain why you're drinking at three in the afternoon."

"You turn back into an ass when he's home," she murmured before downing the rest of the wine.

"No. I'm acting how I always have around him."

"Yeah, like an asshole." She jumped back up and strode to the kitchen. The faucet turned on, and even though I couldn't see her, it was easy to picture it. She did it every day. Rinsed the cup, gave it a quick pat dry, and then stashed it back in the cabinet in the same place it always was.

"I'm taking a shower," she announced, not even looking at me as she went into the hallway.

I sighed. "He's going to catch on. You do anything to prolong seeing him."

"Of course I don't. I love him."

She slammed the bathroom door closed, and I rubbed my temples. She didn't. Not that she'd ever admit it to me. That part of life was behind the curtain that we didn't talk about. The trust wasn't there. And it never would be. She wanted to survive. I was Alex's family. She might tolerate me better than anyone else here, but I was still the enemy.

The screen door creaked when Alex walked in, and I glanced over at him. He tossed his keys on the table before striding across the room and falling onto the opposite end of the couch. Frowning, he scanned the room.

"Where is she?" he asked with a bit of annoyance.

"In the shower."

He shook his head. "How is she?"

My pulse sped up as I faced him. "What do you mean?"

"You see her more than me. I don't know, Niko." He let out a short groan. "What if she never warms back up to me?"

Guilt wormed its way through me as I bit my tongue. This was another reason why I hadn't touched her. She might not love him anymore, but Alex still wanted her. And he was my baby brother. What kind of brother was I to go behind his back?

"She's adjusting," I finally answered. "It's a lot for her. She didn't grow up in it. She saw her sister get killed. By our brother."

"It's been more than two months since she's been here."

He'd die of old age before she adjusted to this life, but I wasn't telling him that.

"Has she tried anything?" he asked in a low voice, even though the shower was still on.

"No." Besides stealing a car key, talking to some woman in Chicago, and hiding the paper. "She visits her dad. We go to the store. She wants to go back to school and finish her degree."

"The group still doesn't trust her," he muttered. "They want her watched longer."

"I already told you, I'd help as long as it's needed." I couldn't deny that I was happy I'd be spending more time with her.

"I feel bad." He shook his head. "You don't have your own life anymore. You're stuck here."

"I'm still making it up to the group for what happened up north." I shrugged. "If this is what it takes, I'll do it."

"What if this was a mistake?" he mumbled, looking conflicted. "I'm stuck too. What if it's like this for the rest of my life?"

I'd been wondering when he was going to bring that up. He'd gone to the group and to the elders, begging to be responsible for Sage. They had agreed. It wouldn't look good for him if he went back and changed his mind. He needed to prove they were happy and would be the rest of their lives. Even if he didn't care for Sage like he used to, it was expected of him to stay with her.

And that reasoning made me feel a bit less guilty about my recent thoughts.

"She'll adjust," I assured him. "Just give her some more time."

With a nod, he focused on the game that was playing on TV as he leaned back and relaxed. I grabbed my bottle of water, freezing when I caught sight of Sage. She was standing in the hallway next to the bathroom door. Only wearing a towel. I glanced at Alex out of the corner of my eye, realizing that he couldn't see her from his side of the couch.

My gaze raked over her still wet body. Her hair was a mess of unbrushed waves that tumbled over her shoulder. Raising an eyebrow, I met her stare. A devilish grin lit up her face, and I couldn't tear my eyes from her as I tried to figure out what she was thinking. Remembering I was still holding my water bottle, I twisted off the cap, keeping my gaze on her as I lifted it to my lips. Tilting the bottle up, I took a sip right as she dropped the towel.

I nearly spit out the water and went into a fit of coughing. Leaning forward, I twisted the cap back onto the water bottle while attempting to control my sudden choking. Alex glanced over at me.

"Went down the wrong pipe," I croaked out once my breathing returned.

Alex chuckled and went back to watching the game. My eyes flew back to the hallway where she was still standing. The towel was around her feet, and I kept my stare fixed on it. If I looked up, that would be it. The last thread of control I'd been holding would be severed. I had a feeling she knew that.

Her feet shifted, and I lost the battle I never had a chance at winning when I lifted my gaze. Her legs still had drops of water on them from the shower. My breath was caught in my throat as I drank in every inch of her naked body. My eyes went to her hand as she raised it to her breast. Her nipples were hard, and her back arched as she grazed her fingers over them.

Her body was as fucking beautiful as I knew it would be. My hand gripped the arm of the couch as I forced myself to stay sitting. I wanted to feel her soft skin against mine as I tasted her. All the dirty images I'd been burying rushed to the surface.

I was so fucked.

Finally meeting her eyes, I was taken aback by the heat in them. A look I hadn't seen before from her. There were no nerves. No regret. No fear. She hadn't had enough wine to forget Alex had come home. She knew he was on the couch. And she apparently didn't give a shit. For the first time, she was putting her trust in me. In a way I never planned for. She was depending on me to make sure Alex didn't catch her. And I would.

Grateful I'd chosen to wear jeans today, I shifted as my dick strained against my zipper. I subtly peeked at Alex, who was still engrossed in watching the game. When I looked back at her, she had her hand on her pussy. Bracing her other palm against the wall, she began touching her clit, and I sucked in a quick breath. She was just full of surprises today.

I didn't move a muscle as my eyes darted between her hand and her face. The pleasure building on her face was intoxicating, and it took everything in me to stay on the couch. I wanted to be the one to draw that reaction from her. I wanted to explore the touch that would entice a scream from her lips.

Her eyelids fluttered the faster her fingers moved. Raising her other hand, she clamped it over her mouth as a tremor ran through her. My teeth slammed together as I nearly fucking lost it and bolted from my spot. She fell against the wall, not slowing down her assault on her clit. Her knees nearly buckled as her orgasm hit. Her body was shaking when she pulled her hand from her mouth.

Raising her eyes back to mine, she lifted her finger that had just been on her pussy and slid it between her lips. A second ago, I didn't think my dick could get any harder. I was wrong. I was willing to bet she tasted more delicious than any dessert I'd ever eaten.

"Dad's calling," Alex said, glancing toward the hallway. He was far enough to the side that he couldn't see where she stood, but it was obvious the shower had shut off a while ago. "I'm going to talk to him outside. We have a trip coming up."

Sage had already slipped into her room and silently shut the door. I turned toward Alex and nodded. It was for the group. He didn't want Sage overhearing.

"I know I don't say it often. But thanks." He grabbed my shoulder. "For helping me with her. I appreciate it, man."

And the best brother award went to me. I was a piece of shit. But even his words couldn't stop me from what I was going to do next.

"No problem," I muttered.

With his phone to his ear, he strode across the living room and went outside. The second the screen door clicked shut, I was on my feet. My back rested against the hallway wall as I waited for her to come out of her room. She wouldn't stay in there long. She had to show Alex she wanted to spend time with him. I wasn't chancing going in. Alex might come back inside. And I couldn't rely on my willpower of not touching her if we were alone in a room. Because I had absolutely none at the moment.

The door opened, and I straightened up, grabbing her wrist before she left the doorway. A cry of protest left her as I pushed her against the wall. Placing my forearm on the wall next to her head, I kept my words quiet.

"That's the second time you had an orgasm while I only sat and watched," I murmured, putting my fingers under her chin and tilting her face up. "There won't be a fucking third time. Do you understand what I'm saying, Sage?"

Her eyes widened in surprise. Nerves filtered through her gaze, but her answer was crystal clear.

"Yes."

That was the answer I needed. There would be no more skirting around the tension we'd built up since she'd gotten here. She'd bulldozed over that line with what she just did. Keeping my hands off her now would be impossible. I shouldn't even be considering it. She wasn't mine to touch. Her life had already been chosen. By the group—who I was supposed to listen to over everything else.

The problem was that right now, I didn't fucking care.

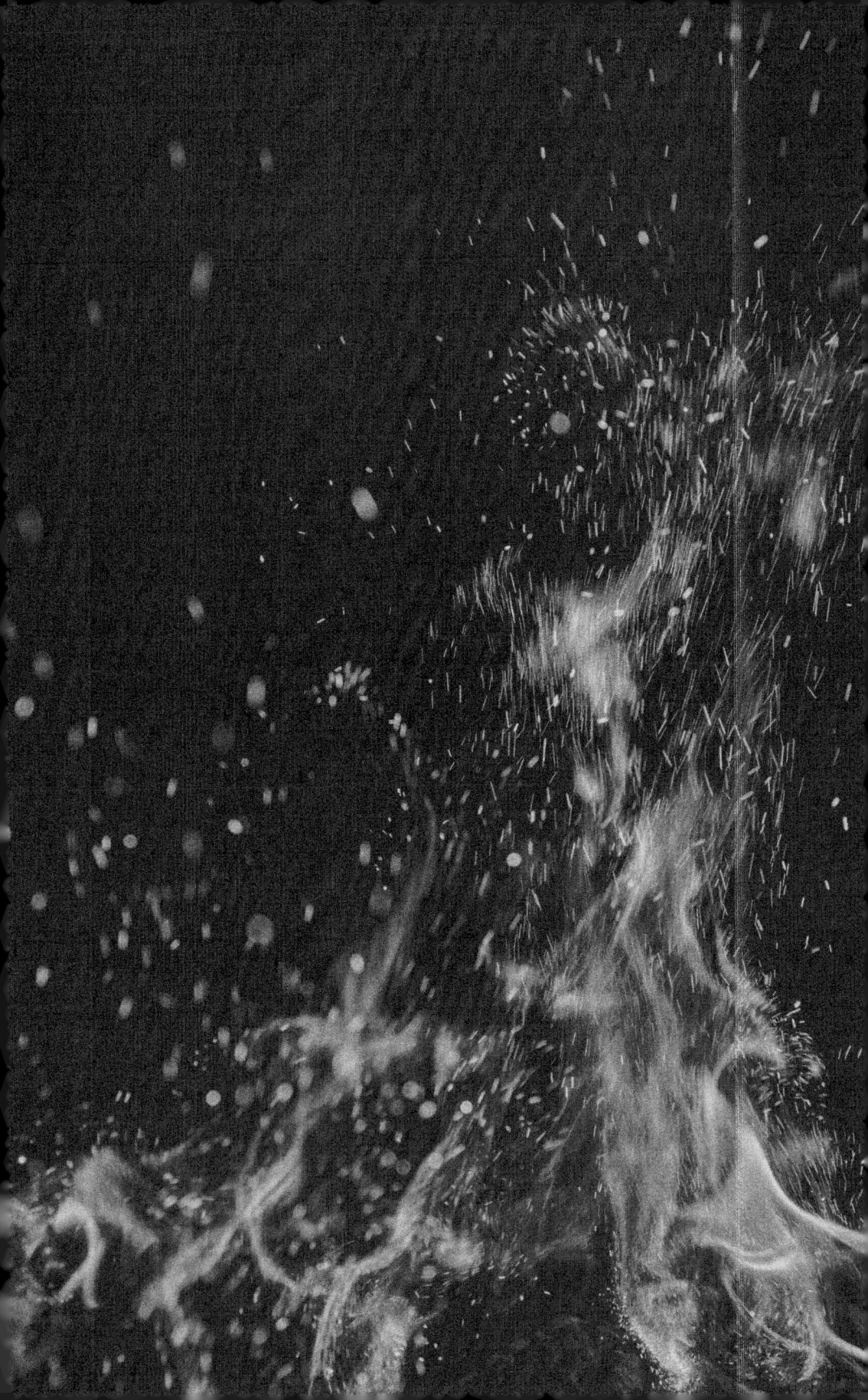

CHAPTER THIRTY-FOUR

Sage

What a shitty three days.

For the two days after I gave Niko the peep show, Alex had taken the days off work. He wanted to spend more time with me and give Niko a break. It was a long two days of acting. Especially when I couldn't drink wine before I had to be nice to Alex.

I could act however I wanted with Niko. When Alex was home, I put up a front. A mask of my former self, even though that girl was long gone.

Today, I was ecstatic when Alex left for work, only to have Geo show up fifteen minutes later. Niko hadn't looked very pleased to see his twin, but Geo stayed anyway. And I spent the whole day in my room. Geo scared me, and if he tried going near me again, I was going to break his nose instead of only giving him a bloody one. Probably not a good idea, since I promised Alex I could learn to love his family.

I cracked my door and poked my head out into the hall. I'd heard the front door slam and hoped that meant Geo had left.

"He's gone," Niko called out from the living room.

A weight lifted off my chest as I walked out of my room. Niko was on the couch, and I bit my lip as I sat next to him. The tension was radiating off him as he stared at the muted TV with his jaw clenched.

"What did Geo want?" I asked quietly.

"Nothing."

I frowned. "He stayed all day."

"He wanted us to hang out. I haven't seen him much," he muttered, running a hand down his face.

Before I could answer, the headlights of Alex's Jeep shone through the windows and my stomach twisted. I didn't even get to drink my wine. Dealing with him buzzed was hard enough. I wanted to be nowhere near him when I was sober.

"Hey, baby," Alex greeted me as he walked through the door.

I cringed to myself like I did every time he said that. It brought back the memory of the night he found me.

"Hi, Alex." I flashed him the brightest smile I could manage.

"I'm going to change clothes really quick. And then, Sage, I wanted to talk to you about something. Alone," he said pointedly, looking at Niko.

"Hey, baby brother, you're the one that wants me here. I'm not going to leave just because you want special time with your girl-friend," Niko replied, his eyes still glued to the TV.

Damn. He really was in a mood. I stood up before they started bickering.

"I'll just wait for you on the porch." I gave Alex a quick kiss on the cheek and resisted the urge to wipe my lips.

"Okay, I'll be out soon."

I nodded and waited until the bedroom door clicked shut. Staring at Niko, I stepped in front of the TV.

"Hey, you're in the way—"

"Do you know what he wants to talk about?" I asked him in a low voice, not wanting to be overheard.

Niko turned his gaze to me. "I have no idea. Sounds like you're going to find out before me."

Fear began to swell up inside me. What if the society changed their mind about me? I brushed my fingers over my shirt where my key sat in my bra.

"I'm sure it has nothing to do with the group. I would have been told if it was," Niko assured me once he caught sight of my panic.

I nodded, although I didn't share his confidence. He'd done next to nothing with the society because he spent all his time with me. How did he know when they made a decision?

Niko leaned back on the couch. "Better go wait outside like a good girl."

I shot him a dirty look before heading out to the porch. He was such a dick when Alex was home. I gazed up at the stars as I waited. It was a beautiful and clear May night. It was hard to believe it had been almost a year since this nightmare began. Lightning bugs filled the cornfield next to the house. The only sound was the crickets chirping. This would have been a perfect place to live. If it wasn't my prison.

"Hey," Alex said as he swung open the screen door.

I swallowed my fear and smiled. He stepped behind me and wrapped his hands around my waist.

"It's so nice out," he whispered in my ear.

Even if his touch had my skin crawling, I relaxed a bit. If this were bad news, he wouldn't be so calm.

"What did you want to talk about?" I asked, ready to get this conversation done with. I was going to claim a headache and go straight to bed.

He paused. "It's been almost three months since we've been living here."

I nodded, wondering where he was taking this.

"It feels like we aren't connecting like we used to. I know I'm not home as often as I want to be. But I was thinking maybe we could start spending more time together. To get it back how it was," he said slowly, as if choosing his words carefully.

"I thought that's what we've been doing the last two days?"

"Maybe we could sleep in the same room."

I went rigid before I could stop myself. His hands left my hips, and he pulled on my arm until I was facing him.

"You don't want to?" He frowned.

"I do," I said quickly. "I want to spend more time with you. But I don't know if I'm ready to be intimate—"

"I wasn't talking about sex." Annoyance crept into his voice.

"Alex, I'm sorry. It just took me by surprise," I told him as softly as possible while panic engulfed me.

"Does that mean you want to?"

I swallowed. "Yes, I think that would be nice."

Alex smiled and kissed me on the lips. I pulled away and hugged him so he wouldn't catch on that I'd rather stab him again than feel his mouth on mine. The thought of sharing a bed with him made me sick to my stomach.

This was the man who I had loved more than anything. He betrayed me. He chose the society over me. Over my mom and sister. I'd come to realize how involved he was with them. He would do anything for them. But I had to get closer to him. So that he would trust me more. I needed to find out more. And if sharing a bed could help, that's what I would do. And unless I made a plan to run again, I really didn't have much of a choice.

We went back into the house and sat on the couch. The couch felt small with all three of us sitting. With me always in the middle. I looked at Niko, and he didn't even glance my way. He had to be curious about what we'd talked about, but he wasn't going to ask.

"Niko, you can move back into your room full time," Alex said as he smiled at me.

He tore his eyes from the TV and looked at his brother. "You really like this couch, huh?"

"No. Sage and I are going to start sharing my room."

I waited for his reaction, but never got it. His usual grin didn't even twitch.

"Good. I missed sleeping in my bed every night," he said as he looked back at the screen.

Well, that hurt more than I expected. Was sex all he wanted from me? He didn't seem to care at all that I was going to be sleeping with Alex. Or he was even better at covering his emotions than I had thought.

We sat and watched a movie that ended all too soon. Going into that bedroom with him was daunting. Alex took my hand as we got off the couch and went down the hallway. Looking over my shoulder, I caught Niko glaring at Alex's back, looking pissed.

Alex tugged me into the bedroom, and I stared at the bed. Suddenly, the queen-size bed seemed so small. I grabbed a T-shirt and shorts to sleep in and went into the bathroom to change. When I came back to the room, Alex was already in bed without a shirt on. My eyes traveled down to the scar on his stomach. He caught my gaze and covered his stomach with the blanket. Still too sore a subject to talk about. For either of us.

I slid into bed and lay on my side, facing him. The urge to stay as close to the edge as possible was overwhelming. I wondered if Alex would want to cuddle like we used to. I got the answer when his hand moved to rest gently on my hip.

He looked into my eyes, and I saw the guy I was once so crazy about. His gaze only showed warmth and devotion. But now I knew who he was. That he would have let the society kill me if that's what they had chosen. *Unlike Niko.* That thought wouldn't leave my head. Niko had kept my secrets. Alex's hand tightened on my hip, and I focused back on him. I had seen the coldness Alex had in him the night he had found me. In my eyes, the man I had fallen in love with was dead.

I woke up with a stiff neck and realized it was still the middle of the night. I didn't want to roll closer to Alex, and lying on a sliver of the mattress wasn't great for deep sleep. My eyes went to the ceiling when Alex's phone went off, making a soft glow light up the room.

My mind went into overdrive when an idea popped into my head. A very stupid idea. But as my heart leaped into my throat, I decided I was going to do it anyway. I'd been here months and hadn't found one single useful thing about the society. It was time to change that.

Carefully rolling out of the bed, I glanced at Alex, who was snoring softly. He had always been a deep sleeper, which worked to my benefit. Tiptoeing around the bed, I reached for his phone on the nightstand. I had been wrong about it being the middle of the night. It was almost six in the morning. I glanced at the notification that had gone off. It was an ad, nothing he'd worry about missing.

Keeping the phone on the table, I quickly typed in his passcode. I'd known what it was for weeks but was never alone with his phone long enough to use it. I peeked at the bed to make sure Alex was still sleeping with his back facing me. My heart was racing, and my fingers trembled as I went into his *Notes*. I frowned, finding nothing useful. Deciding to go through his texts, I scrolled through the conversation with his dad.

My excitement began to fade as I read through the messages. They were careful not to mention anything about the society. If they did, it was so hidden I couldn't even tell. My hope of finding enough to expose them was disappearing more every day. I froze when I saw something I recognized.

His dad had sent him an address. The same address I saw in Geo's phone. It had to be connected to the society in some way. I stared at the address, memorizing it. Closing everything out on his phone, I locked it again. With one last look at Alex, I snuck out of the bedroom.

"Lake Drive," I muttered as I repeated the numbers in my head. The second I read numbers, I forgot them. I needed to remember this until I got to a pen and paper. Running down the hall, I rushed into the kitchen, not even stopping to turn on a light. I'd been here so long, I didn't need a light to see where I was going. I pulled open the drawer and grabbed the notepad before rifling through the junk to try and find a pen.

"What are you doing?"

"Fuck." I nearly shut the drawer on my hand as I jumped.

Whirling around, I could just make Niko out in the darkness as he sat at the table. He had a glass in his hand, and I knew it was tequila on ice. That was his drink of choice besides water. I groaned when I realized the address had disappeared from my mind after him scaring the hell out of me. Now I was going to have to go back into Alex's phone again.

"What are you doing, Sage?" he repeated, standing up and setting his glass down.

"Um." I bit my lip as he advanced closer. I had learned to think fast since I'd been here, but I couldn't come up with one good excuse. "I needed water."

"From the drawer?"

I crossed my arms. "It's none of your business what I was doing. I live here too. If I want to do something in the middle of the night, I can."

"Hmm," he hummed out, leaning over me and grabbing the counter on either side of my waist. His usual minty scent was mingled with alcohol as he brought his face only inches from mine. "How was your first night with Alex?"

His voice had a hard edge, and I scowled. "Fine."

"Are you ever going to admit what we both know?"

"And what would that be?"

"That you don't want him." He lowered his head until his lips brushed my neck. "That the thought of him touching you like this makes you want to run away screaming."

Goosebumps trailed over my skin as his lips grazed down my neck. Niko had kept my secrets so far. But I didn't trust him. Not with everything. He refused to open up about the society, which meant he was still loyal to them.

"What are you doing up?" I asked, changing the subject.

His lips left my body, but he stayed in front of me. "Couldn't sleep."

"Why?"

"Because the thought of him touching you like this is my own personal fucking nightmare."

I sucked in a breath when his hands went from the counter to grasping my hips. I wasn't sure if it was the tequila talking or not. "Is it just about sex to you?"

"What do you think, Sage?"

"I don't know what to think anymore," I muttered, trying to ignore the growing heat between us as he held on to me.

A beeping rang through the silence, and the warmth of Niko's hands immediately disappeared as he hastily stepped back.

"Alex's alarm." He stated what we both already knew. "Better get back in there before he realizes you're gone."

His blank expression was back, which meant he was done talking. Shaking my head, I didn't say a word as I left the kitchen. Hoping I could slip back into bed before Alex woke up, I snuck down the hall. Alex had to set five alarms to wake up. There was a good chance he'd still be asleep.

"It's not just about sex."

Niko's quiet admission hit me like a wall, but I was too tired and confused to think about it. And now I'd have to wait another night to get that address from Alex's phone. It had been a long damn night. I breathed out a sigh of relief when Alex hadn't moved an inch. Lifting the blankets, I lay down and buried my face in the pillow, praying for sleep to claim me.

CHAPTER THIRTY-FIVE

Sage

Opening my eyes, the first thing I saw was Alex staring back at me.

"Morning," he said as he gave me a kiss on my forehead.

"Hi," I replied, after yawning. It felt like I'd gotten absolutely no sleep last night.

"I'm going to take a shower before I go see my dad later," I muttered. The shower was needed to wash the night off. And hopefully, the hot water would help my aching neck.

Alex nodded and stayed in bed. I was relieved. For a second, I was worried he would want to join me.

Stepping into the shower, I didn't move a muscle as I stood under the scorching water. Staying here was bad, but sharing a room with him made it almost intolerable. I had no personal space. Reaching for my body wash, I tossed it back down when I realized it was empty. I eyed the other two bottles before grabbing Niko's. It was better than smelling like Alex all day.

The hot water rolled down my back as my thoughts drifted to sharing a bed with Alex. One night was hard enough. I couldn't imagine doing it every single night. I was falling so deep into this life I wasn't sure I'd make it out alive anymore.

My breaths started coming faster and faster. I attempted to take a deep breath but suddenly had no control of my breathing. My heartbeat was climbing, and I braced my hands on the wall for support. The room started spinning. Panic built as my body spiraled out of control.

This time I knew what it was. It was the same thing that happened in Kalamazoo. A panic attack. Niko's face drifted through my mind as I remembered the concern he'd had. His voice. His touch. Thinking about it wasn't enough to stop my chest from locking up. But the pressure was staying constant instead of building more.

I fell to my knees with the body wash still tight in my grip. Trying to suck in air, I focused on what Niko had done to calm me. Senses. I needed to get out of my head.

Water poured down my head, and I caught a hint of chlorine. But the scent was gone as quickly as it came. Twisting the cap off the soap, I put it under my nose and inhaled as much as I could while my chest continued to tighten. Niko's scent surrounded me, bringing my mind away from Alex and back to last night when Niko's lips were on my neck.

Opening my eyes, I focused on my car key that was sitting on the tub ledge. I had an escape plan if I needed one. I sat there, keeping my stare on the key. The water gurgled as it went down the drain, and I held the soap under my nose, trying to push the nightmares out of my head. After what felt like forever, I was able to start taking deep breaths.

My breathing finally returned to normal, and I dropped the body wash. Slowly standing up, I stepped out of the tub and dried off. After wiping the fog off the mirror, I stared at my reflection. My eyes were red, but nothing too noticeable. I didn't want Alex asking if I was okay. Breaking down in front of him was something I couldn't do. The fact that thinking of Niko helped pull me out of my panic was another thing I didn't want to deal with.

After throwing on a pair of sweats and a tank top, I left the bathroom and crossed the hall to my room. My eyes widened, and I sucked in a breath as I stood in the doorway. All my clothes were pulled out of the dresser. My bags were emptied on the floor. My heart plummeted. The phone. I stared at the room for a full two minutes before Alex cleared his throat from the living room.

There was no point in waiting even longer. I forced my feet to move until I was at the end of the hall to see Alex sitting on the couch with my phone in his grip. A charging cord was connected to it and plugged into the wall behind him. He looked at me, and the eyes that had been full of love were gone. Replaced with the icy stare that sent chills up my spine.

"You have something to tell me?" Alex asked without breaking eye contact.

"No—"

I stopped talking and glanced over my shoulder when Niko's door opened. His basketball shorts hung low on his hips, and his chest was bare as he rubbed his eyes. He glanced up and looked like he was about to start his usual banter until he met my gaze.

"What's going on?" he asked, peeking past me into the living room. A look of understanding briefly crossed his face before his expression went blank. He walked over to the couch and stood where he could see both Alex and me.

"You planning on going somewhere, Sage?" Alex asked.

"Alex—no. That phone was from before you found me." My voice was higher than normal, and I moved closer to him to try to prove my words.

"So why hide it?"

"I don't know. Habit. I only used it to call my dad. You can look at the phone log. That's all that's on there," I told him, grateful I had deleted Kiara's information. Lying wasn't hard anymore. There was no heat rushing to my face. My voice stayed even. I had learned something over all these long months.

Alex turned on the phone, and silent tension filled the room as it powered up. Niko's usual grin was replaced with a pissed-off scowl. I knew he was regretting letting me keep the phone. Alex seemed to be studying my reaction. Finally, the phone was on, and I held my breath. I had checked at least three times that everything except my dad's number was deleted. But that didn't stop the paralyzing fear. Alex took his time looking through it. Eventually, he put it down beside him.

"If that's all it was for, then why keep it hidden?" His voice lost the hardness.

"I didn't really think about it. I hid it the day I got here and just forgot."

Alex nodded. It looked like he believed me. Until he turned his attention to Niko.

"How did you not find it when you searched for the paper? You said you tore her room apart."

"I did," Niko ground out, his face not giving anything away, but at the same time, he didn't try to give an explanation.

"I had it," I spoke up, my gaze cutting back to Alex.

Alex's eyes narrowed. "What?"

"I was scared you'd find it and not understand. I kept it on me most days."

"On you?" Alex asked as the trust I'd been working so hard on was diminishing from his face.

"Yes. In my bra," I muttered.

Why the hell did I say that? There was half a chance he was going to search me and find my key. The one saving grace of getting me out of here if I needed it. I purposely didn't look at Niko as Alex stayed silent and stared at me. Why was I protecting Niko? I should be doing everything for myself. To survive this. I guess, in a way, I was. I'd rather have Niko here than Geo. If Alex didn't trust Niko, then I'd be stuck with someone else every day. That was the only reason I'd lied.

"Sage, this isn't going to work if you're not honest." Suspicion still lit up his eyes as he spoke. "Do you have anything else?"

"No. That was it. I swear," I promised, stepping closer to the couch.

Niko spared me a small glance, but I couldn't tell what he was thinking. Was he surprised I'd lied for him? Because I was still reeling from it. Alex tossed my phone onto the couch, shaking his head.

"Were you searching through my stuff?" I tried not to sound defensive. One night in the same room and this happened. It would only get worse.

"No. I was moving your clothes to make room for mine."

"Oh," was all I could think to say. I should have realized he'd do that.

"Sage, I know these last few months have been hard on you. But if you're thinking of running again—"

"I'm not."

"The group wants to make sure that doesn't happen," Alex said with a cold calmness.

I didn't like the sound of where this was heading. Dread claimed my already growing nerves as I waited for him to continue.

"They wanted me to give you a message. And I've waited this long because I don't want to hurt you. And I don't want you to think it's me that's saying this, because it's not."

Alex paused, and I glanced at Niko, who was trying to cover a confused look. Even he didn't know what Alex was going to say.

"They don't want you running. They want assurance that you won't—"

"I've been here for months, and I haven't," I cut him off, terrified of what he was going to say. They couldn't do much more to me.

"I know, baby. And like I said, this isn't me. But they want me to tell you."

"Just spit it out, Alex," I yelled, tired of tiptoeing around him.

"Sage—"

"I'm so sick of being scared of what might happen. Just tell me so I can deal with it," I said more softly, unable to believe I had just snapped like that. Months of being careful and making sure he trusted me could have just been wiped away.

"They threatened your dad—if you run away again," Alex answered sharply.

All I could do was stare.

CHAPTER THIRTY-SIX

Him

My jaw dropped, and I quickly snapped it shut before Sage looked at me. Her face was impossible to read at the moment. Even I couldn't believe Alex had said that.

"They what?" she asked with a dead stare.

"I'm not going to say it again. I feel horrible for even saying it once. I didn't want to, but they said it needed to be done," Alex said, his tone subdued.

She stood there, her body rigid. My heart jerked seeing the defeated look in her eyes. Her dad was the only important person she had left in her life. Everybody in this house knew it. Without another word, she ran back to the room and slammed the door.

"I think you're going to be back on the couch tonight," I murmured, shaking my head. "What the hell were you thinking?"

He jumped up and motioned for me to follow him. We went out to the front porch, and Alex made sure the door was closed before he started talking.

"I think I'm going to regret that," he muttered as he sat down in the lone chair.

"You think?" I replied sarcastically.

"I just wanted to make sure she wasn't going to run again." He leaned over and put his head in his hands.

"She's been here for months and hasn't done anything," I said, knowing Alex would flip out if I was honest about the paper and truck key Sage had taken.

"I know. Finding that phone scared me."

"Did the elders really tell you that?"

He hesitated. "No."

I breathed a small sigh of relief. The group wouldn't involve innocents unless they absolutely had to.

"Do you really think she still loves me?" he asked.

"After what you just told her, she needs to calm down. But if you make sure she knows it wasn't your idea, I think it'll be okay. You've forgiven each other for worse." I didn't bat an eye as I lied to my brother's face. There was no way Sage loved him. Though she had gotten good at the front she put on for Alex. The wine she drank every night probably helped.

"I just want things to go back to how they were. We would have had a great life if the trip up north had never happened," Alex muttered bitterly.

That definitely would have made my life easier. Then I wouldn't be fighting with myself about the right way of life. The group and the greater good would still be my main focus. Instead of questioning everything.

"I guess we won't have to worry about her running now." There was a hint of remorse, but it was quickly fading.

I didn't say anything. Alex had told her the one thing that guaranteed she wouldn't run again. And we all knew it.

"I think I'm going to go to Mom and Dad's house today. Not sure she'll really want to see me right now." He stood up. "You good to keep an eye on her?"

I grimaced. She wouldn't want to be around either of us today. When I did see her, I was going to get a fucking earful.

"Yeah, that's fine." I leaned against the railing. "I'm always here anyway."

Alex went into my room to get changed before leaving the house. I made some food and settled in for a movie, knowing she wasn't going to come out anytime soon. I almost wished she'd stay in the room. It wasn't going to be a fun conversation when I saw her. But she'd show herself eventually. She had to eat, and I'd quickly learned that she couldn't function on an empty stomach. After a few hours, footsteps padded quietly down the hall.

"He left a while ago, if that's what you're worried about," I called out to her, not having the heart to throw out a sarcastic remark. I knew how badly she was hurting from what Alex had said.

After peeking into the kitchen, she came into the living room. She was wearing a pair of baggy sweatpants and a tank top. Her wild fiery red hair was finally free of the dull brown dye, and it was impossible to ignore her raw beauty.

Except she didn't fully look like herself. Her usually strong-willed eyes were broken. I'd never seen that look on her before. Ever. Not at the house up north. Or when I found her in Kalamazoo. Or even when we found her in Chicago. She finally understood there was no way out.

"Was he telling the truth?" she asked the second she sat down on the couch next to me.

I knew this was coming. I was caught in the middle again. Between my family and this woman who, for some reason, made me question everything.

"What if I say he wasn't? You going to leave?" I asked, treading carefully. I didn't want her thinking her dad was in danger. But I also wasn't about to call out my brother for lying.

"No. I just want to know."

"Don't run and everything will be fine."

"That's not an answer."

"Yes it is, Sage. You told me you're in it for the long haul. Because you *love* Alex."

Her eyes gleamed dangerously. "It's my dad. I need to know the truth."

"You were going to try to leave, weren't you?" I asked quietly. That was the reason she was so angry. Alex had ruined whatever she had planned. Since she was already mad, I might as well get everything out on the table.

"Who was that woman you were meeting down in Chicago?" I asked, curious if she'd tell me the truth.

She swallowed her shock quick, but not fast enough for me not to notice.

"I don't know what you're talking about."

"The day we found you. I saw you in a café with her."

"If Alex saw me with anyone else—"

"Alex didn't see you. I did. He didn't catch up to me until you were leaving the café. I never told him."

She stared at me in disbelief.

"Who is she? You hugged, so you have to know her pretty well."

She didn't answer, so I asked a different question.

"What did you clear off your laptop the night you got here?"

She kept her mouth closed, with obviously no plan to answer me, and my annoyance flared.

"Really, Sage? I've done all I could. I've kept your secrets. I'm still keeping them. From my own family. And you can't come clean about two questions?"

"Come clean? To you? To the man tasked with babysitting me?" she sneered. The broken look was gone and was replaced with a fierceness that unnerved even me. She would never stop fighting.

"I've helped—"

"You've helped because of your guilt. Your twin killed Lacey. You were there. Part of your fucked-up cult ceremony." She was throwing it all out there.

I stayed silent, knowing it was about time we talked about it. I had been dreading it. I barely liked thinking about it.

"My life is so messed up that I don't completely loathe the guy whose job it is to watch me." She laughed darkly. "Do you realize how messed up all of this is?"

"Yeah, I do," I muttered.

"You do? You don't think it's some normal thing because that's what your society thinks? It's just normal to sacrifice people. It's normal to hunt down people who find out about their secret. I'm going to be stuck with you and your brother for a long time. I really want to know what you think about all this." She took a breath, glaring at me.

I averted my gaze. She clearly wanted an answer. But nothing I said would make her feel better. To my group and my family—yes, that was normal. But now, I wasn't as sure. The questions I'd been asking myself ever since this all started had been taunting me.

"Why don't you wear your ring anymore?" she asked me quietly.

"What?"

"Your ring. The ring the society wears. Before the trip up north, you wore it all the time. I never saw you without it. Just like Alex. You had it around your neck when you found me in Kalamazoo. But I haven't seen it since I've been here."

"Aren't you observant? That doesn't mean much. Half of the group doesn't wear theirs in public. The thing can attract attention." I didn't know why I was being defensive. The loyalty to the group, that's why. It was engrained in me. The group came before anything else.

"Or maybe it's because the guilt of what you've been a part of has made you see things differently," Sage said softly.

I became guarded. What was she playing at?

"Niko, I can see you've changed. The way you are with me when Alex isn't around. Even back when you found me. You still had your asshole attitude, but something was different about you. For one, you came to warn me. You don't talk about the society like Alex does. You seem to have distanced yourself. Even from your parents. It's okay to change." She finished her speech and watched me thoughtfully.

I was irritated with how easily she'd picked up all that. Sharing my thoughts wasn't something I ever enjoyed. "Doesn't matter what I think. Your life. Your dad's life. Not up for me to decide anything. You chose to be with Alex. To be with him and survive. You got your wish."

"But if you feel different, then you can stand up and do something. You could help me—"

I bolted off the couch. "And there it is. You want me to help you? I have helped you, Sage. There's only so much I can do, and I've done it."

"But you could—"

"That whole speech was just to soften me up, to get my help. Wasn't it?" I asked harshly, hating that her manipulation had actually struck a chord inside me.

She stood up and faced me. "No. Not entirely. I have seen a change in you. I'm just not sure it's enough. That I can trust you fully."

At least she was honest. But I couldn't have her thinking that I would do anything for her. Not at the cost of hurting my family. Or the fact that no matter what she did, there was no getting out.

"Let me spell it out for you. I helped you. I'll keep helping you in the small ways that I can. I will not help you leave. I won't do anything that hurts my brother, my family, or the group. So, if you have plans to do that, better keep your mouth shut." I didn't take my eyes off her. I had gotten good at being able to tell how she was really feeling, even when she tried hiding it.

"You're lying."

"What?" That was about the last thing I'd expected to come out of her mouth.

"You're lying. I think you would do whatever you could to make sure I'm okay. I think you and Alex are both lying about going after my dad. If it were true, you would've been trying to convince me not to run straight from the start of this conversation. Like you tried to convince me to keep hiding when you found me." Her stare seemed to be piercing through me.

"You're really going to take that chance with your dad?" I asked, gulping down the shock her words caused.

"I don't know. But let's be honest. My dad is sick." She stopped and took a deep breath. "He doesn't have a lot of good years left. When he is gone, your group won't have anything to threaten me with."

I was speechless. She must be very comfortable with me to blurt that out. She finally admitted she wasn't planning on living happily ever after with Alex.

"Are you going to tell them that? Or are you going to keep another secret for me?" she asked with faked sweetness.

Anger shot through me. She was so confident that she was right about me. That I would keep lying for her. And it made me even more irritated that she was right. I would keep this to myself, like I had everything else. But it wasn't a danger to the group. She hadn't done anything. I didn't have to tell them yet. My eyes narrowed as a smug smile lit up her face.

"Listen, don't you dare think—"

I was cut off when she shoved me, knocking me back a couple of feet. Before I could get a word out, she shoved me again.

"Sage, what the hell—"

She raised her hand, and unlike the last two times, I wasn't fast enough. The sting spread over my entire cheek, and I scowled.

"Are you going to tell Alex now? Tell the group? Spill all my dirty little secrets?" She was yelling as she went to hit me again. But I was ready this time. I grabbed her wrist and gripped it tight enough to hold her still. Only for her to try hitting me with the other hand. I eventually got a hold of that one too.

"Answer me! After this, are you going to tell Alex—your baby brother—that I really don't love him?" She was still screaming, trying to squirm out of my grip.

Then she started kicking me. I grunted, attempting to get her arm behind her back and retake some kind of control, but she was struggling too hard. Letting go of her wrists, I wrapped my arms around her waist and knocked her legs out from under her. We fell in a heap on the floor. She was on top of me in a second, grabbing my arms. Twisting out of her grasp, I got a hold of her shoulders and forced her to roll until she was on the floor under me. I straddled her hips and grabbed each wrist, pressing them to the floor near her head.

"Are you going to tell him?" Her chest heaved with each breath. "You've been saying it since I got here. You're right. I don't love him. I never could again."

I didn't say anything as I caught my breath. My jaw ticked, still feeling the heat of her slap on my cheek. She was trying to crawl out from under me, but I wasn't budging.

"I'm not getting up until you stop trying to attack me," I growled. Flashbacks of getting tased were enough to know that I wasn't taking any chances.

"I want to know. If you're going to tell Alex about this whole thing."

She looked me square in the eye. I glared as she smirked. She had started this whole thing to hear the answer. The answer we both knew. But I didn't want to say it out loud. She was right. I wouldn't tell Alex. But for her to know I would go that far to protect her was dangerous. It gave her power. Control. It would give her more strength to do whatever she was planning. I couldn't protect her forever. Not from the entire group. This life was the only one she had a chance of surviving.

"What do you want from me?" I grumbled, my thoughts tearing me in two. Here I was, thinking of ways I could protect her instead of doing what the group asked. I was betraying them by keeping these secrets. But for some fucking reason, I couldn't betray her either.

She moved under me, and I realized my body hadn't gotten the memo that we were fighting. My dick was hard and pressing into her stomach as I held her down. Raising myself off her, I arched an eyebrow when she lifted her hips.

Her hazel eyes darkened. "What can I ask of you?"

I frowned, not sure where she was taking this. "I won't help you run. There's nowhere you can go that they won't find you."

"But you'll help me. In other ways. Right?"

The tension suddenly shifted as her eyes went down to my bare chest. Biting her lip, she raised her gaze back to mine, and an entirely new emotion took over her face. She wasn't struggling to get away anymore.

"I need to hear you say it, Sage," I demanded gruffly. If she gave me the answer I wanted, it was only going to make my conflicting thoughts worse.

"I don't want to take care of myself anymore," she murmured, need filling her voice. "I want you to do it. Can you help me in that way?"

Ignoring the internal screaming that this was a bad idea, I released her wrists. Pulling her off the floor, I lifted her up, and her legs wrapped around my waist. I walked forward until her back hit the wall. I waited for her to stop me. To come to her senses. But she didn't.

I shouldn't get in any deeper with her. It was too big a risk for either of us. Her arms went around me as I pressed my body into hers, and I realized it was too fucking late. I was already in so deep with her that I didn't want to reach the surface again. Not if it meant I had to leave her alone.

I trailed my lips up her neck. "I can do that."

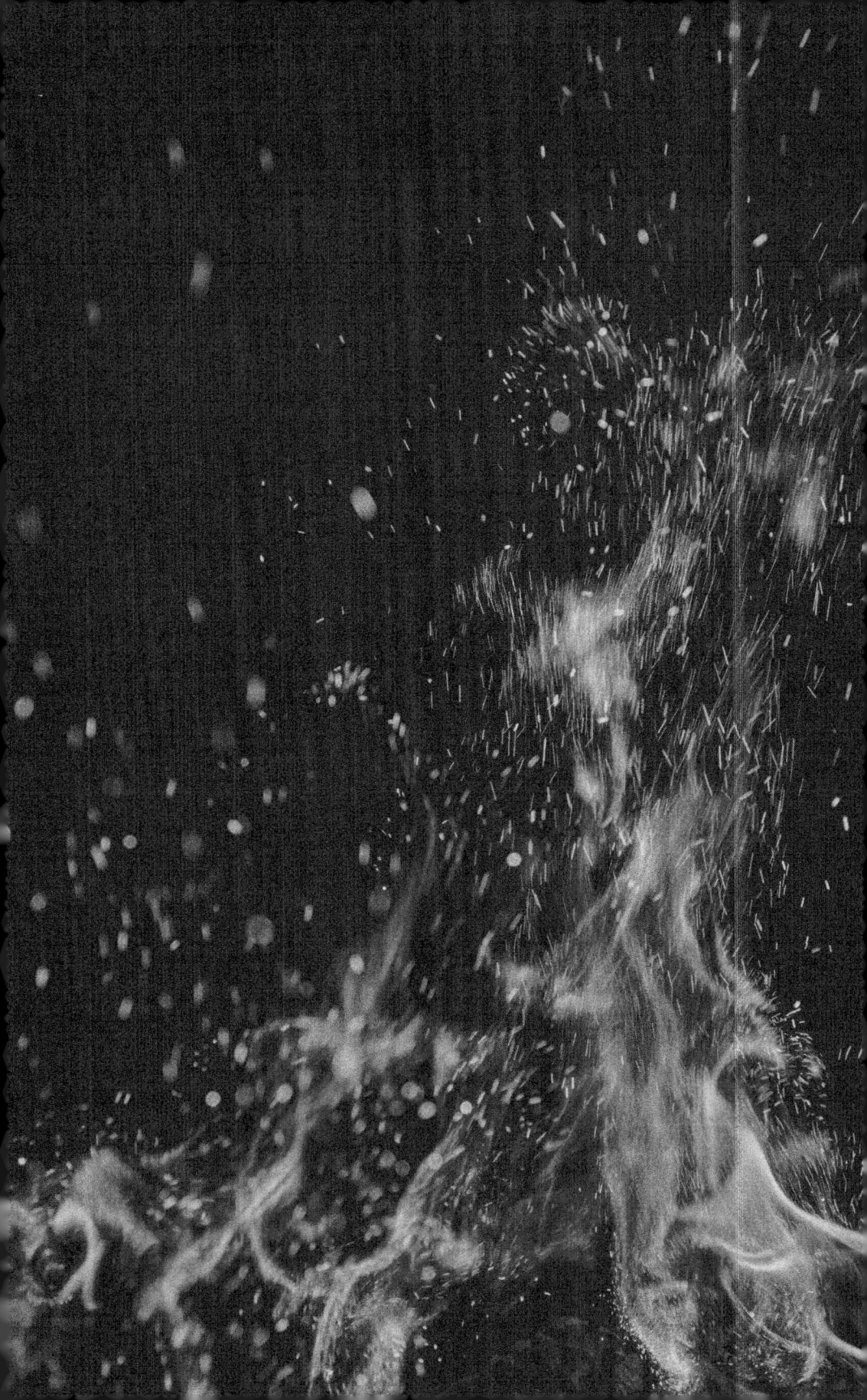

CHAPTER THIRTY-SEVEN

Sage

His hands were all over as he kept me pressed against the wall. His fingers drifted up my stomach and then under my shirt, causing my heart to thrash. I still had the key in my bra. I might trust him with certain things, but my only way out of here was not one of them. If his hands went up any farther, he was going to find it.

"Condom," I muttered, pulling away from him. "Do you have one?"

He froze, lifting his head from my neck. "Yes."

"Go get it."

He chuckled. "After all the tiptoeing we've done around this, believe me, we won't need it for a while. I want to enjoy every inch of you first."

Heat spread everywhere from his words, and I moaned as his mouth went back to my collarbone. My eyes fluttered closed before his hand got way too close to the key. I let my legs drop from his waist, and he grumbled under his breath when I pushed him away.

"Get it," I repeated. "I'm not chancing anything."

He blew out a breath. "Fine."

He stalked down the hall, and I trailed behind him. The second he was in his room, I slid into the bathroom and crouched down. Grabbing the key from my bra, I shoved it to the bottom of the closest tampon box. The last place in this entire house either of them would look. Darting up, I got to the bathroom doorway right as Niko was leaving his room. I glanced at the condom in his hand and grinned. Deciding to distract him from why I was in the bathroom, I lifted the hem of my shirt. I didn't get a chance to pull it off before he grabbed my wrists.

"Don't deny me the things I've wanted to do for months." His heated gaze roamed my face. "That includes taking off your clothes. Piece by piece. Exposing your body little by little and tasting every part as I go."

I bit my lip as my stomach flipped. It had been so long since I'd been touched like that. My body was craving it, and I wasn't even going to try to deny that it was Niko I wanted touching me.

"The couch. The kitchen counter. Or against the wall." Releasing my wrists, he stepped back. "Take your pick."

I raised an eyebrow. "The bed isn't an option?"

Hesitating, he glanced to the front window, and I realized what he meant. This wasn't some relationship where we fell madly in love. It was about the tension we'd built up over the last few months. It was a release. Nothing more.

We needed to make sure no one caught us. I was pretty sure Alex wouldn't want to keep me alive if he found out I wanted his brother instead of him. All the places Niko said gave him a view of the window so we'd know if someone pulled into the driveway.

"The couch it is," I answered, bending down and grabbing the condom he had dropped. I yelped in surprise when he picked me up bridal style and strode to the living room. Setting me down, he got on his knees between my legs as I sat on the couch.

"Watching you take care of yourself is burned into my brain," he murmured, lifting the hem of my shirt and pulling it over my head. "I can't wait to hear you. No need to be quiet this time."

He didn't waste a moment as he pulled me to the edge of the couch. His kisses were soft as he moved down my ribs. My heart beat faster when he switched to the other side, making sure his lips touched every part of me. A jolt of pleasure went straight to my pussy as he kissed my lower stomach.

Goosebumps raced over my skin when he unclipped my bra, letting it fall to the floor. My nipples grew hard, and his tongue gave them the attention I wanted as my back arched. I let my head fall back, my eyes closing as I soaked up every wave of pleasure he was giving me.

He tugged at my shorts, and I lifted myself off the couch a little to let him slip them off. My panties came off at the same time.

"Fucking perfect," he muttered, his gaze darting to every part of my body. "Do you know how much self-control I had to use the last time you were naked in front of me?"

I giggled. "I was honestly a little worried you weren't going to be able to stay on the couch once I dropped the towel."

"Believe me, so was I."

He stayed kneeling between my thighs as his mouth grazed down my leg. He was keeping his word about tasting every inch of me, and my body was on fire. He trailed all the way back up to my neck. His lips reached my jaw, and I tensed.

He noticed my change and froze. Pulling his face away from me, he raised higher on his knees until we locked eyes.

"Don't kiss me," I breathed out. "Not on the lips."

A muscle in his jaw tightened. "Why?"

"I already gave my heart to someone I thought loved me," I

muttered, not meeting his eyes as I talked about his brother. "And he chose your society over me. I won't do it again."

Without a word, he moved to stand, but I grabbed his shoulders, keeping him on his knees.

"I want this. I want you to touch me," I promised him, making him frown in confusion. "But I need to remember that this is only about sex. I can't let myself think it's anything more. If you kiss me on the lips, it'll become too personal. For me, at least."

He stared at me thoughtfully for a few moments. "If that's what you want."

"It is."

I sucked in a breath when he ran his thumb over my lips. "What if I ever change my mind?"

"About what?"

"What if I decide I need you more than the group?"

I blinked in shock, not sure what to say. I hadn't expected him to ask that. This could never be anything more than sneaky fun. We both knew that.

"Then you can kiss me," I whispered.

He nodded, ending the conversation. For a half second, I thought he was going to walk away until he grabbed my hands and pulled me up. Leading me behind the couch, he moved my hands until I was holding on to the top of the couch. Looking over my shoulder at him, I raised an eyebrow, curious about what he was doing. He shot me a mischievous grin before lowering his mouth and trailing his tongue down my spine.

I fought to stay still as he gave the back of my body the same attention as he had given the front when I was on the couch. He kissed and tasted every inch of my skin as he moved lower and lower. My thighs clenched together when his lips grazed the bottom of my spine. Tingles shot through me, and he must have realized he'd found one of my sweet spots because he paid special attention to it.

"Niko," I cried out in torment when his fingers stopped just short of my pussy for the third time. "What are you waiting for?"

"Well, now that I just heard you begging my name, I think my motivation has changed," he said, his voice low and husky. "I want to hear it again."

I bit my tongue in frustration when his thumb barely grazed my clit while his other hand focused on my nipples. Every little flick and pinch sent a spasm straight to my pussy, making my body beg for more.

"Tell me what you want, Sage."

"I want you to touch me," I whimpered, spreading my legs wider.

"I am touching you."

My face flushed, wondering if he really wanted me to spell it out to him. It was obvious he was playing at something. A shiver rolled through me as he rested his chin on my shoulder, his breaths hitting my neck.

"I want you to tell me exactly what you want me to do," he murmured in my ear. "Do you want my fingers? My mouth? Do you want me to make you beg before I make you scream?"

"Why are you asking?" I breathed out as he kissed my neck.

"Because you've lost control of everything in your life. When you're with me, I can give you a little back." I held my breath as he spoke. "You're controlling this. Whatever you want, I'll give to you."

A feeling I shouldn't let creep through me smothered my chest. He cared. Even if it was about sex, he still cared to some extent.

"I want it all," I said firmly, through ragged breaths. "Everything you want to do to me, do it."

He groaned. "Good. Because I've been dying for a taste."

Before I knew it, I was in his arms, and he was knocking the remote off the coffee table. Grabbing the throw blanket from the couch, he spread it over the table and then laid me down on my back. Dropping to his knees, he pulled me to the edge. Anticipation had me nearly clamping my thighs together when his breath hit my clit.

He delved his tongue into my pussy, and I cried out from the much-needed contact. His mouth covered my clit, and then he sucked, circling his tongue on my most sensitive spot. My hands gripped the side of the coffee table as my body quickly climbed to the edge. His arms were wrapped around my thighs, keeping his face right where he wanted it.

"Ruined," he muttered, barely lifting his head. "I'm fucking ruined."

His words didn't register with me as the strokes of his tongue overloaded my senses. I sucked in deep breaths while my legs trembled in his grasp. There wasn't a coherent thought running through my head as I crashed over the edge. I cried out as my thighs clenched, my whole body shaking.

Once my orgasm faded, I attempted to lift my legs from his shoulders, but he tightened his hold, popping his head up to glance at me.

"You gave me free rein to do whatever I wanted to you," he murmured, his eyes dark with need. "And I'm still hungry."

With those words, he dove back down. My clit was already still throbbing from my last orgasm, and it didn't take much before I was struggling against him as another overwhelming crash of pleasure hit me. This time he didn't slow down at all. His tongue lashed against my clit repeatedly until I was a trembling mess when my third orgasm ripped a scream from my lips.

"Niko," I cried out when he didn't let up. "I can't take anymore. Please."

"I could live down here and die happy." He lifted his head to look at me. "This might have been a mistake."

I went rigid, my sex daze lifting. "Why?"

"Because now I don't know how the fuck I'm going to stay away from you when my brother is home." I nearly jumped off the table when he ran a finger over my pussy. "I don't know which one I crave more. Hearing you scream my name or how you react to my touch."

He released his grip enough that I was able to pull my legs away from him. With a grin, I sank to my knees. "Want to see how you react to my touch?"

His eyes flared with heat as the bulge in his shorts grew.

Reaching forward, I grabbed his hips and pulled him closer. He grabbed my wrists, stopping me from yanking his shorts down.

"This is about what you want," he murmured, as I tilted my face up to look at him.

"You said I could control this." I shook his hold off my wrists. "So let me."

Raising an eyebrow in surprise, he raised his arms, letting me grip his shorts. I pulled them down, and his cock was rock hard as it sprang out. My heart raced as I wrapped my hand around it. He might have seen me naked before, but this was my first time seeing him. And he didn't disappoint.

I opened my mouth, running my tongue over the head of his cock. He groaned above me as I opened wider, slowly taking him in my mouth. I needed a break after the three orgasms he'd given me, but hearing how much he was enjoying this was getting me bothered all over again. I affected him too. Creating a suction, I pressed my tongue against him and sucked. He grabbed the arm of the couch, his eyes staying locked on me.

"Fuck," he ground out. "I'd be happy dying this way too."

Hollowing out my cheeks, I took as much of him as I could, moving faster until he stiffened. I knew he was close, but before he finished, he pulled away.

"Not yet," he muttered, tugging me to my feet.

He backed up and fell onto the couch, bringing me with him. I straddled his legs as he grabbed the condom and ripped open the foil. He rolled it on as I bit my lip. There was no going back after this. I shook my head. It was too late for that the second he'd put his mouth on me. And I didn't want to go back. His touch was everything I needed.

"Are you sure, Sage?" he asked, seriousness coating his voice. "Your life is already chaos. Doing this might make it worse."

Grabbing his shoulders, I lifted myself up and slid down onto his cock. He hissed out a breath as he filled me.

"I'm sure," I answered when he was fully inside me. "It's just sex."

His gaze dropped to my lips. "Right."

A bit of tension raised between us, but he didn't make a move to kiss me. I didn't know if I was happy or disappointed. I knew how he felt about the society. He might care for me, but he was still loyal to them. At least he was honest about it.

"Take control, Sage," he told me, grabbing my hips. "This is about what you want."

Without another word, I began grinding back and forth. I couldn't help but think about the first time I was sitting on him like this back in Kalamazoo. So much for my promise of it never happening again. I went slow at first and then faster once I found a rhythm. His hands left my hips before traveling up to my breasts. He gently rolled my nipples between his fingers, his touch growing firmer the more I moved. He pinched them right as I came again.

I went still, wrapping my arms around his neck as I caught my breath. He put his arms around me before standing up. He moved forward until my bare back hit the wall. He pulled away, only to plunge back into me. My arms stayed wrapped around his neck as he continued to ram into me.

I clawed my nails across his back, forgetting we shouldn't be leaving physical marks on each other. At the moment, I really didn't give a shit. It felt too good. He pummeled into me, and I tried keeping my shaking legs around his waist. He grunted, slamming into me one more time before going still. Keeping me pressed against the wall, he rested his head on my shoulder.

"Watching you spiral from pleasure is something that will play on repeat in my head," he muttered.

"You won't need to do that," I managed to say between breaths. "You can see it in person whenever you want."

"I'll hold you to that."

CHAPTER THIRTY-EIGHT

Him

S ex.
　　　Food.
　　　　　Naked conversations.
　　More sex.
　　I'd be lying if I said the past month hadn't been one of the best times in my life. It was obvious she didn't trust me fully. I expected it. I still hadn't kissed her on the lips. I didn't think I ever would. This wouldn't last forever. It had been ten months since she ran from up north. Four months since we'd been in this house. And I had a feeling Alex was getting sick of having me around. He'd been trying to get closer to Sage, wanting things to start moving forward.
　　I was going to enjoy every second with her. Which was why I was tongue deep in her pussy right now. She was leaning against the

wall, and her thighs were clenching around my head as I kneeled under her. The way she reacted to my touch made my thirst for her never-ending. When I used my fingers. Tongue. Cock. It didn't matter. Anything I did had her writhing. I fucking loved it. Every moan. Every scream. I swallowed it all up and dove back in to do it again.

Her legs shook as she tried to stay standing, and my grip on her hips tightened to keep her upright. Her fingers were knotted in my hair, silently pleading for me to go faster. Usually I would have given her an orgasm already, but this time was different. We were going to have a conversation first, and she wasn't getting off until she gave me the answer I wanted. There was more than half a chance she was going to tell me to fuck off.

"Niko," she moaned out my name, making my dick twitch. "Please."

I pulled away from her pussy and glanced up at her, ignoring her protests. "I need you to do something for me."

Curiosity flared in her eyes as she grinned. "Miss my mouth already?"

Jesus. If I didn't spit it out right this second, I'd put it off another day. Like I'd been for a week. Standing up, I pressed against her, letting my fingers replace where my tongue had been. The back of her head hit the wall when I circled her clit.

"Sage. Look at me," I ordered, making her gaze snap to mine. "After today, the drinking is done. You need to stop."

Her relaxation fizzled out as her eyes went cold. "No."

"You went from a couple glasses to almost two bottles a night—in four months." I didn't stop rubbing her clit as I spoke. "It's only going to get worse. Soon, drinking at night won't be enough. It's going to turn into an all the time thing."

"It's the only thing that numbs me," she muttered as she failed to stop reacting from what my hand was doing. Her back arched when I slowed down. "When I have to look at him. Talk to him. It helps me not feel."

I knew that. And understood it. But she was slipping away. Every time she drank, her eyes glazed over into someone I didn't recognize. It made me sick. If she kept going, the things that made her who she was would disappear.

I couldn't sit here and watch that happen. Even though I'd been trying to block it out, it was becoming impossible. Because it wasn't just about sex. Even with everything still between us, she'd opened up a lot in the last month. I'd heard her laugh. Her infectious giggling until she worked herself up so much that she snorted, and then her face would flush pink. I'd try to get her to laugh just to see that blush.

She'd tell me sly jokes and then explain them as if I didn't get it, laughing until tears filled her eyes. She had an obsession with reality shows and would binge one until she finished the entire series. I acted like they bored me, but she always filled me in if I missed any episodes so we could keep watching together. I enjoyed everything we did together. Fuck. It would have been easier if it were only about sex.

"No more drinking." I stood my ground as she glared at me. "Or no more orgasms."

Her mouth fell open. "What?"

She nearly jumped when I pinched her clit. I didn't stop moving my fingers, and she dug her nails into my wrist. Her breathing quickened, and she lost focus of the conversation. She bit her lip, and I froze before she got to the edge.

"Promise me that after today, you'll stop drinking," I murmured in her ear, sliding a finger inside her. "Then you can come."

She blew out a shaky laugh. "Why? So, I can trade one addiction for another?"

I frowned. "You think I'm as bad as the wine you drink?"

"No." She locked eyes with me. "I think you're worse."

Damn, that hurt.

"You're an addiction I never want to quit," she whispered, a bit of fear flashing through her gaze. "Only I know this won't last much longer. Once it ends, I'll be craving it every single fucking day. Then I feel guilt. Because I shouldn't be thinking about you like this. Your brother—your twin killed my sister. I should hate you as much as I hate Geo and Alex. But I don't. And I don't know why. At least I know with alcohol, I can numb all that too."

The pain in her eyes held me hostage as we stared at each other. I couldn't tell her it was going to be okay. She couldn't just choose me over Alex. She'd be with him for the rest of her life. Even if she did have the chance, so much shit had happened. There would always be doubt and resentment.

I tore my eyes from her when I heard something from outside. My jaw clenched, and I hurriedly stepped away from her as I watched Alex park his Jeep in the driveway. We'd been ridiculously careful this last month, but I'd lost track of time while we talked. The passenger door opened, and dread swamped me as Geo stepped out. We'd barely talked the last couple of months.

Sage peeked out the window, going tense when she saw both of my brothers. Snatching her jeans off the floor, she shoved past me.

"I'll be in my room." She didn't even turn to look at me while she got to the hall.

"No more wine," I reminded her. Even though the conversation had gone sideways, I was still going to get her to stop.

Shooting me a death glare over her shoulder, she didn't say a word before disappearing into her room. A few seconds later, the front door opened, and Alex strolled in with Geo right behind him.

"She's in her room," I told Alex before he could ask. Glancing at Geo, I added, "She saw you through the window."

"Thanks," Alex muttered, heading straight to the bathroom.

"What's his problem?" I asked as he sat at the kitchen table. The shower turned on, and I sat down across from Geo, leaning back in the chair.

"Dad still isn't happy about Sage being here." He kept his voice quiet, glancing at the hall. "He thinks she's too big a liability."

"She's done everything we've told her." I shut my mouth when Geo raised his eyebrow.

"I thought your babysitting job was a burden?"

"I've learned to coexist," I snapped, feeling my usual defenses pop back into place. "For my sanity."

"Alex says she wants nothing to do with him."

"She spends every night with him."

He scoffed. "You know what I mean."

Letting my face stay neutral, I kept the surprise to myself. Alex and Geo had gotten closer this last year. If I was being honest, it had been like that for the last couple of years. Even before all this happened. Geo and I used to be connected at the hip. That slowly changed once we graduated from high school. Alex and Geo went headfirst into anything that dealt with the group. I did what was asked of me but didn't do it in my spare time like they did.

Alex wanted to please our father. The best way he knew to do that was through the group. It worked. He and our dad had the best relationship, and now Alex was close to the elders. Geo seemed to enjoy all the worst parts of the group. The kidnappings. Keeping the women in the house. The sacrifices.

The women were supposed to be respected. They were the reason for our entire belief. But Geo felt they were beneath him. That they were there for the sole purpose of dying for the group. He didn't care how they were treated, as long as the ceremony got done. A few years ago, when he told me his thoughts and found out I didn't agree, he began distancing himself. We were still close, but there was a ripple that never left.

He pulled out his phone. "I'm going out on a date tonight. And she has a hot best friend who wants to meet you. We're meeting them at six for dinner."

"And if I already had plans?" I had no desire to go out. There was only one girl I wanted to spend time with.

Geo scowled, glancing up from his phone. "What fucking plans?

You've barely left this house in months. Even when Alex is here, you don't want to go anywhere. Don't you miss how it was?"

No, I didn't, but I wouldn't admit that to him. Our days had consisted of working, while we spent the nights out partying. Drinking, girls, and hangovers that lasted the entire next day. It wasn't like I didn't enjoy it. We always had fun. But I did it because after doing everything for the group, it felt like all the partying was a slice of normalcy. When I went out, I was like every other person in their twenties, having fun.

"Is it because of Sage?" he questioned, staring at me. "Is she giving you what she refuses to give to Alex?"

I rolled my eyes as my heart rate increased. "No. You really think she would want anything to do with me after the part I played in her sister's death?"

Geo didn't answer as he studied my face. He could usually pick up on my lies better than anyone. But not this time. This was one secret I'd take to my grave. After a few moments, he shook his head and laughed.

"Come on, let's get some drinks before we meet the girls for dinner." He stood up and gave me a pointed look as he waited for me to follow him. I glanced down the hall before getting up and grabbing my keys. I didn't have one logical reason to not go. Maybe it would ease his suspicion. I wasn't going home with whoever he was trying to set me up with. I'd go to dinner and act like Geo wanted me to, and then I'd come home.

I hated leaving Sage alone with Alex. I wondered if she'd actually listen to me about not drinking. I guess I'd find out.

CHAPTER THIRTY-NINE

Sage

I'd heard the front door slam over an hour ago, but I was still hiding in my room. I wasn't sure if Geo was still here, and I didn't want to see him at all. Or Alex. Since Niko hadn't come knocking, I was almost positive he was the one who left. Which meant Alex was here. I knew I'd have to show my face eventually. My body was still on edge from the orgasm I didn't get, thanks to him coming home. I'd almost finished myself off, but the chance of Alex walking in on me vetoed that thought immediately.

My gaze went to the phone sitting on the dresser. Alex had given it back to me, apologizing for how he'd acted. He told me I could call my dad any time I wanted. I was guessing he was trying to build trust. There wasn't any. He or Niko could check the phone whenever they wanted. Although I had snuck a few texts to Kiara and then deleted any evidence of it.

"Sage," Alex called from somewhere in the house. "If you're not busy, I need to talk to you."

Ice chilled my veins as I stayed frozen on the bed. Anytime he wanted to talk, fear took over. The chance that the society had changed their mind about me was always in the back of my mind. Sneaking around with Niko only made it worse because it was one more thing I needed to worry about. But it didn't scare me enough to stop what we were doing.

Taking a large breath, I forced myself to stand and made my way to the door. My steps were slow as I moved down the hall, and I scanned the empty living room before turning to look at the kitchen.

"Hey," Alex said softly as he looked up from his laptop. He was sitting at the little card table and looked to be waiting for me to come out.

"Hi." I unclenched my fists and tried to relax. He looked nervous, and I had a feeling I wasn't going to enjoy this conversation. I needed wine.

With hesitation, I sank into the chair across from him. An awkward silence settled over the table as I waited for him to speak up.

"Tomorrow is Sunday. And my parents would really like both Niko and me to come. It's been a while since we've all had dinner together." He paused, as if thinking of what to say next.

A rush of renewed hope flowed through me. Did he trust me enough to leave me alone? Being in a house with no one else for the first time in months would be a dream. Maybe the threat of my dad was enough that he thought I wouldn't run. I could call Kiara. I had texted her a few times, assuring her that I was safe, but talking to her would help so much. To hear a friendly voice.

"I was thinking we could all go."

Alex's words broke through my excitement. Reality crashed down on the feeling of hope. Of course I had to go with them.

"Your parents want to see me?" I asked while holding back tears of disappointment.

He sighed. "I know this is hard for you. But if we're going to be together, my parents come along with that. We aren't going to talk about anything you don't want to."

That meant they wouldn't talk about the society. They planned to keep me in the dark forever. But maybe there was something at their house. Evidence about the society. If I was going to be forced to go there, I could at least try to be productive.

He continued, "I think it would help them feel better to know that you're trying to become part of the family."

"Sure, I'll go," I mumbled. Like I had a choice. I didn't know who would feel better, his parents or the society, but didn't care enough to ask. It would only cause an argument.

He beamed and leaned across the table, kissing me on the cheek. It took all my strength not to dodge it.

"Want to watch a movie together?" Alex asked, hope in his voice. He wanted everything to be good. For it to be normal again. It never would. There was no way I was spending the rest of my life like this. But for now, I would. To keep my dad safe. It was hard to admit, even to myself, that for the last month, escaping hadn't been on my mind as much as it should.

"Do you want some wine?" I asked nonchalantly, Niko's words rushing through my head. Technically, he told me to stop drinking *after* today. I could enjoy my wine one more night.

"Have you even eaten dinner yet?" he asked.

"Yes," I lied, my usual appetite gone from our conversation. "It's always nice to watch a movie with some wine."

He shrugged. "Sure."

I smiled. "I'll get it. You pick the movie."

Alex headed to the couch as I opened the cabinet. I took out the bottle of wine and saw Niko's stash of tequila. I debated for half a second. He probably wouldn't even notice. I quickly twisted the cap off the liquor and took a long gulp. The bitter taste traveled down and warmed my chest. Usually, I needed a chaser after liquor, but there wasn't time for that. I reached for the glasses in the other cabinet, and after setting them down, took another shot from the bottle. Opening the wine bottle, I took one more drink before quietly putting the tequila away. That should help make watching the movie more bearable.

I took a sip of the wine as I walked to the couch to help hide the smell of the tequila. Alex patted the couch right next to him. A hint that he wanted me closer than my usual attempt at sitting on opposite ends. Grateful I had found the tequila, I sat down close enough that we were almost touching.

He slipped an arm around my shoulders and pulled me to him. It was the closest we'd been since everything had happened. Even in bed every night, I kept my distance. The fresh scents of his cologne and body wash engulfed me. That smell used to be intoxicating but was now just an ugly reminder of the memories I would rather forget.

During the movie, I made any excuse I could think of to sneak another shot of tequila. By the time the movie finished, I was still feeling good. Better than good. Drunk. Numerous shots and two and a half glasses of wine were a lot, even with how much I'd drunk these last few months. Alex stretched, finally releasing me from his arm.

"I think I'm going to bed. I've been up since four this morning. I'm exhausted. You ready?"

I shook my head. "No, I'm just going to relax on the porch for a while."

Lying in that bed was the last thing I wanted. I wanted to enjoy this feeling without him being around.

"Okay. Goodnight." He gently kissed me on the cheek before heading to the room.

It was a surprise that he was going to let me go outside while he slept. Since I'd been here, going outside alone hadn't been an option. He must have really believed that I wouldn't run after threatening my dad.

Before he could change his mind, I raced outside and stepped onto the porch. It was pitch black out, and only stars lit up the sky. The usual June humidity was absent. I inhaled the fresh air and then leaned against the house when my head began spinning. I'd had way too much to drink. The light breeze shook the leaves on the trees, and I stared at them, making sure I kept still so I wouldn't spin again. Even with the amount of alcohol running through my veins, it was peaceful. Quiet. For once, no one was watching me. I was alone. Well, as alone as I could get. But that moment was short-lived when, just a couple of minutes later, Niko's truck pulled into the driveway.

Nerves jolted me from my calm state. He wasn't going to be happy when he found out I'd not only been drinking but was an inch away from being wasted. I almost went back inside but decided I'd rather deal with a pissed-off Niko than speak a word to Alex.

Niko stepped out of the truck and walked over to the porch. He stood at the bottom of the porch steps and looked up at me.

"Where's Alex?"

"Sleeping."

The look on his face showed that he as was surprised as I had been that I was out here by myself.

"Where'd you go?" I asked, curious about what he'd done all evening.

"Dinner and drinks with Geo." He paused for a moment. "And two girls."

I swallowed the hurt those words hit me with. Apparently drunk me couldn't hide my emotions well because he moved up the porch steps when he saw my face.

"I did it to get Geo off my back. Believe me, I'd rather be here."

I raised my chin, trying to keep my words clear. "You're free to do whatever you want, Niko. We aren't a thing. We fuck. That's it."

His anger brewed as he narrowed his eyes. "Are you drunk?"

I ignored him and turned away, looking back through the window to make sure Alex was still in the bedroom. Footsteps came up behind me before he grabbed my elbow and spun me around to face him.

I bristled. "Get off—"

"Really? The smell is dripping off you. Did you down a whole bottle of wine?"

"No, I only had two glasses. While watching a movie with your brother," I replied as I pulled my arm away and sauntered over to the other side of the porch.

Realization came over his face, and he frowned. "Got into my tequila, huh?"

I just giggled.

"You're going to say something stupid in front of Alex if you keep getting wasted. It's only a matter of time," he hissed, making sure to keep his voice low.

"That's why I came outside." I trailed my gaze down his body. "So I could be alone. Obviously, that's impossible."

"You're choosing to keep drinking instead of what I can give you?" he asked with a hint of resignation.

"You said I needed to stop after today." I shrugged. "It's not midnight yet. But I will take an orgasm tomorrow though."

His head snapped to the side as he checked to make sure his brother wasn't somehow listening. Seeing as how I'd just checked, I didn't share his worry. Alex was probably already passed out.

"You need to be careful of what you say when he's home," Niko snapped, his anger rising.

"Why? You worried he's going to find out you've been taking care of my needs instead of him?" I couldn't stop the words from coming out, even as his jaw ticked. Drinking when I felt all this anger probably wasn't a good combination. I wasn't in control of my emotions.

"Come on, you need to sleep this off," he said as he reached to pull me into the house.

"Don't touch me. I'm not going in that room right now," I told him, standing my ground. The fuzzy feeling was disappearing at the thought of being near Alex.

"Go lay down on the couch then. You're not staying out here by yourself like this."

He grabbed my arm again and tried to pull me to the door, but I gripped the railing and held on tight.

"Oh yeah, I forgot. Can't do what I want. My life isn't my own anymore."

He sighed and thought for a second. "Fine, stay out here. Probably better than Alex seeing you like this if he wakes up."

"Oh, did Alex tell you?" I asked, changing the subject.

"Tell me what?"

"Tomorrow we're all going to your parents' house for dinner. I'm sure it'll be a big happy family event," I exclaimed sarcastically, clapping my hands.

Apparently, he hadn't known. He stalked into the house without saying anything. I watched as he sat in the folding chair that was right near the window. I shot him a dirty look and turned around, trying to get out of my head.

I'd learned to get comfortable in this trapped life. Going to their parents' house tomorrow was not in my comfort zone. I had a feeling it was going to be terrible.

CHAPTER FORTY

Sage

I woke up feeling better than I'd expected. It probably had something to do with throwing up in the grass before I went to bed. Niko had seen me getting sick through the window and had come out to check on me. After holding back my hair, he practically carried me into the house and ordered me to go to bed. I was still so drunk I had barely cared that I had to sleep next to Alex.

After stretching, I turned around and froze, seeing Alex still sleeping. He was usually up when the sun rose. Not wanting to force a conversation, I silently slipped out of the room. I fell onto the couch and rubbed my eyes.

"Mornin', sunshine."

I groaned. "I really don't feel like talking right now."

"I'm surprised you're awake already," Niko said, sitting next to me. "After how much you drank last night, I thought we'd have to drag you out of bed."

"I'm not awake. Leave me alone."

"Might want to start getting ready if you want to shower before we leave in an hour."

My head snapped up. "What time is it?"

"Ten."

"I thought we were having dinner, not lunch."

"Dad wants us to spend the whole day over there," he said unpleasantly.

I finally glanced at him and realized he looked about as excited as I was to go.

"You don't want to go?" I asked, curiously.

"Don't know if you've noticed, but I spend most of my time here," he said sarcastically. "And with you going, I'm sure this day is just going to be great."

My stomach twisted with dread. Seeing their dad was one of the last things I wanted to do. Now I had to spend the whole day with him and be nice.

"I'm going to shower," I mumbled, heading to the bathroom.

Once I finished, I got changed, deciding to go with a sundress since the day was supposed to be scorching. I scavenged the fridge for food. Alex had jumped in the shower right when I got out. He looked so excited to be taking me to his parents.

He was living in a dream world.

Nothing in the fridge looked the least bit appetizing. I eyed the cabinet where I had drowned my problems last night. I peeked into the hall and made sure the water was still running and stepped near the door to see Niko messing with his truck. Deciding I had a minute before I got interrupted, I swung the cabinet open.

"Oh, come on," I muttered, staring at the empty shelf.

Niko must have moved his tequila. And my damn wine. I needed something to help get me through the day. For a second time, I glanced out the window, making sure Niko was still occupied. I rushed down the hall and opened his door with some hesitancy. I'd only been in here a couple of times. The room was almost identical to mine. A queen-size bed with one tall dresser. The only difference was the furniture was black, instead of light brown.

Moving to the other side of the room, I opened the drawers, quickly pushing the clothes aside and then back to their proper place. Nothing. Getting on my knees, I dropped to the floor and looked under the bed.

"Really?"

I jumped up, bashing my head on the wooden frame of the bed. Muttering curses, I rubbed my head as I turned to the door. Niko was standing there, and he looked more than a little irked.

"It's not in here. You're not getting drunk before we spend all day at my parents." He leaned against the doorframe. "I thought you weren't going to drink at all anymore."

I scowled. "You expect me to do this sober?"

He stepped farther into the bedroom and glanced back at the bathroom door before speaking.

"Get over it. You do fine faking it with Alex. And with me. You can do it for one day." His voice was just above a whisper.

"I don't fake it with you."

I darted around him, but he wrapped his arm around my waist, and he tugged me closer until my chest hit his. I tilted my head up, and my glare went ice cold as I met his eyes. He was taking advantage of Alex still being in the shower.

"You do fake it with me," he growled, his fingers digging into my hip. "Unless you really do think all we do is fuck, like you said last night."

I bit the inside of my cheek, remembering my drunken words. "This isn't going anywhere. Let's enjoy it while it lasts."

I caught the hurt before he masked it. It was more than just sex, and we both knew it. But what was the point of admitting it when neither of us could change the life that was slowly suffocating me?

"Let's try something else then." His arm tightened when I attempted to pull away. "Tell me who the woman in Chicago is."

I didn't answer as I successfully shoved him back as the shower water turned off. I bolted down the hall, purposefully not glancing behind me.

"That's what I thought—faking," he muttered from behind me.

I sat on the couch, ignoring Niko's last words. I gave him an option. Kiss me or choose them. He'd made his choice. He had to know I wasn't going to be completely honest with him. Even if he did choose me, I wasn't sure he could ever turn his back on the society. It was his entire childhood. His life.

"Ready?" Alex's voice jerked me out of my thoughts, and I looked up.

I attempted a tight smile. "Yeah."

When the house came into view, my stomach bubbled like I was going to throw up. I didn't want to do this. I'd forced myself to learn how to handle Alex. I could barely look at Geo. Their dad had never liked me. Even before I'd stabbed his son and got people of his society killed. From the small amount of things Niko had told me, his dad wasn't happy I was with Alex. He had strong ties with higher people in the society. He wasn't someone I wanted mad at me; he held my life in his hands.

Alex took my hand once we were out of the Jeep, and we walked around to the back of the house. It was a beautiful day to be outside. The clouds covered the hot sun, and the breeze was just enough to make it comfortable. The back patio came into view, making memories of our last visit invade my mind. I couldn't believe it had been over a year since I was here. With Lacey. And Jamie. When Alex was still mine, and Niko was just the annoying older brother. It was the night we had made the plan to go up north.

"Alexandros and Nikolas. I've missed you both so much." Caitlin drew both her sons in for hugs once we stepped onto the deck. "Geoffrey is in the house. He'll be out soon."

The tension was thick as both Alex and Niko hugged their mom. Niko met my eyes, not even trying to hide his worry. At least I wasn't the only one who thought this was going to be a bad day.

"Sage, you look well. It is so good to see you," Caitlin said as she leaned in for a hug. I stiffly hugged her back. So, this was how it was going to be. Pretend that everything was completely normal.

"Hi, Dad." Niko's tone was formal and filled with respect.

"Nikolas," Theo Rossi said as he nodded to him.

I couldn't help but notice that their relationship was much more strained than the last time I had been here. It was no surprise when Theo warmly greeted Alex. It made sense. Alex spent much more time with him. Niko was always watching me.

"Hello, Sage." Theo turned his attention to me with a formidable stare.

"Hi." I tried to sound pleasant, but from the looks both Alex and Niko were giving me, it probably wasn't as good as it sounded.

We all sat at the patio table, and no one said a word for the first five minutes. Geo joined us, and besides a small smirk he shot at me, he kept quiet too. Even he realized how bad this was. I could have cried. It wasn't even noon, and we were supposed to stay there until after dinnertime.

Finally, Caitlin spoke up. "Sage, how are you liking the house Alex rented? It's a cute place, right?"

"Yes, very cozy," I replied, fidgeting with the hem of my sundress. It was a great little house. The house I could never leave. They were crazy to think we could all have a normal dinner. I didn't know how I was going to make it through the day.

"I'm sure it's a bit crowded with Niko there." Caitlin chuckled.

"Oh, Mom, she loves me," Niko said as he flashed a half grin. He was acting like the person I now knew was a front. Or at least part of it. Because when it was just us two, he was completely different.

"I'm sure it won't be too much longer until Alex and Sage can be on their own. You two are perfect." She smiled as if she was trying to make me feel better.

Instead, panic flared in my chest. To live alone with Alex. I couldn't think of a worse fate. Niko was the only reason I was still sane. I could be myself around him. Subconsciously, I counted on Niko to fall back on for anything. And even if he wouldn't admit it, I had a feeling he would, no matter what. Hopefully. If he didn't live at that house and if I could never get away, I would drink myself to death.

I attempted to keep my eyes free of my true thoughts as I joined back in on the conversation. Alex, Niko, and Geo were discussing some sports team. My gaze wandered to the pool. In the stress of thinking about coming, I didn't bring a bathing suit. I was regretting that now. It would have been a much easier day if I could spend all of it in the pool without talking to anyone.

"Sage, want to help me get the snack tray ready?" Caitlin asked.

I nodded and got up to follow her into the kitchen. Anything to get away from that table. Caitlin opened the screen door, and I walked into the homey kitchen. It was clean but old. It hadn't been updated in decades. The floor was the iconic black-and-white checkered design, and all the cabinets were a dark brown. She walked over to the counter to the tray, and my face scrunched in confusion when I realized it was already full.

"I know this must be hard for you," she said gently, grabbing my hand.

I didn't move, not sure what to say.

She continued, "I met a woman who wasn't born into our beliefs. She married into it. One of the Elder's wives. At first, she was apprehensive, like you. But now she believes. She does everything for the greater good. As you will in the years to come. I'm sure this year hasn't been easy. But your choice to stay with Alex was the right one. Don't mind Theo. He doesn't like change, but he'll get used to it."

Caitlin smiled at me warmly as she let go of my hand and grabbed the food tray. I followed her back outside, still processing what I was just told. Years to come. I couldn't do this for years. I needed to get whatever I could to make the society pay for what they'd done.

These last few months, I had nearly lost sight of that. Being watched all the time and having to play happy when Alex was around. The stress was almost too much. Then Niko began making it bearable. More than bearable. I enjoyed my time with him. It wasn't enough. I still had to drink to cope with being around Alex. Niko was right. I was spiraling with the alcohol, and if I kept drinking, I'd never have a clear brain. I'd succumb to this life.

I sank back into the patio chair, and Alex glanced at me, his eyes warming. He wanted me to be comfortable here. In that moment, I remembered why I was doing all of this. It wasn't just to survive. It was to make these people pay. For what they did to Lacey and my mom. To Kiara's girlfriend, Valerie, and all the other women in the past. Surviving was part of it. But now it was time to do more. A small twinge struck my heart. Taking them down included Niko.

"I'll be right back. I have to go to the bathroom," I told Alex quietly before I could change my mind.

"I'll show you where it is. I need to grab a drink anyway," Niko piped up from across the table.

I pursed my lips. This wasn't what I wanted to happen. Niko opened the door, and we both went inside.

"I know where the bathroom is," I muttered impatiently. Before he answered, I was already making my way down the long hall.

The bathroom was at the end of the hall at the back of the house. Right next to the office—the place I really wanted to go. I peeked over my shoulder to make sure Niko hadn't followed me and nearly jumped when I turned back around. I had forgotten there was a giant mirror at the end of the hall. Fear was evident in my eyes, but I opened the office door anyway.

The office was small and organized. There was one massive wood desk that took up the whole back wall. It had enough space to fit at least three computers. But there was only one small laptop in the middle. There was a small reading chair in the corner to the right of me and a stand-up light in the other. The desk had lots of drawers and two small cupboards. I looked in the hall again. My heart was racing, and every noise I made seemed deafening.

I didn't know when I'd be back in this house, and I needed to know if there was anything here that was useful. The thick beige carpet masked my footsteps as I crossed the small room. Opening the top drawer, I peered inside. Only pens and some empty notepads. The next couple of drawers were just as disappointing.

I was about to open one of the cupboards when someone cleared their throat behind me. My stomach plummeted as dread froze me in place.

Fuck, I hoped it was Niko.

CHAPTER FORTY-ONE

Sage

I slowly turned around, coming face to face with Theo Rossi. And he was not happy. My face flushed, and I racked my brain for a logical excuse to tell him.

"What are you doing in here?" he asked, his voice venomous.

Before I could say a word, Niko came up behind his dad.

"Sorry, Dad. I asked Sage if she could grab the phone charger for me. I thought there was one in here," Niko explained smoothly.

"I couldn't find it. Sorry," I mumbled, my voice shaking slightly.

"Who knew finding a charger would be that difficult for you?" His tone was sarcastic, but the anger brewing in his eyes was unmistakable.

Theo looked from me to his son and seemed to believe Niko's lie. He mentioned something about the charger being in the living room before walking back down the hall. My gaze darted back to Niko, and when his dad turned his back, the nice-guy charade ended. His teeth were clenched, and his entire body was tense. His hands were balled into fists as he stood perfectly still. I could tell it was taking everything in him not to lose it. He knew exactly what I had been doing.

Letting my gaze fall to the floor, I rushed forward to leave. A gasp escaped me when he shoved me against the wall next to the open door. My wrists were trapped in one of his hands and above my head before I got a word out. His hold tightened when I tried wiggling away.

"Niko," I hissed, fear buzzing through me. "Let me go."

His eyes went between me and the hall while he stayed silent. Giving up on freeing my wrists, I huffed out a breath, waiting for him to come to his senses.

"If you're going to sneak around," he murmured as he leaned closer, "you should make it worth the risk of getting caught."

Rage still simmered in his voice, but his eyes were darkened with something else. His free hand drifted up my bare thigh and didn't stop until it was under my sundress. My breath hitched, my fear giving way to shock. This was *not* coming to his senses.

"Someone's going to walk in—"

"After the show you put on for me the first time I saw you naked, I know you can be quiet." He pushed my panties to the side. "Well, at least when you're touching yourself. You think you can stay silent when it's me fingering you?"

The panic of being found mixed with pleasure when his fingers grazed my clit. His gaze was on the open doorway more than on me, and a bit of tension left me when I realized what he was doing. He was watching the mirror at the end of the hall, which meant he'd be able to see anyone who was coming before they got close enough to catch what we were doing.

I relished in the waves of pleasure rolling through me. My pussy pulsed as he sped up. The stress of the day began to leave my body while my eyes closed, letting him take the burden of keeping our secret safe. He wouldn't let anyone catch us.

My legs began trembling when he pushed one finger and then a second one inside me. His thumb stayed on my clit as his fingers curled and he moved them slowly.

"Quiet, Sage," he ordered when I moaned. "You get too loud, and I'm going to have to stop."

I clenched my teeth together, swallowing my cry as he plunged his fingers deep inside me. My knees nearly buckled, and his hold on my wrists was the only thing helping me stay standing. The pleasure built until my entire body was on fire. I held my breath while going rigid as I got to the edge.

"Hey," I protested when everything stopped as he pulled his hand away.

Tearing his eyes from the mirror, he met my glare. Raising his hand up, he sucked on the fingers that had just been in my pussy.

"You really shouldn't have been drinking last night," he murmured, releasing my wrists.

"Are you kidding me?" I snapped when I realized he really wasn't going to finish.

"I told you. No orgasms until you stop. I really hope it's soon. For both our sakes."

"I didn't drink today."

His eyes narrowed. "Only because I got to the wine before you did. Be good, Sage. That includes not sneaking around, looking for things that don't concern you. Then you'll get as many fucking orgasms as you can handle."

"I wasn't looking for anything—"

"Do not lie to me," he cut me off sharply. "You're going to get caught doing shit like that."

Niko glanced at the mirror in the hall, and his face went dark as he shuffled away from me right before Geo walked into the office. He looked between Niko and me, not hiding the suspicion burning on his face.

"What are you two doing?" Geo asked, looking at his brother to answer.

"Sage had a small freak out from being here," Niko replied casually. "I was making sure she was okay."

"Isn't that Alex's job?" Geo asked, arching an eyebrow. "Or do your babysitting duties include emotional support too?"

"I just needed a second to breathe," I forced out. "I'm trying to be okay with everything. For Alex."

"If you say so." Geo shrugged, still staring at Niko questioningly.

Without another word, I slipped past them, wanting to get far away from Geo. I could hear them following behind me as I slid open the back screen door. I sat back down next to Alex, feeling how wet my panties were from the teasing Niko had done. *Asshole.* I couldn't believe he'd just stopped like that.

Alex's hand went to my thigh, and I painted on a smile as I listened to him talk about something that he wanted to do to fix up the house. Niko and Geo sat across from me. With how Niko was acting, no one would ever guess what we'd just done in the house. The way he could cover his emotions kept surprising me. And made me wonder if he was only acting when we spent time together.

"You okay, baby?" Alex asked. "You haven't said much."

What the hell did he expect me to say?

"I'm okay," I assured him. "I have a headache."

"If it's that bad, I can drive her home now," Niko offered as he looked at Alex for permission.

I bristled. Again, they were talking like I wasn't even there. I couldn't live like this forever.

Alex thought about it for a second before nodding. I swallowed, not sure which was worse. Staying here and pretending or going back to the house with Niko. He was still pissed about what his dad had caught me doing, and I had a feeling he'd want to talk about it.

"Go home and rest. I know this has been hard. Dad and I need to talk about...business anyway," he said, brushing a kiss on my forehead.

Alex tossed Niko his keys, and I got up and made my way off the deck. Niko walked next to me, not saying a word. Once we were in the Jeep, I waited for him to go off, but he stayed silent. After a few minutes, I tried starting a conversation.

"Niko—"

"Unless you plan on telling me what you were doing in that office, I don't want to hear it," he cut me off, his voice scary quiet.

I tried biting my tongue, knowing he was still trying to calm down. But I couldn't help myself. "Maybe I was waiting for you. Although, I never would have, if I'd known you weren't going to let me finish."

The glare he shot me proved he didn't believe me. The rest of the ride home was silent. I understood why he was so angry. He'd covered for me. Lied straight to his dad's face. He easily could have kept quiet and let me fend for myself, but he didn't. He protected me. Again. Against his family.

He pulled into the driveway and jumped out of the car the second he took the key out. I stayed in my seat, watching through the windshield as he opened his truck door. After grabbing something from the back seat, he kicked the door shut and strode to the house. The sun reflected off what he was carrying, the clear liquid sloshing in the bottle with every step he took.

Now I knew where he had hidden the tequila. I quickly decided to stay outside instead of letting him confront me in the house. Looking up, I groaned as dark clouds were approaching. The nice day was about to turn into a stormy one.

With a sigh, I slowly made my way through the front door. Niko was sitting at the table with a shot glass full to the brim. He swallowed it in one gulp and poured another one as I debated over attempting to talk or just going to the bedroom. The bedroom idea won, but as I walked past him, he grabbed my hand, halting my steps.

"You really think we aren't going to talk about this?" he asked, standing from the table.

"You're the one who didn't want to talk," I snapped as I wrenched my hand away and created some distance between us.

Niko followed, looming over me, his face inches from mine. He was trying to intimidate me. I stood my ground, matching his gaze. He might have his own suspicions but couldn't prove what I was doing in the office. I didn't think that's what he was mad about anyway. It was the fact that he'd lied to his dad for me. We stood there for over a minute, glaring at each other. Until Niko shook his head and turned away to down his second shot.

"So, that's your plan," he stated before facing me again.

"I don't have a plan—"

"Come off it, Sage. You were looking for something about the group," he spat out.

He was so close that I could smell the liquor on his breath. The rain had started and was pounding violently on the windows as thunder cracked in the distance.

"That's why you haven't run. You're trying to get information."

"I was just looking around. I haven't left because I don't want my dad to get hurt."

"Right. You think you can find something and take it to the police? Expose the group?"

"No—"

"I thought I was pretty damn clear about how impossible that was. They are everywhere."

"They," I repeated quietly.

"What?"

"You said *they*. It used to be *we*. Don't feel like part of your group anymore?" I regretted saying it the second the words left my lips. His mouth scrunched into a scowl and his eyes narrowed.

"They're my family," he growled.

"The family you've been lying to for months. To help someone who could be a threat," I shot back.

His lips curved upward. "A threat? One girl, a threat to a group that's been around for centuries."

"They didn't stop looking until I was found—"

"If you were that big a threat, you really think you'd still be alive? Sure, they don't like loose ends, which is why they wanted you found. But if they thought you were a threat, you wouldn't be here now. No matter how badly my baby brother loves you. If you get caught doing something like what you did today, your cozy little life is going to be gone."

My heart pounded as chills raced down my body. "You're saying that to scare me."

"You think so? Alex doesn't have the pull you might think he does. If they want you gone, it will happen," he threatened.

"You never answered me. About being a part of your group," I said, trying to shift the conversation.

He was silent, looking like he was internally fighting what he wanted to say.

"What do you think, Sage? You think I've changed and I'm a good person now? After what I was a part of?" he asked quietly.

I sucked in my breath. The last thing I expected was for him to bring that up.

"We're not talking—"

His shadow fell over me before his hand caught my chin. He pulled my face up until I was staring right into his eyes. The eyes that a second ago were filled with rage now looked sad and curious.

"Everything I've done has been for my family. For the group. It's how I was raised. It was all I ever knew. I was ready to do what was expected of me. But ever since that night, I've been questioning everything. I thought that feeling would go away. But you. You make me think about it. You make me want to set it right. So, I want you to tell me. Have I changed?" His eyes searched mine. "Can you ever fully trust me? Or forgive me for the part I played in Lacey's death? Or the fact that I can't completely turn my back on my family?"

I didn't move as I processed his words. He had never been so honest. So open. I didn't know if it was the alcohol that had made him say it or if it had just been building since this had all started.

All these months, I had been hiding. Staying alive to get justice for my sister. Sometimes I would feel a stabbing jolt because when I noticed I was enjoying myself with Niko, I'd remember why I was with him. Guilt always invaded me with those thoughts. Because I looked at him differently from his family. He helped me. Kept me sane while living in this house with Alex. I felt safe when he was here.

The goal of taking down the society was still very much alive. But somehow, in the past few months, I had separated Niko from the society.

"I don't know," I answered softly, not knowing what else to say. "My feelings for you are so confusing, Niko."

The pain that shot through his face was quickly masked as he ripped his hand away from my face. A rush of guilt surged through me, but I ignored it. I didn't want anything bad to happen to him, but at the same time, the society needed to be exposed.

"My parents aren't dumb enough to keep stuff in their house. No point in trying that again," he said gruffly before he took another shot. The honest moment was over.

"I'm done drinking," I muttered, trying to ease the tension between us.

I caught sight of a small grin before he turned away.

"Good."

CHAPTER FORTY-TWO

Him

"What happened to not drinking?" I asked, watching as she grabbed a bottle of whiskey off the shelf.

It had been a few weeks since the day we spent at my parents' house, and she hadn't touched a drop of alcohol since. To say she was cranky for the first week would be an understatement. Sex helped. I kept her occupied whenever I could. But when Alex came home, it was obvious she was more standoffish with him. She hid her emotions well, but even Alex caught on enough to question her about it. She blamed it on her period, and he dropped the conversation in a heartbeat.

"It's not for me," she stated, placing it in the cart. "It's Alex's favorite. I'm trying to be nicer."

"By trying to get him drunk?" I asked with a frown.

She rolled her eyes. "No. I'm trying to show him I still care."

A burn settled in my chest at the image of him touching her. I fucking hated that he was the one to share a bed with her every night. Even though I had no reason to feel that way. I was the one sleeping with the girl Alex thought loved him. Although I wasn't even sure he loved her. He seemed more focused on making it work so the group stayed off his back about it.

I pushed the cart down the aisle as she walked next to me. My questions were on the tip of my tongue, but I held them back. Determination had come back into her eyes ever since she had stopped drinking, and I had a feeling she was up to something. She wanted to go to the store more often. A little over a week ago, she bought sleeping pills. She claimed it was for nights she couldn't sleep. I was calling bullshit, seeing as how she'd put them in the medicine cabinet and hadn't touched them. There was another reason she'd gotten them.

I also researched the number I had taken from her phone back in Chicago. And when I found out who she was, I stayed up all damn night, unwilling to do what I should have. Kiara Jones. A woman who was connected with a woman who had been chosen. I remembered Valerie's ceremony. It was only a few years ago. Sage was tracking down people connected to everything. And Kiara was a cop. If anything was a threat to the group, this would be it. Yet, I hadn't told a soul. Or admitted to Sage what I knew. I had a feeling she'd push me away if I confronted her about it.

Everything added up to Sage planning something other than just running away. It was going to get her killed. I should put a stop to it. But I sat back and did nothing. Because I didn't want to lose her.

"Is that all we need?" she asked as we got to the front of the store.

I nodded, once again deciding to stay quiet instead of voicing my thoughts. We paid for the groceries and headed back out to my truck. She seemed lost in thought as I drove home, and I didn't interrupt her. There was a reason she wasn't telling me anything. Hell, I'd given her the reason. She'd left it up to me to kiss her on the lips, and I still hadn't.

I could admit to myself it wasn't about protecting the group anymore. It was about saving her. Even if she tried to expose our chapter of the group, there were more out there. All over the world. It would be impossible to even get close to the elders before someone silenced it. There were members in the group that held important jobs. Judges. Governors. All that would happen was that Sage would disappear, and nothing would change.

My grip on the steering wheel tightened. She needed to stay here. With Alex. At least that way she'd survive.

"If I told you that I could help you leave and disappear, would you go?" I blurted out the question that had been haunting me for weeks.

Silence. I peeked at her after turning on the dirt road, and she was staring at me in shock. I shook my head, looking back at the road. I never should have brought it up.

"You told me they're everywhere," she said slowly, not understanding why I was asking.

"They are," I muttered. "You'd have to go deep, Sage. Completely disappear."

I had money in savings that could keep her afloat for a while. If she went west, she could most likely live without getting caught. I knew where most of the houses were in the country. Some states had none. I could find her a place where she'd have a near zero chance of being found.

"They'd hurt my dad."

I took a deep breath. "No, they wouldn't. Alex only said that to scare you into staying. Your dad's safe."

Her jaw clenched as she processed that new information.

"I'd have to hide forever," she murmured.

"Yeah, you would."

"I wouldn't be able to visit my dad."

"You wouldn't come back to Michigan. Ever."

Nerves pierced my heart as she looked away from me and stared out the window. If she told me she wanted to go, I'd get everything ready by the end of the week.

"Would you come with me?" she whispered so softly I almost missed it.

I hesitated. "I can't."

It wasn't that I didn't want to. It would be more dangerous for her if I came too. It was one thing for someone to disappear who was aware of the group. It was a completely different situation when a member of the group was a threat. All Sage had was her voice. I knew where the evidence was buried. They'd never stop looking for me.

Even with all the knowledge I had, it wasn't enough to bring down the entire group. It was too large. Too spread out. I'd have to get to the elders, and that was next to impossible. Pulling into the driveway, I ran a hand down my face. What the fuck was I thinking? These thoughts shouldn't even be on my radar. I turned in the group and people went to prison. People I grew up with. My family. Me.

"No," she said loudly, turning toward me after I parked. "I don't want to leave my dad. I'm not going anywhere."

"Okay."

That was the end of the conversation. She hopped out of the truck and grabbed a couple of bags, leaving the rest for me. I stared at her as she walked into the house. It wasn't just about her dad. She was planning something.

CHAPTER FORTY-THREE

Sage

I tensed when an arm draped over my stomach. Blinking my eyes open, I didn't move a muscle as I glanced at the clock on my nightstand. It was nearly eight in the morning. I relaxed, knowing Alex was already at work. Sometimes Niko would open the windows and sneak in here after Alex left in the morning. If the bedroom door and windows were open, we could always hear if someone drove up.

Glancing over my shoulder, I saw half his face was pressed into the pillow. His black hair was a mess, and his eyes were closed. I doubted he was sleeping since he always kept an ear out for Alex. But it was always nice to lie in bed together since we usually avoided the bedrooms.

Turning around, I got comfortable again, dragging my fingers up his arm as I enjoyed the silence. My fingertips brushed over his palm, and I frowned. Callouses met my touch. Niko always had callouses, but I didn't remember them being that rough. A flash of panic coursed through me as I lifted his arm to look at the inside of his wrist.

There was no fucking birthmark. It wasn't Niko.

I tried shooting up as fear stole my breath. His arm locked around my stomach, pulling me into his chest. I rammed my elbow into his ribs, and his hold loosened enough for me to roll away from him. A hand tangled in my hair, and I cried out as he yanked me back. He grabbed my arm and turned me until my spine was pressing into the mattress.

He jumped on top of me, his body pinning me to the bed. He practically sat on my stomach as he got a hold of my wrists.

"Get the hell off me, Geo," I screamed, terror seizing me. "What are you doing?"

Geo smirked down at me. "The bigger question is, what are you doing?"

"I was sleeping," I snapped.

"I thought for sure you would have tried getting away the second my arm went around you." He raised an eyebrow. "Are you used to my brother touching you like that?"

My heart thrashed. "I thought you were Alex—"

"Hold on." He cut me off with a cold laugh. "Wrong brother. My bad, I should have been more specific. Are you used to *Niko* touching you like that?"

"No," I hissed as his nails dug into my wrists. "I told you, I thought you were Alex. Get off me."

He tilted his head to the side. "You could tell I wasn't Alex by looking at my arm?"

"Your ring," I bit out. "Alex wears his around his neck, not on his finger."

Truth was, I didn't notice the ring until after looking for the birthmark, but he didn't know that. Geo didn't say a word as he stared down at me. I couldn't tell if he believed me or not, but he had no proof. He did have a whole lot of suspicion, which wasn't good.

"What the fuck?"

My eyes flew to the doorway where Niko and Alex were standing. Alex looked taken aback at seeing Geo on top of me. And Niko...he looked murderous. He was staring at his twin with rage I'd never seen before. Geo seemed surprised that we were interrupted, and hastily released me before scrambling off the bed.

Alex stepped into the room, glaring at Geo. "What are you doing?"

"Calm down." Geo raised his hands in mock surrender. "I was just playing around. We used to mess with her all the time."

"Not like that," I argued, rubbing my wrists after I stood up. "And that was before you killed my sister. I don't want anything to do with you."

I peeked at Niko, who was still standing rigidly in the doorway. His eyes were still on Geo as his hands were clenched in fists.

"That's no way to talk to your future brother-in-law," Geo quipped, even though he still looked uneasy as he glanced back at Alex. "It doesn't sound like she's coming to terms with our beliefs, does it? I don't think she'll ever get over it. Maybe it's time to think of other options."

My eyes widened as panic washed over me. "That's not true. There's a difference between accepting your society and wanting to be around the person who took my sister from me."

"But if you accept it, then you understand why I had to do it, right?" Geo murmured as more tension blanketed the room.

My stomach plummeted when Alex turned his attention to me. Instead of sticking up for me, he seemed like he agreed with Geo. Forcing myself to move closer to Alex, I grabbed his arm.

"Alex, I promise I'm learning to accept your life." Tears filled my eyes. "But with Lacey, it's different. You know how close I was to her. I just miss my sister. You can understand that, right?"

"Yes," Alex answered, his eyes softening a fraction. "But Geo is my brother, Sage. You can't avoid him forever. It's been nearly eleven months. You need to learn how to get along with my family."

"It would probably help if Geo didn't keep trying to scare the shit out of her." Niko spoke up, not moving from the doorway. "What were you doing in here anyway?"

Geo scowled. "I wanted to ask her a question."

"You had to pin her to the bed to do that?" Niko scoffed. "Crossing a line with your brother's girl, don't you think?"

My jaw dropped before I could catch myself. He was purposely trying to get under Geo's skin, and I didn't understand why. Until I saw uncertainty pass over Alex's face. Niko was trying to drive a wedge between Geo and Alex. Diminish the trust. My guess was because Niko knew Geo wasn't going to drop his suspicion of me. But if Alex had any hint that Geo wanted me, any of Geo's future arguments could be tainted. I shuddered with disgust at the thought of Geo looking at me like that. But it was better than Alex finding out that I was sleeping with his other brother.

Surprised rage lit up Geo's eyes as he stared at Niko. I swallowed hard, worried Geo was about to voice the thoughts he had about Niko and me. After a long moment, Geo only huffed out a chuckle.

"Alex. Come here," a voice called from outside. A chill ripped through me. My gaze darted between Alex and Niko.

"Your dad is here?" I whispered, wondering what the hell was going on today. Their dad hadn't come to the house since I'd gotten here.

"Yeah," Alex answered, already moving toward the door. "He's helping me work on the Jeep. It's time to get back to normal, Sage. Which means spending more time with family."

Normal. Nothing about this life would ever be normal. But I wouldn't have to deal with it for much longer. I'd been slowly getting things ready to execute my plan. This time I wasn't running. I was bringing the society into the public eye.

My gaze wandered to Niko. Every time we went to the store, I got something I needed. None of it was out of the ordinary, though they were things I didn't usually buy. If Niko had questions, he hadn't voiced them. I still needed to buy one more thing that would make it glaringly obvious that I was planning something. Niko was still adamant that the only way for me to survive was to accept this life. Besides his offer to help me leave. If I were smarter, the answer would have been yes. But I couldn't stand the thought of hiding forever like I had for six months. That meant staying here and pretending with Alex. For now.

I'd rather die trying than live like this forever.

Every day I struggled about whether I should tell Niko what I was going to do. There was no denying that I trusted him. But what I was planning would put his entire family in prison if I succeeded. Including him. Because I couldn't think of a way to keep him out of it and expose everything else. He was connected to it all.

Which was why I'd been taking my time getting everything in place. I didn't want to lose him. I couldn't see my life without him. But I was doing this for my freedom. More importantly, for Lacey and my mom. And for any future woman whom the society chose. If I accepted this life and did nothing, women would continue to be murdered. I couldn't live with that when I had a chance to change it.

It was bigger than Niko and me. No matter how much it hurt to think about.

"Why don't you go say hi to Dad, Sage?" Geo's words jolted me out of my conflicting thoughts. "It might help you accept everything if you can stand to be in the same room as our parents."

I shot him a glare before walking out of the room. Niko moved out of the way so I could get into the hall. He didn't say anything, but I could feel his stare on me as I went to the living room. I was relieved to see Alex and his dad outside. I didn't want to talk to Theo any more than I wanted to be in the same room as Geo.

"You're going to have to forgive Dad, along with me, if you really want the family and group to accept you."

I spun around at Geo's words to see them both behind me. My

body went cold when a slice of panic hit Niko's eyes, sending fear rippling through me.

"Forgive him for what?" I asked.

Geo shrugged. "That our dad—"

"Not now," Niko hissed, glancing at me. "You're going to tell her when he's here?"

"Are you worried about how she's going to take it?" Geo asked, frowning. "Or are you concerned about her feelings? You've been spending too much time with her. It's making you soft."

"I'm thinking of the fallout," Niko argued back. "Alex hasn't told her. It's not up to you."

"Tell me what?" I spoke up, dread sliding down my spine.

Geo locked eyes with me. "I'm honestly surprised you haven't put it together yourself yet."

"Geo. Don't." Niko warned, stepping closer to me. "Let Alex tell her."

Geo ignored him, keeping his gaze on me. "Why do you think it was Lacey we chose for our family's ceremony? Why we chose your family specifically."

Confusion rocked me. "Because of our hair color. I already knew that."

"Alex is younger than you, isn't he?" Geo asked, clearly already knowing the answer.

"Yes." I couldn't see where he was going with this. Why did it matter that Alex was ten months younger than me?

"He was born premature. At six months." Geo paused as if waiting for me to suddenly understand.

My conversation with Niko filtered through my head about his mom getting pregnant with Alex the same month their ceremony was held.

"When did your mom go missing, Sage?" Geo asked without a flicker of remorse or concern.

My chest went tight when I realized what he was saying. My gaze darted to Niko, who was failing to keep his face blank for once. The apology and pain I saw flash through his eyes confirmed what I was thinking.

"She went missing in June. When I was two months old," I whispered, tears of anger falling on my cheeks.

Geo nodded. "An interesting timeline, don't you think?"

"Your dad. He killed my mom," I choked out. "She was the one chosen for his ceremony."

"Why do you think he wanted you or Lacey to be chosen for ours?" Geo cocked his head to the side. "Alex was a miracle baby. Mom got pregnant nearly immediately after the ceremony. He was born premature but was in perfect health. Your mom's ceremony proved how important your family was. You and your sister were chosen from that moment."

I grabbed the back of the chair, sucking in deep breaths. Not only had Geo killed Lacey, but his dad had murdered my mom. Niko stared at me, keeping his distance as Geo shook his head.

"If she's going to learn to live with everything, she needs to know," Geo said, his cruel words taunting me. "You can get over it all, right Sage?"

My chest heaved as I kept my screaming thoughts to myself. Anger built as I looked between them. Niko had kept this from me. To protect my feelings or his family, I wasn't sure. Either way, betrayal filtered through my anger. As much as I trusted him, there were things keeping the wall up between us. And I didn't know if we'd ever break through it.

"Hey." Alex pulled the screen door open and poked his head in. "Dad and I have to go get some parts and then we're going to help a friend out with something. Probably won't be back until late tonight. Want to come, Geo?"

"Nah." Geo threw an arm around Niko's shoulder. "I'm going to hang out here. Maybe I can prove to Sage that we can play nice."

A slight frown played on Alex's lips at that response, but he only nodded and muttered a goodbye to me before shutting the door. Bile burned my throat when I met Geo's smug face. Pretending all day with him would be a hundred times worse than with Alex. I was still reeling from what I had just learned about their dad, and I wanted to be alone.

Raising my chin, I strode toward the hall, only for Geo to step in front of me. I gave him a silent warning, which he ignored.

"Where are you going?" he asked, knowing full well what I was doing.

"Back to sleep."

"Now, how can we work past everything if you do that?"

Continuing to move past him, I went rigid when he grabbed my arm. Niko moved next to me, his attention on Geo.

"After what Alex just caught you doing, you probably shouldn't put your hands back on her," he murmured, his voice quiet yet threatening.

The atmosphere between them had been bad for a while, but they weren't hiding it anymore. Geo kept his fingers around my arm as he met Niko's gaze, while I stayed stuck between them. Anger saturated the entire room as Geo slowly let me go.

"You go into your room, I'll follow," Geo told me, keeping his eyes on his brother. "You chose to be a part of this family, Sage. I'm the only brother you haven't spent quality time with. That's changing now. I plan on getting to know you better."

Niko studied Geo's face, as if trying to figure out what he was up to. I backed away from them both and went to the kitchen to get some food. I had no doubt Geo really would follow me to my room, and I'd rather stay out here than be trapped in a smaller room with him. I also suspected Niko was close to his breaking point. If Geo touched me again, he was going to snap, and Geo's suspicion would become tangible proof.

It was going to be a long fucking day.

CHAPTER FORTY-FOUR

Him

"Pizza's here," Geo announced as he came through the door.

Sage didn't even try to smother her groan before mumbling under her breath. "I'm about to break my no drinking promise."

I was almost tempted to agree with her. Because dealing with Geo all day had been exhausting, and he didn't seem to have plans to leave anytime soon.

"We threw the wine and tequila away," I muttered.

"We have the whiskey I bought."

I raised an eyebrow. "The one you bought for Alex and never gave him?"

"I'm waiting for an important time."

Sure she was. Whatever she was planning, I bet it included the whiskey somehow. Not that I was going to bring it up with my brother in the house.

"Pizza's going to get cold," Geo sang out from the kitchen. "I drove all the way into town to get it. One of the negatives of living in the country—no one delivers here."

All day Geo had been making small talk about anything he could think of. Sage had spent the day on the couch, pretending to be interested in whatever was on the TV. It wasn't just Geo she was ignoring. It was me too. She was angry I hadn't told her about her mom. It was one thing Alex and I agreed on. Telling her would only cause more pain. Geo didn't care about that.

"I'll get you a slice," I told her as I got off the couch. I knew she was hungry, but her unwillingness to be near Geo was winning against her rumbling stomach. She mumbled a thank you as she continued to mess absentmindedly with the giant candle that sat on the table at the end of the couch.

Geo was leaning against the counter, opening a beer as I pulled out two plates. The strain between us had only grown all day. For the last few years, we hadn't been as close as when we were kids, and now it felt different. The connection we had was all but gone. And it wasn't only about Sage. We'd drifted apart after graduating from high school, and it had never gotten back to how it used to be.

"You get food for her too?" he asked, eyeing the plates in my hands. "What else do you do for her?"

"I spend more time with her than anyone," I snapped, grabbing a few pieces of pizza. "I'd rather play nice than fight constantly."

"That sounds like no fun."

Ignoring him, I grabbed some napkins and turned around to an empty kitchen.

"Shit," I muttered, picking up the plates and rushing around the corner so I could see the living room. After what he'd pulled this morning, I didn't want to leave him alone with her at all. My gut churned when I saw him sitting in the middle of the couch. Sage was curled away from him, but he made sure there was no space for me to sit between them.

Geo glanced at me and grinned, nodding to the empty spot on the other side of him. "Are we going to watch this movie or not?"

Sage leaped from the couch. "I can't do this anymore. I'm going to bed."

"It's not even six," Geo said.

"I don't care."

Before she could walk past him, he jumped up and grabbed her wrist. My grip on the plates turned painful as anger overtook anything else. Sage glanced at me, subtly shaking her head, not wanting me to interfere.

Fuck that.

There was no way I'd be able to just stand here if he did anything like he'd done this morning. I had barely stayed in control then. Obviously, Sage was thinking more clearly than I was. If Geo caught on to how much I cared for her—that was it. He'd tell Alex and my family.

"Let me go, Geo," she demanded, her voice eerily calm. I didn't move a muscle as I watched her face lose every other emotion except downright hatred. "If I have to be around you, then you better learn to keep your hands to yourself."

A surprised chuckle left him. "You think you can give me orders, Sage? What did Niko tell you all those months ago? The society owns you. You do as we say. And I'm telling you, sit your ass back on the couch."

Instead of answering, she brought her knee up, ramming it into his groin. He turned just in time that she hit his inner leg instead of what she was aiming for. With her free hand, she slapped him across the face. The plates fell from my hands as I raced across the room. Geo's eyes were radiating with rage, and I knew what he was going to do before he even moved.

"Geo, stop," I yelled as he raised his hand.

He backhanded her across the cheek hard enough for her to

tumble onto the couch. A snarl burned my throat as I rammed into him. We fell onto the wooden coffee table, and it broke under our weight as he punched me across the jaw.

"I knew it," he hissed, betrayal written all over his face. "You're fucking her. Do you actually care about her too?"

I didn't answer, digging my fist into his kidney. Nothing I said would change anything. He knew me well enough to understand my reaction. The fact that she meant something to me wasn't a secret anymore. He clipped my chin, making my tongue knock between my teeth. The taste of blood filled my mouth as I swung my fist into his ribs.

"What the fuck were you thinking?" Geo grunted out after my next hit landed on the side of his head.

"What about you?" I grabbed his arm when he tried to slug me again. "Since when do you hit women?"

His eyes glittered dangerously. "Since my own twin betrayed our family. Our entire fucking belief. And it's her fault."

We had both stopped fighting, and I was still on top of him as we glared at each other. I could see Sage sitting on the couch out of the corner of my eye. Geo tried shoving me off, and I grabbed his shoulders, pushing him back onto the broken table. The second he left this house, he'd go to our parents. They'd take her.

"You messed up, Niko," he spat out, squirming to the side. "Don't worry. I'll help clean it up."

"I don't need your help." My panic escalated as I tried to figure a way out of this. Whatever he was thinking, it wasn't going to help her.

"Sage, go pack a bag," I said gruffly, digging my fingers into Geo's shoulders when he attempted to shoot up.

"Niko—"

"Go. Now," I cut her off.

I kept my eyes on Geo as she ran through the living room and down the hall. His face turned menacing when she left the room.

"You can't let her leave," he snapped, struggling against me.

"You're going to die right along with her. The group doesn't tolerate traitors, brother. You know that."

She was leaving. She was getting out of this house before he was. It was the only way she'd have a chance. A searing pain shot down my leg, and I winced, my hold on him going slack. He pushed me off him, kicking me in the gut as I rolled to the floor. Glancing down at my leg, I saw a slim piece of broken wood sticking out of my thigh.

"You really should have kept up with our boxing workouts," Geo murmured from beside me. "Taking this last year off made you slow."

"Believe me, I've been working out plenty." Ignoring the stabbing pain radiating through my leg, thanks to the piece of coffee table lodged inside me, I stood to keep myself between him and Sage's room.

"I hope her pussy was worth it." He stepped up to me, and I straightened my spine, curling my hands into fists. My heart was hammering as I stared at my brother. He used to be the person I'd do anything for.

Now she was.

A thud came from the hall, and I glanced over my shoulder, making sure Sage was still in her room. I turned back toward Geo, and his leering grin had me lunging at him. I wasn't sure what it was, but he was about to do something.

"Choosing anyone over the group was a mistake." His words were the last thing I heard before he slammed Sage's candle into the side of my head, and everything went black.

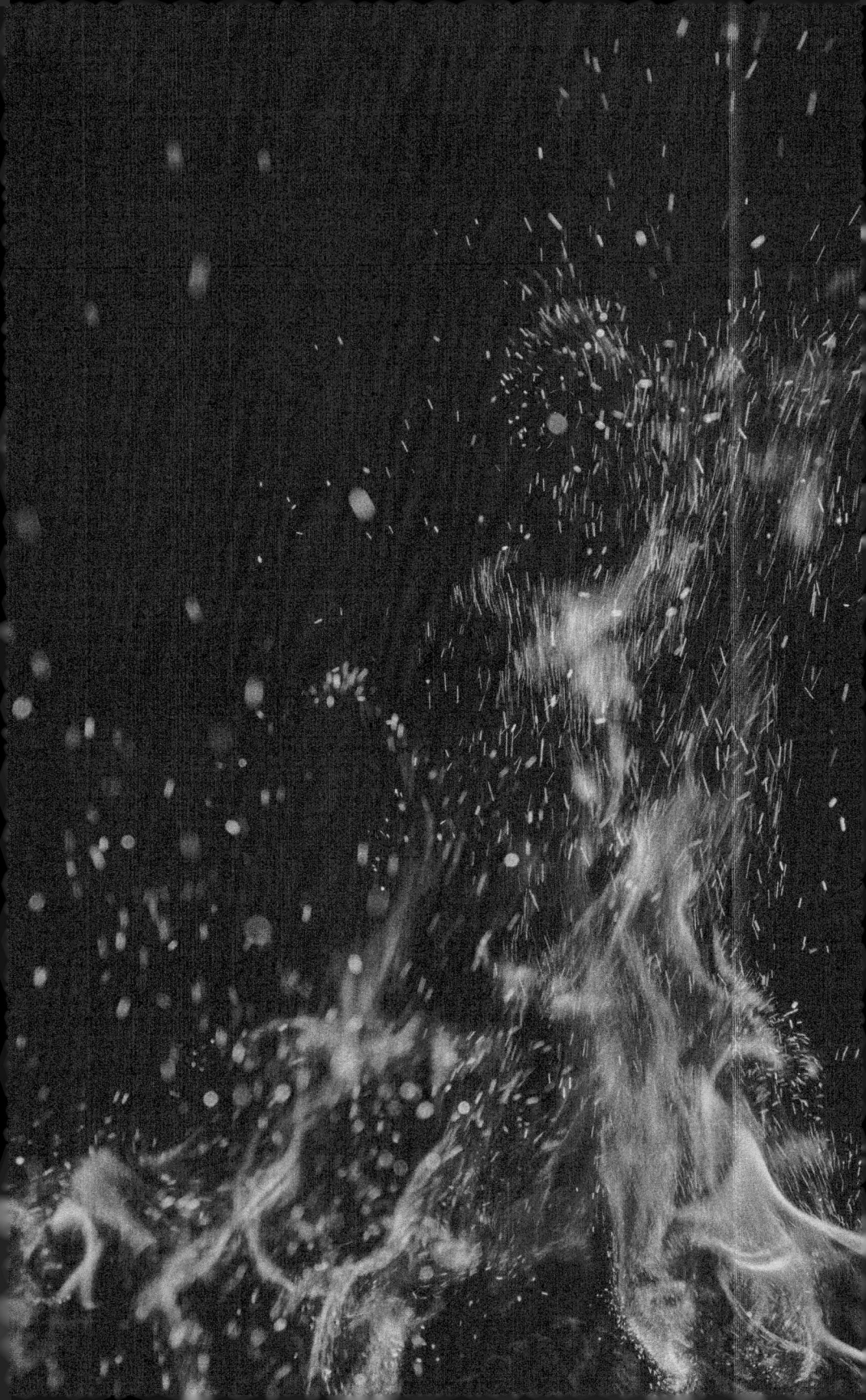

CHAPTER FORTY-FIVE

Sage

I slid my phone into my front jeans pocket before grabbing my small duffel bag. I glanced at the open door and debated running across the hall to the bathroom. My car key had been in the tampon box ever since I'd hidden it there months ago. A thump came from the living room, and my chest constricted, not knowing what was going on.

My hands trembled as I grabbed some clothes from the dresser. This wasn't supposed to happen. I had a plan, and now it was torn to shreds. I had to disappear again before Geo told Alex everything. Fear racked my nerves as I thought about Niko. He was in as deep as me now.

I froze when the screen door creaked open. Someone had either left the house or come inside. What if Alex had come home? I waited to hear anything else, but it was silent. Creeping to the doorway, I peered down the hall. All I could hear was my deafening heartbeat. I tiptoed down the hall, a lump growing in my throat when I saw Niko slumped on the floor.

Running to him, I fell next to him and rolled him onto his back. I blinked back tears when his chest rose and fell. Blood ran down the side of his face from a gash on his temple. Fuck, I couldn't handle any more death.

"Niko. Wake up." I shook him hard, but he didn't move. "Come on. Get up."

The screen door creaked again, and I scrambled to my feet, spinning around. Geo was already rushing toward me, and I didn't have a chance to move before his arms wrapped around my waist, knocking me down. Pain ricocheted through my skull when the back of my head smacked the floor. I flailed my arms, not seeing where I was swinging as the room spun.

"Don't make this worse on yourself," he grated out when my palm connected with his ear.

"Fuck you," I screeched, knowing I wasn't going to get out of this alive if he did whatever he was planning.

Panic suffocated me when he got a hold of my arms. A ripping sound filled the room before something sticky wrapped around my wrists, securing them together in front of me. His weight shifted on top of me before he grabbed my ankles and taped them together too. He climbed off me, and I struggled against the duct tape as he moved toward Niko.

"What did you do to convince my brother to protect you?" he asked as he started dragging Niko toward the front door. "To turn his back on everything he's ever known?"

"He hasn't," I forced out. "He refuses to tell me anything about your society."

He stopped and stared at me. "He was about to let you walk out that door, Sage. Don't fucking lie to me."

Before I could respond, he dragged Niko onto the porch, and I heard the duct tape ripping again. Wriggling around, I managed to sit up. The tape wouldn't budge when I tried moving my wrists. Reaching down, I began tugging at the tape around my ankles but got nowhere before Geo came back into the house.

"I'm not sure Alex will be surprised when he finds out." He crouched down next to me, one of his eyes swollen from Niko's hits. "His patience with you warming back up to him was already at the breaking point."

I screamed in protest when he flipped me over his shoulder. He carried me outside and set me down on the porch with my back leaning against the side of the house. Looking to the other side of the porch, my gaze landed on Niko. His hands were taped above his head to the metal railing. Guilt washed through me. I'd heard what Geo had said earlier. The society would never trust him again. His life was on the line as much as mine was.

Geo went to Niko, and I flinched when he hit him across the face. Niko groaned as his head snapped to the side.

"Come on." Geo hit him again. "I want to talk before Alex gets home."

"Stop," I cried out when he punched Niko for a third time. "Please."

He turned toward me, curiosity flaring in his eyes. "Are you worried about him? I thought you were using him to get out of this. But the look on your face says differently."

I bit my tongue, not saying a word. Niko's head rolled as his eyes fluttered open. His gaze was unfocused until they landed on me. He saw my taped wrists and ankles and tried bolting up before realizing his hands were bound above him.

"You know this hurts me as much as it hurts you," Geo murmured as rage covered Niko's face. "You're my brother. My twin. Hurting you goes against everything."

"The piece of wood in my leg says differently," Niko snapped.

Geo grabbed my arm, hauling me to my feet. I gritted my teeth, refusing to acknowledge the pain his bruising grip was causing.

"I had to stop you," Geo said, shaking his head. "Because the group—the secret of our belief—comes before anything. You know that. And you chose to ignore it."

"I haven't told her shit." Niko's eyes went frigid. "We were fucking. You realize how boring it is being stuck in a house for months? It was a way to pass the time."

I was positive his words were lies, but they rolled off his tongue with ease. Geo's gaze darted between us, a vile smirk forming on his lips. My mouth went dry as his free hand slid under my shirt. He grazed his fingers up my bare stomach while his other hand locked tighter on my arm as I attempted to twist away from his touch.

"If it's only about sex," he kept his stare on Niko, "then you wouldn't mind if we shared. Would you?"

"Get the hell off me," I shrieked, disgust rolling over my skin. A whole new type of terror seized me when he let go of my arm, only to use that hand to fist my hair, wrenching my neck back painfully. I swung my arms toward his gut, but his hand left my stomach and grabbed my wrists.

"Stop," Niko snarled. "You fucking touch her—"

Geo's cruel laugh cut him off. "You just can't stop with the lies, can you? You do care about her."

"Geo. Don't do this," Niko tried unsuccessfully to speak more calmly. I couldn't see his face, but his voice was shaking with anger. "I'm asking you as my brother—"

"You're fucking the girl our other brother is with," Geo spoke sharply. "You've attacked me twice when I've touched her. I'm not looking at you like a brother anymore."

My stomach heaved when hot breath hit my exposed neck. His hold in my hair tightened, keeping me in place. My head was throbbing from hitting it, and him pulling my hair was nearly unbearable. I could hear Niko's threats as he shifted around.

"What do you say, Sage?" His lips brushed the skin right under my ear. "You give me what you've been giving Niko, and I'll keep this a secret too."

Niko went silent as Geo continued to press kisses onto my throat. My entire body trembled no matter how hard I tried to stay still. My breaths were short and fast as my eyes stayed on the dimming sky above me.

"Give me an answer, Sage." Repulsion crawled through my body when his teeth grazed me before biting me hard enough to leave a mark. "I don't see what the issue is. You've fucked Niko. My identical twin. You probably wouldn't even tell a difference."

I couldn't do it. There was no way in hell I could willingly let him touch me. But if I agreed, maybe he'd free me long enough for me to get away. Or not. I wasn't sure I could take that chance. But what other choice did I have right now?

"Your silence speaks volumes." He released my hair, and a small amount of relief filled me when the pain in my head eased. "I thought you were using him. But shit, I really think you care about him too."

Niko's eyes lost their fury when we locked gazes. He was on his knees, his arms pulled behind him.

"Alex won't be back until later," Geo said, glancing at his phone.

"Are you going to leave me out here until he comes back?" Niko spat out. "Or are you going to run to Dad like you do with everything else?"

"Neither." He dangled Niko's car keys from his finger. "She already got through Alex once. I'm not taking the chance that she'll do it again. She's been nothing but a wedge. I'm fixing it."

"No," I screamed as he threw me over his shoulder again. I pounded my taped hands on his back as he carried me toward the truck.

Niko was bellowing at his brother to stop as he tried to yank his wrists free. Geo ripped open the back door and tossed me onto the seat. Reaching around, he snapped the seatbelt in place.

"Don't fucking move, or I'll tape your hands behind your back." After he finished talking, he slammed the door and went around to the driver's side. I stared at Niko through the window, my heart lurching when I saw him free. He was racing toward the truck, favoring his hurt leg, as Geo backed out of the driveway.

Right as the truck was straightened out in the road, Niko hit the window, trying to pull open the locked door. Geo gunned it, making Niko lose his grip. Twisting my neck, I peered out the back window to see Niko coughing from the dust the truck had kicked up.

"Where are you taking me?" I asked, my words barely coherent as dread took hold of me.

"I'm doing what should have been done when we first found you," he replied coldly, turning to glance at me. "You miss your sister so much, Sage? It's time for you to reunite with her."

CHAPTER FORTY-SIX

Him

"Fuck," I screamed at the empty road after Geo had turned the corner.

He was going to kill her. And I had no way to leave this house. Sage's car sat in the driveway like it had for months, but her key was on my key ring, which Geo had. I ran my hand down my face and flinched. My temple was still trickling blood, and the pain hadn't dimmed at all. Probably had something to do with Geo waking me up with his damn fist.

Pain throbbed in my leg when I limped back toward the house. Sage consumed my thoughts. The fear in her eyes when Geo hauled her away—while I was fucking useless—was haunting me. Rubbing the tape against the edge of the metal railing had worked, but it took too long to free myself.

Headlights brightened the darkening sky, and I cursed under my breath as Alex's Jeep pulled up beside me.

"What the fuck happened to you?" Alex asked, his eyes widening at the blood on my face before he looked toward the house. "Where's Sage?"

"Geo. He fucking took her." A combination of truth and lies might help me twist the conversation. When we found Sage, it would be our word against Geo's. My heart seized. Hopefully, she'd still be alive.

"What? Why?" Alex parked the Jeep and jumped out. "He did this to you?"

Leaning against the car, I hissed out a breath as I yanked the wood out of my leg. I tossed the bloodied piece of coffee table onto the ground and pulled my shirt off. The stab wound wasn't deep, but blood still gushed out. Alex was asking question after question as I wrapped my shirt around my leg, tying it tightly.

"You saw him this morning," I finally cut off his endless questions. "He wants her. Why do you think I've kept her away from him? He snapped tonight when he made a move and she slapped him."

"He what?" Alex growled in disbelief. "Geo wouldn't do that to me."

"I didn't think he'd stab me and knock me out when I tried stopping him," I pointed to my temple, "but here we are."

"When did he leave?" Alex was already texting on his phone. Geo really must have thought Alex was going to be gone longer because there was no way he'd chance letting me talk to Alex first.

"Not long. Maybe ten minutes," I answered, heading back to the house to grab another shirt.

"Where do you think he went?"

"Anywhere we wouldn't be able to find him," I muttered, trying to think of one place Geo would go. He would stay clear of anywhere that was connected with the group. He hadn't gotten permission to hurt her. He was doing it on his own.

I nearly ripped the screen door off the hinges as I stormed into the house. Alex sucked in a breath as he came in behind me. Splintered wood from the coffee table littered the living room floor. The glass plates of pizza I had been carrying were shattered into small pieces. Small drops of blood stained the carpet where Geo had struck me.

"Son of a bitch," I roared, ramming my fist into the drywall. "I'm going to kill him."

Alex's hand clamped on my shoulder. "We'll find him. Calm down. He's still our brother. But Niko...you know the group will want him dealt with. The elders ruled that Sage stay with me. Him taking her like this. It's against a direct order."

For the last couple months, I'd expected it would be me the group would be hunting down for that exact reason. What an odd turn of events. I'd take Geo's place in a fucking heartbeat if it meant Sage was safe.

"Are you getting someone to track his phone?" I asked as I moved down the hall to my room.

"Yes. But he knows how we work. He probably already turned it off." Alex trailed behind me as I rummaged through the dresser before pulling out a clean T-shirt.

"Let's go," I pushed out through clenched teeth. My head was vibrating with pain, and my leg hurt with every step. I got to the living room before Alex grabbed my arm.

"I'm going to meet with Dad and a few others. Stay here and rest—"

"Are you serious? I'm not staying here."

"Niko, you look like you stepped out of a horror movie. You need to clean yourself up and shower all the blood off. You can't walk without limping." He shrugged. "You're going to slow us down."

"No, I'm fine—"

"Dad agrees," Alex cut me off. "He wants you to stay."

He held up his phone, showing me the text messages as proof. I scowled, knowing Alex wasn't going to back down. My father's word was the group's word. What they said was law. If I sat here and argued, it meant fewer people looking for Sage. I didn't exactly want Alex or Dad finding her first, but it was better than Geo killing her. If they got to her, there was a chance I could get her out of town before they caught on to the truth.

"He's going to hurt her," I muttered, careful to keep the concern I was consumed with out of my voice.

"We'll find him," Alex reassured me. "But do you think he's right?"

My eyes snapped to his. "What do you mean?"

"It's been almost a year. Don't you miss your life?" Alex asked hesitantly. "Maybe it's better if she disappears—"

"And then what?" I snapped, my anger barely in control. "That nurse at her dad's nursing home is already suspicious of you. She disappears, guess who the prime fucking suspect will be?"

"You're right," he agreed in a rush. "It's just been stressful."

My guilt about going behind his back with Sage cleared up in that moment. He didn't love her. He'd be fine if she died. I barely breathed as I tried to stay in control. I wanted to rip the keys out of his hand and look for her myself. But that would only make this whole fucked-up situation worse.

"Go," I said gruffly, going into the kitchen. "Call me when you find him."

Wetting some paper towels, I wiped the drying blood off my face as the screen door slammed shut. Resting my forearms on the counter, I closed my eyes, willing my pounding headache to go away. The second they found her, I was getting her the hell out of Michigan.

CHAPTER FORTY-SEVEN

Sage

"How long have you and Niko been sneaking around?" My grip tightened, and I glanced at him, making sure his eyes were still on the road. I managed to slip my phone from my pocket, and it was hidden between my thighs. Now I just needed to text Niko without Geo realizing what I was doing.

"Are you really going to stay quiet the entire drive?" he asked, tapping his fingers on the steering wheel when traffic slowed down again.

"Are you really going to kill me?" I shot back. "If so, then no. I really don't feel like talking."

He chuckled. "You always were feisty."

Keeping my gaze on him, I turned the phone on. The second the screen lit up, I turned the brightness down as low as it would go.

Texting while the phone was between my legs was hard enough, and having my wrists taped was going to make it even more difficult.

After we left the house, Geo had gotten on the main highway to go north. I wondered if we were heading to another house owned by the society. My eyes lowered back to the screen, and I clicked on Niko's name. After Alex had found the phone and gave it back to me, Niko insisted on putting his number in there. I had argued about it, saying it made no sense because I was always with him. I guess it was a good thing he didn't listen to me.

"Fuck," Geo muttered when traffic slowed to a crawl again.

"Is there a reason you won't turn your phone back on to check if there's an accident?" I asked, my voice filled with sarcasm. "I saw you turn it off. Or are you hiding me from your precious cult?"

He slammed on the brakes when a car cut into our lane in front of us. I was grateful the distraction was keeping his eyes on the road instead of on me.

"They'll know everything once you aren't a problem anymore," he grated out. "Unlike my twin, my loyalty still lies with them."

I didn't answer as I peeked back down at the screen, quickly typing out a message.

Spare car key in tampon box. Heading north on I-69.

Without even hesitating, I hit send. That key was my one escape route. But Niko proved he'd help me leave back at the house. I had no doubt he'd keep this secret for me. If I made it out of here alive.

"Where are we going?" I asked, looking up once the text was delivered.

"Oh, now you want to talk?"

"Has the society ever accidentally killed a woman who wasn't a true redhead?" I asked the random question that popped into my head. It was better than him bringing the conversation back to Niko.

Even with the traffic, his head whipped to the side to glare at me. "I'm sure by now Niko has told you everything."

"I wasn't lying when I said he hadn't told me about the society." I stretched my legs, freezing when my feet hit something solid. "I only know what Alex told me the night Lacey died."

"You answer one of my questions, and I'll answer yours," he replied. "But I hope you understand, Sage. You can't sweet talk your way out of this like you did with my brothers. Your tears. Your words. Neither will help you."

I swallowed the fear from his threat. The second he had hit me in the living room, I knew he had no issues with hurting me. After what he did to Niko, I was positive he'd do whatever was needed for me to disappear.

"Why are you sleeping with Niko instead of Alex?" he asked.

"What?"

"Alex did everything to protect you." He sped up once traffic thinned out. "Niko was right at my side when I killed Lacey. He was a part of it. How can you be okay with Niko and not Alex?"

"I don't know," I answered, refusing to tell him everything. "Maybe because I've spent almost every waking second with Niko since I came back."

I moved my bound feet to the side, feeling the edge of Niko's toolbox. He always kept it under the passenger seat. Sliding it closer to me, I tried thinking of a way I could reach down without Geo noticing. There had to be something in there I could use to free myself.

"Did Niko tell you that you were the chosen sister?"

My eyes widened as I stared at the side of his face. "No."

"Years ago, it had been decided that it would be you. Until Alex fell in love with you. He saved you."

"By sacrificing my sister," I hissed, anger clouding my judgment.

"It had to be one of you."

"That was two questions. Now, you answer mine." I changed the subject, not wanting to talk about Lacey. I needed to keep a clear head.

"We're going to a vacation house I rented in Traverse City. Niko and the group know nothing about it, so don't think he's coming to rescue you." His confidence in telling me the truth only added to my panic. "As for your other question—every woman we've chosen has been a redhead. We don't make mistakes."

"Women dye their hair all the time. What if you killed someone who didn't have natural red hair?" As I spoke, I sent another text to Niko, telling him where Geo was taking me.

Geo scoffed. "Your lack of confidence about our reach is almost insulting. It isn't a spur-of-the-moment decision. Every ceremony takes months to plan. Sometimes even longer. We study the women and their heritage. Parents, grandparents, and extended family. We know everything about them before they're taken."

"I think you're all fucking insane," I stated, keeping my voice strong.

He chuckled. "Think whatever you want. It won't change anything."

Slumping back into the seat, I kept my feet beside the toolbox. I slid the phone back into my front pocket, hoping Niko got my messages. Just like I did up north, I wasn't giving up. I'd survived too long to do that.

The entire way, I'd been texting Niko whenever Geo made a new turn. We were in Traverse City now, hours from Capac. Geo turned on a small road, and I glanced at the street sign when the headlights shined on it.

I texted the road name to Niko as knots grew in my stomach. Geo had gone quiet, and I was sure we were close to wherever he was taking me. After about a mile, he turned into a narrow driveway. Trees covered both sides of the driveway, and the house didn't come into view until he drove around a curve.

I searched the front of the tiny house and panicked when I didn't see an address. As fast as I could, I texted a short description of the driveway and the house. It was a small, orange-brick home with a one car attached garage. Two large windows sat on either side of the front door. My heart jolted when my phone vibrated. Before I looked down, I peered at Geo to make sure he wasn't watching me.

I'll be there soon. Don't give up.

Niko's short text gave me a dash of hope as Geo pulled in front of the garage. He took the keys out of the ignition before he jumped out. Shoving my phone into my pocket, I reached down and flipped open the toolbox. Peeking above the seat, I saw him pulling up the garage door. It was too dark to see anything, and I brushed my fingers over the different tools until I found something with a pointed end.

I held the handle of a Phillips head screwdriver and straightened up. Flipping it in my grip, I stabbed the tape between my wrists. Nerves swarmed me as Geo opened his door back up. I leaned forward a bit, hiding my hands. He barely glanced at me before turning the truck back on and slowly pulling into the garage. It was a tight fit with Niko's large truck.

I continued to poke at the tape until I felt it loosen around my wrists. My heart was racing as sweat dripped down my spine. Geo turned off the truck and turned to look at me. I froze my movements as I met his gaze.

"I'm surprised you haven't started begging for your life yet." His voice was full of cruel mockery, and I let loathing fill my eyes.

"If hearing a woman beg is what gets you off, you'll be waiting a long fucking time. I've been through too much to have my last words give you any happiness."

His eyebrow arched in surprise. "Stay there."

Again, he took the keys with him as he moved to shut the garage door. Pulling my wrists apart, I cried in relief as I dove down and attacked the tape around my ankles with the screwdriver. I pulled and twisted, feeling the tape loosen. The broken pieces were still stuck to my skin, but I didn't bother with them as I got to my knees. Glancing out the window, I watched him unlock the door that led into the house.

Pulling the handle of my door, I sucked in a breath when it

wouldn't open. Even when I pulled the lock up, the door didn't budge. The damn child locks had to be on. I was gripping my only weapon so tightly that pain shot through my palm. I stayed on my knees as Geo moved around the truck to my door.

He pulled open my door, and once he was standing in front of me, I lunged at him. Throwing all my weight into it, I plunged the screwdriver into his body near his shoulder. I stumbled to the floor; my movements slow from my muscles not moving for hours.

"Shit," he roared, his hand flying to the screwdriver.

I kicked him behind the knees, giving myself a head start as I darted to the only door that was open, which led into the house. I rushed through the doorway and pushed my body into the door, yelling out when Geo shoved from the other side. I leaned against it, trying to get it closed. Panic clawed my chest when his leg shot through the small opening, preventing me from closing it all the way.

"I was going to make this fast and painless," he shouted, his voice shaking with anger. "Not anymore."

I scanned the room, searching for another way out or something I could use as a weapon. It didn't take me long to take in the small space. The kitchen was nothing but a short island with a stove and fridge on the opposite wall. Stairs led up to an open loft. The living room had one couch in front of a large fireplace. A full-length wide mirror was on the small wall that separated the kitchen and living room. There was nothing that could help me against him.

My throat tightened when I saw a large board nailed in front of the only other door. I'd gotten out of the truck only to be trapped in this house. My planted feet did little to stop the door from moving when Geo rammed into it again.

Knowing I wouldn't be able to hold the door much longer, I bolted forward, running around the kitchen island. Geo burst in, his eyes wild with rage. The screwdriver wasn't in his shoulder anymore as blood dripped down his shirt.

All that was on the counter was a coffee pot with a jar of sugar next to it. I kept my gaze on him as I slid open the drawers in front of me. Geo didn't move an inch as his chest heaved. Glancing down inside the drawer, I was met with silverware and cooking utensils. A pair of scissors caught my eye, and I grabbed them.

"If you're going to stab somebody, you should go for the heart," Geo said, taking a step closer toward me. "You should know that, seeing as I'm the second Rossi brother you've tried killing."

"For that to work, you'd need a heart," I shot back. "Something you're seriously lacking."

"Give it up, Sage," he warned. "You're not leaving here alive."

All I needed to do was keep him talking until Niko got here. He strode closer, and I backed up against the stove with the scissors tight in my grip. His gaze trailed down my body, and his jaw clenched.

"What the fuck is that?" he snarled, staring at my jeans.

My stomach dropped as I glanced down to see my phone sticking out of my pocket. Shit.

"Did you text someone?" he asked, rushing toward me until he was just on the other side of the island. "Does Niko know where we are?"

"If you're going to kidnap someone, you should probably search them." I reached forward and grabbed a handful of butter knives from the drawer. "Seeing as you kidnap women for your fucked-up belief, I'm surprised you don't know that."

His eyes darkened from my taunting as I threw a butter knife at him. He ducked away as I hurled another one at his face. It hit the side of his head, and he grunted, shooting around the island. The next knife hit his gut, not slowing him down in the slightest as he charged at me. Switching the scissors to my right hand, I used my left to knock the lid off the jar of sugar. Grabbing a handful, I threw it at his face right before he reached out to grab me. Some must have gotten into his eyes because he staggered back, wiping his face.

"Bitch," he screamed as I climbed onto the island and jumped to the floor on the other side. My feet hit the floor, and I looked to the garage door that was less than ten feet away. His footsteps pounded behind me, and I raced toward the door.

"No," I shrieked in pain when a hand wrapped in my hair. He yanked me back, grabbing my arm with his free hand. He swung me around, and I flinched before my back connected with the mirror hanging on the wall.

Shattered pieces of mirror fell around me as I slumped to the floor. My breaths were locked in my chest, and pain pulsed throughout my body. Rolling over, I began crawling away, but he grabbed my legs, pulling me back.

"You should have died the night I took Lacey's life," he muttered, flipping me onto my back as I struggled against him. I'd lost the scissors when I fell, so I clawed my nails at his face when he slapped me across the jaw. "You're a cancer to my family. But not anymore."

His hit made my ears ring, and his hands closed around my throat, cutting off my air. I smacked his face over and over, but his hold didn't ease. My lungs begged for air as I fanned my arms out, sliding them on the floor. My fingers brushed against something, and after fumbling, I was able to get a hold of the scissors I had dropped.

I could feel my strength leaving me as I stared into his eyes. He was looking at me with complete hatred as he continued to keep my air cut off. Forcing my arm up, I went for the most fragile part of him I could reach.

I stabbed the scissors into the side of his neck as hard as I could. His eyes bulged as I yanked them back out. Blood spurted out, covering me as he finally released me. I gulped in air, not moving as he fell to the floor next to me, trying to stop his bleeding. Turning my head, I met his gaze as his movement slowed.

Even though it was most likely less than a minute, it felt like an eternity until he took his last gurgling breath. I stared at his lifeless eyes, bile rising in my throat. Getting to my hands and knees, I inched away from him, dry heaving with each breath. My throat burned with pain as I threw up everything that had been in my stomach.

I'd killed him. When I wanted revenge for my sister, I never thought it would be with my bare hands. My body shook violently as I brought my shirt up and tried wiping his blood off my face. Tears mixed with the blood as I rubbed my face again and again. The blood seemed endless. Climbing to my feet, I stumbled to the sink.

I turned the water on full blast and stuck my head under, not caring that it was ice cold. Pink water swirled down the drain as Geo's last breaths haunted me. I didn't move even when the water ran clear.

A hand touched my back, and a scream scorched my already sore throat as I whipped my head up from the sink. Spinning around, I sagged in relief to see Niko. Until I remembered what I'd done. To me, Geo was a monster. But to Niko, he was his brother. His twin.

"I'm sorry," I sobbed, my voice hoarse. "I didn't have a choice—"

"Sage. Calm down." His voice was soft, but the pain in his eyes was all I could focus on. "You did what you needed to survive."

"I didn't want to kill him," I choked out as he wrapped his arms around me. "He's your brother—"

He pulled away from me, gently gripping my chin with his fingers. My breathing was climbing out of control as we locked eyes.

"He wasn't going to let you live, Sage." He sounded so sure, but sadness was etched on his face. "It was always going to come down to you or him. I came here knowing that. And I would have chosen you."

"Niko—"

His phone went off, and he pulled away as he put it to his ear.

"No, he hasn't called me," Niko grated out, turning away from me. "When will you be back at the house?"

I was guessing he was talking to Alex. I crossed my arms, holding myself as chills ripped through my body. Water from my hair dripped down my clothes as I froze in place when Niko slowly walked toward Geo's body. He stopped a couple of feet away, and his whole body moved when he inhaled a deep breath.

Guilt I never thought I'd feel about Geo's death squeezed my heart. After a few moments, Niko reached down and grabbed Geo's phone from the pocket of his jeans. He finished his call and faced me.

"We need to go," he said, coming back into the kitchen.

"Where?"

He lifted me in his arms before heading toward the garage. "I'll take care of everything. You just need to relax, okay? We need to get back to the house before Alex does."

I nodded, having no energy to question what he meant. The large garage door was open, and my car sat in the driveway. He set me in the passenger seat and went back to close the garage door.

My gaze stayed on him, wondering what was going to happen now. This changed everything.

CHAPTER FORTY-EIGHT

Him

I blew out a breath when Alex's Jeep was absent from the driveway. This wouldn't have worked if he'd gotten home before us. After parking the car, I rested my head against the steering wheel. Geo's face hadn't left my mind since I'd seen him lying on the floor. It didn't feel real.

I waited for Geo's phone to power on as I glanced at Sage. She had slept nearly the whole way home. Her face was free from blood, but the bruises were beginning to grow darker. I nearly lost my shit when I saw what his hands had done to her throat. He had almost succeeded in killing her.

Once Geo's phone was on, I found my dad's number quickly. They were tracking his phone, and odds were someone already knew it was on. My gut twisted as I hit the call button.

"Geoffrey? Where are you?" my dad screamed into the phone. "Do you realize what you've done?"

"I'm sorry, Dad." Apology saturated my voice. Geo and I sounded as identical as we looked. Even my parents wouldn't be able to tell my voice from his, especially over a phone. "I made a mistake. I hurt her. I wasn't thinking—"

"Come home. Right now. We can fix this," my dad begged. "I'll talk to the elders—"

"It's too late," I cut him off. "I know going against their word is unforgivable. I brought Sage back."

"Good. That's good, son. Alex will be there soon. We've all been looking for you."

"I won't be here."

Silence. I waited for him to process that before continuing.

"I can't show my face to the group. Not after this. I'm leaving." I took a deep breath. "And I'm not coming back."

"You can't do that," he hissed, anger mixing with concern. "The group won't allow you to do that. You know too much."

"I'm sorry," I repeated before hanging up.

Tapping the phone against my forehead, I almost jumped when Sage spoke up.

"What did you just do, Niko?" she asked quietly.

"Alex will be here soon," I told her. "I'm sure he's bringing the doctor to check you out—"

"Wait. Where are you going?" Her voice rose with each word.

"I need to go back and clean everything up." *And bury my brother.* I didn't want to go back up there. If I had gotten there earlier, I would have killed Geo. I had no doubts about that. Guilt weighed me down, knowing I wouldn't have hesitated. He wouldn't have let her go. It had to be done.

"Let's run." Her eyes were wide with panic. "Please. We can leave now."

"We can't. Everyone is on edge with what happened. They'll be on high alert looking for him. There's no way you'd get out of Michigan." I reached over and grabbed her hand. "Everything will be fine. Alex has no idea. Things will go back to how they were. You'll still be safe."

"After what I just did, I can't pretend anymore."

"You can," I said sharply, seeing her begin to spiral. "You're going to go into the house and tell Alex that Geo made a move on you and when you denied him, he went into a rage. Tell him Geo nearly killed you but couldn't finish it and brought you back. That's it. Do not mention the house you were at. Or what happened there. Nothing else."

"Okay," she whispered. "You're coming back, right?"

"I'll be back sometime tomorrow."

"I'm sorry, Niko."

"You have nothing to apologize for. You saved yourself, Sage."

Getting out of the car, I carried her into the house and laid her on the couch. I ran to my room and grabbed a change of clothes before going back to tell her goodbye. Leaving her was hard as hell, but I needed to finish this. Giving her a soft kiss on the forehead, I went back to her car and headed back to Traverse City.

Smoke filled the morning sky as I sat on the dew-covered grass. My arms were resting on my knees, and I swung the bottle of tequila back and forth. The house was as clean as I could get it. Dad had called, telling me to stay at his house tonight because Alex needed time with Sage after what happened.

I had no logical argument against his reasoning, so here I was. Drinking my fucking sorrows away. After everything she'd gone through, I wasn't able to reassure her that I didn't hate her. I'd seen it on her face before I left, but I needed to make sure I was long gone before Alex showed up. He wouldn't have let me leave if he had seen me. I was the last person they wanted looking for Geo, seeing as it would be too emotional for me. They were worried I wouldn't be able to think straight since he was my twin.

I wonder what they'd think if they knew I had just buried my brother.

My gaze stayed on the bright flames as I took another swig of the liquor. I built the fire to hide the fresh dirt. Now I just needed to wait for it to die out. The closest neighbors were a half mile down the road. Even if Geo hadn't told the group about this place, it was obvious he liked the seclusion like they did.

I groaned when my phone rang. I was nowhere close enough to sober to talk to anyone right now. But this was the fifth call from him. They'd start searching for me if I didn't answer.

"Yeah?"

"Niko?" Alex questioned. "Where are you?"

"Don't worry about me, baby brother." I let myself fall back until I was staring at the rising sun. "I'm not off looking for him. I'm holed up somewhere, drinking."

"This isn't your fault," Alex snapped. "I told you to go see Dad."

"I didn't want to."

"The group is pissed," Alex stated. "First everything that happened with Sage last year, and now this. Dad is not happy that our family is in the spotlight again."

"I figured."

"You need to come home and help. Go see Dad."

"I will. Later. I'm too fucked up to drive right now. How is she?"

"She's okay." He lowered his voice. "The doctor checked her out, and she went right to bed. Other than telling me what happened, she hasn't said a word."

I nodded, forgetting he couldn't see me through the phone. "It's been a long night for her."

"How'd you get her car key?" Alex asked. "I thought it was on your truck key ring."

"I took it off a few weeks ago," I muttered, surprised he had paid enough attention to realize that. I changed the subject before he could question it more. "Have you gotten any sleep? It's nearly eight in the morning."

"No. It's going to be a long week," Alex grumbled. "Let's hope we find him soon."

Sitting up, I looked back at the dying fire. The search for him would be long. The group didn't want rogue people running around with secrets at stake. Getting Sage out of town was out of the question now.

"Get some sleep," I told him. "I'll be home as soon as I'm sober enough to drive. I can watch her while you go talk to Dad. I'm sure you want to be involved with everything."

"No. I'll be staying with her," he answered sharply, making my blood run cold. "I haven't been home nearly enough. And Dad made it clear that after everything, I need to make sure my relationship with her is everything it's supposed to be. She needs to accept our life. The faster, the better."

He made it sound like a damn business transaction. Lifting the bottle, I drank the last few drops. If Alex was going to be at the house, that meant I'd have absolutely no time with Sage. I probably wouldn't even be at the house. Dad would want one of us helping with the group.

"I'll see you when I get back," I mumbled, not waiting for him to respond before I hung up.

Standing up, I whipped the tequila bottle into the fire. I stumbled back a few steps as my head spun. My clothes were covered in dirt and blood. Ripping my shirt off, I tossed it in the fire before doing the same with the rest of my clothes. If someone was walking into the woods right now, they were getting a show.

Grabbing the hose, I rinsed myself off. The alcohol was successful at numbing my body against the cold water. Childhood memories took me hostage, like they had all night. That was the Geo I missed. The version of him I'd known for the last few years—especially after seeing what he'd done to Sage—I fucking hated.

I stayed under the hose until I was confident that I was as clean as I could get. The fire wasn't as large anymore, and I aimed the water at the flames. The sun dried me as I waited for the fire to die out. After a while, all that remained were wet ashes. I stared at the ground for another few minutes before turning the hose off.

    I headed back to the house, planning to sleep until the alcohol worked its way out of my system. Then I was going to see Sage. My dad could wait. The strings that once tethered me to the group were gone. The pressure of the never-ending loyalty to them had disappeared. She came before them. Before anyone.

    And I was tired of fighting it.

CHAPTER FORTY-NINE

Sage

Alex hadn't let me leave his sight for the last three weeks. It had been fucking miserable. My cuts and bruises were pretty much gone. But I'd been exaggerating my fake back pain so I could spend most of the day in bed, away from him. I'd barely seen Niko. He came and saw me after everything happened, but Alex didn't give us a moment alone. Then his dad blew up his phone until Alex pretty much told him to get the hell out of the house. His dad's been making him help with the society. When he was here, he kept his distance since Alex was always in the room. Always.

He made Niko go to the store if we needed something. Anytime I was on the couch, Alex was touching me in some sort of way. I wasn't sure how much longer I could do this.

Last week, Alex had been in the shower, and for once, Niko had been here. I asked him to get me the last thing I needed to complete my list of what I needed to leave. Before he could respond, his mom had walked in with a tray of food. Both their parents had been spending way too much time here.

"Would you like another piece, Sage?" Caitlin asked, passing the tray of meatloaf to Alex.

Ever since her son had disappeared, Caitlin had lost the happiness in her eyes. But she had been putting on a strong front for the rest of her family. She'd been bringing us meals so often that our fridge was overflowing with leftovers.

"No, thank you," I responded quietly, feeling the weight of her joyless gaze.

I wasn't sad about what I'd done to Geo. He was going to kill me, and I did what I needed to survive. But guilt had been eating me up every time I saw the pain in Niko's eyes. We hadn't had a chance to talk about it, and I wasn't sure he'd want to discuss it with me. Or talk to me at all.

Theo and Caitlin were here for dinner for the third time this week, and acting in front of them, on top of Alex, was exhausting. Every time Theo glanced my way, his stare was filled with loathing. He blamed me for everything that had happened.

"I think I'm going to lay down for a bit," I announced, ready to get away from them. My gaze slid to Niko, and my eyes narrowed in surprise when I saw a small smile playing on his lips. That was the most happiness I'd seen from him in weeks.

"Hold on," Alex said, grabbing my hand to keep me at the table. "I'm going somewhere with Dad for the next two days. I feel horrible for leaving you, but something needs to get done."

Excitement hit me for the first time in weeks, and I swallowed it while everyone's attention was on me. Caitlin was giving me an encouraging smile, as if I were devastated that Alex was leaving. Niko kept eating, keeping his eyes off me. Theo was engrossed in his phone.

"I'll call to check up on you," Alex continued. "And I'll be back as soon as I can, okay?"

"I'll be fine," I assured him. If the smile Niko was trying to hide was any indication, it was him who would be staying with me.

The next twenty minutes dragged on while we finished dinner. Alex went to pack a bag while his parents said goodbye and left the house. Niko began washing the dinner dishes, and I moved beside him and started drying them. Neither of us said a word, but anticipation was heavy in the air.

I caught myself from flinching when Alex grabbed my hip, turning me around. Pressing a kiss to my cheek, he kept me in his hold longer than I wanted.

"I'll see you later," he said, exhaustion filling his voice. "I know you've had a horrible few weeks. But don't worry, baby. When I come home, we're going to move forward. We'll talk about it when I get back."

Panic flared from his words, but I didn't ask what he meant. I was going to enjoy these next two days being free of him. He muttered a goodbye to Niko before heading to his Jeep. I watched him drive away through the window, feeling the constant weight on my chest ease a fraction.

"Do you know how long I've been waiting for this?" Niko murmured from behind me, his arms going around my waist. "It's been hell not being here for you."

"Have you been sleeping at your parents'?" I asked as he pulled me toward the couch. Since everything happened, he'd barely spent a night here.

"Yeah." He frowned as we sat down. "They've been watching me as much as they've been looking for Geo. They think I'll be the first person he contacts. Or that I might try to search for him. They're worried I'm about to snap."

"Are you okay?" I whispered. "You had to see what I did. And then you went back to clean it up. I'm sorry, Niko."

"Listen to me." He turned until we were facing each other. "I am not mad at you. You protected yourself. Yes, I miss my brother. But I do *not* blame you."

"How can you not hate me? I know how it feels to lose a sibling. I could never forgive Geo for what he did." I shook my head as tears filled my eyes.

"That was different," he murmured, pulling me into his chest. "I can mourn the brother I loved. The one I grew up with. The man he became was someone I didn't recognize."

"I thought you were avoiding me," I mumbled into his shirt.

He pulled away, meeting my eyes. "Believe me, if I could, I'd be spending every fucking second with you."

Relief flooded me. "It's not going to stay like this, is it?"

"Everything's different right now, Sage," he said hesitantly. "Our entire family is in a spotlight for a reason none of us want."

"I'm done." I kept his stare, making sure he knew I was serious. "I can't do this anymore. Especially with you not here."

"You can't run. There are too many eyes. If that's what you want to do, we'll plan something—"

"I'm not leaving," I cut him off sharply, being completely honest with him. "I'm doing what I promised myself a year ago. I'm exposing the society. They can't keep doing this to innocent women."

His jaw ticked, and I couldn't decipher his thoughts as he stared at me. He scrubbed his hand over his mouth before letting out a long breath.

"I figured you were planning something like that." He jerked his head toward the window. "I got the smartphone you wanted. It's in your car under the floor mat right next to the spare key."

"Thank you."

He raised an eyebrow. "Is that what you've been waiting for to do whatever you're going to do? You needed the phone?"

"That's part of the reason."

"What's the other part?"

I shrugged as if it were obvious. "Because if I do, it'll hurt you."

Surprise gleamed in his eyes before the smile I had missed lit up his face. I cried out in surprise when he grabbed my wrist and pulled me to my feet. One of his hands wrapped around the back of my neck, pulling me closer.

"You have a lot of motivation to make sure this plan of yours works," he murmured softly. "And I'll help. Whatever you need, I'll do it."

My jaw fell. "Niko. You realize I'm talking about the entire society. Alex. Your dad—"

"I know what it means." He pressed his finger to my lips. "And when that happens, I'll most likely go down with them. I'm connected in every way, Sage. There's no way to keep me out of it. And that's okay. After the shit I've done and the things I've helped with, I'm just as guilty as the rest of them."

"No—"

He shook his head, warning me to let him finish. I swallowed my arguments as his hand tightened on the back of my neck.

"You are going to survive this. I'll make sure of it. You're the reason I didn't go down the same path as Geo. I was already shutting everything out. It wouldn't have taken much longer for me to lose the last shred of empathy I'd been holding on to.

"I used to think the others in the group were my family. But they were bound by blind loyalty. You have every reason to hate me, yet you're the only one who sees straight through me. And I keep waiting for you to put an end to whatever we have. Because I sure as fuck don't deserve the warmth you've given me."

"You do," I interrupted firmly, my heart hammering. "You do deserve it."

"When I look at you, I see a future outside this small town. Outside the group. And I want it. So damn bad." He tucked my hair behind my ear. "But for you to be free of all this, the group needs to be brought down. And unless we find some miracle, that includes me too."

Tears rolled down my cheeks. "I've lost so much. I don't want to lose you too. These last three weeks without you, they've been horrible. I missed you. Our talks. Your touch. Even our bickering. Everything."

He smiled sadly. "You wouldn't be losing anything, Sage. You'd be living the life you were meant to."

"We'll figure it out." I grabbed the front of his shirt. "We'll find a way to keep you separate from the group. Because I have to do this, Niko. I couldn't live with myself if I didn't."

"I know. You can't survive in a trapped life. Your spirit burns too bright for that, Sage."

"You're choosing me over the society," I whispered, flutters swarming my stomach.

He grabbed my cheeks, tilting my face up. "I will choose you over everything. Always."

With those words, his lips crashed to mine.

CHAPTER FIFTY

Him

I was a fucking idiot.

I'd known for months that I would do whatever I needed to protect her, yet I'd still resisted kissing her on the lips. Why? Right now, I had no damn idea. Because kissing her felt as natural as breathing. I didn't know how I'd gone this long without kissing her. But I knew without a doubt I'd now be doing it every fucking chance I got.

She moaned into my mouth as our tongues met. My hand got lost in her hair as I kept her pressed against me. Her taste was everything I knew it would be. There was so much darkness spiraling around us, but none of it could touch us in this moment. Our problems were long forgotten as I kept my lips on hers.

Without breaking our kiss, I lifted her in my arms, carrying her toward my bedroom. Her eyes popped open, and she pulled away.

"Niko. We can't see the driveway from back here—"

"It's fine," I told her, setting her on my bed. "They're gone for the weekend. If they come back, my dad will call."

"Are you sure?"

"Yes." With that answer, I crawled on top of her and leaned down to kiss her again. Alex and my dad were doing research for the group, and it had been planned for a while. They were most likely already halfway out of Michigan by now.

Raising her head, she met my kiss, wrapping her arms around my neck. She opened her mouth, allowing my tongue to slip back inside. I was going to savor everything about this night. Because I wasn't sure when it would happen again.

Her hands went under my shirt, her fingers trailing down my spine. She gripped the bottom of my shirt and pulled it over my head. It only took a few moments for the rest of our clothes to end up in a pile on the floor. I lay back on top of her, relishing feeling her soft skin against mine.

"You know, this is the first time we're actually going to sleep together in a bed." Her giggle turned into a moan when my tongue traced her collarbone.

"Not sure how much sleep we'll get," I muttered between kisses as I moved lower down her stomach.

No more words were spoken when my tongue reached one of its favorite places. She kept her legs spread as I licked and sucked liked she was my last meal. I slowly slid a finger inside her, keeping my mouth on her clit. I added a second finger, and her thighs began tightening around my head.

My cock was hard and aching to be inside her, but I wanted to savor this for as long as I could. Things were changing. Our sneaking around wasn't going to happen anymore. Not when my dad wanted me to help with the group. I'd seen it in her eyes earlier. She was at her breaking point about being here. She'd leave soon, and her future wasn't going to have me in it if she was successful with whatever she was planning.

Her cries made my cock twitch when she came hard. Her thighs crushed the sides of my head as her body heaved with every breath. Once her hold loosened, I lifted my head up to see her looking back at me. Her gaze that once held pure hatred for me was now full of emotions I'd never expected to see from her. Warmth. Trust. Desire.

I couldn't wait anymore. I had all night to taste her again. Reaching into the nightstand drawer, I grabbed a condom and ripped it open, sliding it over my cock as she stayed still underneath me. My hands pressed into the mattress on either side of her head as I eased inside of her.

Her pussy clenched around my cock as I inched deeper. My eyes were locked on hers as I started moving. Her legs wrapped around my waist, giving me a better angle to hit her sweet spot.

"I don't know if I can do it," she mumbled breathlessly. "I don't know if I'm strong enough to leave and do this, not knowing if I'll ever see you again."

I didn't stop my slow strokes as I answered. "You are. You're going to leave and end this, Sage. Then you're going to live. And enjoy life."

"Without you?" she choked out. "I don't want to."

"You don't want to stay trapped here." I pulled out and plunged back inside her, making her cry out. "I'll help however I can. But you're going to do it. Understand?"

She nodded. "I'll tell you what I'm planning."

"Tomorrow," I told her as I lowered myself down on top of her, both of us sinking into the mattress as her legs began trembling.

Her arms went around me as I continued to plunge inside her. This time was different from what we'd done in the past. There were no barriers between us anymore. I gave her what she wanted. I chose her. And I always would.

Her breathing quickened as she climbed to the edge again. My face was in the crook of her neck, her scent surrounding me as I moved faster. She felt so fucking good. I wanted to remember every single detail about her because those would be what I lived on once she left.

My balls tightened as pleasure ricocheted through me, her screams heightening my climax as she came too. I stayed on top of her as we caught our breath. Her heart pounded against my chest as she ran her hands through my hair.

After a while, she broke the silence. "I don't want this night to end."

Lifting my head from her neck, I kissed her on the lips. Neither did I. When Alex came back, everything was going to change. I was going to make every single second of this weekend count before we were forced back to reality.

CHAPTER FIFTY-ONE

Sage

I tensed when an arm went around me until I remembered whose bed I was in. His lips grazed my neck as his scent surrounded me. Turning around, I hungrily kissed him on the lips, convinced I could never tire of his taste.

He pulled away and grinned. "Mornin', sunshine."

"I thought you called me that to get under my skin." Giggling, I pushed him away when he came closer for another kiss.

"I told you, Sage. You burn bright. I knew that even when you first got here."

He groaned when his phone rang, bringing me back to reality. Last night had been amazing. But life wasn't that easy.

"Hi, Dad," he answered, clearing his throat to get rid of the sleep in his voice.

He went rigid, his stare going toward the door. Before I moved a muscle, he climbed over and nearly fell out of the bed. With the phone to his ear, he slid jeans on. A pit formed in my stomach, but I still didn't leave the bed.

"Yeah, Dad. I got it." He hung up and glanced at me before digging through the dresser for a shirt.

"Someone's coming over?" I asked, sounding calmer than I felt.

"Alex will be here any second," he muttered. "My dad and his friend are on their way too."

"What aren't you saying?" I asked, noticing his hesitation.

"He told me to pack a bag."

"You're leaving?" I finally stood up.

"I have no idea. He didn't elaborate."

"I can't do this anymore." I crossed my arms. "Being near Alex all the time is driving me insane. I'm going to snap."

"Sage." His tone was sharp. "You want to have a chance to carry out whatever you're planning? Because if Alex walks in and sees you naked in my room, you won't have a chance to do anything. I'll be gone. You'll be gone. That will be it."

He was right. And I knew it. But I was so tired. Worrying every time I opened my mouth that I was going to say a truth instead of a lie. It was exhausting.

"If I could, I'd walk straight out that door with you and never look back." He glanced down the hall where he could see the front window. "But that would get you killed. We have to play this smart."

"I know," I muttered, pushing past him to go to my room. "I'm just sick of it all."

He grabbed my arm. "If I find out I won't be coming back for a while, I'll tell you. Then I want you to do it, Sage. Leave and start whatever you've been planning. Call me when you need my help."

I opened my mouth but didn't have a chance to answer when Niko pulled me into the hall and pushed me into my room right as the screen door creaked open. Silently shutting my door, I leaned against it, listening to their conversation.

"What happened to the weekend with Dad?" Niko asked.

"Something came up," Alex answered, sounding stressed. "But he's leaving and wants you to go."

"Why?"

"Because with Geo gone, you're his oldest son. Get used to it, Niko. He's going to fully expect you to pull your weight for the group."

"I have been," Niko snapped. "I've been helping you, like they've asked—"

"And I appreciate it. But that's done. I'll be staying with Sage. And you're going to go stay with Mom and Dad for now. If I need to go somewhere, then she can come to the house and spend time with Mom."

My heart stopped as Niko started arguing. I slid down to the floor and hugged my knees. There was no way in hell I was staying here with Alex for who knew how long. I had everything I needed to leave. I could have it ready by tomorrow.

Tonight was the last night I was spending in this house.

It had been a long day of pretending. I'd caught a bit of doubt on Alex's face more than once since this morning. Last night while he slept, I'd finished everything I needed to so I could make this happen.

I sat down on the couch next to Alex, plastering on a huge smile. He smiled back, even though confusion flashed through his eyes.

"Alex, it's been a year since everything happened," I said softly, grabbing his hand. "I know this has been hard on both of us. Trying to find a new normal. I'd been keeping myself closed off. But I'm tired of it. I want to move on. I want us to be happy again."

His gaze lost the uncertainty. "That's all I've been wanting, baby."

"I think we should get married." I had practiced saying that over and over, making sure I could do it with the right emotion. "I'm ready, Alex."

His eyes bulged in disbelief as I kept the smile on my face.

"You want to get married?" he asked, astonishment smothering his voice.

"Yes. I want you to know that I'm here to stay. And I love you." I swallowed the vile taste in my mouth. I could do this. Only a little longer.

I relaxed when he beamed. He jumped up, pulling me into his arms.

"It will be amazing, baby. We'll forget about this whole year and start new. It's going to be great."

"It will. And I was hoping you'd say yes, so I got something to celebrate."

Pulling out of his grip, I went to the kitchen and pulled out the whiskey I had bought. Last night, I'd crushed sleeping pills and mixed them in. It was enough to drop a damn elephant. I raised the bottle, showing it to him, and he laughed.

"Kind of early to drink. It's what, one in the afternoon?"

"Come on, Alex. You're not going in to work today, right? Let's enjoy the day and then maybe later...we can spend some time alone." I shot him a flirty grin and fought the nausea trying to overtake me.

His eyes couldn't get any bigger. "All right. Let's have some drinks."

"Let me grab the tequila. You know whiskey and I don't mix." Going back to the kitchen, I grabbed the empty bottle I had told Niko to save weeks ago. It had been sitting in the cabinet, filled with water. I poured myself a shot and then grabbed an extra glass for Alex.

"It's going to be great, Sage," Alex told me as I poured his drink to the brim. "My family will be happy to hear the news. And it'll be so much easier to combine everything once we're married."

A chill tore through me as I glanced at him curiously while he downed his shot. "Combine things?"

"Yeah." He poured himself another drink. "Having separate bank accounts doesn't make sense when we're married. I'll add you to mine so our money is in one place."

It took everything to keep my emotions off my face. I wondered how long he'd been wanting to say that. It was the society who wanted to make sure I couldn't leave. Without access to my money, I wouldn't have a chance to go anywhere. Good thing I wouldn't have to worry about that after today.

I coaxed him to have one more shot before I headed to take a shower. I wasn't sure how long it would take for him to pass out, but I wanted to be ready to leave when it happened. If he wasn't drowsy when I got out, I'd try to get him to drink more. After taking the fastest shower possible, I slid on some shorts and a tank top.

Voices drifted through the door, and I froze when I heard him. I ran a brush through my still wet hair and flew out of the bathroom. Rounding the corner into the kitchen, I stopped short, seeing Niko sitting at the table. Glancing around, I saw Alex outside the window, talking on the phone.

"What are you doing here?" I asked, keeping my voice low. "I thought you were going somewhere with your dad."

He chuckled. "And here I thought you'd be more excited to see me."

My gaze drifted to the whiskey bottle sitting on the table. My heart thudded when I noticed it wasn't as full as it was when I went to take a shower.

"Niko," I nervously ran a hand through my hair, "did you drink that?"

"I was going to ask if you knew that Alex found the whiskey you got him. I thought you were saving it for whatever you're planning." He looked out the window at Alex. "He seems excited about something. But he said he wanted to tell Dad first."

"Did you drink that?" I repeated.

He nodded. "Alex poured me a couple shots, and he drank it too. I wasn't going to say no. I'm supposed to drive his Jeep back to Dad's since everyone thinks Geo has my truck. Drinking just prolongs me having to drive back."

I swallowed hard. "Shit."

Raising an eyebrow, he stood up. "What's wrong?"

"I gave him the whiskey, Niko," I whispered. "After yesterday, I didn't think you would be coming back for a while. I'm leaving. Today."

His eyes widened as he looked at the bottle and then back at me. "Did you poison it?"

"No. Not exactly." I bit my lip. "But there's enough sleeping pills in there to knock someone out for hours."

His posture relaxed at my words, and he let out a laugh as I stared at him in confusion.

"Don't look so worried," he told me, still looking amused. "I don't mind a few hours of uninterrupted sleep. And no one will suspect that I'm helping you if you drugged me too."

"What I'm doing is going to expose everything," I reminded him. "If it works."

He grew serious. "Whatever it is, you better be careful. I would go with you if I could, but I'd only lead them right to you. They're still waiting for Geo to contact me. If I disappear, they'll be searching for me too."

"I know," I murmured. "I'm getting the evidence I need, Niko."

"Call me before you do it," he said, worry covering his face. "I'll do whatever you need so you can get it."

I wanted to argue with him. The evidence I got would most likely implicate him too. But he already knew that. And he still wanted me to do it. I didn't know if I'd ever see him again after today.

"Sage. You want to tell Niko the good news?" Alex asked as he came back into the house.

I forced a smile. "You can."

Alex wrapped an arm around me as he looked at Niko. "We're getting married."

There wasn't a hint of Niko's real feelings as he grinned and offered his congratulations. He must have realized that was the news I was using to give Alex the whiskey. We all sat on the couch, and I grew anxious about my plan while Niko and Alex talked. Alex's arm stayed around my shoulders as I waited for the sleeping pills to take effect.

It felt like forever until Alex's arm slipped from its spot around me. Niko was staring at me as his eyelids drooped closed. I stayed perfectly still as Alex's breathing evened out into steady, deep breaths. Niko was slumped back—out cold.

Glancing over my shoulder, I made sure Alex was sleeping too before I grabbed his arm and pushed it off me. Then I coughed as loud as I could a few times. Neither of them flinched. My stomach bubbled with nerves, knowing there was no going back now.

Facing Alex, I slid two fingers into his pocket and slowly pulled out his phone. I held my breath, terrified he would somehow wake up. Once his phone was in my hand, I ran to my room and grabbed the smart phone Niko had bought for me. I scrolled through Alex's texts, finding the address his dad had sent him months ago. Once I typed it into my phone, I went back to the living room and put Alex's phone back in his pocket.

Eyeing Alex's keys on the kitchen counter, I took a deep breath. I really hoped he had drunk enough to stay passed out for as long as I needed. Swiping the keys up, I rushed out the door and got into my car.

After driving for twenty minutes, I pulled up to the hardware store. Forcing myself to act normal, I walked into the store and searched for an employee.

"Hi," I said, finding a guy stocking shelves. "I need to copy my keys."

Looking annoyed that I had bothered him, he pointed to a small counter near the back of the store.

"Thanks," I muttered, hurrying back to where he'd pointed.

I greeted another employee who was behind the counter. "How long to make a copy of six keys?"

The guy glanced at the keys I set on the counter. "About a half hour."

I smiled. "Perfect."

He grabbed the keys, and I rushed out of the store, driving one block to my bank. Luck was on my side because there wasn't a line at all. I pulled out nine thousand dollars, knowing the society would be watching my account once they realized I was gone. But this would be more than enough to keep me going until I did what I needed.

I went back to the hardware store and waited impatiently for the keys. I tapped my fingers on the counter, watching other customers go about their day. I hadn't even been gone an hour, but I was getting nervous. I wanted Alex's keys back where I'd found them before he woke up. If he knew I had them, then they could move things before I got the evidence I needed.

Alex's key ring had six keys on it. Three of them were for his car, his house, and my house. The other three keys were a mystery. But I knew they had something to do with the society. Because when I had asked about them a few weeks ago, he was vague. The usual reaction when it had something to do with them.

"Here you go," the guy said, dropping the two sets of keys on the counter.

Handing over some of the cash I had just pulled out, I paid for them. "Thank you so much."

The whole way back to the house, my heart was racing. If Alex was awake, this would all be ruined. And I'd be screwed. I pulled into the driveway and quietly shut my door after I got out. Peering through the front window, I relaxed when they were both still on the couch. I quickly walked in and put Alex's keys back on the counter exactly where they had been. Then I double-checked that his phone was back in his pocket.

The bag I had packed yesterday was waiting under the bed. I slung it over my shoulder and grabbed the empty sleeping pill bottle from the dresser drawer. As I passed the kitchen table, I placed the pill bottle right next to the whiskey. Because fuck him. I hoped he was pissed when he realized what I'd done.

I glanced at Niko and felt a pang of guilt. I didn't want to leave him. I had thought for hours to come up with a way to keep him out of what I was going to do. But it wasn't possible. Unless Kiara could come up with something.

Stepping out of the house, I grinned. I had no plans to ever come back here. And it felt amazing. I pulled out of the driveway, wondering how long it would take them to wake up. It didn't matter. By the time Alex found out I was gone, I'd be far enough away.

Last time I fled, I had no plan, only the will to survive. This time, I was running straight for them. And I was going to get what was needed to expose it all. No matter what the cost.

CHAPTER FIFTY-TWO

Him

My head was still groggy from the sleeping pills as I watched Alex tear the house apart. Once he understood what Sage had done, there was no stopping his rage. The whiskey was dripping off the wall from where he'd thrown the bottle. He had gone to her room, searching for anything to tell him where she'd gone.

I glanced out the window as my dad pulled up. Three other men stepped out of the car with him, and I stood from the couch. I hoped by now she was somewhere she couldn't be found. Because the group was going to use every resource they had to find her.

I checked my phone again, waiting for a text or call from her. I didn't have the number for the phone she had. Her old phone was hidden away in my room. The front door opened, and I let my face go grave as I met my father's gaze. I didn't think it was possible for anyone to be angrier than Alex. But my dad's eyes were burning with more rage than I'd ever seen.

"I knew this was going to happen," he spat out as Alex emerged from the hall. "She should have been dealt with a year ago."

"We'll find her," Alex snapped.

"I'll go look at her old house in case she stopped there," I told them, holding my hand out. "Let me use your Jeep."

Instead of giving me the keys, he exchanged a look with my dad. I tilted my head in confusion as nerves brushed my confident act. Something was wrong. They were all staring at me without saying a word.

"What did you and Sage do when I left with Dad two nights ago?" Alex asked quietly.

"Watched a movie before she went to bed," I answered, giving him a questioning glance, not letting my nerves get to me.

"The trip got postponed. I planned to come back home that night."

I could see it on his face. He fucking knew.

"I trusted you with her," Alex murmured as panic crawled through me. "You lived with us to make sure she stayed where she was supposed to. I noticed how she warmed up to you. She didn't spend all day in the room anymore. I was happy and thought it would make all our lives easier. I never would have imagined that you were fucking her."

The color drained from my face as my eyes went to my dad. Disappointment and betrayal were written all over his face. But not surprise. Alex had already told him. Fuck.

"Alex—"

"How long has it been going on?" Alex cut me off sharply.

I hesitated, debating on denying it. It was obvious he had proof, or he wouldn't have told our dad.

"I came home in the middle of the night. Only to find her in your bed," he said bitterly, his eyes filled with hate. "What a great fucking brother you are."

"I'm sorry," I pushed out with as much sincerity as I could muster. "We drank. And things went too far. That was the only time it happened."

"The second I saw you two, I wanted to bust in there and kick your ass. But I stopped myself." He looked at our dad again. "Because Sage isn't just mine. Her life is owned by the group. So, I went back to Dad's. And I waited. The elders told me to wait. Until a plan was in place."

I gritted my teeth, realizing he'd been acting all weekend. And that was why he'd pushed me so hard about leaving with Dad. To separate me from her.

"I didn't know what she was pulling with the marriage shit, but I went along with it," Alex continued. "I didn't fucking expect her to drug me."

"How could you, Nikolas?" my dad asked, shaking his head. "Family is everything."

"Sage must be pretty fucked up to sleep with you," Alex muttered, his hands clenched into fists. "You were a part of Lacey's ceremony."

My anger surged. "I told you, it was a drunken mistake. My loyalty is still for my family. And the group."

"Have you forgotten who you are?" Alex seemed like he was trying to comprehend why I'd done it. "You've helped with how many other ceremonies while we were growing up? Your name is signed in that book right next to mine. Although, over the last year, you really took a step back. At least now I understand why."

"I raised my sons to be future leaders. What did I do wrong?" my dad said, stepping up beside Alex. I tensed, realizing what was happening. "What happened with Geoffrey? Were you protecting her somehow?"

"He attacked Sage. Exactly like I said. He fucking stabbed me," I said gruffly, having no intention of ever telling them what really happened. "I don't know where he is."

"Give me your phone," Alex demanded.

My gaze darted between him and my dad. I was grateful Sage had left already because I had a feeling they had been planning something for her. Alex had played into Sage's act of wanting to get married when he was fully aware I had been sleeping with her.

"Are you expecting a call from her?" my dad snarled, his trust in me completely gone. "Did you help her leave?"

"I was drugged right along with Alex. I had no idea she was leaving."

"How'd she get the pills, Niko?" Alex prodded. "You were the one with her all the time."

"I don't know."

"Give me your phone," Alex said again.

My jaw clenched as I pulled my phone from my pocket. I couldn't take the chance that Sage would call or text if they had my phone. It could ruin whatever she was doing. Staring at Alex, I dropped my phone to the floor. Then I smashed my foot on top of it. I felt it crack under my shoe, and I stomped on it again for good measure.

"You son of a bitch," Alex hissed. "You'd rather help her than your family?"

I saw his punch coming too late for me to dodge it. His fist collided with my cheek, and I charged forward, ready to fight back until the barrel of a pistol pressed into my chest. One of the men who had come with my dad kept the gun on me even as I backed up a step.

"Can't fight your own battles, Alex?" I taunted as my chest heaved. "Come on. Fucking try to beat my ass and see what happens."

"I don't need to. The group has my back for anything I need. Too bad that's not something you can count on anymore."

"Your mother is already so heartbroken over Geo," my dad muttered, looking pained. "Now her other son has betrayed us. You'll stay in this house until the elders decide what's going to be done with you."

"Don't worry, I'll call and let you know when we find Sage," Alex said with a small smirk.

Alex and my dad left the house while the other three men stayed. They looked at me like I was scum. Falling onto the couch, I ran my hands down my face. I really hoped Sage could pull off whatever she was planning without me. Because I was as fucked as she was now.

CHAPTER FIFTY-THREE

Sage

It had been three days since I'd left. This time I wasn't holed up in a shitty motel. I'd been on the move constantly, getting what I needed for the next step. After I had left Alex's house, I went to my house and switched out my car for Lacey's truck. Niko still had the spare key, but the original was still in the toolbox where I had put it a year ago. I seriously doubted they would even look in the garage. The last thing they expected me to do was use a massive, stand out truck to leave. Which was exactly why I'd done it.

Now, I was up north, staring at the Mackinac Bridge while sitting in the truck. It was bringing memories that made it difficult to push away. Being here used to be my favorite place. Now it plagued my nightmares. But the address I had found in Alex's phone was in the UP. I looked it up on the map on my phone and researched the whole area. My bet was it was another house the society owned. Like the one I'd burned down, this one was in the woods in the middle of nowhere.

I had been keeping in touch with Kiara ever since I'd left. The first day, I told her everything that had happened in the past four months. How hard it was to pretend with Alex. How I almost lost sight of everything from the drinking. I even told her about Niko and how he helped me stay sane and kept my secrets.

Sighing, I looked away from the bridge and dialed Kiara's number.

"Sage?" she answered.

"Hi. I just wanted to check in."

"Where are you?"

"Still in Michigan," I responded vaguely. I didn't want Kiara to come meet me. I didn't want someone else to get involved and get hurt if the plan didn't work.

"I can help you if you tell me what you're doing," she pleaded.

"All I'm doing is researching," I lied.

"You can do that from Chicago."

"No, I can't. Once I get the evidence we need, then I'll come see you. We have nothing right now. Except my story." What I'd done to Geo popped into my head. I had my own secrets to hide too. "And we have no idea who we can trust, even in Chicago. What if you tell someone and they bury it, or worse, hurt you?"

"It might be time to take that chance—"

"No," I said more sharply than I intended. "We need to do it so that they don't have a chance to get away with it. I got an address from Alex's phone. I'm going to send it to you. Maybe you can find out who owns the land? That could be the start of a lead."

"Sure, I'll see what I can do. You're not going there, are you?"

"Of course not. Not without knowing more about it," I replied. In the last year, my lies had become second nature. If Kiara knew my plan, she would come to Michigan to try to stop me. But nothing was going to get in the way of what needed to be done. And I had to do it within the next few days for it to work.

"Okay, I'll send you the address now. I've got to go. I'll call back soon."

After hanging up, I pressed on another number. The number I'd called and texted so many times I'd lost count. Yet Niko still hadn't called me back. Worry had set in when his phone went straight to voice mail. Either something was wrong, or he was choosing them over me.

He was the one who'd told me to go ahead with my plan. I wanted him here with me, but I could do it without him. I didn't want to. But I would. I had to. Because this was my only chance at surviving.

I glanced behind me at the snacks I'd bought for the next few days. The least amount of stops I made, the better. I only had one specific stop planned before I got to the house. The sheriff up there was in on it, and who knew how many others. I needed to stay off their radar. After I went over the bridge, it would take less than two hours to drive to that address.

Shaking off my fear, I put the truck in drive and made my way over the bridge.

I found it. The house wasn't visible from the road, and I wasn't about to just waltz up the driveway. But I knew exactly where it was. I drove down the road another two miles and pulled into a public parking area. A place where people parked when they went to hike, hunt, or enjoy the beach of Lake Superior. The truck would fit right in, and people kept their cars parked there for a day or even longer.

I'd marked this place on the map and knew this was perfect. The parking area was busy with summer tourists, and no one glanced my way when I parked. Just like the other house, this one was right on the water and away from any city. This public parking was the closest thing to civilization for miles.

Before I had lost signal, I wrote an email to Kiara and explained exactly where my truck was going to be parked. But instead of sending it, I scheduled it to get sent in two days. If Kiara got that email now, she would drive here as soon as she could. I didn't want her to get hurt, especially if this lead didn't come to anything. Two days was all I needed.

If I succeeded in finding what I was looking for, I could cancel the email. If I got caught, Kiara would have the information to find my truck and any evidence that I had gotten so far.

It was early morning, and the sun was already hot. I got out of the truck and packed my backpack with some snacks and water before heading toward the beach. I stayed near the tree line and walked in the direction of where the house was. Slowing my steps after walking about fifteen minutes, I scanned the trees for any sort of trail.

After a few more minutes, I spotted a small opening in the dense trees. It was easy to miss, and if I hadn't been searching for it, I would have walked right by. I stepped onto the narrow trail and then froze.

My heart was racing like I had just run a marathon. For the last year, I had done everything to stay as far away from them as possible. Now, I was in their backyard. The last few days, I'd moved nonstop to make this plan a reality. There was no turning around now. Even though the terror that invaded every part of my body was begging me to flee.

I closed my eyes as I sucked in deep breaths. I could do this. After a couple of minutes, I forced one foot in front of the other. My eyes swept the area for any movements. I noticed a private property sign nailed to the tree next to the trail. I was getting close. I stayed on the trail, getting farther from the beach. Fear lit inside me when the house finally came into view.

It was smaller than the other house, and it didn't have the grand elegance either. It was still large but looked old and decrepit. The outside was dark stone, and it seemed no one had done work on it in years. The porch wood was rotting, and the roof shingles were falling off. Two of the upstairs windows had large cracks in them. But I knew this was the right place when I saw bars. Although only one window upstairs had bars while none of the others did.

Staying between the trees, I stepped off the trail. I circled the house until I found a little spot that was perfect. There were views of the driveway and the entire front and side of the house. No one would be able to leave or come without me seeing. I was surrounded by thick bushes and was confident that I couldn't be seen. Now it was time to wait.

There was a lone beat-up truck in the driveway. No other cars joined it as I sat for the next four hours. I was waiting for whoever was here to leave. I had used my debit card in a city right after I crossed the bridge. If they were watching my account, they should see that transaction soon. When that happened, they would call anybody in the area to go check it out, and that would most likely include whoever was in this house.

An hour later, a man rushed out, making sure to stop and lock the door behind him. My heart stopped. It was Eric. The same man who'd lived at the house I had burned down.

I ducked down even farther into the bushes as his truck raced down the driveway. Once the sound of his engine had faded away, I looked back at the house and waited to see if there was any movement. I'd learned from Niko that they never got together unless there was a ceremony. Eric was the only one who lived at the other house. I was almost positive there was no one else in the house.

But fear still kept me rooted in my spot. Tomorrow was the last night of a full moon for this month. August. If they were going to kill another woman, it was going to be within the next couple of days. I had circled the entire area, and there were no other cars anywhere. There was an open area in the backyard with tire tracks, but it was empty. There was no one else there. Except maybe there was. What if there was a woman locked in that house? I was going to find out. Along with any other evidence I could take without them knowing.

Moving away from the bushes, I ran to the front door. I peeked in the windows and saw no one. The bars on the window above me looked new and shiny. They must have been making this into their new murder house. The windows that didn't have bars probably would soon. I gulped as I looked at the lock on the door. The copied keys from Alex's ring were pressed tightly in my hand. I tried one key and let out a frustrated groan when it didn't fit. If I couldn't get into the house, this would all be for nothing. The second key didn't work either.

When the third key slid in, I didn't know whether to jump in excitement or run away screaming. Slowly, I cracked open the door just enough to see inside. No sound or movements. I slipped inside and locked the door behind me. My hands shook as I turned the key. The vivid memory of when I had escaped through the front door of the other house tore through my mind.

I had fought for my life to get out of that house, and now I'd just turned the key that could lock me in to another nightmare.

CHAPTER FIFTY-FOUR

Sage

I glanced around and déjà vu spread through my senses. The wood floors were the same color as the other house. But they were in much worse shape, just like everything else in the entrance. The walls were covered more in yellow stains than the white paint. I could see the kitchen was straight down the end of the hall. The staircase was to my left, and there was a room with the door closed on my right.

Finding the basement was my first goal. I crept toward the kitchen, but it was impossible to be quiet. The old floors creaked with every step.

The countertops in the kitchen were just as empty as the last house. I hurriedly opened the two doors, only to find a pantry and a laundry room. The need to leave was starting to consume me. I had never been claustrophobic, but this house felt like a coffin. I needed to get out of here before Eric returned.

Going back down the hall, I began to open every door. Finally, I tugged the third open and was met with a set of concrete steps. Taking two steps at a time, I raced down. There was no other door; it was an open basement. The only light was from the one above the steps, making the whole room pitch black.

I pulled out my phone, turned on the flashlight, and scanned the room. There wasn't much to see. It was small. There were no crosses on the walls and only three tables. My heart stuttered when my light shined on them. Scissors, twine, and knives covered the first two tables. The third table was against the back wall and was empty. Except for the metal cuffs chained to it.

My stomach threatened to heave everything up. I bent over, wrapping my arms around myself. I had to fight it. There could be nothing that showed I had been here. After many deep breaths, I straightened back up and looked for the whole reason I'd come down here.

There it was. On a small shelf against the wall. The book.

Carefully picking it up, I opened it, and my eyes widened. It was the same book I had ripped the page from. Tears sprang to my eyes when I turned the next page. There was Lacey's full name and the date she had been killed. The words gave me what I needed to keep going and reminded me of why I was fighting so hard.

There would be no new name for them to put in this book.

Setting the book down, I tugged my backpack off my shoulders. I pulled out a book that looked identical to the society's book. Well, almost identical. It wasn't as thick, but the outside black leather looked the same. It had taken me two days of scouring antique bookstores to find one that could pass as real. As long as they didn't look inside it.

I took the book from the shelf and replaced it with the one I had brought. With low lighting, no one would be able to tell the difference. At least until they opened it. The book was everything. It had names of victims and names of people in the society. It was the main reason I had come. I glanced one more time at the book I'd replaced and hoped they didn't plan on using it within the next few days. I wanted to give it all to Kiara before they even knew it was gone.

I made sure everything was back in place before running back up the stairs. The feeling I got in that room was almost unbearable. Racing down the hall, I looked out the window to the empty driveway. My phone showed I'd only been in the house for twenty minutes, but it had felt like an eternity.

"One more thing," I muttered, my eyes going to the second floor.

I needed to make sure there wasn't a woman trapped in here. With one last look at the driveway, I bounded up the steps. There were four doors upstairs, and all the rooms were empty. Each of the three bedrooms only had a bed and nothing else. Everything looked rushed and made me think that my guess was right. This house was replacing the one I had burned down.

Back down on the first floor, I scanned each room and was satisfied that no one was there. I walked back out the front door and locked it. There was no sound of any cars approaching, but I ran back to the safety of the trees like I was being chased.

I pushed through the branches until I was back on the beach. After running nearly the whole way back, I unlocked the truck and got into the passenger seat. I pulled the book out and slid it under the seat, along with my phone. Leaning back in the seat, tears fell down my face. I had done it. I'd gotten what was needed to at least start an investigation into the society. Wiping the tears away, I packed some more snacks and water into my bag. After locking the truck, I slid the key on a little ledge of metal under the truck near the rear tire. If I got caught, I didn't want them to know what I had driven here. It was time for the next part.

I was going back to the house. To wait and watch. There wasn't a woman in that house, which meant they were going to be bringing one if they planned to do a sacrifice. I was going to be there when it happened. There was no way I'd be able to rescue someone by myself. I'd record it and blast it on social media. Then I'd run back to my truck and go to the major city, two hours away.

I would go into the state police station and start screaming about how a woman had been kidnapped. It was risky. That sheriff was in on it, but he wasn't part of the Michigan State Police force. It was still possible others were. The plan rested on me being so loud and insistent that the whole building would hear, not only one person. The best-case scenario was that I staked the house out and they didn't bring a woman back at all. But if they did, I'd do whatever I needed to rescue her. I didn't want one more woman dying by their hands.

With my stomach rolling, I walked down the beach again until I found the trail. I went right back to the hiding spot in the bushes. The truck was still gone. It felt like I'd been here for days, but the sun was still in the sky. I felt so vulnerable just sitting outside the house. It was a well-hidden spot, but that didn't stop the fear from claiming me.

I wished I wasn't alone. Niko's face flashed through my mind, and I closed my eyes for a moment. I wanted him to be here. I didn't believe he would turn on me. Not after everything he'd done for me.

My eyes popped back open when the loud revving of an engine filled the air. The truck was back, and Eric and another guy jumped out. I peered through the gaps in the bushes to study the new guy. Something about him looked so familiar, but I couldn't place where I'd seen him before. The guys didn't say anything as they went into the house.

I breathed a sigh of relief when a woman didn't come out of the truck. Maybe they weren't doing it this year. They didn't have a lot of time left before the full moon was gone for the month. I still wasn't leaving until I knew for sure. I'd brought enough food to last the next day. These shrubs would be my home for at least the next twenty-four hours.

The feeling of terror never left. It lingered front and center in my mind as I stared at the house. Fear of them knowing someone had been there was keeping my exhausted brain wide awake.

My eyelids began to get heavy. I had been running on little sleep over the past few days and staring at nothing was getting to me. That changed when the front door opened. Eric walked out with a beer in hand and started making his way to the trail that led to the beach. Dread swallowed me as Eric kept walking away from me. What if they knew I was here?

I shoved that thought away. If they had found me or the truck, he wouldn't be walking slowly with a beer in his hand. He disappeared into the trees, and I hoped he wasn't going to the public parking area. Now I was really stuck in these bushes because he had walked right into my escape route.

Hours went by and nothing happened. The sun began to set, and Eric still hadn't emerged from the woods. The other guy was still in the house, and I was trying to remember where I had seen him.

A branch snapped behind me, and before I could turn around, it suddenly felt like my hair was being ripped out. The shrubs scratched at my arms as I grabbed the hand that was wrapped in my hair. His grip was iron tight, and when I let out a piercing scream, a hand covered my mouth roughly as I got pulled into his body.

"This is seriously the last place we would have ever looked for you. How nice of you to come on your own," the voice hissed in my ear.

I craned my neck as much as I could with his hand still in my hair. It was Eric. I flailed, trying any way to get out of his grip, but it was no use. Terror invaded my bones as I struggled. My fast breaths were shallow from his hand covering my mouth. He dragged me to the house until we got inside the front door. The side of my head hit the wall as he shoved me out of the way. My chest went tight as the sound of the lock turning sliced through the air.

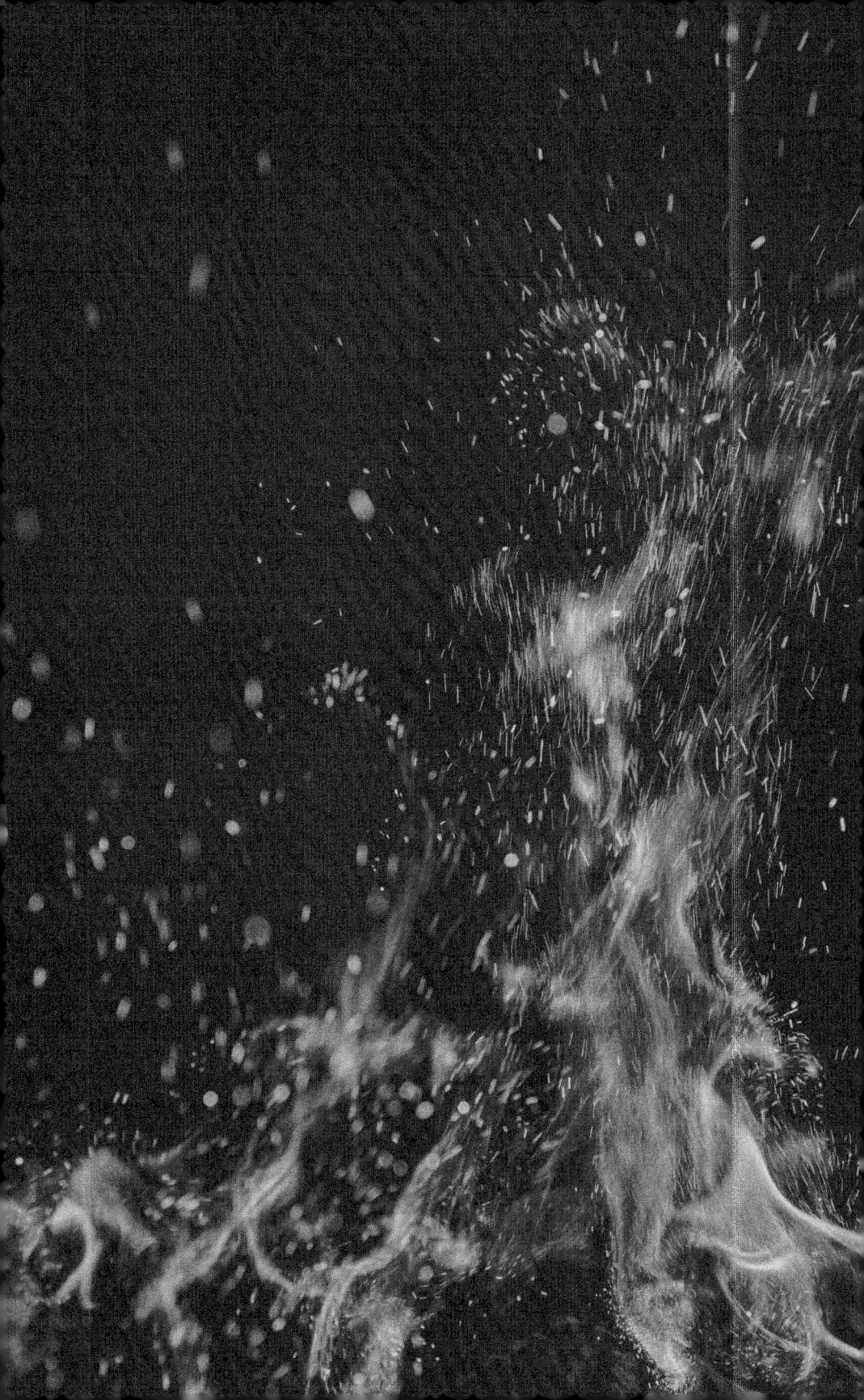

CHAPTER FIFTY-FIVE

Him

"Here. He wants to talk to you." Mark shoved the phone in my face, and I scowled as I grabbed it from him.

I'd been stuck in this house for the last four days. Mark and two other members of the group had been here the entire time, taking turns watching me. There was always at least one of them awake at all times. They'd been making me sleep on the couch, where it was easier to keep an eye on me.

Putting the phone to my ear, I walked into the kitchen to get as much privacy as I could in this fucking house.

"What?" I grated out, not giving a shit who it was.

"I thought you'd want to know," Alex's smug voice came through the phone, "we found her."

My heart stopped. "Where?"

"We found her yesterday." Alex ignored my question. "She made it easy."

The front door slammed, and I spun around to see two guys rushing out. Mark stayed near the door with his glare pointed at me. He was holding the gun in his hand as if waiting for me to try something.

"You're doing a ceremony," I muttered. That would be the only reason they'd leave me here with only one person. They needed a minimum amount of people for a ceremony.

"Yes," he answered coldly. "After tonight, she won't be a problem anymore."

"Alex, you're rushing this. These need to be planned and you know it. Have you even thought of the story of her disappearance? It usually takes months to plan all that." I was trying anything to get them to wait and give me a chance to get to her.

"We changed our minds. And even if you somehow get out of the house, you won't find us. We aren't at the other house in Wisconsin. We got another house. You've been out of the loop for so long you don't even know where it's at."

I froze. If they weren't at the house in Wisconsin, I had no idea where they were.

"She's been a loose end for too long. We'll figure it out. The elders already agreed," Alex continued. "And they have a plan for you too. You broke Mom's heart, you know. Now, she has to say goodbye to another son."

"You're going to be fucked if you can't explain her disappearance," I pressed, trying to change his mind. "You'll be a suspect. You know that."

"That's group business. Something that doesn't concern you anymore. See you later, Niko."

Alex hung up, and I gripped the phone, keeping it to my ear. My gaze went to Mark, who was still watching me intently. I'd been thinking of what I could do to get out of here, and I needed his phone to do it.

Turning around, I lowered the phone and went to the settings.

"Hey," Mark growled. "Give me the phone back."

Ignoring him, I scrolled down and changed the lock screen time to five minutes. I needed to be able to get into his phone.

"If you don't want a bullet in your back, you better turn the fuck around," Mark warned.

Reaching for the cabinet above me, I spun around to face him. Grabbing the tequila bottle, I set the phone on the counter.

"Want a drink?" I asked casually. "I know I could use one."

"Give me the phone."

"Can't do that," I muttered, whipping the bottle at his face. "I need it."

Mark ducked away as the bottle went flying at him. I lunged, going straight for the gun in his hand. He blindly pulled the trigger and the shot went wide. I got my hand around the gun as he punched me with his other fist. Kneeing him in the gut, I pushed him back against the wall, trying to pry the weapon from his grip.

We fought for control, and I shoved my elbow into his throat. He choked out breaths as his hold went slack. Ripping the gun away from him, I rammed it into the side of his head. His eyes rolled as he slumped to the floor.

Sticking the gun in the back of my jeans, I went back to the phone and made sure it hadn't locked. Leaving it on the counter, I raced to my room and grabbed a couple of belts. I didn't want to kill Mark. There wasn't time to figure out a way to cover his death up. I quickly secured his hands behind his back and then wrapped the other belt around his ankles. Once I was confident he wasn't going anywhere, I grabbed the phone again.

Deciding to search his phone before using my last option, I went through the texts and everything else. I grumbled under my breath, finding nothing. The phone had been wiped. Most likely to stop me from doing this if I got a hold of it.

Opening the web browser again, I typed in what I was looking for. I couldn't just call her. Her number was in my phone that I had destroyed. But I remembered where she worked. I could call her office and get a hold of her that way. And hope to everything she didn't hang up on me. I found the number I was looking for and pressed the call button.

"Yeah, can I please talk to Kiara Jones?" I asked as my heart thudded.

"One moment, I'll transfer you."

I paced the house as elevator music hummed in my ear. Less than a minute later, a brisk female voice came on the phone.

"This is Detective Jones."

I took a deep breath. "Ms. Jones, I need your help."

"Who's this?"

"I'm...a friend of Sage Taylor."

There was silence for a few moments.

"A friend?" she asked icily.

"Yes. Look, she's in trouble—"

"What's your name?"

"That's not important right now. What's important is I need help."

"If you're really a friend, then tell me your name."

I debated lying for half a second. "Niko."

"Niko?" The shock in her voice told me immediately that Sage had told her about me.

"Yes."

More silence.

I grew annoyed. There wasn't time for this.

"Listen, they got her. And she'll be gone by tonight. But I can help. I just need to know if you know anything about where she went. What area was she in?"

"You're a part of it. Of them," Kiara said, her voice shaking.

"Obviously, Sage told you who I am. Did she tell you that I've been helping her for months? I found her and didn't tell anyone. I've been hiding her secrets since they found her." I tried keeping calm, but there wasn't time to argue.

She paused. "Yes, she did tell me that you helped. But you were part of her sister's death."

"Listen, I know what you do for a living. But I'm telling you, Sage is in trouble. I can get to her if you have a way to help me," I snapped, not admitting to anything.

"If they took her, then why don't you know where she is? You're with them."

"Because they have an idea that I helped her run. They cut me from everything."

"I don't know if I can trust you," she said coldly.

"Trust me? Do you really think that I would call someone who knows everything about us—who works for the police—if you weren't my one and only option? Why in the hell would I try to contact you for anything—except to help her?"

"I have to go. I'll call you back."

"Wait, what? No—"

Kiara hung up. I fought the urge to throw the phone across the room. I had to hold out hope that maybe she would call back. I stared at the empty driveway, thinking about my next fucking problem. I needed a car. Wherever they'd taken her, it wouldn't be around here. The houses were always far from cities. I'd most likely have to drive for hours.

It was still early morning. They had to wait for the moon to be full to do the ceremony. I'd have time to get to her if I found out where the house was. Looking at the phone again, I took a deep breath before making another call.

CHAPTER FIFTY-SIX

Sage

I awoke with a start, the soreness of my arms reminding me where I was. With a groan, I tried pulling my wrists free again. I had been pulling at the cuffs for...I didn't know how long I'd been here for. But the sun was up, which meant it was a new day. Both my wrists were handcuffed to the iron bed frame with my arms raised near my head. I could sit up and scoot down a little if I stretched, but it was impossible to get comfortable in any position.

Eric had come in twice to let me go to the bathroom, and he brought me food, which I ate with one hand still cuffed to the bed. My wrists were raw and bruised from trying to slide and pull out of the restraints all night. My head was still aching from Eric dragging me by the hair and then slamming me into the wall. The blue comforter had fallen off the bed at some point during the night, and the pillow behind my back didn't help soften my position at all.

Footsteps started to come down the hall. The creaking floorboards were my alarm that someone was coming into the room. I sat up as straight as I could while the door opened.

"Hey, baby," Alex purred quietly as he closed the door behind him.

I glared. He was taunting me by calling me that. By now, he knew I hated it. I was surprised it had taken this long for him to come see me. I had expected him to make an appearance last night. Fear was coursing through my veins, but I focused on the rage instead.

"It didn't take long to find you at all this time. I can't believe we found you at our house. What were you doing? Trying to spy on us?" he asked as he sat at the end of the bed.

I stayed silent.

"You're not going to start saying you want to marry me again, are you?" he asked with a smirk.

"Fuck you."

"At least that made you say something. I need to ask you some questions, and I need answers." His eyes turned cold and threatening.

"Or what? You'll kill me?" I scoffed. "You're going to do that anyway."

He frowned. "You'll want to do this the easy way, Sage. There are men in this house who want answers, and they're going to get them. One way or another."

My gaze went to the door, wondering how many men were here. I didn't want to talk to Alex, but I sure as hell didn't want to see anyone else in this house either.

"What questions?" I asked through clenched teeth.

"Let's start with—how you found this house."

"I watched you put your passcode into your phone for the last month. Memorized it and searched through your phone while you slept and found the address."

"Where's your car?"

My heart raced. "I didn't drive it up here."

"So how did you get here?"

"Hitched rides from the rest areas."

He raised his eyebrow. "Pretty gutsy of you to trust total strangers when you're on the run."

"I decided I had a better chance if you couldn't get a hit on my car," I said as I tried to stretch my burning arms. "And I wasn't running away. I wanted to know more about the society."

"Look where that got you."

"Still better than playing pretend with you."

He ignored me. "Where'd you get the keys?"

I sucked in a breath. If they knew I had those, then they might realize I had come in and taken the book. Alex was reading my face, and I snapped my teeth together, realizing I'd let my guard down. He got up and scooted closer before sitting back down while turning a little to face me. He was close enough that if he leaned in more, his leg would touch my hip. I tried to move away, but the cuffs prevented that.

"The keys. How'd you get them?" he repeated impatiently.

"I made copies of them while you were passed out," I answered. For once, it was the truth. I didn't know what else to say.

"What were you planning on doing with them?"

I could have sagged with relief. He didn't know the book was gone. They didn't know I'd been in the house before Eric had found me. Suddenly, Alex grabbed my thigh. His grip turned painful when I struggled against him.

"Don't touch me—"

"Then answer me. What were you going to do with the keys?" he asked menacingly.

"I don't know. I hadn't gotten that far. I didn't even know if those keys were for this house. I just made copies of all your keys."

His hand stayed on my leg as I tried to control my breathing. I hated that I was so vulnerable right now. I knew there was a possibility of getting caught when I first started this. And I was okay with that. I'd gotten the evidence I'd come for. But I hadn't expected to be cuffed to a bed and threatened by Alex. I thought they'd kill me and get it over with. This was much worse.

"That wasn't so hard." He squeezed my thigh. "Next time, answer the question the first time I ask it."

I tugged against the unforgiving cuffs as I glowered at him.

"How did Eric find me?" I asked my first question.

His chuckle lacked humor. "You really thought you could come straight to our house and not get noticed? He walked down the path and could easily see where someone went off the trail and into the trees. He's lived up here his whole life. He tracks and hunts. Finding your path through the shrubs and trees was easy. But it was a shock when he found you. He thought it was some tourists that had come in from the beach."

I leaned my head back on the iron bars. I had thought of everything. A few broken branches and crushed leaves were the reason they'd caught me. I'd been so close to being free. I would have been long gone if I hadn't come back to watch them. But regret would have burned through me if they'd had killed another woman.

"Are we done?" I snapped. "I told you everything."

"Not everything," he murmured, meeting my eyes.

"What are you going to do with me?" I asked, avoiding whatever else he wanted to talk about.

"You know what's going to happen."

"No, I don't," I lied as terror slid over me. "How are you going to do it?"

Alex didn't say anything as he turned his gaze to the window.

"You realize tonight is the last day of the full moon?"

My heart dropped. I knew there was a chance of that, but I figured they'd do something else to explain my death. For them to use me for their benefit had disgust churning in my stomach. Pushing past my hesitation, I asked the one question that could give me a chance.

"Is Niko coming?"

The second the words left my mouth, I could see it was a mistake. His jaw tightened as his eyes darkened in anger. The hair on the back of my neck stood up. He looked the same as the night he had found me all those months ago. Cold and cruel.

"Let's talk about my brother," he hummed out with his hand still wrapped around my leg.

"Talk about what? He's part of your society. I figured he'd be right at your side the whole time." I didn't let my disappointment show. Niko was my small hope of getting out of here alive.

"How did you get my brother to turn his back on us?" he asked as his rage climbed.

"What?" I asked, playing dumb.

"I know your little secret, Sage. You were sleeping with him. I came home that night instead of leaving for the weekend and saw you in his bed."

All the words I had been prepared to say disappeared from my head. Panic for Niko tore through me while a small amount of relief trickled in too. He hadn't chosen them. If Alex had found out, that meant there was a reason Niko hadn't been able to contact me.

"You acted like you wanted to marry me," I mumbled, too scared to ask about what happened to Niko.

"And we were going to get married. For a year. Then next year, you were going to be the sacrifice. Turns out, we're just doing it a year early."

I gaped at him. "You were going to stay with me a whole year?"

"Believe me, it wouldn't have been a nice year for you," he growled. "It would have made the last six months with me seem like a cakewalk."

I sucked in a breath, trying to control the sheer terror taking over my body. I didn't want to die by their hands. For their fucked-up ritual that my sister and mom had died for.

"You had this plan since you found me?" I wondered if all my lies and acting with him had been for nothing.

"No," he answered sharply. "I was really trying to make a life with you. To be happy. But after I saw you and Niko, it wasn't going to happen."

"You can forgive me stabbing you, but not for what I did with Niko," I said, my voice full of contempt. There wasn't any reason to care what I said to him now. "Are you mad that your brother can fuck better than you?"

Without warning, he reached over and grabbed my hair, yanking until I was inches from his face. My head was still sore from when Eric had dragged me into the house, and I let out a shriek. My cuffed wrists were screaming in pain as I tried to struggle out of his grasp.

"You should have been grateful to me. I took you in. I spoke up in front of the group. For you. To keep you alive. And you repaid me by sleeping with my brother and drugging me so you could leave," he spat out, his eyes crazy with fury.

"Alex—"

"Did Niko help you run?"

"No," I cried out as I tried to think through the searing pain from his grip.

"Did he help you run?"

"No. He had no idea. Why the hell do you think I drugged him too?" I screamed.

"You're lying," he hissed.

"No, I'm not. Please," I begged him, my head throbbing.

He loosened his grip slightly but still held on to my hair as he studied my face. I glared back. He could do whatever he wanted; I wasn't going to give up Niko.

"He was part of Lacey's ceremony. I thought you'd jump at a chance to get him in trouble."

"Is that what you want me to say? That he helped me, even when he didn't? I did everything behind his back. I got the pills when I told him I was grabbing tampons. I went through your phone when you both were sleeping. I never got a chance to run when I was with him."

Alex finally let go, and I ripped my head away from him. Leaning back, I slowed my breathing, trying to calm down. I met his gaze again, not recognizing who was in front of me. The man I knew was gone and had been replaced with a cold, cruel monster.

"Doesn't really matter anyway. They know what he did with you. And Niko outed how much he cared about you when he refused to help find you. I wanted to see what you'd say," he said as he finally moved off the bed and stood up. "You've truly learned how to lie. I don't believe anything that comes out of your mouth anymore."

"I wish I'd never met you," I screamed at him. "And that's a fucking truth. I hate you."

"One of you would have been sacrificed, even if we'd never met, Sage," he murmured as he stood up from the bed.

I looked away from him and stared at the wall. There wasn't anything else I wanted to say to him.

He sighed. "Enjoy these last few hours. When the sun goes down, it'll be time to start."

"I'd enjoy it a lot more if I wasn't handcuffed."

"After everything you did at the other house and this past year, that's not happening. Sorry." He sounded anything but sorry.

He moved toward the door before stopping. He faced me, and I stiffened, wondering what he was about to say.

"What happened with Geo?"

I didn't hesitate. "Exactly what I said happened. He attacked me. Almost killed me, then changed his mind."

I didn't care if he knew what I really did. I wasn't protecting myself. I was lying to keep Niko out of it. If they knew Niko had covered up Geo's death, that would be even worse than what he'd done to help me.

"We'll find him," Alex said quietly. "Whether he's alive or not."

I shrugged. "Good luck."

He stared at me for another few moments, as if he wanted to say something more. He shook his head and left the room, shutting the door behind him. Only then did I allow the tears to fall. I took shallow breaths, trying to cover up my sobbing. I didn't want them to hear. The shadows from the bars on the window covered the grimy wood floor. The sun was already starting to lower in the sky, and my entire body began to tremble. I had put on a brave face in front of Alex, but I didn't want to die. Especially not at the hands of him and the society.

A sob caught in my throat as I thought of my dad. This would break him. I was all he had, and he was about to lose that too. Kiara wasn't going to understand why I went alone. But tomorrow, she would get that email and find the evidence. Alex still had no idea I'd driven Lacey's truck up here. Even if they realized the book was missing, they wouldn't know where to look. Until it was too late. A slice of peace calmed me. Kiara would do what needed to be done. It would happen even if I wasn't here to see it.

My thoughts drifted to Niko as I stared at the slowly darkening sky. He'd chosen me over his society. His entire life had been for them, and he'd turned his back on it to help me. Not Alex, who I had shared my life with for over three years. Niko found it in himself to realize that the way he had grown up was wrong. I regretted not saying goodbye to him now. My heart stuttered when I let myself admit what I already knew.

I was in love with him. In a different life, I could have been happy with him.

But it was too late for that.

I sat in the dark, tensely waiting until I heard footsteps out in the hall. The door swung open before Alex stepped in. Behind him was the man that had gotten out of the truck with Eric.

"Don't make this harder than it has to be," Alex said without an ounce of emotion.

"What, no needles full of sedative this time?" I asked sarcastically. My last moments on this earth would not be spent begging for my life. But that didn't mean I was going to go quietly.

"Since this was decided so last minute, we don't have any."

I didn't answer and braced my body to get ready for when they uncuffed me.

"Robert, you hold her legs down while I get her arms," Alex muttered to the man behind him.

My eyes went wide. Robert. Robert Dailey. The husband of one of the other victims I had looked into. I remembered him from the news clips I had watched. That's why he looked so familiar. I felt sick. His poor wife. She had no idea who she had married. I was glad it was Kiara I had chosen to visit first. If I had gone to see Robert first, there was no doubt—I wouldn't have survived this long.

Robert's hands wrapped around my ankles, and I flinched but didn't fight back. His grip wasn't tight. I wanted to wait until Alex freed my arms. He went for my right arm first and unlocked the handcuff. Grabbing my freed wrist, he gripped it as he unlocked my other cuff. The second the lock clicked, I moved.

I slipped my right hand out of Alex's grasp as I pulled my leg back before ramming my foot right into Robert's face. I swung my fist, smashing it against Alex's cheek. But it wasn't enough. He was ready for me to fight back. He practically lay on top of me, pinning my arms under him as he unlocked the handcuff from the bed.

Then he grabbed one of my arms and snapped the cuff back on. I was straining to move under his weight as he grabbed my other wrist, cuffing my arms together in front of me. Once they were locked, he climbed off me and pulled me up with him.

"That bitch," Robert cried. He had both hands over his nose, and blood was pouring out. "I think she broke it."

"Go get cleaned up. Eric will help me downstairs," Alex said without his eyes leaving me.

Robert ran from the room while Alex's grip on my arm tightened.

"Let's go," he demanded.

I dug in my heels, refusing to walk. He shook his head and lifted me up, throwing me over his shoulder. I flailed and screamed, but he easily carried me to the basement.

The room wasn't dark like it had been earlier when I had snuck down there. There were candles lit everywhere and a lantern on each table. Flashbacks of what had happened to Lacey claimed my mind. I knew exactly what was going to happen, and that made it so much worse.

Alex carried me to the back table and laid me down. Eric came up from behind and pushed my shoulders down as Alex locked the cuffs around my ankles. He unlocked my wrists, only to lock them into the giant metal restraints that connected to the table.

Alex and Eric walked back up the stairs once I was secured. I twisted and pulled, but the chains were impossible to escape from. I yelled as loud as I could. Screamed until my voice grew hoarse. And then I heard them. The chanting.

My heart was beating out of my chest, my body cemented with dread. This was it. My worst nightmare since this had all started. Craning my neck, I saw them walking in with the same long hooded cloaks they had worn last year. There were only four men.

Once they surrounded the table, I was able to look at their faces. Eric, Alex, Robert. The man I didn't recognize was right above my head. This was his sacrifice. He looked to be around my age. My screams were locked in my throat as I stared into his eyes, seeing only determination. No fear or guilt. Like everyone else around this table, the guy had been born into it, and he was going to do what was expected of him.

Alex left for a few moments, only to return with a knife. He handed it off to the man who stood above me. I stopped struggling because I wasn't going to beg or plead. Their chants grew louder, and I tried to shut them out. To find my own peace in my final moments.

I thought of my family. Lacey. My parents. I had faith that Kiara would get justice for them. And now for me. Their secrets would be revealed, and the society would crumble. I wouldn't be there to see it. But everything I had done in the past year had led to this. It was worth it for all the future women who wouldn't be killed. For all the families who wouldn't wonder for years what had happened to their loved ones.

I even had a chance to love one more time before it came to this. Niko was who I last thought of as the man raised the knife above my heart. I wasn't scared anymore. I was grateful I'd had one more year to live. It had all been worth it.

CHAPTER FIFTY-SEVEN

Sage

"Stop."

That one word sliced through the chants. My eyes snapped open to see the glint of the blade inches above me. That voice. It once shot hate through me, but now I welcomed it with everything I had. Niko was standing near the steps, pointing a handgun directly at the man holding the knife. They stopped their chanting and pulled back their hoods as they all stared at him.

"Niko. What the hell are you doing?" Alex growled through his shock.

"Let her go," Niko ordered in a low voice.

Tension blanketed the room while the men didn't make a move. The man was still holding the knife above me. Alex took a step toward Niko.

"Are you fucking crazy? Put the gun down. How did you even get into the house?" Alex asked, trying to keep his voice even.

"This house isn't a fortress like the other one was," Niko answered, his gaze never leaving the guy holding the knife. "All I had to do was bust through a window."

"Niko—"

"I said let her go. Unlock the cuffs. Now."

Beads of sweat formed on Alex's forehead. Niko's glare finally shifted to his brother. His hands unwavering as he pointed the gun. His face showed no emotion other than being dead serious. The man holding the knife took a step back.

"You know we can't do that," Alex forced out.

"You know what a good shot I am, baby brother. Better do as I say."

Alex's glare was filled with hatred and disbelief. "You think you two are going to walk away from this? She knows too much. God, she turned you against your family. Do the right thing and put the gun down."

"No. I'll say it one more time. Unlock the cuffs. Now. Or someone is going to get a bullet in the shoulder."

"You wouldn't—"

A shot pierced through the air, making me jump. The noise echoed off the walls, and for a minute, all I could hear was ringing in my ears. But the man dropped the knife before grabbing his shoulder.

"You could have killed him," Alex roared.

"He'll be fine, besides not being able to use his arm for a while. The next shot will drop him. Now let her go."

Eric took keys out of his pocket and started quickly unlocking the cuffs that had me trapped on the table.

"What are you doing?" Alex snarled at him.

Eric paused and looked at him. "Your brother's gone off the deep end. I'm not about to get all of us shot. It'll be fine. The group will find her. And him."

Finally, my legs and then my arms were free. I sprang off the table and ran over to Niko. I looked at Alex, but he was still staring at his brother. Shock, anger, and sadness were all over his face.

"Throw your keys. All of you," Niko demanded.

"Only Eric and I have keys to the house," Alex said stiffly.

"Yeah, well, I don't want any of you following us out of here. Everyone throw over your keys." Niko pointed the gun at Eric.

Everyone except Alex threw their keys across the room, and I hurriedly picked them up.

"Come on, Alex. Don't make this difficult," Niko said. I glanced at him, hearing how his voice was shaking.

"I can't believe this. You're choosing a girl over me? Over the group? This is our life." Alex was trying to reason with him.

"That life is over," Niko stated. "Throw your keys."

Alex shoved his hand in his pocket under the robe and threw the keys. I picked them up and noticed the copies I had made were on the key ring too. Alex was glaring at me as I stood back up. I looked him right in the eye as I stepped back next to Niko. He looked like he was about to say something, but I turned my face away from him. He wasn't worth another look—or another word. I never wanted to see him again.

"You've just signed your death warrant," Alex yelled, but Niko ignored him.

"Let's go, Sage," Niko told me quietly. He let me go up the steps first and then followed behind, still pointing the gun until we shut the basement door. He took my hand before we ran to the front door. I unlocked it, and once we were both out, I locked it back up.

"I cut some wires under the hoods of their cars. That should give us a good head start," Niko muttered as he pulled me down the driveway. My eyes widened in surprise when Niko opened the door to my car. The one I had left in Capac.

"You need to drive me to my truck," I told him as soon as we were both in the car.

"We can get it later. We need to go."

"No." My voice was reaching hysterics. I didn't do all this to leave that book here. "It's only down the road. Niko, I need what's inside. Please."

He ran a hand through his hair and looked over at me. "Fine. But you need to follow me back."

"Back where?"

He sighed. "The house Geo took you to. The group doesn't know about it. It'll be safe for now."

I nodded, gazing at the house as he pulled away. It felt surreal to be leaving. I didn't think I was going to get out alive. I turned to Niko and saw his hands shaking as he gripped the steering wheel. His eyes were hard and unreadable.

"Thank you. For saving me," I said softly.

"I told you, Sage. I'll choose you over anyone." He gave me a small smile.

"How'd you get my car?" I asked, wondering how he'd known I had left it at my house.

"I still had the truck keys. I went there, only to find your car instead. Good thing I had the extra key for that one too."

He frowned, and I rested my hand on his arm.

"What's wrong?" I asked.

"I didn't have a way to get to your house." He sighed, his eyes not leaving the road. "I called my mom and told her I was sorry and that I'd come clean about everything. When she got to the house, I told her I was sorry and then took her keys."

"Niko," I choked out. "I'm sorry."

"I'm fine," he said gruffly. "I don't think I've ever seen my mom so disappointed. But she's fine. I'm sure my dad got her hours ago."

"I'm sure it was hard," I mumbled, not sure what to say. He'd done it for me.

"Is this the parking area?" he asked, changing the subject.

"Yeah," I answered as Niko pulled up next to the truck.

"They never would have thought to look for that beast of a truck," he said as he shook his head.

"That was the point."

"What's so important that you needed to stop and get the truck?" he asked curiously.

I hesitated. "I'll show you when we get to wherever we're going."

"Are you good to drive? Or do you want to leave one of the cars here?"

"I'm fine," I promised, not wanting to come back up north for a very long time. "I can drive."

I slid behind the wheel and followed him out of the parking lot. The full moon was still high in the sky, and a shiver ran through me. I had almost died. If Niko hadn't shown up, I would have disappeared like all those other women. Getting that book to expose them would have been worth it. But the happiness was pumping through my body.

I couldn't wait to get out of the car and look through that book. My stomach dropped when I remembered who that included. Niko. I didn't know exactly what was in the book, but I knew it would be enough to get him taken down with the rest of them.

I was so torn. I didn't want him to be a part of them anymore. I wanted him to be free. But I didn't think it was possible if I turned over this book. I tapped my fingers on the steering wheel. It wasn't if. It was when. I wouldn't be able to live with myself if I didn't do it.

I was going to give it to Kiara, and the society was going to be in the public eye.

I parked behind Niko in the driveway and stared at the small brick house. This was another place I never wanted to come back to. But Niko was right. It was safe. After turning off the truck, I grabbed my phone and canceled the email to Kiara. I could give her the book in person now. I texted her the address and that I had what we needed.

I slid the book out from under the seat and stepped down from the truck. The sun was just starting to come up, and the sky was a beautiful pink. With the book in my arms, I followed Niko to the garage door he had already opened. His truck sat there, like it had been since Geo had taken me.

A lump grew in my throat as I walked into the house. There wasn't a trace of what happened. The mirror that Geo had thrown me into was gone from the wall. I couldn't see any blood on the floor.

Meeting Niko's gaze, I stiffened when his eyes traveled down to the book in my arms. His face changed to surprise and then understanding.

"You did all of this for that book, huh?"

"Yeah."

I gripped the book tightly, not sure what was going through his head.

"How did you find me?" I asked, trying to change the subject.

"Kiara Jones."

My eyes widened in shock. "Kiara?"

"I convinced her I was helping you, and she gave me the address you'd given her of the house up north. I guess it was a good thing that you told someone about me. Or I never would have found you."

"How did you—"

"I went through your phone the night we found you. At the motel when I got your bags. Saw her name and number and kept it in case I ever needed it."

I didn't say anything as I absorbed what he'd just said.

He continued, "I understand why you kept her such a secret. If they found out you were working with the police—"

"She didn't have anything to go on. I didn't want her to get involved until I had enough."

"With that book, you have more than enough. They're going to realize it's gone real quick."

"Maybe. I found a book that had an identical cover and switched it out. If there's no reason for them to look at it, then we may have some time before they figure it out."

He raised his eyebrow. "You really did think of everything."

"I texted Kiara. She's driving up here from Chicago."

"I'm pretty sure she started driving after she gave me the address."

I swallowed around the lump in my throat. "I have to do this, Niko. I can't let them keep killing when I have a way to stop them."

"Sage, I know." His gaze softened. "We talked about this before. Quit looking like I'm about to rip the book from your arms. After everything, you think I'd try to stop you?"

"I don't want you to go down with them." I cried as he wrapped his arms around me. "Maybe we can talk to Kiara about a plea deal—"

"After the things I've been a part of, a plea deal won't be enough. I'd still get time," he said quietly.

How could something so right be burdening my mind so badly? The society needed to be stopped. I only wished it didn't include him. Niko sat on the small couch and pulled me down next to him. He reached over and brushed my hair out of my face.

"You look exhausted. Did you get any sleep in the last four days?"

"Barely."

"Kiara won't be here for a while. Go up in the loft and sleep a little. I'll wake you up in a couple of hours, and we can talk some more."

A bit of suspicion hit me at how he ended the conversation. He leaned over and brushed a kiss over my lips.

"I don't care what happens to me," he murmured. "As long as you're safe. And you will be."

Ignoring my protests, he lifted me in his arms and carried me up the stairs.

"Get some sleep. I'll be here when you wake up." He gave me another kiss before going back downstairs.

My body was still hurting from being cuffed to the bed the whole night before. Relaxing into the pillow, I turned onto my side with the book next to me on the bed. My fear of being found was nonexistent. I trusted Niko to keep me safe. My eyelids grew heavy, and I drifted into a deep sleep.

CHAPTER FIFTY-EIGHT

Him

I waited thirty minutes before quietly going back up the stairs. She was sound asleep, looking more peaceful than I'd ever seen. She thought that getting the book would be the end.

I didn't have the heart to tell her that she was in even more danger now.

That book wasn't the only one. There were many others. That book only had information about the people who lived in this area. Each area had its own. Sage and Kiara would be able to bring down one chapter of the society, but never the whole thing. It was too big. But I had thought of a way to possibly change that.

I sighed when I realized the book was under her arm. If I woke her, this wouldn't work. I crouched near the bed and very slowly slid the book away from her arm. Freezing when she moved, I waited to make sure her breathing was still even. After a few moments, I pulled the book from her and went back downstairs.

I sat back on the loveseat, my eyes glued to the book that sealed my fate. Alex's. My dad's. And everyone I had known while growing up. Instinct screamed to burn it. But I wouldn't. She needed to do this.

Opening the book, I flipped through until I found the page I was looking for. My gaze trailed down the names scrawled from top to bottom. At the bottom of the page was my name, both printed and signed. Every man who helped in ceremonies would sign the book when they turned eighteen.

I had questioned my dad about why everyone had to sign it and was told it was tradition. But in the years after, I learned what it really was. Insurance. That if any man decided to talk about what they'd done, they were just as guilty as the rest. It was just another way to make sure the group was kept a secret. There were over seventy names signed in this book from all the previous years. There were the names of all the victims and the dates they were sacrificed. In further pages were the sites of where they were all buried. It had everything Sage needed to start an investigation.

I hesitated for a second before I ripped out the bottom of the page, tearing the small area out that had my name. And Geo's. I didn't need anyone to be searching for him either. I flipped a few more pages and tore out another full page. Folding them up, I put them in my wallet before sneaking the book back upstairs.

Going back downstairs, I quietly opened the garage door and slipped out. I rested against the brick on the front of the house and pulled out Sage's old phone that had been in my room. I took a deep breath, mentally preparing for this conversation. I punched in the number I'd memorized years ago and put the phone to my ear.

"I was wondering when you'd call. Your brother beat you to it."

"Samual, we need to talk," I said, my voice cold.

"Where did you take the girl? This can all be fixed, Niko. Go home. See your father," Samual ordered softly.

"No."

"No? What else are you going to do? You can't turn your back on us," His voice went from concerned to angry in a matter of seconds.

"She found something. Something that is going to take down at least part of the group."

"Then get it from her," Samual hissed.

"I can't. It's too late. But I managed to take the paper that implicated you. And the other elders. As of right now, you are safe. Unless you don't do exactly what I'm about to say next," I drawled, trying to stay calm as nerves pierced me.

"You can't threaten me—"

"I can. I have the evidence to do it. The Midwest chapter is about to get ripped wide open. Nothing you or I can do about it. Your best bet is to start distancing yourself. But like I said, I took the paper that named you. You can still stay in the shadows if you listen to me."

There was a long moment of silence.

"I'm listening," he finally snapped.

"Sage Taylor is no longer going to be in danger. The group will not touch her. She will live her life as she chooses. If she even has an accident, this paper goes straight to the cops. And they'll come straight for you. Everybody in the group needs to know that she is not a target. You understand?"

I waited for an answer but was met with another long silence. I could only imagine what Samual's face looked like at that moment.

"I'm going to need you to answer," I said, enjoying the power I now held over him.

"Nikolas, you aren't thinking straight. Spend some time before you do anything rash," he implored, trying to keep the anger out of his voice.

"Believe me, I'm thinking more clearly than I have in years."

"This is your life. Your family's life. You can't turn your back on us."

"Your chance of saving your own ass is running out," I snapped, losing patience. "Agree or don't. But I want an answer. Now."

He paused. "It'll be done. I'll start informing everyone tomorrow—"

"No. You start when we get off the phone," I interrupted sharply.

"Fine."

"Another thing. I don't want to be running my whole life, so I'm going to add my name on the list of being safe. Everyone needs to know that I'm off limits—"

"Not possible. Not after what you did."

"Yes, it is. You and the other elders control everyone. You say jump and they ask how high. I don't care what you have to do. Threaten them. Threaten their families. Do what has to be done to make sure that no one comes after me." I knew it was possible. They had information on everyone in the group. Their word was law.

"You're really going to turn your back on your family?" Samual asked, almost pleadingly. We both knew this was going to change everything. Nothing like this had ever happened before.

"I'm done with it all. The group. The beliefs. It has to change. It's not the way anymore."

"It's our way of life."

"Maybe. But it's not mine anymore. And you'll make sure no one comes after me. Unless you want to rot in a cell for the rest of your life."

"Okay," he whispered.

"What was that?"

"I said okay," he snarled. "You and the girl will not be harmed. But that will change if you involve me or the other elders in whatever mess you made. Understand?"

"Good."

I hung up, my hands shaking a bit. I wasn't sure if that was going to work. Samual, along with the other elders, knew how fucked they'd be if they were exposed. They were going to do anything to save themselves.

My excitement faded and guilt set in. No one in the group knew what was coming. It felt wrong to betray them. My parents. Even

Alex. I was turning my back on everything I'd ever known. I had half a mind to grab the book and tear out their names too. But if I did that, Sage would always be in danger.

Alex would never let her go free. I doubted even the elders would be able to sway him from trying to find her again. Out of the corner of my eye, I caught Sage peeking her head out of the garage door. I forced out a smile.

"I was looking for you. I thought you may have left," she said.

"No, just needed some fresh air. It's been a long night."

She stepped out and leaned against the wall, right next to me. Our shoulders touched, and we stayed like that for a while as we stared at the trees across the street.

Finally, she broke the silence. "You have no idea how grateful I am for all you've done, Niko. I can only imagine how hard it's been. Choosing me over your family. You betrayed them because of me."

Pushing myself off the bricks, I twisted until I was standing in front of her. I rested my arm near her head and lifted her chin with my fingers. Pain clouded her eyes when I met her gaze.

"I didn't do this because of you," I murmured. "I did this for you. I'll do anything for you, Sage. I love you."

"I love you too," she choked out as tears covered her cheeks. "There has to be a way for you to stay separate from the rest of the group. I need you, Niko. I don't want to lose you."

"I can't promise anything. I wish I could stay here." Using my thumb, I wiped her fresh tears away. "But I can't."

"You've helped. You can still try to talk to—"

"I'm leaving. Before Kiara gets here."

"You're going to run?" she asked in surprise.

"No. There's something I need to do."

"Where are you going to go?"

"I'll be busy. And don't worry about hiding anymore. You're free. The group isn't going to try to touch you anymore. You can have a life. Go back to school. Move back home." I smiled while my heart was shattering.

Hope rushed into her eyes. That had been her dream for the past year. To stop fearing for her life. And I'd made sure she was going to get it.

"How am I safe?"

I paused. "Let's just say I had a little pull left and used it. You don't have to live in terror anymore."

"But what about you? The society will be looking for you. And when I give this book to Kiara, the police will be looking for you too."

"Don't worry about me. I have it figured out. I'll be okay."

"Are you going to stay in touch?" she asked quietly.

I chuckled. "I'm surprised you're not tired of me yet."

I couldn't help but throw in a joke. I didn't want to leave on sad terms with her. She looked at me, rolling her eyes. The fire in them that I had fallen for was still alive and bright. She would get past this and live out the rest of her life exactly how she wanted to. That's what I wanted for her. Even if I might not be a part of it.

"I'd never get tired of you," she admitted, wrapping her arms around my waist.

When she touched me, it felt like everything was right in the world. It was going to be hell being away from her. I closed my arms around her, committing everything to my memory.

"These last six months have been anything but normal," I said as I rested my forehead on hers. "I want you to go back to living life. You need to heal from all this, Sage. That includes me. You were stuck with me. The feelings you have for me might change—"

"They won't," she snapped as she pulled away, realizing what I was doing. "I didn't fall in love with you because I was trapped with you, Niko. I'm not the one who changed this last year. You are."

"I know. And I'm glad I did."

"Don't leave," she pleaded.

"I have to. I need to finish something."

"Let me come with you—"

"No. Kiara is going to need you. They're going to want your testimony and everything for the case. You have to stay here."

This was it. I didn't know when I would see her again. It was for the best, but that didn't make it any easier. I put my hand on her cheek and gently tilted her head up. She met my kiss, not holding back. I grabbed the back of her neck, pressing her as close to me as I could. She was intoxicating. It would take every ounce of my fucking willpower to leave. I finally pulled away, breaking our kiss.

"Stay out of trouble while I'm gone," I told her, running my fingers down her face.

She forced out a giggle while her eyes were heavy with sadness.

"Bye, Sage."

"Be careful, Niko," she said as she wiped a tear away.

I went into the garage and got into my truck. She watched as I backed out and got to the street. I waved before I got out of view. She waved back, sorrow etched on her face. I forced away the sad thoughts of saying goodbye and planned what was next.

I knew what I was going to do the second I'd seen the book in Sage's arms. The police would never be able to find all the chapters of the group. But I could. I was going to start looking for the other books. To completely end it. And once I got as many of the books as I could before they caught on, I was going to give up the paper with all the elders' names on it.

That would make the entire group crumble. It would be done. I wasn't worried about what would happen to me once it was all over. I needed to do this. To make up for all the evil I'd been a part of. For all the other women and their families.

The hardest part was leaving Sage. I wanted to stay near her. But I didn't want to be a constant reminder of the horrors of what had happened to her family. She needed time away from me to realize how she really felt.

She was safe from the group. She'd be okay. And that was all that mattered.

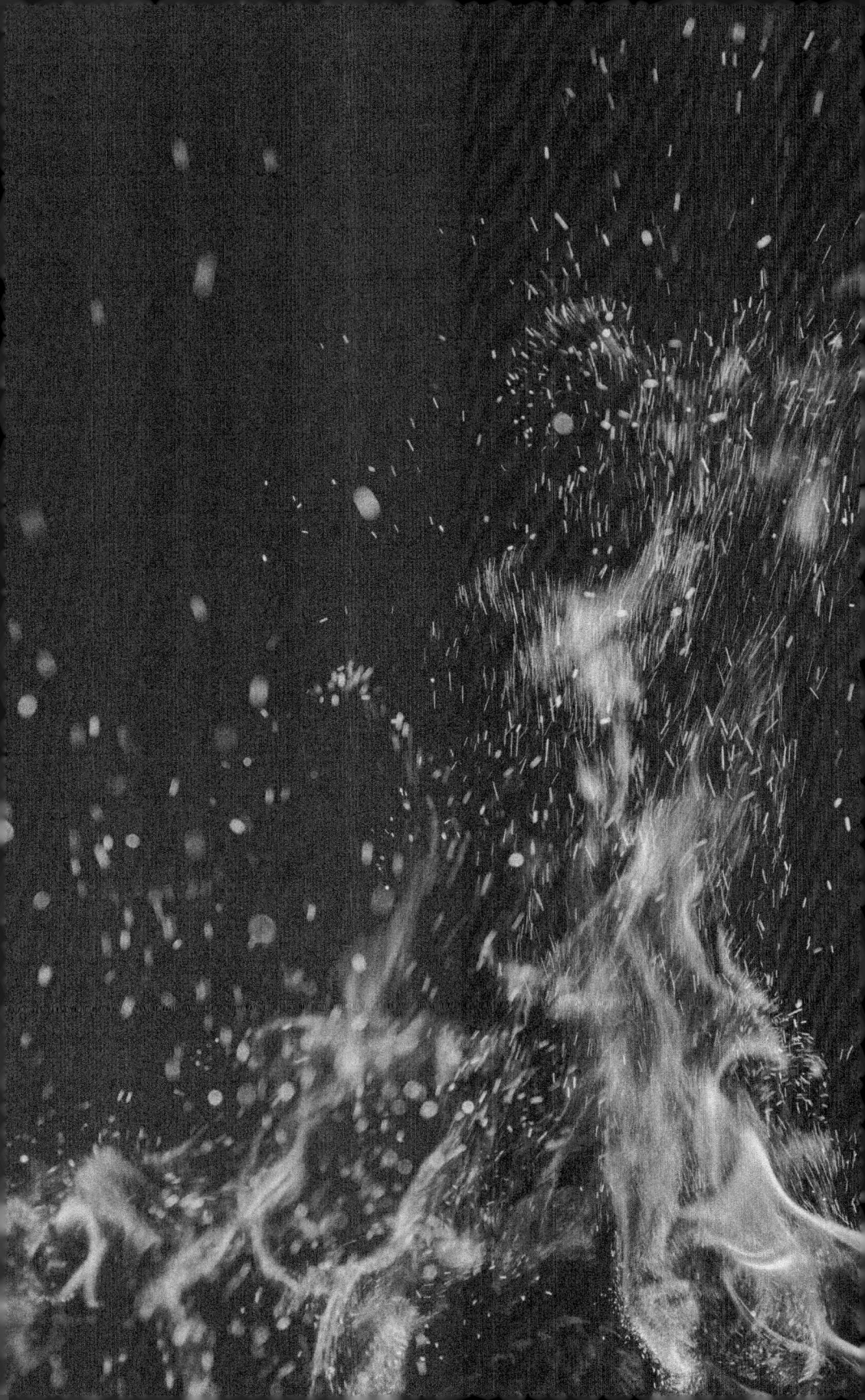

CHAPTER FIFTY-NINE
THREE MONTHS LATER
SAGE

Sage

Sipping my coffee, I stared out the back window as the sun rose. The large kitchen table was lonely when it was just me here. I'd been back at my house ever since Niko left. Kiara had stayed for a while, but after a few weeks, she needed to get back to Chicago. These last months had been a whirlwind, and it was just starting to slow down.

Immediately after Kiara had made it to Michigan, we opened the book and looked through it. It would incriminate them all. I had noticed another page was ripped out, along with a tiny area on a different page. Kiara had asked me about it, and at the time, I had been honest about not knowing. But now I did.

Niko's name wasn't found anywhere in the book. I had no idea what the other page had on it, but I had a feeling it had something to do with Niko telling me that I was safe from them.

He was true to his word. No one had come looking for me. There was always a nagging thought in the back of my mind that they would come for their revenge.

Once Kiara pushed the book into the right hands, things moved fast. To make sure nothing got buried, I had contacted the family members of all the victims that were listed in that book. Not in person, but by phone or email.

I wasn't about to walk into something like I almost did with Robert Dailey—who had been a part of the society. Many family members joined together and kept badgering the police to make sure it was a top priority.

Not even three weeks after I had taken the book, arrests were already being made. The police in different cities were working together, and the FBI got involved because it crossed state lines. While people were getting arrested and taken in for questioning, they started digging at all the burial sites that were listed in the book. By now, the media had gotten a hold of the story, and it had exploded over social media. A secret society—that so many seemingly regular people were a part of—was the talk of everyone, everywhere. The public knew, and the outcry made sure it would not be forgotten.

Kiara had made sure that I was at the police station when they brought Alex in for questioning. I had sat impatiently in the waiting area, and when he had seen me, his rage was uncontrollable. He had lunged at me, and it took two officers to hold him back.

But he didn't scare me anymore. His secret was out, and he couldn't hurt me. I had smiled smugly at him as the officers held him back. I wanted to show him that it was me who had done this. That there was nothing he could do anymore. That had been the last time I saw him, but I was planning on being at his court date whenever that would be.

The one surprising thing was that there had not been one

mention of Niko. His name was obviously missing from the book, but I had expected his name to come up from someone else. The more people they questioned and arrested, the more the society turned on each other.

The man who had supplied the sedative drug had told officers about the man who got the coffins for the burials. They were all fighting to release information in exchange for reduced sentences. But not one of the group members uttered Niko's name. I didn't understand why. What could he be holding to have everyone protect him?

The police took my statement when this had all started, and it gave them an inside look into what the society did. I had told the police everything—except every single detail about Niko. I told them all about what happened with Lacey and the ceremony. About how they were all in hooded robes during the ceremony and I couldn't see their faces. Which was the truth. They didn't have to know Niko had been part of it.

Kiara had told me that with the book, they had more than enough evidence if I didn't want to sit on the stand inside a courtroom and tell my story. And I was relieved about that. I didn't want to be a part of the media circus.

A week after I had given the book over, Kiara had asked why I was protecting Niko. She couldn't understand why I was letting him walk free when he was with the society. I tried explaining it to her. Yes, Niko was part of the society. But he had changed. He conquered a life that could have devoured and spit him out into a person who was cold and soulless.

That was what made him different from Alex, or from anyone else I had met from the society. Alex would have done anything to protect the society. He was a diehard believer, just like his father, and most everyone else in the society. If it hadn't been exposed, it would have kept happening for years to come.

I waited every day for Niko to call. I was still fucking waiting. I was so angry at him for leaving. Especially when it was clear the society wasn't naming him in anything. Until something was dropped off at Kiara's office. Now I understood why he'd left. It didn't make it any easier. I still missed him.

Everything I'd done had been worth it. And I'd do it again if I had to. But now that it was over, I was alone. Setting my coffee down, I wiped my tears away as I thought of my dad.

A week ago, he'd passed away peacefully in his sleep.

I would always be eternally grateful that I had these last three months to spend with him. And that my mom's disappearance had been solved before he passed away. Kiara had come for a couple of days, but her caseload had been crazy with the society, and she couldn't stay long.

Today was my dad's memorial. And then I was going to make plans to leave Capac. It would always be home, but there was nothing left here for me. And no one. I had as many good memories as I did bad. I needed a fresh start.

My phone went off, and I looked down to see a number I didn't recognize. I warily picked it up, my fears about the society running rampant.

"Hello?" I asked timidly.

"Hey, Sage."

My heart stuttered. "Niko?"

"It's so good to hear your voice," he breathed out.

"I don't know whether to yell at you for not calling or to tell you how much I miss you," I muttered, unable to stop smiling.

"Yell all you want. I'd stay on the phone all day and listen."

I giggled before growing serious. "Have you been keeping up with what happened?"

"How could I miss it? It's been everywhere. I'm sure the elders are freaking the hell out."

"We did it," I whispered. "We exposed them."

"You did it, Sage," he said softly.

"Are you coming home?"

He paused. "I'm sorry about your dad. I know how close you

were to him."

"I'm okay." I took a shaky breath. "I really am. I'm sad he's gone. But he's not in pain anymore. This week has been hard though."

"I'm sorry I haven't been there for you." Regret filled his voice. "I've been busy."

"It's been three months since you left," I stated.

"I know."

"My feelings for you haven't changed," I murmured, recalling his words from the last time I saw him. "I still miss you."

Glancing at the clock on the stove, I jumped from my chair when I realized it was almost nine. I was supposed to pick up a platter of sandwiches at nine o'clock for the memorial service. After smoothing out my black dress, I grabbed my jacket.

"You still there?" Niko questioned.

"Yeah. I'm sorry." I grabbed my purse from the hall table on my way to the front door. "I have to be somewhere."

"I can call back—"

"No," I cut him off. "I can talk and drive."

I tugged open the door, only to freeze. My purse slipped from my arm and fell to the floor. I lowered my phone as I stared at him. He was leaning against the doorframe, his green eyes brightening when he met my gaze. A light stubble covered his jawline, and his black hair was longer than it used to be. He was wearing black slacks with a matching jacket and a crisp white collared shirt underneath.

"Mornin', sunshine," he murmured, putting his phone in his pocket without looking away from me.

"Niko," I choked out as I flung my arms around his neck.

He picked me up, and I wrapped my legs around him as he walked into the house. Not even bothering to close the door, he pressed me against the wall. I didn't want to let him go. Being in his arms was everything I'd been wanting for the last three months.

We stared at each other before his gaze traveled down my face to my lips. Hesitation brewed in his eyes, and I frowned, not understanding what he was thinking.

"Part of the reason I left was to give you a chance to see how you really felt about me," he explained quietly. "So much had happened in those six months. I wanted you to have a slice of normal again before I came barging back in."

"You could have left for a year and my feelings wouldn't have changed." Pulling my hands from his neck, I grabbed his face in both of them. "I want you. Now. Tomorrow. Forever. I missed you. It felt like a piece of me was gone."

He grinned for a split second before I pulled him closer and crashed my lips to his. I melted into the kiss as one of his hands went to the back of my neck. His taste was exactly like I remembered, and my craving for him only intensified. I understood why he wanted to give me a chance to live without him after everything that had happened. The thing was, I didn't want to. He was what I wanted.

He pulled away after a while, catching his breath. "I thought you had to be somewhere."

"It's fine. People can live without sandwiches." I glanced at the clock on the wall, making sure I still had a couple of hours before I needed to leave to get to the church on time. "Did you come back for the memorial?"

Setting me down, he glanced down at his suit. "I didn't want you to be alone."

"Then don't leave again," I mumbled under my breath, terrified that it was what he planned on doing. "How did you find out about it?"

"I was in Chicago yesterday. I met with Kiara."

My mouth fell open in surprise. "She didn't tell me."

"I know. She knew I was going to surprise you." He chuckled. "When I first saw her, I thought she was going to arrest me."

"She wouldn't," I said quickly. "She knows what you did to help me—"

"I know that now. Plus, I'm more useful to her when I'm not in prison."

"You sent her another book from the society." I stated what we both already knew.

A month ago, another leather book ended up on Kiara's desk. On the outside, the book looked identical to the one I had taken from the house up north. But the pages revealed a whole new set of victims, names, and burial sites. From states that were up and down the East Coast. One page had been ripped out of that one too. That was when I realized what Niko had been up to when he left.

"I did. And I gave her three more books yesterday. That's why I went to see her. And she told me about your dad."

"Three?" I repeated. "Niko, how many books are there?"

He frowned. "I'm not sure. Enough to cover more than half the states in this country. More in other countries."

"You plan on finding them all?" I asked, my stomach sinking. He was going to leave again.

"As many as I can. I'm pretty sure they'll start hiding them better real soon, and it will be harder to find them."

I raised an eyebrow. "They wouldn't get rid of them?"

"The belief runs strong, Sage. Those books are part of it. It would take a lot for them to do that. But it's okay; when I can't find any more books, I have a plan to take them down from the top," he replied.

"The elders?"

"Yeah."

"No one has mentioned your name at all. I'm guessing that has something to do with those missing pages?"

"Yes. I needed leverage." He pulled me back into his arms. "For you to be free. And me. I've been waiting for them to come after me. I'm not sure they've caught on yet."

I swallowed. "What happens when they do catch on that it's you doing all this?"

"I'll be fine. If I do give Kiara those papers, I'm sure the police have something that can prove they came from those books." He shot me a confident smile. "If that happens, they'll have much bigger problems to deal with than tracking me down."

I didn't share his confidence but decided to ask the other question that was bothering me. "If Kiara hadn't told you about my dad, would you have come back?"

"Yes," he said softly. "After seeing her, I was coming here. I couldn't stay away from you much longer. Not talking to you was driving me insane. I needed to see you. I just wasn't sure you wanted to see me."

I rolled my eyes. "Next time, pick up a phone and ask."

"I have no self-control around you, Sage." He shrugged. "If I called, I wouldn't have been able to stay away. I need to get those books."

"Take me with you," I pleaded, grabbing his jacket. "I don't want to be here anymore. I want to be with you."

He hesitated. "It's dangerous. If I get caught—"

"Niko, I want the entire society brought down," I interrupted. "I spent a year surviving a dangerous life. I can handle doing it again if it means the society is gone. I want to help. And I want to be with you."

He ran his fingers down my cheek as he blew out a breath. "See, this right here is why I didn't tell you what I was doing. And why I didn't call."

"You don't want me to go?"

"Because I wouldn't have been able to tell you no."

I tilted my head in confusion before grinning. "So, that means I'm going with you?"

"Is that what you want, Sage?"

"My home is anywhere you are."

He broke out into a smile before giving me another kiss. I felt whole now that I knew he wasn't leaving again. Whether we were running around the country searching for books or living in the suburbs, I didn't care. As long as I was with him.

"Then it looks like you're stuck with me." He ran his lips down my neck. "Again."

"It's exactly where I want to be."

EPILOGUE
TWO AND A HALF YEARS LATER

Him

"Cheers." Kiara raised her glass as she smiled at Sage, who was sitting next to me. "To ending all of this."

We all clinked our champagne glasses over the large round table. We were at one of the nicest restaurants in Chicago, celebrating the official end of the investigation. Next to Kiara were the two FBI agents we'd been working with over the last two years. Without them, getting the books from other countries would have been impossible.

"You okay?" Sage murmured under her breath when my hand tightened on her thigh under the table.

"More than fine," I answered, giving her a soft kiss on her forehead. "It's hard to believe it's over."

It felt surreal. Even as closely as I worked with the police and FBI,

I kept waiting for them to turn the tables and take me in. Everyone at this table knew I had been a part of the group. It was the only way they'd gotten enough inside information to get to the elders.

The entire time we'd been getting the books, I'd waited for the elders to come after me. But they hadn't. As more books got released to the public, the more they went underground. Completely cut themselves off from things concerning the group. But it was too late. I saved every piece of paper I ripped out of each book.

"They can't touch us anymore," Sage said softly, knowing where my mind was at. "We're free, Niko."

More than eight months ago, the elders were arrested. It was a madhouse all over the world. People had been following the news ever since the first book was exposed, and with each one I brought to Kiara, it only increased the public's shock. There wasn't a place where this hadn't made the evening news.

Every elder got a life sentence. Sage and I watched the trials on TV. Neither of us wanted to be there. My name had been buried from everything concerning the group, and I wanted it to stay that way.

Sage had been worried that other people in the group were going to come after me once they realized what I was doing. But the only person who ever knew I took the paper from the first book was Samual. And to my knowledge, he never told another soul. Except when he tried getting a plea deal. He named every single member he could think of.

My gaze went to the two FBI agents sitting across from me. They were the ones who interrogated Samual. When my name was brought into the conversation, they acted like they were going to come after me. But my name didn't leave that room. There was no evidence trail connecting me to anything. It had all worked out better than I imagined.

"Niko, how's it going at the center?" Kiara asked while the server brought our food.

"Good. We got more investors last month, which helped a lot."

With Kiara's help, Sage and I opened a facility for the kids who were hurt the worst by all of this. So many parents were arrested, leaving children to become wards of the state. Most of them were already fully immersed in the beliefs of the group. I wanted to help break the cycle. The center was a place where the kids could come and talk to counselors and therapists. It was a place for them to talk to other kids who were dealing with the same things.

"We're opening another one in a few months," Sage told Kiara as she glanced at me. "So many investors have come forward wanting to help."

We planned on opening one in every state where there were kids who needed it. Finding the money wasn't difficult. So many people wanted to help and be part of something that had to do with one of the largest news stories in decades.

For the past six months, I'd been taking college courses to get my psychology degree so I could become a counselor to help the kids. I had done almost two years of college when I got out of high school, and luckily those credits transferred, so it wouldn't take long for me to get my degree.

"And I thought you two were going to have a chance to relax once this was all finished." Kiara chuckled. "You're going to be busy. Are we still on for lunch this weekend?"

"I am," Sage spoke up as she cut her steak. "Niko's busy. But he'll be back later in the afternoon to help us move into our apartment."

We'd been staying with Kiara for the last six months—ever since we settled in Chicago. Now that we weren't traveling everywhere, I was excited that we were getting a place of our own. Three blocks away from Kiara. Sage considered her family. She didn't want to be far from her.

I lost my appetite as I thought of where I was going this weekend. To visit my mom. I'd visited her a couple of times already. I had expected her to want nothing to do with me, but after everything, she still loved me. Even though she couldn't comprehend how I could choose Sage over my family. Seeing her was always strained. But if she wanted me to visit, I would.

Most of the wives didn't get the long sentences that the men received. They only kept the secrets, while the men were the ones who kidnapped and killed. Although some did help with the small aspects of the ceremony. The wives' names were in the book too, but not to the extent of the husbands and sons. My mom would most likely get out and enjoy freedom again.

Unlike my dad and Alex.

They were in for life. I hadn't seen them once since the day I rescued Sage. A small amount of guilt would always stay with me. Even though I didn't regret it.

Sage had talked to Kiara about everything. I opened up a bit to her as well, deciding that if I could trust someone, it would be her. If she wanted to put me in prison, she would have done it already. Sage told her what really happened with Geo, and although I disagreed with that, I understood why she needed to admit it. She didn't want us to live in fear of his death hanging over us.

Geo was still considered missing, and that was how it was going to stay. I bought the house in Traverse City that Geo had rented. We never went there, but we'd never sell it either.

Kiara kept our secret about Geo, and the talks we had with her helped Sage and I become stronger too. There was so much trauma from the past. So much death. I had been consumed with thoughts about how Sage would come to resent me for what my family did to hers. She felt guilty she took my brother from me, even after what he'd done.

Kiara became almost like a therapist for us, and we worked through it all. Which I would be forever grateful for. It wasn't like we could go to an office and talk to some stranger about it all.

Standing from the table, I took Sage's hand. "Come on, let's get a drink from the bar."

We went to the balcony that overlooked the Chicago skyline as the bartender mixed our drinks. I stood behind her with my arms around her waist as she leaned on the railing. This was home now. Neither of us had any desire to ever move back to Michigan.

"Are you ready to start your new job next week?" I asked, resting my head on her hair.

She'd finished her teaching degree this year and would be teaching at a local middle school. Kiara was right about us being busy. Sage wanted to teach but wanted to help with the centers too. I was working construction on the side to pay the bills until I got my degree.

"I'm ready for everything," she murmured, resting her head on my shoulder. "I'm happy, Niko. It's all over. We can start our lives."

I spun her around until she faced me. Her eyes were bright with excitement, and a contagious smile played on her lips.

"My life started when you walked into it." Placing my fingers under her chin, I tilted her face up before kissing her.

There were no doubts about my love for Sage. She'd saved me as much as I'd saved her.

She was mine and always would be.

THE

END

ACKNOWLEDGMENTS

It's hard to believe this book is out in the world! Although it wasn't my first published book, this was the first story I'd ever written, and their love holds a special place in my heart. I want to thank you all for taking the time to read Ruby Revenge and I hope you enjoyed watching their story unfold. If you enjoyed reading, please consider leaving a review. It helps authors so much!

Honestly, I never thought I would publish this. When I first wrote it, I thought it would only be a thriller. But rewriting it into a romance made all the sense since my characters deserved their happily ever after!

Writing can be lonely, but I had some amazing people help me on the journey to get this book published! I want to thank Jenna and Jess for reading Ruby Revenge early and helping me make it the best it can be. Jen, I am so glad we met and became friends! Thank you for being there to let me ramble and plot out the harder parts of the story. Your comments and love of the characters helped me stay on track to finish! And last but not least, a huge thank you to Jo. I feel so lucky to have met you! Thank you for always reminding me to write what I love and stay true to myself.

And words can't express how thankful I am to everyone who reads my books and falls in love with them as much as I do when I'm writing them! I appreciate you all so much. You are all the reason I keep writing. I can't wait to share more stories with you all!

Xoxo Kay Riley

ABOUT THE AUTHOR

Kay Riley writes dark contemporary romance. She loves writing feisty, strong heroines, and keeps things interesting with unexpected twists. Kay grew up in the Midwest but has lived in some amazing places, including Japan.

When she's not writing, she is spending time with her husband and kids. She loves cats, coffee, reading, and her guilty pleasure is watching reality shows.

You can follow Kay on social media to keep up with her newest stories.

ALSO BY KAY RILEY

SUNCREST BAY SERIES

FATEFUL SECRETS

TREACHEROUS TRUTHS

RUTHLESS ENEMIES

Printed in Great Britain
by Amazon